BITTERSWEET PASSION

Their lips met eagerly. He kissed her in frantic haste, desperately trying to put all his love and passion and desire into this one last embrace. For that's what this would be, if his plans worked out.

When they finally drew apart, she had tears in her eyes. He did, too. He could feel their sting.

"Don't worry, Will," she said quietly. "One of these days I'm going to succeed in my major mission in life."

He stared through her, hearing her words, knowing only that he was about to succeed in *his* major mission in life, and it didn't feel anything like it was supposed to.

"Aren't you curious what it is?" Priscilla teased.

He tried to grin. "What is it, cowboy?"

"To love every last trace of sadness out of you."

PUT SOME PASSION INTO YOUR
LIFE . . . WITH THIS STEAMY SELECTION OF
ZEBRA *LOVEGRAMS!*

SEA FIRES (3899, $4.50/$5.50)
by Christine Dorsey

Spirited, impetuous Miranda Chadwick arrives in the untamed New World prepared for any peril. But when the notorious pirate Gentleman Jack Blackstone kidnaps her in order to fulfill his secret plans, she can't help but surrender—to the shameless desires and raging hunger that his bronzed, lean body and demanding caresses ignite within her!

TEXAS MAGIC (3898, $4.50/$5.50)
by Wanda Owen

After being ambushed by bandits and saved by a ranchhand, headstrong Texas belle Bianca Moreno hires her gorgeous rescuer as a protective escort. But Rick Larkin does more than guard her body—he kisses away her maidenly inhibitions, and teaches her the secrets of wild, reckless love!

SEDUCTIVE CARESS (3767, $4.50/$5.50)
by Carla Simpson

Determined to find her missing sister, brave beauty Jessamyn Forsythe disguises herself as a simple working girl and follows her only clues to Whitechapel's darkest alleys . . . and the disturbingly handsome Inspector Devlin Burke. Burke, on the trail of a killer, becomes intrigued with the ebon-haired lass and discovers the secrets of her silken lips and the hidden promise of her sweet flesh.

SILVER SURRENDER (3769, $4.50/$5.50)
by Vivian Vaughan

When Mexican beauty Aurelia Mazón saves a handsome stranger from death, she finds herself on the run from the Federales with the most dangerous man she's ever met. And when Texas Ranger Carson Jarrett steals her heart with his intimate kisses and seductive caresses, she yields to an all-consuming passion from which she hopes to never escape!

ENDLESS SEDUCTION (3793, $4.50/$5.50)
by Rosalyn Alsobrook

Caught in the middle of a dangerous shoot-out, lovely Leona Stegall falls unconscious and awakens to the gentle touch of a handsome doctor. When her rescuer's caresses turn passionate, Leona surrenders to his fiery embrace and savors a night of soaring ecstasy!

Available wherever paperbacks are sold, or order direct from the Publisher. Send cover price plus 50¢ per copy for mailing and handling to Penguin USA, P.O. Box 999, c/o Dept. 17109, Bergenfield, NJ 07621. Residents of New York and Tennessee must include sales tax. DO NOT SEND CASH.

RELUCTANT ENEMIES

VIVIAN VAUGHAN

ZEBRA BOOKS
KENSINGTON PUBLISHING CORP.

ZEBRA BOOKS are published by

Kensington Publishing Corp.
850 Third Avenue
New York, NY 10022

First Printing: May, 1995

Printed in the United States of America

To Andra and Vonnie
My Sisters—My Friends

Prologue

Philadelphia, 1856

" 'Evening, Mr. Seth." Young William Radnor hailed the elderly night watchman who paddle-footed around the street corner just as the family's carriage pulled up to the arched red awning that stretched from the Radnor Building to the curb.

" 'Evening, Master William," the old man replied.

"Run fetch your father, William," Ann Radnor told her son. "And don't tarry. The Murphys are waiting."

Years later Will Radnor marveled that the only thing he couldn't recall about that cold misty evening was the reason the Murphys were waiting. Everything else had been graphically etched into the fabric of his ten-year-old brain.

He'd been wearing short black pants, knee-high socks, and new shoes. He recalled looking down at his shoes after he entered the door opened for him by the night watchman. *Mud.*

"Your father's working late, is he, Master William?" Seth, the night watchman, was a jovial sort. William had known him all his life. "Must have a big case comin' up in court."

"Yes, sir. 'Night, sir." Inside the marble and brass lobby, William knelt, spit on a finger, and rubbed mud off the toe of one black patent-leather shoe.

Years later he still remembered the sound made by the

rigid soles of his new shoes slapping against the marble floor, echoing through the cavernous interior of the building in which his father and grandfather and his great-grandfather before them had practiced law. William took the stairs with extra care. He trailed an open palm along the brass banister, pivoting on his slick soles at the landing, continuing to the next level.

Outside the glass-paneled door to his father's suite of offices, he paused to tug up his socks; his new shoes ate them at the heels. Swirling gold letters were etched into the frosted door pane: *Radnor, Radnor, & Kane, Attorneys at Law.* William remembered when the door had read: *Radnor, Radnor, & Radnor.* It had remained so for years after his great-grandfather's death. William wondered when they would get around to removing the name of Charles Martin Kane, his father's Harvard roommate, the first lawyer outside the family ever admitted to the firm. Just last week Charles Kane resigned; William still recalled his parents' bitter words over the affair.

They probably wouldn't leave Charles Kane's name on the door any longer than necessary. They should have saved the other pane; the one that read: *Radnor, Radnor, & Radnor.* When they replaced the glass this time, maybe they would leave space for his own name—William Penn Radnor IV. The fact that he would practice law in these offices had never been in question.

That he would not do so with his father, however, soon became all too apparent. Inside the spacious offices of the most prestigious law firm in the City of Brotherly Love, William found everything in disarray. For a moment he stood as though glued to the spot. Wide-eyed, he gazed from overturned chairs to files strewn across the wine red carpet. An unfamiliar sense of foreboding crept up his spine. His heart began to pound. He peered down the long hall.

A man's arm . . . a gray pinstripe sleeve . . . His father!

William moved. Racing through the outer office, he jumped over a toppled chair, waded through piles of paper and books, and knelt beside his father, who lay sprawled in the hallway outside Charles Kane's vacated office. Blood pooled in a black circle beneath him.

William reached forward; his hand hovered above the still body. Except for the fixed stare in his lifeless brown eyes, his father might have been asleep.

"Father?" The word choked out; William felt his own heart beat in heavy thuds, constricting his throat. "Father, wake up."

He experienced a strange sensation, as though his voice and his brain operated from separate bodies. His brain knew that his father would not awaken to his call, no matter that his gray pinstripe suit was unrumpled, that his brown hair was slicked to the side, unmussed, that his white collar was crisp and pristine.

A vivid ink-stain of red blood dried on the starched white shirt. It had run down his father's side, exited again, and formed a black circle beneath him. Already the stench of blood rose from the wool carpet.

Although his stomach had begun to tumble, William could not tear himself from his father's side. Looking closely, he saw where the bullet entered through a small tear in his father's jacket. Then he noticed the gun in his father's hand—one of a matched pair of engraved pearl-handled Colt Pocket Dragoons presented to Charles Kane at last year's Independence Day celebration. The pistols had been the award for winning the sharpshooters' contest. Charles Kane always won the sharpshooters' contest.

The sight of the pistol grasped in his father's lifeless hand brought William to his feet.

His father had been murdered!

By whom? Terror froze William in place. Was the criminal even now lurking somewhere in this suite of offices? Although his heart raced, his feet seemed rooted to the floor.

Like a marionette, he turned his head this way and that. Everything was scattered—papers, books, files. Inside Charles Kane's office, the polished oak case for the matching pair of Colts stood open, velvet-lined like a coffin, he thought. Like an empty coffin.

William sprang to life. Clutching the pistol to his chest, he raced from the offices. By the time he reached the carriage where his mother waited, tears streamed down his face. His father was dead.

Shot to death.

The police came, investigated, pronounced the motive for the killing to have been robbery, and took the pearl-handled pistol from William.

"When we find that matching gun, we'll have the murderer," the captain explained. "Then we'll return the pistols to you, son."

The hearse arrived. Men in gray suits covered his father with a white sheet and carried him away. William stood on the curb beside his weeping mother. Together they watched draft horses pull the hearse bearing his father's body down the street.

"Don't cry, Mother," William soothed. "If the police don't find Father's murderer, I'll do it."

Spanish Creek Ranch, New Mexico Territory, 1870

Creeping toward the corral, Priscilla McCain squinted against the dazzling reflection of a steadily rising sun. She shivered in the crisp air coming off distant mountains and hurried through patches of ground fog that tickled her bare feet. Arriving at her destination, she slung her blond pigtails over her shoulders and cast a furtive glance back the way she'd come—to the sprawling adobe house where her mother prepared breakfast, to the closer adobe barn where her father fed his saddle horses and Uncle Sog milked Tequila, their Jersey cow.

So far, so good. No one had seen her. Yet. From beneath her flowing cotton nightgown, she withdrew an old pistol she'd found in her father's trunk the day before.

Supporting her right arm with her left hand, like she'd seen her father do, she took deliberate aim at the first of five empty tomato cans she'd lined up on the far side of the corral fence. She squinted along the barrel and pulled the trigger.

Even though it was a small gun, its repercussion jolted her. She steadied herself, took aim, and fired again. And again. And again. None of her five shots hit a target, but two came close.

"What in thunderation d'you think you're doing, Miss Priss?"

Priscilla reloaded the pistol, ignoring her father, who stomped toward her from the barn. Before he reached her, she repeated her shots. This time she hit one can.

Charlie McCain waited until she finished, then jerked her around by the shoulders. He took the pistol from her hand. "Where'd you get this old thing?" His voice was gruff.

Priscilla regarded him solemnly. He was already dressed for the day's work—with heavy brown duck britches stuffed into knee-high, work-scarred boots, covered by a pair of worn leather chaps. His leather vest topped a blue chambray shirt, the only concession Priscilla had ever known him to make to her mother's attempts at sprucing up his attire. Priscilla could hear them now.

"Blue brings out the color of your eyes, dear," her mother would say.

"Hell, Kate, d'you think those ol' cows are gonna give a damn what color my eyes are when I stick that brandin' iron to 'em?" her father would reply.

Her mother was like that, always trying to make her father into a gentleman—and Priscilla into a lady. But her mother was right about the blue shirt bringing out the color of his eyes. Leveled on her now, they were as vivid a blue as the sky on a clear summer day.

They didn't intimidate Priscilla, though. She returned his glare with a matching pair of blue eyes, even though her neck had to stretch to meet his gaze. "You know where, Pa. In that old trunk in the barn—with all that old iron junk."

Charlie removed his sweat-stained Stetson and ran a callused hand through dark, wiry hair. "Artifacts," he corrected, "not junk. And you're to stay out of that trunk, young lady." He frowned at the small pistol. "This is no toy. I won't have you using—"

"A man's gotta learn to shoot, Pa." She watched his mouth twitch, but he didn't laugh at her. Pa never laughed at her, not even when she knew he wanted to, like now.

"Dadburnit, sugar. You're not a man. You're a ten-year-old girl. Your mama'll have my hide for this. And yours, too."

"She expects me to learn to protect myself. She told me so."

"Protect yourself, yes. But she won't cotton to you takin' target practice. Learn to load and fire a gun, for protection. That's what she meant. Not target practice. Your mama expects you to be a lady. And so do I."

Priscilla shook her blond pigtails. "What you need on this ranch is a *son*."

Charlie's expression softened. "No, sugar, what I need is a daughter just like you. A daughter who'll grow up to be a lady like her mama."

"I'll never be a lady like mama. She's the most beautiful woman in the world. You always say so. And the best cook, and the best seamstress, and the best—"

"And you're the spittin' image of her. Don't I always say that, too? Look at this head of golden hair. You'll look just like your mama one day, mark my word. And you'll learn the rest. We aim to see to that."

Priscilla rammed fists to her hips. "I'm not going back East to school."

Sighing, Charlie held up his hands in defense. "The sisters in Santa Fé told your mama about a good girls' school in St. Louis. That's not too far away now, is it?"

Priscilla concentrated on the four cans still standing on the fence. She took the pistol from her father and began to reload it. When he tried to stop her, she pulled away. "I'm not going, Pa."

"You will if I say so."

Priscilla took aim, steadied her arm, and hit the first can. A thrill tickled her insides. The repercussion wasn't as strong this time. Of course, she'd learned to brace herself against it.

"Miss Priss."

Priscilla fired again, hit the second can. And the third.

"Miss Priss, you look at me."

She missed the fourth, frowned at it, then cast a stern look at her father. Along with his blue eyes, she had inherited a strong stubborn streak, or so her mother claimed. "I told you not to call me that."

The absurdity of the situation struck Charlie like a fist to the gut—his beloved, headstrong young daughter sneaking off to the corral at dawn in her ruffled nightgown, demanding to be treated like a man, and taking target practice with a pistol he should have thrown away years ago.

Exasperated with both Priscilla and himself, he reached to embrace her, but she backed away. He stared down at the top of her head, at her hair the color of young corn silk. It would one day be as thick and golden as Kate's. But Priscilla's pigtails were lopsided and irregular, and her part meandered down her head with as many crooks and turns as the Pecos River. She wouldn't hear of her mother combing her hair. Kate said she'd learn, to give her rope.

But Priscilla didn't want to learn. Somehow she'd managed to get it in her head that Charlie was sorry she wasn't a son. He must have done something to give her that idea, but for the life of him, he couldn't think what. Sure, it had come as a blow that after Priscilla's birth, Kate hadn't been able to conceive again. But that meant they had more love to give Priscilla.

And love her he did. The older she got the more she looked like her mother and the prouder Charlie was of her. It would hurt to send her away to school, but Kate wanted it. And Charlie wanted what Kate wanted. They both wanted Priscilla to have all the advantages they could provide—which meant she had to learn to behave like a lady.

Priscilla didn't want that, either. Charlie recognized the problem—she was afraid of not measuring up to her mother, so she took the opposite tack. Kate said Priscilla had been born a tomboy, and there was nothing they could do about it until the right young man showed up. Then Priscilla would take on the role of a lady too fast to suit either of them.

"Until that time she's better off in britches," Kate argued. "I expect her to behave like a lady, but the less feminine she looks, the better."

Kate had good reason to want Priscilla to mask her femininity. At fifteen Kate had been assaulted by a stepbrother. With Charlie's love and help her wounds had healed, but he knew she harbored fears for their daughter.

Charlie had fears, too, fears of sending Priscilla away to school. He worried that she would have trouble fitting into an all-female society, unless she began taking an interest in more feminine things. If this morning was an indication, that wasn't likely to happen anytime soon.

Why, she hadn't even put on a dress in two years, and she'd worn that one only once. Later, when Charlie asked, she claimed it was too small. To no avail he had argued that her mother could easily let it out—or sew another.

"You'll make a fine lady, sugar," he assured her now. "Just like your mama—"

Priscilla glowered at him. "I've never heard you call Uncle Crockett sugar."

In spite of the situation, Charlie smiled at the thought of calling his crusty old foreman sugar or anything akin to it.

"Or Uncle Sog."

"No, Miss Priss, I've never called Crockett or Ol' Soggy Bottoms sugar. Even if you *are* only ten, I think you're smart enough to figure out the difference."

Priscilla elevated her chin to an angle that would have befitted the First Lady of the United States of America. "Then don't call me sugar, either."

Charlie stared dumfounded at his gangly yet proud young daughter.

"All right, Miss Priss, if that's what you want."

"And don't call me Miss Priss."

"Now, sug—" Removing his Stetson again, Charlie slapped it against his thigh. He glimpsed Crockett and Ol' Sog standing in the barn door, pretending to mind their own business. Seems Priscilla's gunshots had called all hands. Before he could think of a response, Priscilla added,

"Call me Jake."

"Jake?"

"Tell mama you can hire a tutor, if it'll make her happy. But I'm not going off to try to become a lady. I'd rather work at something I can do. Like being a cowboy."

Without another word Priscilla clutched the pistol to her chest and stomped toward the house, her proud little chin jutting toward the tier of mountains that encircled Spanish Creek Ranch. She left Charlie with no illusions that she intended to join her mother in the kitchen or would take up sewing.

Nearer the house stood Joaquín, son of the Apache woman Nalin; he also watched Priscilla's progress, his face an emotionless mask. Not quite a year separated the two, with Joaquín being the younger. Charlie turned his attention back to his daughter.

Jake? Where in hell had she come up with such an outlandish demand? Yet, wouldn't it be a whole lot simpler as she grew to womanhood in this wild country if all hands considered her one of the boys?

One

New Mexico Territory, 1879

"Sorry to tell you this, Miss Jake, but Ol' Sog here ain't goin' nowhere no time soon. A broke femur's a mighty dangerous thing."

Priscilla McCain turned away from Ol' Sog's pain-pinched countenance. Big man though he was, he'd passed out when Doc Sloan pulled his thighbone back in place. He was still so pale the sunspots on his aged, leathery face looked faded. Priscilla studied the fly-bespecked adobe walls of the hovel that served as both home and office for the only doctor within fifty miles of Chimayo. How could she leave Uncle Sog in such a place, so dirty and so far from home? "We'll take the stage—"

"Too risky." Doc Sloan's red face and stubbled chin gave him the appearance of a man who was just coming off a drunken binge. His hand had been steady enough, though, when he set Uncle Sog's leg.

Sog tried to move, but the doctor pushed him back to the narrow table where he lay. "Aw, Doc, I can't lie here and let Jake ride off by her lonesome."

"A lot of good you'd do her," the doctor countered. "In your shape, you'd likely die afore you reached Santa Fé."

"But I'm responsible for her, Doc. Her pa put me in charge."

Priscilla leaned over the stricken old man, frowning in

her best imitation of anger, which didn't fool either of them. "I've ridden these trails all my life, Uncle Sog. Nothing to it. Besides I'll make better time without your carcass slowin' me down."

Ol' Soggy Bottoms, range cook for Charlie McCain's Spanish Creek Ranch for twenty-odd years and for outfits clear across Texas for who knew how many years before that, was accustomed to giving orders, not taking them. Priscilla had learned that, early in life.

"A range cook answers to no one," her father had told her, when at twelve she'd had the audacity to suggest that Uncle Sog not make any more pies with canned peaches.

"They make the bottom soggy," she complained.

"Where in tarnation d'you think I got my name, Jake?" She could tell by his peppery tone that she'd hurt Uncle Sog's pride.

"You eat, or you don't eat," her father said. "But Sog here runs the show."

Since that time she hadn't given him any trouble, and certainly no one else had. But now a broken leg had grounded him, and he wasn't taking the matter with grace, like her mother would have said. In fact, he was being downright ornery.

"Your pa sent me along on this horse drive to chaperon you, Jake," Sog argued. "He'd have my hide if I let you ride fifty miles through these mountains alone, jes' 'cause a horse went an' busted my good leg."

"Not until he recovers, he won't," Priscilla returned. "Doc says you'll have to stay here awhile, Uncle Sog. But I can't dillydally. With both you and Pa laid up, and Uncle Crockett off in Texas buying cattle, Pa needs me at home. No telling what the Haskels have tried since we've been gone."

"That's my point," Sog persisted. "Bad as that Haskel bunch wants Spanish Creek Ranch, ain't no way of knowin' what they'll do next to take it. Why, they've got hired guns that wouldn't blink an eye at snatchin' you, Jake. That'd get to Charlie real quick, an' they know it."

Priscilla focused on the earthen floor. Uncle Sog had a point, but she was a good enough shot that she wasn't afraid of a Haskel hired gun. Of course, if they came at her with more than one—"They've let up since their attack on Pa," she said. "Pa says they've turned things over to their crooked lawyers."

The old man's gray eyes narrowed, whether from pain or worry, Priscilla couldn't tell. "I don't like it, Jake."

"I know, Uncle Sog." She stroked his thinning, once-sandy hair, then grinned when he winced, knowing it was as much from embarrassment at her show of affection as from pain.

Uncle Sog wasn't really her uncle, but he'd come to the territory with her pa back in the early sixties. Sog and ranch foreman Titus Crockett were the only family Priscilla had ever known, outside her mother and father. They'd practically helped raise her. Since she got old enough to sit a saddle, she'd gone along on horse and cattle drives, but always with her pa, Uncle Sog, or Uncle Crockett to see to her safety. Pa had intended to head this drive to Chimayo himself, before he caught a couple of Haskel bullets.

Priscilla wasn't afraid of the Haskels, they just made her fighting mad. With the territory still recovering from the Lincoln County War, the Haskel Land Grant Company had stepped in and claimed thousands of acres of land on irregularities in Spanish Land Grant surveys. And they'd hired a passel of guns and lawyers to back them up.

Three weeks earlier they'd attacked her pa and his cowboys while they were rounding up cattle to fulfill a government contract. In the skirmish Pa took a bullet through the thigh and another in the shoulder. Afterward, his cowboys quit, saying they weren't drawing fightin' wages and claiming the climate was healthier down Texas way. Only Uncle Sog and Uncle Crockett stayed on.

And Red Avery, she thought, recalling the red-headed archaeologist who couldn't be numbered among those capable of defending Spanish Creek Ranch. Red was long on education and short on everything else. As far as Priscilla was concerned he was less than worthless on a ranch. She knew he entertained romantic designs on her, which she considered equally misplaced.

Priscilla had no time for romance. Not as long as Spanish Creek was in trouble. Her mother and father had bought that ranch with their blood and sweat. And as long as there was breath in her body, Priscilla vowed to fight the Haskels and anybody else who tried to take it.

She smiled to herself. They'd outwitted the Haskels this time. With the cattle gone, the Haskel bunch figured they had the McCains over a barrel. But they hadn't counted on one factor—the horses in Spanish Creek Canyon. Pa sold these horses only when a situation could not be resolved by other means. Such as at present, when a government contract waited to be filled. Competition was fierce for government contracts, since they went a long way toward helping turn a profit in lean years.

With her father laid up, Priscilla had persuaded him to let her drive the horses. Truthfully, he'd had no choice.

"Uncle Sog and I can trail that herd to Chimayo, Pa," she'd argued, "while Uncle Crockett rides down river to buy more cattle."

"With what?"

"With the government gold we'll bring back from selling the horses," she retorted. "Any cattleman in Texas will honor an IOU from Charlie McCain."

Which was true, except they hadn't counted on Uncle Sog's horse stepping in a varmint hole and breaking a leg. Nor had they counted on that horse falling on Uncle Sog and breaking his leg, too. All of which was unfortunate. None of which Priscilla would allow to stand in the way of ranch work.

"I have to get this gold back to Pa, Uncle Sog. You know that."

"Now missy—"

"You always said I'm handier with a rifle than you are. I can dispatch any hombre who sets out to take our gold, same as you."

"It ain't only the gold, Jake."

"I can protect myself, too." She reached for the saddlebags, which were heavy with government gold. "I'm going."

When the old ranch cook stirred, Doc Sloan laid a hand on his shoulder. "Wouldn't be movin' around if I were you. I'd hate like the dickens to have to pull them bones back together again."

Sog settled back. "Do me a favor, missy."

Priscilla eyed him.

"Take the derned stage into Santa Fé. An' get that Holbert feller to ride on out to the ranch with you."

"No tellin' when a stage'll come through—"

"One's arrivin' this afternoon from Springer," Doc Sloan allowed. "If you two'll quit jawin', you can catch it, an' I can get my patient settled down."

Although she hated the thought of a jolting stagecoach ride over narrow mountain roads, Priscilla knew when to fold, as she'd heard the cowboys say, times when she'd sneaked off to the bunkhouse to play poker with them. Paying the doctor for Uncle Sog's treatment in advance, she forewarned him.

"We expect the best care you can give him, Doc. My pa will come personally to fetch Uncle Sog, and he won't settle for less than your best shot."

The stagecoach driver was already stepping onto the box when Priscilla approached the station. Recognizing him, she hailed, "Hey, Zeke, don't leave without me."

"Wouldn't think of it, Jake." Zeke Grayhorse was a big man. His shoulder-length black hair bounced from beneath a high-crowned black felt hat when he jumped to the ground. He met her at the hitching rail. "Buy your ticket while I unsaddle your horse and tie him on behind."

Priscilla dismounted before the low adobe stage station. She removed her spurs and stuffed them inside her saddlebags with the gold. Pulling her Winchester from its scabbard, she lifted the saddlebags from behind the cantle.

"Want me to put them things up top with your saddle?"

Priscilla glanced to the top of the coach. "I'd rather keep them inside if there's room."

"Sure is that."

"Good." She grinned, wrinkling her nose. "For more reasons than one. I'd probably run off any paying customers. Uncle Sog and I've been sleeping with a horse herd for better'n a week."

Zeke laughed. "Wouldn't know you any other way, Jake."

Priscilla took the remark as it was intended, in fun. After paying her fare, she opened the stagecoach door and tossed her gold-laden saddlebags to the vacant seat.

The other seat was occupied by a long-legged man who slouched back in a corner with a hat pulled over his face. He was lanky enough to be a cowboy, but that's where all resemblance stopped. His citified black suit, complete with starched collar and fancy silk tie, would be a laughingstock around a bunkhouse. Priscilla grinned at the hat, a black bowler, wondering what pranks Uncle Sog and Uncle Crockett would think up should such a man foolishly venture onto Spanish Creek Ranch.

When she climbed into the coach, her eyes fell on the man's boots. If you could call them that, she thought. Certainly they weren't the sturdy boots Westerners wore to work cattle. Where in tarnation did this greenhorn expect to go in footgear that flimsy? Why, the first cactus patch would catch him like a flytrap.

Will Radnor pulled his long legs out of the way of the boarding passenger with a brief, "Excuse me, sir."

At the unexpected greeting Priscilla's head jerked up. Her Stetson fell backward. She reached for it with her free hand. In the other she gripped the Winchester.

"It's miss," she corrected in a snippy tone.

Hearing that, Will shoved the bowler back off his face. He'd seen only the scuffed boots and leather-clad knee when he made the assumption. Now he looked at the rest of the package. His brown eyes widened.

Fully aware of his perusal, Priscilla moved inside, leaned her rifle in a corner, and arranged her saddlebags on the seat opposite the greenhorn. She figured him for a drummer of some sort. If he intended to sell his wares in this country, she could tell him a thing or two about how to dress. On the other hand, it might be fun to watch him find out for himself.

Moving his gaze up her buff-colored leather britches, Will did a double take at the gun belt and holsters strapped around her slender hips. What the hell kind of country was this? Here he'd been dreaming about voluptuous, black-eyed *señoritas* and what had he found? A female warrior loaded for bear. He sniffed the air. Actually, she smelled more like a horse. But then he probably reeked malodorously, too. Since leaving St. Louis, he could count the number of baths he'd had on one finger—and that one in an icy mountain stream. He had run out of clean clothes even before that. Civilization couldn't come soon enough.

"ALL ABOARD!" Zeke called from the driver's box. Without further warning, the coach lurched forward. Priscilla, in the process of taking her seat, staggered. She flung her arms wide, clutching at the leather straps to either side of the doors.

Will caught her when she pitched toward him. He steadied her with hands spanning her hips just above the gunbelt. Their eyes met. He thought for a minute he'd grabbed hold of that horse he smelled, and it was a wild one. But no horse he'd ever seen had such startling blue eyes.

"Damn," she muttered.

"Begging your pardon, miss." But he didn't think to turn her loose.

She mumbled another oath, jerked free, and seated herself opposite him. With movements as cocky as a gunfighter's she diverted her gaze. Ignoring him, she settled back in the seat and clamped one booted ankle over the opposite knee in an unladylike pose that caught Will completely off guard.

Unable to stop himself, he allowed his gaze to drift over her once more. Tall for a woman, trim, not a bad face even though it was tanned from too many hours in the sun. But her clothes were what intrigued him. A faded blue shirt, topped by the kind of leather vest he'd seen a lot of lately—on men. Her leather britches were as stained as a painter's palette, and her floppy brown felt hat—he'd heard them called Stetsons—was well worn and misshapen. But her pistols gleamed in their oiled holsters, and she carried an equally well-cared-for Winchester for extra measure.

The outfit intrigued him, yes, and the feel of her did, too. His hands tingled from the soft leather and what he knew would surely be softer skin beneath it.

He watched her performance as attentively as if he were in a theater and she the star performer. She lifted her hat, wiped a dampened brow, and tucked wisps of hair the color of new-minted gold behind her ears. As though he weren't watching, she turned to secure the position of her rifle, giving him a glimpse of an almost perfect profile and a mass of that gold hair that hung in one heavy braid down her back. His mind played games, wondering how long it was when loose, how soft it was, how it would smell against his face. Same as the rest of her, more than likely.

When she turned her head again, he watched her face screw up in a grimace. Following her line of vision, he caught her sneering at his feet. His feet? He searched his boots for a scuff or a tear in the fine leather, but saw neither.

What the hell? Probably she'd never seen such a fine pair of footwear.

"Miss what?" he inquired.

Her head jerked up. Her blue eyes glinted with undisguised mockery. She wasn't in the least abashed to be caught sneering at his attire.

But Will Radnor was abashed. Abashed to find himself seated across from such a woman. He hadn't expected to encounter refined ladies in New Mexico Territory, not like the ones in Philadelphia. Actually, he'd looked forward to meeting a few less pretentious women. Well, here was certainly one less pretentious woman. After another snickering perusal of his person, she settled back and closed those sky blue eyes, which were the only feminine thing about her— except for that head of golden hair. As an afterthought, she lifted two slender fingers, whose nails were ragged and dirty, and used them to pull the brim of her Stetson over her eyes.

Guns and britches and a baggy man's shirt. Except when she settled back, her vest fell open and her shirt rested softly across breasts that revealed at least as much femininity as those blue eyes.

Just when he figured she intended to ignore his question, she responded, "McCain."

McCain.

The name did more to undo Will Radnor's composure than Miss McCain's mannish attire, or her weapons, or even her captivating blue eyes. With concentrated effort and the skills of one practiced in interrogation, he kept his voice noncommittal.

"Will Radnor here." He offered his hand but she merely nodded beneath the hat and didn't look up. He turned to the window, watched the country blur past. The coach bolted around one hairpin curve after another, unsettling Will's city stomach, as the vehicle hugged a towering rocky wall here, teased the edge of a sheer precipice there. Tops of trees appeared along breaks in the canyons and lined the banks of a swiftly moving river far below. In the distance mountains rose in tiers, ever higher and bluer. Everywhere he'd been in this country, tall blue mountains rose in the distance, beckoning him onward, always beyond reach.

Beyond reach, like the mission that had driven Will since childhood. A mission of vengeance. When he left Philadelphia, taking a leave of absence from his law practice, he hadn't been certain he could locate his father's killer after twenty-three years. But he couldn't resist following the latest trail, which led to a man by the name of McCain who was thought to have been living somewhere in New Mexico Territory for more than twenty years.

He glanced across the small confines of the coach to the sleeping Miss McCain. She looked to be in the neighborhood of twenty, and she obviously took their harrowing ride as an everyday occurrence. Which to his mind proved she must have been reared in this country. Certainly no one new to these mountains could fall sound asleep while faced with the prospect of being plunged into infinity at any given moment. After twenty-three years, Providence had at last smiled on him.

The mountains fell away. Then no sooner had they reached the lowland, than the coach lurched ahead, whipped by a shouting driver. Will swallowed his stomach and decided the driver must be possessed by demons.

At the change of pace, Priscilla bolted upright, settled her Stetson on the back of her head, and stuck her near-perfect profile out the window.

"What is it?" Will asked.

"Three . . . four men."

"What—" A volley of gunshots answered his question.

Priscilla shoved her saddlebags to the floor and reached for her Winchester, which she loaded with dispatch. Will jerked his feet from under the heavy saddlebags.

"What've you got in there—" A succession of gold coins spilled from the saddlebags and rolled across the floor.

She fired out the window, then turned a silencing glare on Will. He met her gaze, struggling to make sense of the bizarre turn of events. Behind her a body fell from the driver's box and dropped to the ground. Will's stomach lurched again. He wished for his own rifle, which he'd stashed in the rear boot with his gear.

"Hey, Jake," came a call from above. "Whit's been hit. Can you climb up here and give me a hand?"

"Coming." Priscilla reloaded her rifle as she spoke.

"Jake?" Will glanced around as though another person might suddenly appear inside the coach. "Who's Jake?"

"I am." Without a moment lost to indecision, Priscilla wriggled headfirst through the window on the far side from the approaching attackers.

Will stared dumfounded for an instant. Regaining his senses, he grabbed her around the waist and hauled her back inside.

"Turn me loose." She struggled to free herself, but Will held tight. "Don't you know anything?"

"I know better than to let a lady climb on top of a stagecoach when it's barreling over the road at breakneck speed, even if her name is Jake and she dresses like Billy the Kid."

"For your information, greenhorn, we're being attacked. The shotgun rider just got hit."

"Then I'll go up." Will reached for her rifle. They tugged back and forth, and finally he wrenched it away. "Use your pistols from in here." His brown eyes challenged her. "If they get close enough." With that, he climbed out the same window she had attempted to use earlier.

Priscilla watched him disappear. She considered pulling him back inside, but not until it was too late. His actions had come as such a surprise, she hadn't had time to react. What good a greenhorn like him would do on the box, she couldn't imagine.

"If my gold gets stolen, I'll hold you responsible, green-horn," she hollered out the window.

"Then get busy and defend it from down there. If you think you can shoot straight enough."

Livid from the slur on her marksmanship, Priscilla drew her pistols, loaded them, and began firing randomly at the advancing outlaws.

"Don't waste shots," Will shouted down. His mocking tone set her teeth on edge. "Unless that gold they're after has been molded into bullets."

Before long Priscilla realized that although he might dress like a greenhorn, Will Radnor's marksmanship was superior to that of anyone she knew. Except her pa's. And maybe her own.

But using her rifle, Will kept the advancing attackers too far away for her to get off a pistol shot to prove her competence. He dispatched the outlaws in record time, and the stage settled into its normal bouncing gait. Will remained on top, however, leaving Priscilla alone inside the cab to ponder the incongruities between the man's looks and his behavior. She liked the way he had taken charge, pulling her back inside and risking his life on top without hesitation. She liked the way he talked, teasing, yet serious. She wondered what he was doing in New Mexico Territory, and whether she would see him again. She'd like a chance to test her marksmanship against his.

She knew she could outshoot him. But recalling his arrogant insults, her indignation returned. She stuck her head out the window. "You don't have to show off by riding the rest of the way on top. We already know you can shoot—when you have the use of a good rifle."

He chuckled in reply, further irritating her. "Being the expert you are, you surely don't expect me to abandon my post."

"Humph!" *His* post! Zeke had called down for her help, not that of a long-legged greenhorn. Why, she was surprised he knew enough to ride on top without falling off. On second thought, maybe he didn't know as much as he thought he did, not if Zeke could be encouraged to join in a little fun.

"Hey, Zeke," she called up. "While you're stopped, I think I'll pick some of those primroses over yonder."

Zeke hee-hawed from the box, but he didn't whip up the horses like she'd expected.

"Sorry not to oblige you, Jake," he called down, "but the team's winded from outrunnin' them road agents."

Will Radnor spoke, obviously to Zeke, not to her, for his words were lost in the wind. Zeke laughed.

Priscilla replaced the gold coins that had rolled out of her saddlebags. She tried to relax, but with that infuriating greenhorn on top of the stagecoach, pretending to be a shotgun rider . . .

He wasn't half-bad-looking, though, for a greenhorn. And he was tall. With those long legs, he'd likely top her pa by half a head, and Pa stood nearly six feet in his stockings.

No, she decided, Will Radnor wasn't half-bad-looking. She liked clean-shaven men; you could see their features—angular face, strong chin, broad forehead. Except for that city-pale complexion, he wasn't half bad-looking.

But he *was* city-pale, and he *had* taken her place on top of this stagecoach—using *her* rifle.

Like Pa said, a man couldn't get stomped on, unless he laid down. Her pride might be hurt, but she could fix that. She'd demand a rematch.

If he owned a rifle!

Securing the thongs on her holsters, Priscilla hefted herself through the window of the rocking coach. The ground rushed by in a blur below her. She hesitated, reconsidering such a foolhardy move. But Will Radnor had done it, blast him. And he was no more than a greenhorn.

With more trouble than she would admit in a thousand

years, and a goodly measure of trepidation, Priscilla wriggled until she turned herself around in the window frame. From there she reached for a handhold on the luggage rack.

When Will glanced back from the driver's box, he gaped, wide-eyed, as though he couldn't believe his eyes, and Priscilla almost laughed. Then his brows arched in a cocky way and she heard his insulting lilt even before he uttered the words.

"Get on back inside, Miss Jake. I'll protect your gold on into Santa Fé."

"Like hell you will," she muttered. With a heave she hoisted herself until she lay with her belly over the luggage rack. Her arms burned from the exertion and her breath came short. But she'd be damned if she'd let Will Radnor know it.

She half expected him to offer her a hand, but he didn't, which further infuriated her. Of course, she would have refused it, which, something told her, was the reason he turned back to Zeke and continued a conversation she couldn't make out.

By the time she gained the top, Priscilla was breathing hard. She wondered whether the climb had winded Will. Surely. Him being a greenhorn and all. But he certainly hadn't shot like a greenhorn.

And the smile he turned back to her was genuine. He shifted toward the outside of the driver's box, motioning her to the space he'd created between himself and Zeke. When she hesitated, his arrogance returned.

"Sit between us, Miss Jake. Wouldn't want you to fall off the edge here."

Although she hated to admit it, curiosity got the best of Priscilla, and she squeezed into the space between the two men. "You couldn't be trusted to catch me if I did fall off," she retorted. Even wedged between them, she found it hard to keep her balance on the rocking driver's seat. For support, she propped her boots on the box—beside those flimsy things the greenhorn wore.

"Why, Miss Jake," he was saying, "what a short memory you have. Didn't I do a fair job of driving off those highwaymen?"

"Highwaymen?" Priscilla laughed. "Out here we call them road agents—or simply bad men."

"Whatever you call 'em," Zeke put in, "that was mighty fancy shootin', Mr. Radnor. Wouldn't you say so, Jake?"

Priscilla stared straight ahead, over the rumps of the galloping horses. Zeke was laughing at her, blast him. "Fair," she conceded.

"Fair?" Will questioned. "You could have done as well, I suppose?"

"Better." She indicated her Winchester, which he still held across his knees. "If you plan to remain in this country long, you should carry one yourself."

He grinned in a companionable way, before searching the horizon from mountain range to mountain range. "For a woman who lives in such a big, free country, you're certainly quick to put a man in a box. If everyone out here jumps to conclusions the way you do, I'm in serious trouble."

Jump to conclusions, my eye, Priscilla thought. She studied his feet, propped beside hers. The difference between their boots extended beyond size. Hers were no-nonsense work boots, made in the Spanish tradition from bullhide, with high slanting heels and pointed toes, designed to not slide through a stirrup—and to slip easily out of one to keep a downed rider from being dragged. Will's footgear, on the other hand, was of the thin-soled city variety.

"That's the second time I've caught you laughing at my boots."

"My mama's kid gloves are sturdier." Although she had decided against offering any more advice, she couldn't resist. "A word of warning, greenhorn. Don't call those things boots out here."

Soon afterward, the stage rolled into Santa Fé, crossed the Río Santa Fé, and circled the plaza which was studded with cottonwood trees and teemed with people awaiting the arrival of the stage or taking a siesta. Will scanned the scene, preoccupied. Priscilla wondered again what he was doing here, and how long he would stay.

"I feel like I've entered a foreign country," he admitted.

"You have. I don't know where you're from, greenhorn, but this is ranching country, and you're gonna stand out like a lamb licker at the Cowboy Christmas Ball."

He winced. "Sounds bad."

She nodded gleefully. Then, recalling Pa's admonition to play it straight and fair, even with those less fortunate, she added, "Except for your shooting."

Will tipped his bowler. *"Gracias, señorita."*

Priscilla was still pondering Will's having thanked her in Spanish, the language of choice in Santa Fé, when Zeke guided the team to a stop before the adobe station. Will jumped to the ground and reached his hands to catch her.

"Jump," he ordered.

Without fully intending to, she stepped off the driver's box into his waiting hands. He caught her around the waist and lowered her to the ground with the greatest of ease. Their gazes held. He grinned.

"You smell like you've been sleeping with your horse."

His voice held no censure, and she took no offense. Instead, she laughed. "Fifty of them. For over a week."

Will watched her face light up at his teasing. The brilliant blue dome of sky above them seemed to dim at the sparkle in her eyes. Or was it at the thought of who she was? A McCain.

He reached to the box for her Winchester, but made no attempt to hand it to her. "No hard feelings, I hope."

With a cocky tilt to her head and a voice sweet enough—

he had no doubt—to get her just about anything she damned well wanted, she replied, "I demand a rematch, greenhorn."

"By all means, Miss Jake. Name the place and weapons."

"I'll have to think about it. Will you be in town long?"

"I'm here to stay."

A frown creased her brow above a lovely straight nose. Funny, he hadn't noticed how really pretty she was. "I'm a lawyer," he explained. "I've taken a position with Faust & Haskel."

The light in her eyes went out. Her expression turned cold.

Behind them Zeke Grayhorse instructed the station manager to send someone back along the road to pick up Whit, the shotgun rider. "He took it in the shoulder. Shouldn't be too bad off, if we get to him in time."

Zeke clapped Will on the back, announcing to all who had gathered around the ancient plaza in Santa Fé, "This here's our new hero, folks. Saved the day after Whit caught himself a bullet."

The words droned in Priscilla's ears. She stepped away. Retrieving her saddlebags, she threw them over a shoulder and tried to move through the crowd that had gathered to hear Zeke recount the adventure.

"Miss McCain?"

She paused at Will's call, steadied her gaze on a piñon tree in the distance.

"You forgot this."

Turning, she accepted her rifle.

"Thanks for the use. Mine's stashed in the boot." He shrugged. "Guess I have a lot to learn about this country."

His candor surprised her. She was suddenly sorry for her unwarranted attack on him. For a greenhorn, Will Radnor had possibilities.

Everyone out here came from somewhere. That's what her parents always said. "Don't judge a man because he dresses different, or talks different. Most of us came here from someplace else. If we can make a life in New Mexico Territory, others can, too."

"About that rematch—" Will was saying.

"There won't be a rematch." Without explanation Priscilla turned and left him standing in the dusty Santa Fé street.

Two

Spanish Creek Ranch spread thirty miles along the Pecos River in north-central New Mexico Territory, flanked on the west by a triple-decker range of mountains. The distant ridges formed a dusty blue horizon high in the Navajo-blue sky. Priscilla sat her horse at the crest of the nearest hill, scanning the familiar setting below. All looked quiet. No sign of trouble. That established, she allowed the delicious emotions of returning home to sweep through her. Joy. Love. Security.

The rambling adobe ranch house flowed in serpentine fashion around oases of piñon and cottonwoods, with deep verandas for respite from the scorching summer heat. Clay ollas and strings of red peppers hung from vigas. Her mother's prized red roses added an additional touch of color.

Home. Priscilla had been born in this house, back when the structure amounted to only two rooms. The rest, numbering twelve rooms to date, had been added later. As had the barns and corrals and holding pens for livestock.

Home. Where her father and mother had tamed the desert and made friends with the warring Apache.

Home. Which the Haskel Land Grant Company was determined to steal from them. Unwanted visions of Will Radnor flashed through her mind—his angular, handsome face and shining brown eyes, his citified clothing, his expert marksmanship. His hand, smooth from an easy life of office work; his smile, teasing and ready.

His employer, Faust & Haskel.

Nearing the house, she spied her mother and father sitting in the shade of the deep veranda, watching her approach. She slid off her mount, flipped the reins over the pole rail, and bounded up the steps, a broad smile on her face. Ten days earlier, when she and Uncle Sog rode away, Pa had been confined to bed.

"I see Mama let you up while I was gone." She stooped to hug her pa, then stood back and perused him, her blue eyes softening on his bloodless face. His skin was sallow and more wrinkled than she recalled. His wiry hair was streaked with much more gray than she'd ever noticed. Even his blue eyes were dull and lifeless.

She looked to her mother—stately and serene, always the lady. Her blond hair fell in one long braid down her back, as did Priscilla's; her starched white cotton shift grazed a body that was still youthful at forty-five. But her mother's beauty and ladylike ways no longer threatened Priscilla. Indeed, her mother was her best friend—next to her pa.

Priscilla couldn't recall a time when she hadn't idolized her pa; she'd tried to emulate him in every way, and had succeeded in many. Her mother allowed it, for the most part, setting her foot down only on matters of grave importance—such as the time she found Priscilla behind the woodshed, with a wad of chewing tobacco protruding from one jaw.

Seeing Pa now, pale and unable to leave the house, unsettled Priscilla. "How is he?" she demanded of her mother.

"He'll be fine, darling."

"He looks weak. Is he—"

"Don't worry about me, Miss Priss," Charlie interrupted. He'd always had a hard time calling her Jake—except when discussing ranching matters, man to man, as it were. Occasionally he resorted to the childhood name he knew she hated most, just to show her who was boss, she suspected. Although most of the time he used it with such tenderness, she had to pretend to be offended. "Your mama nursed me back to health once before, she'll do it again."

"He's right," Kate agreed. "You're not used to seeing your papa any way but in charge of things. He'll be back running this ranch before you know it."

"I'm still running this ranch, sweetheart," Charlie growled. "Even if neither of you care to take note of the fact."

After Priscilla carried in the gold and related the circumstances of Uncle Sog's accident, assuring her parents she had paid the doctor for his services in advance, she glanced toward the barn. "Any trouble while I was gone?"

"Not a squeak out of the Haskels," Kate answered.

Pa, as usual, was anxious to get on with business. "Crockett drove in that herd of steers yesterday, Jake. Looks like you'll be short-handed for the branding. 'Less you can make use of Avery."

"Red's still around?"

Her pa's eyes flashed. "That dadburnt, red-headed, freckled-faced, over-educated archaeologist—"

"Don't be so hard on Red, Pa," she teased. "It isn't his fault, you know. If he'd been born wearing boots and working cattle, you wouldn't approve of him."

She watched Pa frown. "I'm not that hard on you, am I?"

Priscilla laughed. "We'll just have to wait and see. Don't start worrying right away. I certainly don't have designs on Red Avery."

Kate raised her eyebrows. "I'm afraid he has designs on you, darling."

"So am I." Priscilla turned serious. "I'm surprised he wasn't the first to curl tail and run at the sound of gunfire. But you never can tell about folks. There was this greenhorn on the stage who turned out to be a sharpshooter. He sure surprised Zeke and me." She grinned sheepishly, then added, "With my rifle."

They pressed her for details, and by the time she finished

the tale, Pa's eyes were flashing again. "You seem mighty interested in some feller you met only one time. Where's he from? What's his line of work?"

"He just moved to Santa Fé, Pa. I didn't ask where from, and I'm not interested. He's a lawyer. For Faust & Haskel."

"Humph!" Charlie snorted. "Reckon that puts an end to that."

"Don't worry," she consoled again, only half in jest. "No man's gonna ride in and carry me away from Spanish Creek." She ruffled his hair playfully. "And I promise not to get desperate and encourage Red to stay on."

The next few days were so busy, Priscilla had little time to think about men—even a greenhorn lawyer who worked for the enemy. Branding five hundred head of steers was hard, hot, dusty work—work that began before sunup and ended after dusk. Her mother did her share in the corral, although with Uncle Sog gone, she was left with cooking chores, too. In the evenings, Priscilla helped wash dishes and prepare meals for the following day.

"Sure miss Uncle Sog," she commented while drying the last dish one night.

"I hope he'll be all right," Kate worried. "Sog's been with us since the beginning."

Priscilla wasn't used to seeing her mother with sagging spirits; it worried her. That damned Haskel Land Grant Company. They were the ones to blame. For everything.

By the end of the week all hands were tired of branding cattle, and Charlie was tired of watching from his easy chair. Kate took time out at intervals to keep him company. They watched from the veranda, reflecting on Priscilla's stamina and enthusiasm.

"I was wrong about her outgrowing the tomboy stage," Kate commented once. "By nineteen, girls should want party dresses and beaux. But what does our daughter prefer? Boots and britches and the company of a horse."

"She's a damned fine rancher." Charlie's voice was thick

with emotion. "Good thing we never had another child. Priscilla would be hard put to share Spanish Creek."

"That's why we needed another child."

"If it'd been a boy, woe be to him. Priscilla doesn't like playing second fiddle even to me. She'd've locked horns with a brother, sure enough."

"But you're proud of her, aren't you, Charlie?"

"More than she'll ever know, sweetheart. More than she'll ever know."

Late Saturday afternoon with only a few head left to brand, Priscilla roped a steer and dragged it to the branding arena. Since she was the best roper on the ranch, other than her pa and Uncle Crockett, the roping usually fell to her. Uncle Crockett bulldogged the animal to the ground, but, short of hands as they were, Priscilla had to dismount and help her mother and Red hold the larger animals, allowing Crockett to turn loose long enough to wield the branding iron.

Not that Red Avery wasn't physically up to the strenuous work; he was every bit as large a man as her pa. It was technique he lacked, and heart. No matter how many times they showed him how to do this chore or that, he couldn't seem to learn.

"Beats me how the man can be so dense," her mother had mused. "With all that education, you'd think he could learn simple tasks like tightening his cinch and locking gates behind him."

"It isn't brains, Avery's lacking," Pa had objected. "It's heart." He'd looked at Priscilla then, eyes flashing. "His heart's in the wrong damned place."

But no matter where Red Avery's heart was, since the cowboys quit and since he wasn't inclined to leave Spanish Creek, they had to put him to work.

Priscilla dallied the rope around the saddlehorn, then slid off her horse in one fluid motion, while Crockett grabbed the steer by the horns and threw it to the ground.

By the time Priscilla reached them, her mother had hold of the steer's neck, and Red was attempting to get a grip on its rump.

"Get your knee on him, Red," she encouraged. "Hold him. Don't let the critter loose." With her help, the three of them held down the struggling animal, while Crockett burned the ornate S brand of Spanish Creek Ranch into the hide of its left flank and cropped its right ear with an inverted V.

Finished, Crockett jumped back. "Let 'im up." He returned the branding iron to the fire, which wafted piñon smoke across the dusty corral. Kate and Priscilla rose simultaneously; the steer lumbered to its feet.

"Take the rope off his neck, Red." Priscilla headed for her horse, where she unhitched the other end of the same rope from her saddlehorn. When she attempted to coil it, however, it flew through her hands.

"Catch that rope, Red," she shouted. By the time the archaeologist brought his attention back to the corral, the steer had run him down in the packed soil.

Less than worthless in a corral, Priscilla muttered, dusting her bottom absently with one hand, while she ran after the rope the steer dragged behind him in his race for freedom. Catching up, she reached for the rope, only to have a stranger step from the shade of a piñon tree. He bulldogged the running steer, pinning its shoulders to the ground.

Priscilla stood above steer and man, fists on hips. For a long moment, her brain refused to accept the truth.

"What do I do now?" Will Radnor questioned innocently, as though his presence in a cow pen were an everyday occurrence.

Priscilla's eyes darted to his feet. No thin-soled greenhorn footgear now, but a pair of Santa Fé's finest handmade boots. She took in his attire—leather britches, chambray shirt, leather vest. The transformation took her breath, until she remembered who he was. "Where the hell did you come from?"

"I can't hold him down all day, Jake. Tell me what to do."

Priscilla knelt, slipped the noose from around the steer's neck and stood, coiling her rope absently. "Go to hell."

Will jumped to his feet. Together they watched the steer race around the end of the corral, headed for the herd. "You even curse like a man."

"What're you doing here?"

"If I came for a taste of Western hospitality, I'd be up a creek. Thought sure I'd at least be offered a cold drink of water."

"You certainly shall be," Kate replied from Priscilla's shoulder. "Come up to the house, Mr.—"

"We aren't finished branding, Mama." Priscilla tossed Will a nod of dismissal. "Let's get back to work." She strode to her horse and stepped in the saddle. But when she dragged the next steer to the branding arena, Will Radnor was there. And somehow he managed to make himself useful. He helped Kate and Red hold the animal, then slipped the noose off its neck like Priscilla had done earlier and tossed it to her. Through the remainder of the afternoon, Will proved a respectable ranch hand, and although she couldn't understand why—they certainly needed the help—Priscilla's fury mounted.

When the last steer had been branded and turned out to pasture, Priscilla headed for the barn, leading her horse. For some strange reason, she was infuriated to find Will Radnor looking so much like he belonged in this country. *Her* country. And acting like it. When in fact he had come from the East and worked for the enemy.

"Miss McCain?"

Priscilla stopped with her back to him.

"I've come to discuss a client."

Without facing him, she shrugged and started to walk away.

"May we talk somewhere?"

Glancing to the far end of the corral, Priscilla saw her mother and Red staring at the two of them. "Come on," she told Will. "I have to put Sargeant away." To her mother, she called, "Be along in a minute, Mama."

Will followed Priscilla to the watering trough where they stood silently while the pinto cutting horse drank. Finally she said, "Let me speak frankly, Mr. Radnor. No one who works for the Haskels is welcome on Spanish Creek. I would advise you to leave while I'm the only person here who knows who you are." She looked at him then—a mistake, for standing there in his leather and chambray, with dust on his face, and a new Stetson shoved back on his head of thick brown hair, he took her breath away for the second time today.

She'd never experienced such an embarrassing reaction to a man. "Outfit yourself like a cowboy if you want, but that won't change your stripes."

"My stripes, Miss McCain?"

"Take your pick. The Haskel Land Grant Company hires guns and crooked lawyers. Which are you?"

"Neither. I'm an honest lawyer and a damned good one." He sought her gaze and held it steady. After a long moment he added with a wry grin, "I acknowledge being an expert shot, but my gun isn't for hire."

Discomfited, Priscilla dropped her gaze. "Then why did you come to Santa Fé?"

He scanned the late afternoon sky. "My health?"

She glanced around at that. Their eyes met again. She grinned. His lips tipped briefly before his expression sobered and he turned away. That surprised her.

He followed her into the barn. They walked the distance without speaking. She opened both halves of the heavy door to the stall and led Sargeant inside. Will remained in the threshold, where he grasped the overhead crossbar with both hands, stretching his arms, lengthening his already lanky torso.

"Why do they call you Jake?"

She flipped the stirrup over her saddle seat and tugged at the cinch, ignoring him as best she could. "I told them to."

"Does everyone do everything you tell them to?"

She ignored him.

Finally he offered, "Haskel Land Grant accounts are handled by the firm's senior partners. As the new member, I'm given smaller fish. Today the judge appointed me to defend a horse thief called Wounded Eagle."

Priscilla caught her breath. "Joaquín?"

"They called him Wounded Eagle. He won't talk to me."

"His name is Joaquín. He's half Apache, half . . ." Her gaze drifted toward the house. "Why did you come here?"

"Lady in town said your father—"

"What lady?"

"Miss Laredo, I think."

"You think? Jessie Laredo doesn't leave any man in doubt. It looks like you're a greenhorn in more ways than one."

Before Will could counter, Priscilla lit into him again. "I know what she told you. It's what everybody thinks. But it's a lie."

Will stepped into the stall. He noted the fury in her blue eyes, recalled how they sparkled when she laughed. He wondered if they burned blue fire when she made love.

If she made love. This was one tough hombre, as they said out here. "I didn't come to slap a paternity charge on your father, Miss McCain. Frankly, it doesn't matter to me whether he fathered Wounded Eagle or not. I need to talk to someone close to my client. Find out how I can go about defending a man who refuses to speak to me."

When Priscilla lifted the saddle from the horse's back,

Will removed the saddle blanket and held it until she reached for it.

"Thanks," she mumbled. By the time she draped the blanket over the stall, Will had removed the bridle and held that for her, too.

Together they rubbed down the sweating animal. Finally curiosity got the best of her. "Where'd you learn to bulldog?"

"Bulldog? What's that?"

She raised astonished eyes to his. "Whatever city folks call throwing a steer."

"Throwing a steer?" Will's expression registered recognition. "Oh, that. I just watched the older man. When I saw you in trouble, I thought I'd lend a hand."

"I was not in trouble."

"That cow was getting away from you."

"It wasn't a cow, it was a steer. And I would've caught it."

"What's a steer?"

Priscilla rolled her eyes. "If you think those boots make you a cowboy—"

"I never claimed to be a cowboy. I thought I might not stand out like a *lamb licker at the Cowboy Christmas Ball* if I dressed like everyone else."

She grinned, somehow pleased that she'd had something to do with his transformation. "Until they hear you talk," she quipped.

"What's wrong with the way I talk?"

"It isn't so much the way you talk, as the stupid things you say."

He cocked his head, pursed his lips, and studied her, amused. He'd never met a lady like her. If you could call her a lady.

"Well, anyhow, thanks for lending a hand," she added. "You saved us a little time out there."

He followed her outside into the growing dusk. The air

hung heavy with piñon smoke from the branding fire, blended with the sweet scent of pine. The sun was beginning to set. It streaked the sky with fiery colors, reminding Will of the blankets Indian women sold around the plaza in Santa Fé.

"What can you tell me about this Wounded Eagle . . ." He held up a hand to ward off her viperous tongue. "Except his parentage. I'm not interested in that. I want to know why he won't talk to me."

"For starters you might call him Joaquín."

"If that's important—"

"It is. An animal name dishonors an Apache. The bigots in Santa Fé call Joaquín, Wounded Eagle, because . . . because of his birth."

"Joaquín, it is. What else?"

They walked through the corral. She closed and latched the gate behind them. "Whose horse did he steal?"

"There you go jumping to conclusions again, Miss McCain. You shouldn't assume he's guilty. Unless he has a history of—"

"He doesn't."

"I don't know who the horses belonged to. They claim he was riding with Billy the Kid's gang. The others got away. He got caught."

"Joaquín doesn't ride with Billy the Kid. He probably knows him. But he doesn't ride with him."

"What's his problem, then?"

She walked with her hands stuck in her back pockets. Will couldn't help noticing how that stance stretched her shirt across her bosom, revealing the woman beneath the tough exterior.

"His problem?" she was asking. "Like everyone else, Mr. Radnor, Joaquín wants Spanish Creek Ranch."

Reaching swiftly, Will grabbed her by an upper arm and drew her to a halt. She glared up at him, silent, hostile.

"Did anyone ever tell you, you have a chip on your shoulder the size of a redwood tree?"

"We don't have redwood trees in New Mexico." She jerked to free her arm, but he held on. Inside, her stomach tumbled and she wondered what Will Radnor really wanted at Spanish Creek. She doubted he wanted the ranch itself. If he did, she figured this was one man who'd be honest enough to admit it straight out.

"And I don't have a chip on my shoulder, Mr. Radnor. I just don't like consorting with the enemy. Especially when he makes a habit of ingratiating himself with me."

"I don't ingratiate myself with anyone, Miss McCain. If you people can't accept a helping hand without biting it off, this isn't the kind of place it's made out to be."

Incensed, she tried again to free her arm. This time he turned her loose.

"Do you think I could speak with your father?"

"About Joaquín?"

He held her gaze, steady, warming her beneath the magenta-streaked sky, before he looked away toward the adobe house.

The house glowed in the last rays of the day's sun. Her mother had lighted inside lamps and yellow light streamed from the deep-set windows. Priscilla was suddenly glad Will Radnor had come. Glad he could see her beautiful home. Glad he had proved himself a fair hand in the corral.

When she glanced back to him, he was staring at her. Their gazes locked again, probing. "Among other things," he replied.

Will knew exactly what he wanted at this moment, and it had nothing to do with Joaquín or even with her father. He wanted to kiss her. Right here in front of her magnificent home, beneath the fiery magenta sky, surrounded by nature's majestic mountains. Even knowing she was Charlie McCain's daughter. That was the hell of it. Even knowing she was Charlie McCain's daughter, he was attracted to her, like lightning to dry wood. He turned back to the house.

His voice, as low and dusky as the evening sky, sped along Priscilla's spine. It wasn't the summer evening that warmed her now; she sensed as much. It was the heat in Will Radnor's brown eyes. And the unwanted feelings of camaraderie she felt toward this man who worked for the enemy.

"If he isn't in bed," she agreed at length. "Come on." When they approached the house, she explained. "Pa was wounded a few weeks back in a skirmish with the Haskel bunch. They drove off the cattle we were contracted to deliver to Fort Stanton."

"For what purpose?"

"So we couldn't fulfill our contract, Mr. Radnor. I told you not to ask stupid questions. You should be aware that your employers are determined to take this land, by court order or by running us off. Stand forewarned. They will *not* succeed."

Will followed her up the tile steps leading to the sprawling adobe. On the veranda a gentle breeze cooled his rattled senses. But when they reached the wooden entrance doors, he stopped short at the most incongruous sight he had encountered yet in this strange land: A full suit of Spanish armor stood guard beneath the yellow lantern light, one hand extended as in greeting.

Bowing in pantomime, Will gripped the metal gauntlet. He nodded a silent greeting to the headless helmet. Cold steel though it was, he suspected this was the warmest welcome a Radnor was likely to receive at Spanish Creek Ranch.

Then Priscilla's mother opened the door with a broad smile. "I'm Kate McCain. Come in, Mr. . . . uh . . ."

Will quickly doffed his Stetson to the woman who only a short time before had been scrambling around the cow pen in grimy britches. She had changed into a loose white

cotton gown trimmed with white embroidery. Her golden
hair was braided in one long heavy braid, the same as her
daughter's. Although the gold in Mrs. McCain's hair had
lost some of its color with time, Will realized that Priscilla
must be a reflection of her mother in earlier years. Even
now Kate McCain was an extraordinarily handsome woman.

Except her eyes were hazel, not blue.

Priscilla led the way into the spacious foyer without pausing to introduce Will. "Where's Pa?"

"In the courtyard, darling."

"Come on." She motioned toward Will as though he had
contracted a plague of some sort. Greenhornitis, he suspected. "He wants to meet Pa."

Priscilla strode across the broad expanse of tiled floor.
Will and her mother kept pace to either side. "Joaquín's in
jail, Mama. Accused of horse theft."

"Oh, dear, no," Kate moaned.

They entered a large enclosed courtyard, which was
ringed on three sides by a sweeping veranda. Lighted lanterns hung from vigas, transforming the desert foliage into
shapely silhouettes that undulated in the evening breeze like
sensuous black fingers caressing the pale adobe walls. Will
recalled telling Priscilla that Santa Fé seemed like a foreign
country. Well, the McCains' home was an unexpected oasis
in the middle of a wilderness.

Then he saw Charlie McCain, and his breath caught. The
man sat beneath a deep overhang, with a lantern directly
over his head and a leather-bound book opened on his lap.
His legs were covered with a brightly striped blanket; one
arm was tied in a sling. From the scowl on Mr. McCain's
face, Will figured the man wasn't enjoying his convales-
cence.

"Pa, somebody's here to see you . . ."

When Charlie glanced toward the approaching trio, his
eyes opened wide, and Will saw at once where Priscilla got
her blue eyes. Like her mother's hair, her father's eyes had

dulled a bit with the passage of time, but Will had no doubt
that twenty-three years ago, Charlie McCain's blue eyes had
shone in all their brilliance in the offices of Radnor, Radnor,
& Kane in Philadelphia, the City of Brotherly Love.

". . . about Joaquín," Priscilla was saying. "He's been—"

Before Priscilla could finish, Will stepped forward ex-
tending his hand to Charlie, who stared at it, transfixed.

"William Penn Radnor IV, Mr. . . . uh, McCain."

Charlie gawked, solemn, speechless.

"He's the one who came to our aid in the corral, dear,"
Kate was saying.

"Joaquín's been arrested, Pa. For—"

"Leave us," Charlie interrupted. He tore his gaze from
the vision of his past. "Bring that bottle of good whiskey,
Kate, then leave us." He turned to Priscilla. "You, too, Miss
Priss."

Chagrined at being dismissed so curtly, Priscilla stomped
from the courtyard. No wonder the whole country talked
about Pa. He guarded anything concerning Joaquín as jeal-
ously as if it were that elusive cache of gold in Spanish
Creek Canyon. Perhaps she should talk to him. With
Joaquín in jail, the gossip could get ugly. Even if it weren't
true, it couldn't help hurting Mama.

While her mother fetched the whiskey Pa requested, Priscilla wandered to the front veranda, where she sat on the
steps and absorbed the last rays of the evening sun. Ever
changing, yet always the same, the late-day sky reminded
her of a theater production filled with passion and aggression and an ethereal majesty that never failed to lift her
above the problems of the day. For the moments it took the
sun to disappear beyond the distant ridge of mountains, each
second different and more vibrant than the last, everything
else in the world dimmed, as if eclipsed by the wonder and

the beauty. For those few moments, anything seemed possible.

Even defeating the Haskels. They might be powerful, but viewed in contrast to the power of nature, they were not invincible.

Will Radnor had no part in their schemes. She was sure of that. Not yet, at least. He couldn't have come all the way to New Mexico Territory to aid the Haskels in taking Spanish Creek Ranch. She'd be foolish even to think such a thing. He probably hadn't known about their land-grabbing ways until she told him. Besides, Will Radnor wasn't that kind of man. She could tell.

She'd been too hard on him. That, too, was certain. But that could be remedied. By the time he and Pa finished their discussion, she and Mama would have supper on the table . . .

Jumping to her feet, Priscilla headed for the kitchen, but before she reached the front door, it burst open in her face. Will Radnor stormed past without so much as a by-your-leave.

Until then she hadn't realized she'd been waiting for him. That was a surprise in itself. As was his stormy mood. What could Pa have done to send him off in such a stew? She followed him down the steps.

"Will?" At her call, he stopped, midway between the house and the hitching rail. He didn't turn around, prickling her ire, until she recalled the numerous times she had snubbed him.

"Supper's almost ready." She spoke from the bottom step.

Still he didn't turn. She watched his shoulders bunch in a jerky fashion, a shrug, she supposed. She wondered again what her father could have said. Or had her own rude behavior finally caught up with her?

"We wouldn't want you to go away thinking us inhospitable."

Will moved. Reaching the hitching rail, he turned around. His eyes leveled on hers. His expression was unreadable.

"It isn't safe," she insisted, "riding back to town in the dark. Mama'll be happy to have you—"

Will's gaze held hers, dark and piercing. Even though she had no idea what was on his mind, she stopped speaking. He withdrew a rifle from the saddle scabbard, checked it, then thrust it back in place. Priscilla bristled at his silent rebuff. Venturing forward, she stopped directly in front of him, fists on hips.

"You might be a fair shot from the top of a stagecoach in broad open daylight, but it's dark now, and there're outlaws out there—and Haskels."

Will reached to pick up his reins.

"Blast you, greenhorn. If you think you can get out of our rematch by getting yourself shot—"

Will dropped the reins. His hands shot out. He grabbed her shoulders, jerked her forward, crushing his lips to hers. The impact hit her with the intensity of a thunderbolt. His fingers dug into her shoulders, while his lips moved over hers so fiercely, with so much pressure that she felt his teeth grind against hers through their lips.

Her heart thudded with the cadence of a war drum; tears stung her eyes. Will's day-old stubble scratched her chin. But still she didn't think to move, to struggle.

Suddenly, she realized that his kiss had changed. His lips opened; they stroked hers, gently, sending something tingling and tender racing down her spine.

She felt his tongue, wet against her skin. Something soft took hold of her, something magical. Her own lips began to move, she could feel them, but she didn't know how, or why.

Will's grip on her shoulders eased. His hands slipped up her neck, cupped her face. His tongue breached the opening created by her own moving lips; he dipped inside. She shuddered.

Of an instant, he released her. His gaze delved into hers, holding hers, steady. But she wasn't steady, far from it. She could feel herself tremble. She clasped her arms about her chest but was powerless to turn her gaze away. Behind her, the front door slammed. Will's brows narrowed.

"I work for the Haskels, Miss Priss." His lighthearted tone turned harsh. "Don't you forget that." Turning abruptly, he caught up his reins, stepped in the saddle, and swung his horse around, breaking eye contact.

Stunned by the entire experience, Priscilla watched him ride away. The finality of his statement clashed with the soft, sweet emotions called forth by his kiss. She felt empty with his leaving, confused by his behavior . . . Humiliated.

Suddenly her mother was there, cradling her in her arms, loving, consoling. "There, there, darling. It'll be all right. It was a hard lesson, but a necessary one. That man is no good. He just proved it."

Three

By morning Priscilla had decided to forgive Will Radnor. The magical emotions aroused by his kiss had gone a long way in dispelling the anger and hurt brought on by his rougher treatment. After all, she reasoned, hadn't she snubbed and belittled him every time they'd met, so far? No one could be expected to take such treatment sitting down, not even a greenhorn.

He was due a turn—and an apology. And that's what she would do. Apologize. First chance she got.

That decision made, Priscilla's plan began to take shape. By daybreak, she was chomping at the bit to implement it. The only hitch she could see was finding an excuse to go into town. Then she arrived at the kitchen and discovered that the angels must surely be smiling on her, to use one of her mother's favorite phrases.

"I'm going into Santa Fé this morning, Kate," Pa was saying when Priscilla reached the doorway. "Need to check on Joaquín. While I'm there, I might as well see what Newt's doin' to apprehend those road agents."

Her mother agreed. "Yes, dear, you must see about Joaquín. I suppose we should send word to Nalin." She handed Priscilla a plate.

"Let me see how bad things are, sweetheart. No need to worry his mama until we have to."

"Or Victorio," Mama said. "Didn't Crockett say he was considering taking his people to Mexico?"

"Might've already left," Pa said. "In any case, we can't make it worse by giving those braves of his another excuse to clash with authorities."

"I agree."

Priscilla bided her time, while her parents discussed the Apache war chief, Victorio, and his difficulties with the army. She filled her plate with her mother's breakfast specialty—hash-brown potatoes mixed with sausage, scrambled eggs, and roasted green chiles—and sat down to eat.

At a lull in the conversation, she offered, "I'll drive you into town, Pa."

His head jerked up; he frowned down the length of the table. The ashen cast to his complexion was made even more stark by the dark circles under his eyes. Obviously, he hadn't slept any better than Priscilla, a fact that fueled her suspicions. She fought them down. Of course, Pa would be worried about Joaquín. Why, Joaquín had been born right here in this house. He'd been raised alongside her, for the most part. Even though he had taken off on his own several years ago, Pa still loved him. She loved him, too. Even her mother did. Priscilla could see how folks might get the wrong idea.

That Pa would risk encouraging the local gossips by rushing to Joaquín's side, bespoke the measure of the man. Priscilla's pride swelled at his unselfishness.

But the alarm that passed between her parents at her offer to drive Pa to town had nothing to do with Joaquín, Priscilla discovered.

"Your mama told me what happened between you and young William Radnor."

Priscilla felt herself flush.

"Is your mama right? Have you learned your lesson?"

"My lesson?"

"That he's no good."

"I . . . uh . . ."

Pa's tone changed, softened. "You don't have to talk

about it, sugar. Long as you know to stay away from him and his kind."

Priscilla struggled to suppress a grin. "You mean greenhorns, Pa?"

"I mean any dadburnt feller who'd kiss a girl the first time he laid eyes on her. He's no good. Not for my daughter."

"It wasn't the first time he'd laid eyes on me, Pa," she teased. "We met on the stagecoach."

Pa's eyes flashed.

"Don't worry," she assured him quickly. "I can take care of myself. You taught me."

"Humph!"

"About going to town," she continued between bites. "While you check on Joaquín, I'll haggle with the government officials, wrangle us a contract for those steers."

"Fine, Jake." Pa was all business again. "That's fine."

But when she rose to leave the table, he added, "I expect you to stay away from Radnor."

Priscilla studied him from the doorway. He was serious. Poor Pa. What would he do when she really found a man to court her? "He's defending Joaquín, Pa."

"I know that. But the order stands."

"Order?" The word *order* had never set well with Priscilla; it tended to bow her neck quicker'n an old mossy horn could spook a good horse. She figured Pa ought to've learned that by now. "It was just a kiss, Pa. You taught me how to judge a man's character. Don't you trust me?"

"Trusting you has nothing to do with it," he barked. "It's that dadburnt Radnor. He's—"

Priscilla watched her mother cross the room while Pa ranted. She placed a hand on his shoulder, the time-honored signal for him to shut up. This time it didn't work.

"I mean, he's . . . he works for the Haskels."

Priscilla eyed her parents curiously. "And he's a greenhorn." She grinned. "Likely he'd be about as worthless on a ranch as Red Avery." Will's help in the branding pen popped to mind, but she resisted bringing it up. "He's new to the territory," she added. "He didn't have any way of knowing about the blasted Haskels until he got to town."

Pa's eyes flashed again. Mama looked downright worried.

"I can't believe you're both so concerned about one simple kiss. Why don't you reserve judgment until he finishes defending Joaquín?"

Priscilla watched Pa shovel a forkload of her mother's scrambled eggs into his mouth. He chewed, wiped his lips with his napkin, and looked back at Priscilla. He was glaring.

"That's the same damned thing he said."

While Pa finished breakfast and called Red Avery to hook up the wagon and team, Priscilla headed for her room to dress. Her parents' attitude surprised her, but she knew it shouldn't. Likely any parent would be worried if they saw a stranger kiss their daughter.

And Will was, after all, a stranger. But it hadn't been one simple kiss. Far from it. And she was hard pressed to control her anticipation of seeing him again. But she had to control herself. In Pa's mood, he'd likely leave her at home if he suspected her real reason for going to town. Her real reason—to apologize to Will Radnor.

Searching her closet, Priscilla drew out a new pair of chamois-colored leather britches and a matching silk shirt Mama had tried unsuccessfully to persuade her to wear the last time they went to town. Priscilla could hear her now:

"If you won't put on a skirt, darling, at least wear a more ladylike blouse."

Priscilla had declined at the time. Not that she objected to the blouse. It fit as loosely as her other shirts, but being silk, it required a fancy lace camisole underneath, or so Mama claimed.

Picking up the flimsy bit of lace now, Priscilla tried to decide what the object of wearing such a garment could be. It covered her skin in a few places but otherwise did little to either conceal or contain, which Priscilla had always figured were the two reasons for wearing undergarments.

But when she slipped it on and looked in the mirror she was taken aback. For a moment she thought she must be looking at someone else's reflection. A lady's, for sure. The soft lace brushed against her skin like spring leaves. She gulped, watching her breasts rise and fall with each breath. They mounded above the garment and snuggled softly into the nest of lace. Almost timidly, she tied the peach-colored ribbon that held the camisole in place.

With infinitely more care than usual, she brushed and rebraided her hair in its one thick braid, buttoned on the silk blouse, and tucked it into her fitted britches. In the back of her closet she found her good pair of boots. Fortunately they had been shined. She couldn't recall the last time she'd worn them.

Buckling the gunbelt around her hips, she stopped suddenly, reconsidering. It looked so bulky, felt so bulky. But if the Haskels happened to be out and about, she'd need her guns fast.

"Avery's here with the wagon." Pa's voice boomed down the long corridor from the kitchen to Priscilla's room in the south end of the building.

"Comin', Pa." Hastily she scanned her dressing table. Bare, as she liked it. But she didn't want Will telling her she smelled like a horse today. Today she wanted to smell like a lady. It would make her apology seem more sincere.

On her way to the kitchen she darted into her parents' bedroom, found a bottle of perfume on the dressing table, sniffed it, turned up her nose, then spritzed it in the general direction of her body a couple of times.

"Jake and I'll take Avery along with us," Pa was explaining when Priscilla arrived back at the kitchen. "That'll leave you and Crockett to defend things here."

"We'll be fine, dear."

Her parents were standing in the center of the big room.

Pa was propped up by a crutch under his good armpit. He drew Mama to him from that awkward position and kissed her full on the lips. Her parents had never hidden their passion from Priscilla. Seeing them in each other's arms was a common sight. But today it did uncommon things to her. Uncommon, yet far from unpleasant. She felt again Will Radnor's hands on her waist when he'd helped her down from the stage; but it wasn't her waist that tingled with the memory—it was higher and lower.

To keep from feeling disloyal to her parents, however, she didn't allow herself to dwell on Will, except for the apology she owed him. She was going to town to apologize. That was all.

She worried that her mother might smell the perfume or notice the silk blouse and all would be lost. But Mama's only comment was to raise her eyebrows.

Priscilla shrugged. "If you're right about no-good men, you're probably right about other things." She kissed her mother lightly on the cheek. "You're always saying that silk is cooler in summertime than anything else."

Her mother nodded in an absentminded fashion. Thankfully, her parents were preoccupied with Joaquín. Priscilla was worried about him, too, but that didn't keep her from cringing inside for deliberately misleading her mother.

Kate followed them out back to the waiting wagon. "Be careful, dear. Please."

"I will, sweetheart."

"Keep your guns handy."

"I will."

"He's young, Charlie, but he's been harboring this hatred for a long time. He's dangerous."

Priscilla thought sure she'd misunderstood. "Dangerous? Joaquín?" Mama sounded like she'd been out in the sun bareheaded, which she'd always claimed would fry Priscilla's brains. "Joaquín doesn't hate Pa, Mama. Or any of us. He just wants to be part of—" Her admonition came to a sudden standstill at the shocked expression on her mother's face.

Pa cleared his throat. "Nothin's gonna happen to me, sweetheart, I promise you that. We'll be back before you know it." He kissed Mama soundly, then motioned to Crockett, who fiddled with the harness. "Keep your gun at hand and Kate in sight."

"Will do, Charlie. No Haskel's gonna take this place out of our hands."

Pa's gaze found Mama's. "Don't either of you risk your life for Spanish Creek."

"We won't, dear. Don't you—" She stopped, pinned Priscilla with a haunting look of apprehension. "Be careful, darling."

Priscilla drove the wagon with her father on the seat beside her and Red Avery in the bed behind.

"Keep your eyes peeled," Charlie told him. "Check ahead and behind. Can't have those dadburnt Haskels takin' us unaware."

They rode in silence until they were far enough away from the house for Priscilla to relax. Her plan had succeeded so far, but she knew she'd have an easier time in town if she could keep Pa's mind off Will Radnor. As if in answer to a prayer, she recalled Mama's strange behavior. *Joaquín,* that's how to keep Pa from thinking about Will.

"Why was Mama so worried about Joaquín attacking you, Pa? Joaquín loves us— in his own way."

"I wouldn't go that far."

"Well, he certainly isn't dangerous, not to us. I don't understand Mama's concern."

"Your mama's concern is for you, sugar. And for me. Same as always."

His tone was gruff, and Priscilla turned to see him staring straight ahead, the brim of his Stetson adjusted against the glare of the rising sun, his jaws clenched. Coming after her own sleepless night, his petulance riled her.

"Why do you always clam up when the discussion turns to Joaquín?"

Silence.

"If Nalin would tell who his real father is," she persisted, "it would save all of us a lot of grief."

"And bring more to others," Charlie growled.

"Such as?"

"Don't get smart with me. Nalin has good reason for refusing to reveal who fathered Joaquín. She says it would bring the army down on Victorio's Apaches. Your mama and I choose to believe her. And we'd appreciate it if you—"

"The army? Why?"

"I don't know, Miss Priss. All I know for fact, is what turned up on my doorstep—a dear friend who was suffering from exposure. Nalin wanted to take her own life. Your mama nursed her back to health. We kept her with us until Joaquín was born."

"And Joaquín's blue eyes . . ."

"Joaquín's blue eyes," Charlie repeated as if by rote. His temper seemed to have eased off, and for some reason, he became uncustomarily talkative. She decided to take that as a good sign. If he worried over Joaquín, he wouldn't be stewing over Will Radnor.

"Those eyes aren't the reason I feel responsible for the boy," he admitted. "Nalin's husband was a friend of mine; he was murdered more'n a year before Joaquín was born."

"I didn't know that!"

"Reckon I've always felt responsible. Jessie Laredo's husband—"

"Jessie Laredo had a husband?"

"Man by the name of Suárez. That's where she got the cantina and the shipping company. Inherited them from Rodrigo. He was a bad one, real bad. He'd steal, lie . . ." Pa's words drifted off; then, as though they had rebounded from the high ridge of mountains that ringed the horizon, he continued, "Rodrigo Suárez sold whiskey and rifles to the Indians. That last shipment . . . to Victorio's braves . . . He spiked the whiskey with arsenic. Jessie found out. She came to me, but I couldn't get there in time. Nalin's husband and six other braves were already dead."

"That wasn't your fault."

"Maybe not. But they were my friends. Mine and your mama's. I felt like I'd let 'em down. Still do."

"And you want to make up for it by helping Joaquín."

"Is that wrong?"

"It's admirable, Pa. But I wouldn't have expected less from you." She flicked the reins, encouraging their prized pair of Morgan harness horses, Martha Washington and Betsy Ross. "You're a fair man, Pa. That's why your hasty judgment about Will Radnor is so hard to understand."

"Humph!" He shifted angrily on the wagon seat. "He kissed you, didn't he?"

Priscilla hastened to change the subject again. "Why wasn't I ever told all this?"

"All what?"

"About Nalin's husband and the whiskey? About you and Jessie Laredo?"

"Me and Jessie Laredo? Whoa, now, sugar."

"I mean, I didn't know you were friends, Pa." She frowned at him. "I mean . . . she isn't exactly the type—"

"I'm not sure I like your tone," Pa barked. "When'd you start judgin' folks?"

The team approached a rockslide. Priscilla guided Martha and Betsy deftly around it. "I don't know, Pa. Yesterday, I guess. Same time you did."

He didn't like that, she could tell, but he kept his mouth shut, which, in itself was strange, for Pa always tried to get the last word. She must have really made him mad this time, and in light of what she planned to do in town, that wasn't too smart. She decided it would be in her best interest to make up before they reached Santa Fé.

"When did you meet Jessie, Pa?"

"Way before I met your mama. Jessie and Rodrigo were already livin' in Santa Fé when I got out here."

"When was that?"

Without a moment's hesitation, he responded, "Twenty-three years ago."

"From Texas?"

"In a roundabout way."

"I thought you were born and raised in Texas, Pa. I thought that's where we got our start with these Morgans, from your family. I thought Uncle Crockett and Uncle Sog—"

"Whoa, there, sugar? Why all the questions?"

Priscilla grimaced. Here she'd been trying to settle him down, and she'd riled him again. Since when did she have to handle her own pa with kid gloves? "I don't know, Pa. Suddenly I feel sort of stupid, nineteen and not even knowing where my own father was born and raised."

"Humph!"

"I wasn't very inquisitive, was I?"

"You were busy growin' up. And your mama and I were busy getting this ranch started. It's the present that counts. There's no useful purpose in dredgin' up the past."

"But it sounds exciting. Arsenic-laced whiskey. Murder and assault."

"You wouldn't've called it exciting, if you'd been there. Besides, it's the future that's exciting. Defeating the Haskels. Enlarging Spanish Creek."

He reached over and patted her knee, a peace offering. She relaxed.

"I'll be turning it over to you one day, Jake."

His voice was thick. Priscilla smiled at his uncustomary show of emotion. She knew Pa was proud of her. She could always tell when she pleased him. But he'd never put it into words.

Then they arrived in Santa Fé, and Priscilla, too, put the

past out of mind. Getting a rope on the present promised to be chore enough.

"Cain't let you see that half-breed, Charlie," Newt Haskel, the sheriff, replied to Charlie's request to see Joaquín. "That young lawyer left orders not to let anyone in."

"He didn't mean me, Newt."

"He never said nothin' about you bein' special, Charlie. I got my orders, you know. You'll have to carry yourself up his way and git permission, 'fore I'll let you in."

Pa was fuming. Priscilla could practically see steam billowing from his nose. She figured he had it coming for being so bullheaded about Will. Now at least she wouldn't have to concoct a story to get to see Will. She wasn't good at concocting stories.

She headed the team for the corner of San Francisco and Water Street, where the adobe offices of Faust & Haskel sat next to the offices of the Haskel Land Grant Company. But Pa's mind wasn't on the Haskels today, Priscilla discovered.

"Remember what I told you, Miss Priss," he growled when she drew rein.

"Pa, don't call me that. Especially not . . . in town."

"Humph! Avery, run get that greenhorn lawyer."

"Don't call me that," Priscilla repeated.

"All right," Charlie barked. "But you remember your promise. Steer clear of that damned Yankee."

"I told you not to worry, Pa."

"Not to worry? You think you can come into town smelling like your mama's rose garden and I don't know what you're up to?"

She stared at him, abashed.

"I thought it was your mama wearing that perfume.

Didn't realize it was you till we were too far from the house to turn back. Make sure you mind me about that boy."

Priscilla stopped listening halfway through the lecture, for Will had come to the door. He stood there, staring at her, his gaze intense, unreadable. She couldn't keep her eyes off his lips. She flushed, recalling his kiss, the tender, gentle, exciting part. Why was it so hard to recall the other—the bitter, fierce, angry part? Her parents must be right. They always were. This man was no good.

But when he smiled, she smiled. Then, while she was trying to decide how she could get him alone to apologize, his expression turned to stone and he averted his gaze. She looked quickly away.

A sickening sense of humiliation crept up her neck. She diverted her attention to the street ahead, which was no more than a haze of red earth. She heard Will approach the wagon, but he ignored her as if she weren't even in town, much less sitting right in front of his very eyes. He stopped beside her, but spoke across her in curt tones.

"You want to see my client?"

"That's what I said." Charlie's tone was equally curt.

"Will you persuade him to talk to me?"

"Maybe. If I can."

Priscilla's heart pounded so loud it was downright embarrassing. She didn't look at Will, but she could feel his breath blow against her cheek when he talked in explosive tones to her pa.

"Damnit, McCain, I can't defend the man if he won't talk to me. Quicker we clear Joaquín, the quicker we can get down to business."

"I'll see what I can do."

"Permission granted."

"Then climb in back of this wagon and ride down there with us. You have to tell Newt to let me in."

Priscilla heard the exchange as from afar. She felt the heat that had crept up her neck burn her cheeks. She'd never been so embarrassed. The soft summer breeze blew the silk blouse against her skin, reminding her of her plans.

Did he know? Could he tell she had dressed up just for him? How humiliating! She stared straight ahead, scarcely moving until Pa brought her attention back to the dusty street.

"Whip up the team, Miss Pr— Whip 'em up, Jake. Let's get on down to that jailhouse."

And whip up the team she did. Laying leather the length of their backs, she heed and hawed, and Martha Washington and Betsy Ross leapt to their traces. She'd see how these two surly men liked a taste of their own medicine.

"Hold on there," Pa warned.

Ignoring him, Priscilla jerked the reins to the right, swerving to miss a wagon that had slowed in her path. From the corner of her eye, she saw Pa grip the seat with a white-knuckled hand and wished she could see Will Radnor's face. Maybe she'd thrown him off by now.

She laid the whip across the horses' backs again, first Martha's, then Betsy's. "Giddy-up there!"

"Watch that burro!" Charlie hollered. "Thunderation, Priscilla, slow down."

They arrived at the jail in a cloud of red dust. Priscilla jerked the reins with vigor, bringing the horses to a bone-jarring, stiff-legged halt. The wagon seat bounced beneath her.

She wanted to turn around, but didn't dare. She hoped she'd landed Will Radnor on his greenhorn hind-end. But before the dust had settled good, his insulting lilt cut through the mush in her brain.

"Practicing to drive the stage, Miss McCain?"

She locked her jaws against a retort.

"Careful, Radnor," Charlie growled. "A deal's a deal." He turned to Priscilla. "Park under that tree yonder."

"I'm not coming in, Pa. While you talk to Joaquín, I'll

go down to the Palacio and check on a contract for those steers."

"Well, park this rig and walk. Avery'll drive me down there when I'm finished here. Avery!" he called. "Get that dadburnt walking stick from the bed and help me down off this seat."

When Red Avery came around the side to help Charlie disembark from the wagon, Priscilla allowed herself a brief glance to the boardwalk. No sign of Will Radnor.

That greenhorn! Here she'd worn a fancy silk shirt and a stupid contraption underneath it and her mother's perfume . . .

Haggling with the government officials took her mind off Will Radnor. When she exited the Palace of the Governors, she was feeling somewhat less chagrined. One thing she could be glad of, she hadn't found a chance to talk to that greenhorn; he certainly didn't deserve an apology. Jessie Laredo hailed her from across the plaza.

"*¡Hola,* Jake!" She fell in step with Priscilla. "The whole town's talking about the way you handled that runaway team."

"Runaway team?" Priscilla studied Jessie with renewed interest, recalling Pa's story. Jessie certainly didn't look like a widow—or dress like one. From what Pa said, she must be at least Mama's age, but she still looked and dressed like a girl, a slightly disreputable girl, of the sort men liked to ogle—unruly black curls, flashing black eyes, breasts that bulged above the low cut of her white blouse.

Jessie's familiarity surprised Priscilla. She'd always been friendly, but Priscilla couldn't recall ever really talking with the woman, not alone, much less having Jessie initiate a conversation.

Yet, Priscilla was pleased. A woman like Jessie could answer any question an unschooled girl like herself might have.

Jessie linked arms with Priscilla, drawing her at a leisurely gait around the plaza. "That Will Radnor's some kind of man."

"I wouldn't know."

"He's renting a room from me. Above the cantina."

"Really?" Priscilla strove to sound uninterested. As tempting as confiding in Jessie might be, she could *never* do it.

"He certainly is a fine specimen of a man. He's single, you know, and smart, and . . ."

"Stop, Miss Laredo."

"Jessie, please. Everyone calls me Jessie."

"Jessie, you'll have to find someone else to harness up with that greenhorn."

"*¿Sí?*" Jessie patted Priscilla's arm. "A lovely blouse. And the lace camisole—just the right touch."

"The right touch?"

"Seductive, but not brazen."

Priscilla felt herself blush. "I don't know what you're talking about." She stopped in the path. Jessie stopped, too. "I have to go get Pa. Good-day—"

"Charlie's still at the jail, *chica*. I just came from there. He and Newt are discussing those road agents that handsome Will Radnor dispatched for you."

"With my rifle," Priscilla retorted.

"Now, Jake, you'll have to soften your attitude just a bit. Not much, he might like strong women— "

"Jessie, I have to go, really."

"Priscilla . . . *Sí*, we must call you Priscilla from now on. You have plenty of time, *chica*."

"Time?"

Jessie winked. "For a little rendezvous, *¿por qué no?*"

Priscilla blinked. Surely, she'd misunderstood. "I have to get Pa."

"I'll let you know when Charlie's ready, *chica*. Why don't you walk down to the river, cool off in the shade of those nice piñon trees? Unless you'd like to come into the cantina. I have to get back to work."

The cantina? Priscilla could see Pa's reaction to that. "I, uh, I shouldn't. The river sounds nice."

Jessie squeezed her arm. "Walk on down there, then, and let your senses cool off. And *chica,* when you're chasing a man, don't be so obvious."

Priscilla's heart skipped. "Chasing . . . ?"

Jessie winked. "The runaway team. You didn't really want to throw Will Radnor into a pothole on his *sentaderas,* did you?"

Priscilla wasn't sure what a *sentaderas* was, but since Jessie had been right about everything else, she probably knew what to call his hind-end, too.

"It was that obvious?"

Jessie nodded.

"Do you think he knew?"

"No sé. I don't know him that well. But he's old enough—and handsome enough—to have had women chasing him before."

"Chasing him?"

"There's nothing wrong with chasing a man, *chica.* But you must go about it the right way. You could try pouting . . . or flirting? Flirting always gets them. What about Red Avery?"

"What about him?"

"You could use him to make Will jealous."

"Jessie. I . . . I think you're right. I need to walk along the river and cool off. That's all." She disengaged herself from Jessie's hold. "Thanks for the advice. I'll try not to get carried away again."

"Oh, no, *chica.* It's all right to get carried away; just don't let him catch on . . ." Jessie winked. ". . . until you've snared him."

Priscilla took the alley leading from Water Street to the river and came upon a peaceful oasis. The Río Santa Fé flowed in lazy fashion through the width of town. Piñon trees lined its banks. Peaceful. Yes, Jessie was right. She inhaled the naturally perfumed air and wondered quite suddenly why anyone needed bottled scents.

She mustn't let Will get the best of her again. Not that he would have a chance. Lost in thought, she strolled down the riverbank until she'd left the buildings behind. Presently she came upon a patch of sunflowers that looked like they'd been created from pure gold, highlighted as they were by a shaft of sunlight.

The sunflower heads were huge this year, a good foot in diameter. Picking one she attached it to the trunk of a piñon tree, with its stem twined around the bark. Counting off fifty paces, she drew a pistol and began to fire at the petals.

Shooting targets was such a common pastime, Priscilla really didn't have to think about it. Her mind drifted to Will Radnor, to his thick brown hair.

She hit a petal. "He loves me."

To his lean, angular face.

She hit a second petal. "He loves me not."

To his soft, sensuous lips. She hit the third petal. "He loves me."

She aimed at a fourth petal, but before she could pull the trigger, a bullet ripped into it.

"She loves me not."

Embarrassment swept over Priscilla in a heated rush, leaving her so weak, she feared she might crumble to the ground. She gripped the pistol tighter, hoping to still, or at least conceal, her trembling. Without turning to look at Will, she aimed at the next petal, fired, and hit it. "She hates him."

His hands clasped her shoulders from behind; his touch burned through the silk. Or was it her skin, burning from embarrassment.

"Hmmm . . . roses. I've never shot against such a sweet-smelling opponent." His face was near, so near his cheek touched her hair, so near she felt his warm breath against her ear. Before she could control it, a soft shudder coursed down her spine. His grip tightened.

She took aim, fired, and hit the next petal, and the next. Her pistol was empty. She felt his right hand leave her shoulder. From her peripheral vision she watched him extend an arm in front of her. She saw his gun. A small, pocket-sized pistol. He fired. Once, twice, three times, four, hitting a petal dead-center each time.

"That's five shots," she mumbled. Will dropped the little pistol to the grass and turned her by the shoulders.

She stared down at the gun.

"It's a little hot to stick back in my britches," he explained. "I mean . . . uh . . ."

Priscilla looked up. His face was mottled, like he was embarrassed about something, but his eyes smoldered with something different, an emotion she had no name for—one that left her feeling warm and giddy all over, nonetheless.

"You need a holster," she said quietly.

He didn't respond right away, but kept looking at her with that expression that made her knees go weak. It reminded her of his kiss, the good part. Even though she was mad enough to feed him horseshoe nails, all she could think about was kissing him again.

"It wasn't my idea to ignore you, Miss Priss. Your father ordered me to never so much as look at you again."

"Pa?"

"Humm . . . last night and again today."

Priscilla felt herself engulfed in flames. But they were no longer flames of embarrassment or anger. They were something way beyond her experience. They made her feel terrible and wonderful and giddy and weak. She recalled Jessie's warning not to let a man know how she felt. How could she keep such an obvious fact a secret? She tried not to look at him.

"I'm not supposed to speak to you, either."

Will's hands slipped up her arms, clasped softly around

her neck, traveled to her face. He cupped her jaws in his palms and lifted her face, staring into her eyes with an expression that stopped her heart. Jessie was right. She had a lot to learn.

"But he didn't say I couldn't apologize." Will's whispers blew against her lips.

Apologize? Him? She was the one who needed to apologize. She'd snubbed and belittled—

"I was aggravated last night," he was saying, "but not with you." His breath tickled her lips seductively. "I took it out on you. I'm sorry."

Her eyes searched his. He was sincere . . . or awfully good at acting like it. Were her parents right? They usually were.

Then his lips claimed hers, and all thoughts of parents and no-good men evaporated. There went that shudder again. How embarrassing.

How wonderful. Now he was kissing her. Really kissing her. His lips caressed hers, softly, tenderly. Slanting, moving. Without realizing it she reached out; her hands touched his body, grasped him around the ribs. She felt him tremble.

Or had she imagined it? Was it she who trembled? She felt like her body was full of light and life, glowing and quaking like aspen leaves in late fall.

His tongue touched her lips again, parted her lips again, dipped inside. Her breath came short. When he tugged her to him, she went willingly.

The sheer lace of her camisole and the thin silk of her blouse did little to protect her from the impact when her chest met his. One of his hands was on her back, splayed across her shoulders, supporting her, pressing her to him. When her breasts flattened against him, she felt her nipples grow taut.

Again, embarrassment coursed through her—could he tell? She knew he could. But her embarrassment was swept away by another wave of sweet, fiery, spine-tingling passion, as Will continued to kiss her with the softest, tenderest, wettest kisses this side of heaven.

She was only half aware of his hands moving around her sides. When the heels of his palms rested against the edges of her breasts, pressing them together in front, another wave of fiery heat chased the last. She sighed into his open lips.

At the sound, Will drew back. He looked into her eyes, deeply, as if searching for something. "Priscilla McCain."

She suppressed a shudder at the musical way his strange accent played with her name.

Then his eyes turned cold. "Hell fire and damnation!"

She froze. He'd done that before. Confused her by saying something soft or teasing, then following it with something cold and harsh.

When her breathing steadied, she felt awkward, standing there in his arms, with them staring into each other eyes, neither of them speaking. "How did you find me?"

"Jessie said you were waiting for me."

Their expressions registered the truth simultaneously. Will laughed; Priscilla blushed.

"She came over to the jail and whispered it to me. Said you asked her to. You didn't?"

"Of course, not. I never wanted to see you again."

He grinned. Then he did the most unusual—and wonderful—thing. He kissed her again. Quick. Hard. Solid. Yet tender, oh, so tender. "How'd you feel about it now, Miss Priss?"

She grimaced. "I could shoot Pa for calling me that."

Before the words were out of her mouth, Will had stiffened.

"I didn't mean it," she assured him. "It was just a . . . a phrase we use out here."

"I know." But the spell had been broken. He stepped back, picked up his little pistol and began reloading it.

Priscilla took it from him, turned it over, wondering

whether her trembling would ever cease. "I've seen a gun like this somewhere."

"I thought you might have. It's an old gun. Not many people would know it only holds five shots."

"That was instinct." She squinted at the pistol. "Or memory. I don't remember where I saw one." She looked at him and was surprised to see his face grim. "Where'd you get it?"

"Belonged to my father's law partner. It's one of a matched pair."

Priscilla laughed, hoping to lighten his mood. Wanting to bring back the magic. "Matched pair or not, it won't do you much good out here. It isn't a Western gun, greenhorn."

And then he did the strangest thing. Strange and wonderful. He took her in his arms and held her tightly against his chest. She could hear his heart beat against her. She wrapped her arms around him and held him tight.

It was her first real embrace. And it was wonderful beyond all her expectations. For a man who was no-good, Will Radnor knew how to do some pretty wonderful things.

Four

Will left first, and Priscilla gradually regained her wits. Whether he was no good or not remained to be seen, but one thing was certain—Pa thought he was. Pa would have a conniption fit if he so much as suspected she'd been with Will.

She touched her lips. And she'd certainly been with Will! Pray God, she would be again. But first things first. She had a cattle drive to organize. That ought to take Pa's mind off Will Radnor.

On her way back to the jail, she located Clem Holbert and arranged for him to find some cowboys to help with the drive. All the while, she was practically bursting with plans, plans totally unrelated to driving a bunch of steers to market. Even the necessity of lying to Pa about seeing Will, was alleviated by her scheme to make things right. Her parents would come around once they got to know Will—if she didn't slip and ruin things first. As soon as Joaquín was free, she would set about convincing them to give Will another chance. They would come around. They had never denied her anything she wanted.

And she'd never wanted anything like this in her life.

Pa was waiting for her in front of the jail, propped against the adobe wall, his walking stick, as he called it, stuck under his good armpit. If he'd had two good legs, he would have been pacing.

No, Priscilla reconsidered, *if he'd had two good legs, he would have come after her.* The idea of Pa discovering her in Will's arms jolted her.

"Took you long enough," Pa barked.

"Where's Red?" she asked, attempting to divert his attention from her tardiness.

"Took off chasin' some dadburnt bones a feller found on a place north of town. Run over there and fetch the wagon." He squinted at her, heightening her rising feelings of guilt by several degrees. "Looks like you got that burr outta your saddle. How'd you make out with the government folks?"

Priscilla leveled her matching pair of blue eyes on his, realizing this was the first time in memory hers had ever lied to this man, whom she loved and admired above all other people.

"Sure did, Pa. We're to drive the steers to Fort Stanton soon as possible."

"Fort Stanton. Hell, that means you'll have to go with 'em, Jake. Without one of us along, Victorio's braves'll raid 'em sure as shootin.' "

With a bit of a shock, Priscilla realized that she wasn't all that anxious to go on a cattle drive. She wasn't even anxious to return to Spanish Creek. Not with Will's kisses so fresh and sweet, not with the promises his embrace had awakened inside her.

"Uncle Crockett can go," she suggested. "Victorio's braves know him. I ran into Clem Holbert. He's bringing three or four cowboys out in the morning. They'll be at the ranch ready to ride by first light."

Pa's eyes flashed. Dismally, she wondered why she ever tried to fool him. He was smarter than just about anybody she had ever known. And had more common sense, too. But leaving on a trail drive right now was out of the question, so she continued her argument.

"I wouldn't feel right going off until Joaquín is free, Pa. How was he?"

"Wouldn't talk to me. Except to say he wanted no help from me or mine."

"What about the horse he stole?"

"I asked him about that. He said it was none of my affair, that . . ." He looked off toward the plaza. His words drifted on the piñon scented air.

"That what, Pa?"

"Never mind. There's nothing more we can do here. If things don't change, we'll have to ride out to the ranchería an' tell his mama."

"I'll talk to him."

"Why would he listen to you? You two don't get along; haven't ever since you grew up."

"I know, Pa, but—"

"Did you convince my client to talk to me, McCain?" Will's voice boomed from behind Priscilla, cold and harsh, as far from the seductive tones he had murmured against her skin only minutes before as snow was from a warm summer rain.

She turned, but he wasn't looking at her. Instead he glowered at her pa. She glanced back in time to see Pa's eyes flash in a way she knew well.

"You're the one claimin' to be a lawyer, Radnor. Get him to talk on your own." Charlie turned to Priscilla. "Help me over to that wagon, Miss Pr—"

"Pa." Her warning stopped him. But Will still ignored her, or was trying to. He seemed to be focusing too intently on her pa. As if he was afraid to take his eyes off Pa, lest they stray to her.

And what would she see if they did? Would he glare at her with that same menacing expression? "How can Will, uh, Mr. Radnor defend Joaquín, if Joaquín won't talk to him?"

"Humph! That's none of my affair."

Exasperated, Priscilla decided she'd have to take control.

"What about the horse Joaquín's accused of stealing?" she asked Will. "Whose is it?"

"That's plural, Miss McCain." Will's coldness confused her. Pa, she understood. He'd made his feelings about Will kissing her perfectly clear. Besides that, Will worked for the Haskels, which would have been reason enough in itself. But Will had no reason to hate her pa.

"Horses," Will explained.

"How many? And whose?"

Will shrugged. His coldness was almost more than she could bear. Although she couldn't recall the last time she'd cried, she felt like crying now. And that made her mad. Fighting mad. What right did these two bullheaded men have charging at each other and putting her in the middle?

"Horses carry brands, Mr. Radnor." She spat his name, hoping to give him a taste of his own medicine. "Whose brand was on the horses Joaquín is accused of stealing?"

"I haven't seen them," Will admitted. Although he had turned her way, he still refused to meet her eyes. "My information says there're six horses. From what I understand, they don't carry brands—"

"No brands?" Priscilla rolled her eyes. "I told you not to say stupid things, greenhorn. A horse with no brand has no owner. And if a horse has no owner, it can't be stolen."

"These horses have an owner. Some fellow outside town claimed them. I'm not, however, *stupid or green* enough to take the sheriff's word for it."

"THE SHERIFF!" Charlie spat. "That dadburnt Newt Haskel. He'd tell a lie if the truth served him better."

"I intend to ride out and take a look, McCain," Will assured him. "The horse Joaquín was riding is a different matter. According to the sheriff, that horse carries the Spanish Creek brand."

"Well, he damned well didn't steal it," Charlie barked. "Leave it to a Haskel to make something out of that."

"I understand your position with the Haskels, sir—"

"You don't understand coyote cookies, Radnor."

"Pa!"

Will bowed his neck; his eyes bore into Charlie's. "Don't push me, McCain. I gave you until—"

Priscilla stalked between the two men. She pushed them apart with a hand to each chest. "While you two tangle like a couple of mule skinners in an augurin' match, I'm going to talk to Joaquín."

"No, you're not." Charlie grabbed for her, lost his precarious balance, caught the crutch, but missed Priscilla.

"Yes, she is," Will countered. His voice lowered. "She's right, McCain. If you care anything at all for that man's life, you'd better let your daughter have a try at what you failed."

Priscilla spun to face Will. "Failed? My pa wasn't undergoing a test, Mr. Radnor. He was visiting a friend. For a man to ride twenty miles over rough roads with two unhealed gunshot wounds, you'd think—"

"Whoa, there, Miss McCain. Don't get all worked up."

"Worked up?" She rolled her eyes. "You're despicable."

"And you're . . ." A grin quirked Will's mouth in a delicious way that reminded Priscilla of how his lips had felt on hers. For an instant, her anger dissipated. Pa interrupted.

"Get your eyes off my daughter, Radnor."

Priscilla gasped. "Both of you are despicable." She scowled from one to the other. "Entertain yourselves. If you think you can do it without bloodshed."

Without further ado, she stormed into the jailhouse, where she came face to face with Newt Haskel, who refused her entrance, as he had done her father before her. "Radnor's in charge of who his client sees, Jake. Cain't go against his wishes." His tone implied that he wouldn't if he could.

Newt Haskel was as tall a man as Will, and bulky, although half the size of his older brother, Oscar. He sported a thin brown handlebar mustache, again a weak copy of the flourishing mustache his brother wore. Newt's clothes were neat enough, considering the fact that he was a bachelor and lived alone. He always wore a black bolo tie with an ornate silver concho that matched the buckle on his belt. The silver conchos and his sheriff's badge were always polished, showing pride in his profession, Priscilla had thought on other occasions when she tried to follow her parents' dictate to find something good in everyone.

"Show the lady in, Newt." Will's voice startled her, for she thought he'd remained outside arguing with her pa.

She flinched at the sound of it, softer, respectful, even. *Lady.* The word sifted through her layers of anger and confusion like a sprinkling of stardust. She'd never been called a lady before. Of course, she'd never allowed it.

Strangely enough, it felt good. Not highfalutin and stickysweet, like she'd always thought, but sort of soothing after their recent confrontation. Her eyes sought Will's, even as she accepted the fact that it was *who* had called her a lady that made the difference.

His brown eyes gleamed; he winked.

She smiled.

Winked? The nerve of him. The arrogant, dastardly nerve of him! "You aren't as suited to this country as I'd thought, greenhorn."

Will's expression turned quizzical, arrogantly so, she thought.

"We don't play games out here, Mr. Radnor. When we like someone, we like them. When we don't, we don't." She turned quickly, lest he respond, hurried through the door Newt had unlocked, and stomped down the corridor to the back of the building, her march accompanied by the resounding jangle of her spurs.

Two cells were located on opposite sides of the narrow hallway. One was empty. Joaquín lounged against the far wall of the other, a cigarette between his lips. Smoke curled upward on a draft from the window above his head. Light from the window highlighted his glossy black hair.

He stared impassively at Priscilla. She stopped before the bars. For a moment they stood, each taking in the other. Priscilla broke the silence.

"I know you're not a horse thief, Joaquín."

His face showed no trace of emotion.

"I also know you don't ride with Billy the Kid. So why are you in here?"

For another lengthy moment they stared at each other. Finally, Joaquín pushed his boot against the wall, shoved off, and ambled toward the bars. He stopped before Priscilla, grabbed a bar in each fist, and stooped to bring his eyes level with hers. Long straight hair swung to either side of his face, falling from the red flannel headband to well below shoulder length.

"You know why, Jake. Look me in the eyes and admit it, if you can."

Joaquín wasn't much taller than Priscilla, but he was often mistaken for a larger man. He was well proportioned, sleek, Priscilla had always thought, like the puma that ranged in the Sangre de Cristos. He was easily recognizable as an Apache—earth-toned complexion, broad nose, high cheekbones, squared chin—until he looked you in the eye. Those brilliant blue eyes gave away his parentage, and had caused him untold grief since he had reached an age to know the difference.

He and Priscilla had played together as children. They'd roughhoused, then, back when they were young. Friendly competitors, like the best of brothers and sisters, they fought over who could shoot the straightest, who could run the fastest, who could ride the wildest bronc. Then Priscilla grew up to become Charlie's tophand and heir apparent, and Joaquín turned bad.

At least, that's what folks around the territory said. Priscilla had her doubts. Disillusioned, perhaps. But she knew he hadn't turned bad. He was searching for his identity, Mama claimed. Priscilla couldn't recall precisely when she realized the key to Joaquín's identity was the word father.

It had taken her even longer to understand the underlying injury that resulted from, not the fact that he didn't have a father, but from the obvious truth revealed by his clear blue eyes. A truth denied by the very father he sought to claim.

Joaquín didn't belong to either world—not the white man's world with his Apache coloring and features; nor to the Apache world with those startling blue eyes. His shame was obvious to the most casual observer. It couldn't be hidden by clothing or masked with war paint.

Joaquín—unlike his half-brother José Colorado, an honored Apache warrior—belonged nowhere. Not even to the one place in the world he yearned to call his own—Spanish Creek Ranch.

He took the cigarette from his mouth, flicked off the ash, and shoved it back between his slightly parted lips.

"How've you been?" she asked.

He chuckled, but the sound was derisive rather than mirthful. He glanced around at the cell he'd occupied for three days straight. "Never cared much for locked doors."

"You've never been in jail before, but I guess it wouldn't matter—"

"I've been locked up all my life, Jake. And locked out."

She ignored his petulance. "Pa wants to help."

Joaquín's blue eyes turned as hard as flint. If she hadn't known him well, his expression would have been frightening, or at the very least, intimidating. "I don't want anything from Charlie McCain. I don't need his help."

"Yes, you do. Will says—"

"Will?"

"Your lawyer. Will Radnor."

Joaquín snorted. "Charlie teamin' up with the Haskels? Never thought I'd see the day. Of course, he'd take sides with the devil himself against me."

"That isn't true."

Joaquín reached through the bars and caught a loose strand of blond hair, which he tugged through callused fingers. "Don't worry your pretty blue eyes over it, little Miss Priss. You've got Spanish Creek. That oughta be enough for you to count coup over."

"Don't—" She reached to touch his hand, but he dropped her hair and pulled his hand back inside the cell. "You're hurt, Joaquín. You have reason to be, but—"

Joaquín turned his back abruptly. "I don't want your damned sympathy. Or Charlie's. Especially not Charlie's."

Priscilla studied him from the rear. His shoulders bunched forward, tensed, as if against physical blows. His hands gripped in fists at his sides. It was a stance of defiance. She tried to recall what Joaquín had been like before he turned bitter, but the only image that would come to her was of a small dark boy with clenched fists.

"They said the horses were unbranded," she told him.

"I didn't take anything that wasn't mine."

"I know you aren't a horse thief," she said again. "But if you won't help Will, how can he prove it?"

Joaquín remained silent and motionless. He stood that way for long moments—his back to her, his shoulders hunched. Finally he ground out the stub of his cigarette on the stone floor. He stalked toward the mattressless bunk, where he picked up a tobacco pouch and a pack of cigarette papers. With his side to her, he rolled another cigarette, licked the length of the paper edge, and stuck it to the other side. When he turned back, it was to look past her. She might as well have been invisible.

"Newt! Where the hell are you? Bring me a damned light!"

Priscilla hadn't been aware of Will, standing in the shadows of the corridor. At Joaquín's call, he stepped forward, struck a match on the heel of his boot—as casually as though he had been born to the Western gesture—and offered the flame to Joaquín.

When the cigarette took light, Joaquín stepped back. Priscilla watched Will shake the flame out and toss the burned match to a spittoon near her feet. It missed. Without looking at her, he bent at the knees, picked up the match, and tossed it into the spittoon.

He rose slowly, coming at length face to face with her, eye to eye. She felt weak at his intense, searching perusal. When he spoke, it was a low, soft command.

"Introduce me."

Priscilla stood mesmerized. She stared into Will's questioning gaze. At length, she complied with his command, hoping her voice wouldn't quiver.

"Joaquín, this is Will Radnor. He's been appointed by the court to defend you."

"I know who he is."

"The Haskels had nothing to do with hiring him."

"The Haskels had everything to do with it."

"With your capture, maybe, but not with appointing Will—"

"Who the hell did the appointing?" Joaquín demanded. "You think Judge Sanders isn't in Oscar Haskel's pocket?"

"Why do you have to be so stubborn?" She immediately regretted the outburst. In a lower voice, she said, "Will wants to defend you. He can get you out of here. But you have to help him."

Joaquín turned hooded eyes to Will.

"She's right, Joaquín. Horse theft is a hanging offense. If you'll cooperate, I can help you."

"What can I tell you, lawyer? You learned my name." He glared at Priscilla, then back to Will. "From the looks of things, you two are thick enough that you've learned every damned thing about me."

"I've heard a lot of gossip, yes. Priscilla says you're no horse thief. I'm inclined to believe her. But whether or not

you are, you deserve a fair chance. If you'll help me, I can
convince a jury of your peers—"

"A jury of my peers?" Joaquín hissed. "Who the hell
are *my* peers?" Coming forward, he stopped in front of Will,
glared into his eyes. "Take a good look at me, white eyes!
Who are my peers?" He turned those furious eyes on Priscilla. "Look at me! Who am I? NOBODY!" Joaquín's barbaric cry echoed through the empty room.

Priscilla shrunk back involuntarily. Will took her by the
shoulders, stopping short of drawing her into the protection
of his arms.

"Joaquín, please, talk to Will," she begged.

"Come on, Priscilla." Will turned her toward the hall.

Joaquín stared, stolid, his face revealing no emotion. Will
dragged her down the hallway.

"Talk to Will, Joaquín," she called. "It's your only
chance. Talk to him. For Pa's sake. And for yours."

When they entered the front office, Newt Haskel greeted
Will with a slap on the back.

Newt was a jolly sort, Priscilla recalled, if he liked a
person. Obviously, he'd taken a liking to Will.

"Will, I've been lookin' for you, son. You know that little
matter we were discussing?" Newt's mustache, thin though
it was, waggled when he talked. He clapped Will around
the shoulders like they were the best of friends.

Joaquín's accusation sliced through Priscilla. She knew
it was true. The Haskels owned every lawyer and official
in this territory, why not the judges?

"Need a word with you, son," Newt was saying, " 'bout
that little piece of business." He remembered Priscilla, then.
His eyes traveled over her, reminding her of the silk blouse
she wore . . . and of the wispy bit of lace beneath it.

Something that felt like fear welled inside Priscilla in a
sickening rush. It clogged her throat and brought moisture
to her eyes. She jerked free from Will's hold and fled.

"Priscilla, wait," Will called. But she didn't dare look back.

Not until she and Pa were seated in the wagon and headed out of town did she regain her sensibilities enough to realize Red Avery wasn't with them.

"Where the hell is that worthless—"

"Calm down, Miss Priss. When he came back from looking at those bones, I sent him on home ahead."

"Ahead? On what?"

"Joaquín's horse. Don't figure he'll be needin' it anytime soon. Since it was wearin' a Spanish Creek brand, Newt couldn't very well refuse to give it to me."

Priscilla eyed him sharply, then turned her attention back to the road. As usual Pa didn't miss a lick.

"You gonna tell me what happened inside that jail to set you off like your mama's steam kettle?"

Will watched Priscilla rush out of the jail. "I want to see that sworn statement against my client, Sheriff," he demanded. "And the information on those horses."

Newt changed the subject in tones that sounded accusatory. "Looks like you an' that little gal are gettin' thick. Don't know what a feller could see in a woman who dresses like a man—"

"You'd do well to stop right there, Haskel."

"Oh, I'll stop all right, son, if that's what you want. Figure you bein' down here without family o' your own, though, someone oughta look out after you. There's some things about McCain you might wanta know."

Will glanced through the open doorway. Priscilla was helping Charlie across the street. Except at the clip she was dragging him, Charlie might end up with more injured than one gunshot arm and leg. Lordy, that was one spunky lady. She might act tough, but that didn't keep her from fighting for those she loved.

"McCain ain't his real name," Newt was saying. "Of course, that ain't uncommon out here. Lot of folks shed a bad reputation by buryin' the name of the perpetrator. Rumor has it, murder's what he's accused of. 'Course it was a while back. In Philadelphia."

The sheriff had Will's full attention for the first time since Priscilla sashayed out the door. He watched Newt stroke his mustache.

"Suppose you knew that, though," Haskel allowed, "bein' from Philadelphia yourself. And a lawyer, to boot. McCain was a lawyer, so they claim."

For some unfathomable reason Will found himself taking offense at Newt Haskel's allegations, truth that they were. "I'll want directions to where those horses are being held, Sheriff, so I can ride out and have a talk with the man who claims them."

"What for? Ain't my word good enough?"

"One person's word is never good enough when a man's life is at stake."

"That half-breed's no man, son. You're new to this country—"

"I'm not new to the law. I want those directions and the claimant's sworn statement on my desk before closing time."

Outside, Will looked after the McCain wagon, which was by this time no bigger than a thumbnail in the distance. He grinned, thinking of the ride he'd had earlier today on that same wagon. *Ol' Charlie'd better hold on.*

In no more than three minutes, he'd crossed the plaza, climbed the back staircase of the cantina, and walked the length of the corridor to his room. The door was open. He stopped in the portal.

"You oughta slow down, Will." Jessie stood beside his open French doors. Obviously, she'd watched him cross the plaza. "You can run around like a headless chicken up

North. Weather's cool, it won't hurt you. Down here it's too hot. You oughta slow down."

"Thanks for the concern, Jess." Will stepped inside the door, tossed his Stetson to the hatrack, where it landed next to the bowler he hadn't worn since arriving in Santa Fé.

She stared at him with a funny, knowing sort of expression that made him uneasy. He wondered what she wanted.

"I'll buy you a drink of real whiskey for what's on your mind, Will Radnor."

"My mind?" Will hoped the heat racing up his neck at the prospect of sharing his thoughts wasn't a glowing confession.

"Come on in. I won't bite."

Will cast doubtful eyes in the direction of the jail. "Thought you and ol' Newt were, uh, thick seems to be the word around here."

Jessie laughed. "That doesn't mean I can't enjoy talking to a handsome man. In fact, I might be able to help you out of your present dilemma."

"Dilemma?" But Will was intrigued, more by the information Jessie promised, than by entertaining a beautiful woman in his room. Something warned him that he might need just such a woman to dispel the magic that was inching its way under his skin and into his heart.

Magic that would surely turn to a curse before his task was finished. Will motioned Jessie to the one chair. He took the bed. Sitting on the edge he studied her. Jessie Laredo, voluptuous, sensuous, the kind of woman he'd envisioned meeting in Santa Fé. Before that fateful stagecoach ride. Before the magic of looking into Priscilla's eyes and kissing her lips.

"She's grown into an intriguing woman," Jessie was saying.

Will knew it would be best to let his mind wander in other directions. He rested his elbows on his knees and cupped his chin.

"I hope you took notice of the way she dressed up for you."

Will's head popped up. "She told you that?"

"Will, *querido,* she didn't have to tell me. I'm a woman. An older woman, to be sure." She shrugged her still smooth shoulders. "A woman learns to detect such things."

"I'll bet you do. Some of you."

"I'll take that as a compliment, *querido.*"

"As it was meant."

"Her silk blouse," Jessie continued.

Will started to tell Jessie that explanation was unnecessary. He had noticed every enticing morsel of Priscilla.

"And her perfume," Jessie continued. "I've known her all her life, Will, and I can say for a certainty, Priscilla McCain has never, ever worn perfume before today." She cocked her head, teasing. But he detected a serious tone beneath it. "There were other . . . more subtle signs . . . beneath the silk, if you catch my meaning."

Will laughed. "What are you, the town matchmaker?"

"If that's what it takes. Priscilla needs someone and something of her own, something besides her parents and that ranch."

"Newt took the opposite tack. He spent the last half hour trying to discourage me from becoming interested."

"Newt?"

Will kept his silence. He wondered how much Jessie knew, how much more he could learn from her. A woman of her ilk likely knew a lot. "Newt objects more to her father than to Priscilla," he revealed at length.

"That's a bone of contention between Newt and me. It's like Charlie says—the Haskel Land Grant Company is after all the land up and down the river. If you look into it, you'll discover that they have a valid claim to a lot of it. The old Spanish land grants."

"To Charlie's place?"

"Charlie says not. And he should know. He's a—" Jessie

stopped abruptly, then cleverly changed the subject. Clapping her hands as if in sheer delight, she rose and stood in the open French doors. "Isn't this the most magnificent afternoon. Don't you just love our sky? All the layers and shades of blue. And the lazy white clouds. Every time I see the sun stream through little holes in the clouds, I know there's a heaven up there someplace."

"Charlie's a lawyer," Will prompted. "Is that what you started to say?"

"What did Newt tell you?"

Will tried to keep his voice noncommittal. "That McCain isn't his name. That he's wanted for murder." He left out the part about Philadelphia. The folks in Santa Fé could gossip all they liked, but he didn't intend to tip his own hand. He'd waited too long for this opportunity.

"Newt's repeating what he heard," Jessie said. "You know how gossip is, it starts out with the truth, but by the time it's gone through several repeatings it changes color. Charlie's story has had a good twenty years to become distorted."

Will inhaled deep drafts of piñon-scented air. Jessie had told him it came from centuries of campfires that had burned around the plaza. Santa Fé was an old town.

And Charlie McCain's story was an old story. A story not believed by all, Will discovered.

"Charlie is no murderer," Jessie said flatly.

"Seems there's more than one opinion."

"There's a difference between opinion and knowledge. I know. I was in Santa Fé when Charlie arrived."

Will pursed his lips, struggling to keep his interest undetected. "From Texas?"

"Texas?"

"Priscilla said her father came from Texas."

"Priscilla doesn't know the story."

"Come on, Jess. Do you take me for a greenhorn, too? If the whole town is gossiping about it, she has to know."

"The McCains keep pretty much to themselves out at Spanish Creek. They're friendlier with Victorio and his Apaches than to most folks in Santa Fé."

"With Apaches?" Will didn't even try to hid his surprise.

"Something that happened a long time ago," Jessie dismissed. "The whole town isn't gossiping about Charlie. Oscar Haskel would like to use it against him, but he can't figure out how. He doesn't know enough of the truth. Only a handful of people ever knew the story. And they're gone, for the most part. I figure I'm the only one left in these parts, other than Kate and Charlie, who knows the truth."

"The truth? How do you know the truth, if—?"

"Charlie told me."

Will froze, his eyes on the patterned carpet. "Charlie told you?"

"We were friends, back then. He was new in town, lonely and determined to build a new life. Lonely men need a woman to talk to, Will."

"So he told you he murdered—" Will stopped short of revealing any information he hadn't heard in Santa Fé. Newt, after all, hadn't revealed the name of Charlie's victim.

"No," Jessie was saying. "Charlie told me he killed a man in self-defense."

Will trained his eyes on the floor. "Makes sense," he fabricated. "Otherwise he would have been arrested for the crime."

"Oh, he was accused of murder. There was even a wanted poster with his picture on it. I didn't see it, but I heard about it."

"He escaped?"

"He ran. Said he couldn't prove his innocence."

Will felt weak. Sick. "You must have known him well," he retorted.

"Don't worry about it," she evaded. "It was a long time ago. Charlie has proved the kind of man he is."

"Murdering and calling it self-defense? Dodging the law

for over—who knows how long? Stealing land from the Haskels?"

"Whose side are you on, Will?"

Will looked into her deep, black eyes. She was smiling, but it was a wan, sad sort of smile that added years to her usually youthful appearance. "On the side of the law, Jess."

"Where does that leave Priscilla?"

"Priscilla?" Will swallowed the distress that rose in his throat. "Miss Jake McCain can take care of herself. She's definitely her father's son."

Five

"SADDLE UP!"

Titus Crockett's call echoed through the early morning chill. Priscilla wasn't going on the cattle drive willing, but she was going. Pa remained adamant.

At Uncle Crockett's call, she rushed to the tack room to find an extra slicker in case they ran into rain. In her search, she came upon an old trunk. Memories assailed her. Her mind seemed to stand still. The cattle drive forgotten, she stooped, opened the lid. To her surprise, the trunk was empty.

"Get a move on, Jake. Crockett an' those ol' steers are waitin.' "

Priscilla glanced up to find Pa standing in the doorway, his demeanor solemn. Her hand trailed inside the trunk. Her fingers absently picked at the aged paper lining, while her mind played with a nagging memory.

"What happened to the old Spanish armor and stuff that was in this trunk, Pa?"

She watched his gaze fasten on the trunk. He frowned.

"It's . . . completely empty?"

She nodded. "Isn't this where I found that little pistol?"

"Pistol?"

"You remember, Pa. That little pistol I found years ago. You caught me shooting it at tin cans. That's when I told you not to call me sugar or Miss Priss, to call me—"

"Jake," he supplied. " 'You don't call Uncle Sog sugar, or Uncle Crockett,' you said. 'Call me Jake.' "

She smiled fondly, remembering along with him. "You've had a hard time remembering that lately."

But her pa didn't smile. He looked old, his features drawn. The trip to town yesterday had been too much for him. The trip and the argument they'd had later, out at the canyon. That argument had taken a lot out of both of them.

The trunk forgotten, Priscilla rose and went to him. She folded her arms around his middle, laid her head on his chest. "Get some rest while we're gone, Pa." He patted her head in a reassuring manner.

"I'm sorry I jumped on you like that yesterday, sugar. I wish you could understand."

A retort was on her tongue—how could she understand when he was being as stubborn as a jackass? But she held her tongue. She couldn't leave Spanish Creek with another argument between them. The one yesterday had been enough, the worst argument she and Pa had ever had.

Not far out of Santa Fé, Priscilla had realized why Pa sent Red Avery home ahead of them. They'd traveled only a couple of miles past the outskirts of town when he instructed her to take the southern route back to Spanish Creek.

"We're going by the canyon?"

"Might as well."

The thought of seeing Spanish Creek Canyon cheered Priscilla. Joaquín's cynicism and Will's likely collusion with the enemy had left her steaming. She figured that was why Pa decided to go by the canyon. They both needed time to cool off before returning home.

The canyon was hers and Pa's special, secret place; at least that's the way she thought of it. Her mother knew about the canyon, of course, but no one ever talked about it. The few times Priscilla had gone there had been in the company of her pa. She'd been fifteen or so the first time he took her to see the horses. She recalled his warning, still.

"Don't ever come here without me, Jake. And don't tell another soul about this place." They'd been hunting wild horses, just she and Pa. "Spanish Creek Canyon is sacred to the Apache. They trust me to keep it thataway."

They had followed Spanish Creek to its head, where the water burbled from under a mound of rocks at the base of a fir-studded cliff. Priscilla hadn't missed the precautions Pa took to be certain they weren't observed. Only after he'd climbed part way up the cliff on foot and scanned the countryside in every direction, had he pulled aside some low-growing cedars and motioned her into a narrow passageway formed by a split in the cliff. The resulting space was so narrow they were forced to ride single-file.

Priscilla would always remember her initial excitement at such an adventure. Excitement mixed with anxiety. "If it belongs to Victorio, what are we doing here?" she had whispered. She wasn't actually frightened, she'd assured herself. She was, after all, with Pa. He was the best shot in the territory, and she was quickly learning to shoot as well. Between them she and Pa could dispatch most any adversary. But tales of Victorio's merciless wrath speared her excitement with a goodly measure of trepidation.

"Victorio gave me use of the canyon," Pa had explained. "Said I could take horses from here when I needed 'em. Long as I never told anyone where they came from."

Priscilla had always been a romantic where her father was concerned. If Pa said the fierce war chief Victorio gave him use of the canyon and the horses in it, then Victorio gave him the canyon and the horses. At the time it hadn't occurred to her to question the veracity of such a claim, nor the circumstances behind the gift.

But standing there yesterday, watching the magnificent Spanish horses frolic in their natural environment, she had begun to wonder. She knew what was on Pa's mind. Joaquín.

"How did Joaquín find out about this place?"

Pa shrugged, but didn't answer.

"Why would he steal some of our horses?"

"They aren't technically ours, Miss Priss."

"We're the only ones who know about them. The only ones who use them."

Again Pa remained silent. She watched him visually count the herd.

When he finished, she questioned, "How many did he take?"

"Six."

"Why?"

He favored her with a strange sort of smile. "Joaquín figures they belong to him."

"But . . ."

"He's right. They do."

Priscilla's boots slipped on a rock. She caught her balance, physically. Emotionally, Pa's claim had been a wallop to the gut.

"In a manner of speaking," Pa finished.

"In what manner of speaking?"

"They belong to Victorio's Apaches. Joaquín is—"

"I know what Joaquín is, Pa. So does he. What he needs to know is *who* he is."

"I don't know who he is."

Priscilla stalked away. Kicking a stone in front of her she wandered toward the cave where they'd found the Spanish armor. Pa came up behind her.

"I don't know who Joaquín's father is, Priscilla." His voice had softened. He took her by the shoulders. "But it isn't me. If it were, I'd have been man enough to claim the boy years ago. Your mama and I have discussed it many times."

Priscilla watched water bubble from the earth, she imagined it running through the cave and out the other side. Pa had related the history of the canyon on that first trip, what was known, anyway, or more accurately, what he deducted from the evidence. The Spaniards had obviously found this canyon on one of their treks up from Mexico. Some of them were killed here. The armor and other remains testified to that. Their horses had grown and multiplied in the valley unobserved, as Mexicans and later Anglos moved into the area. To the Apache, the fact that the horses had evaded discovery by the white eyes could mean only one thing—the Great Spirit had given them to The People.

And Victorio in turn gave Pa permission to take horses from the canyon when he needed them, in appreciation for Pa's help in solving some difficulty involving white raiders. The only condition Victorio had placed on the gift was that no one else could ever learn about the canyon or the horses. Priscilla wasn't even sure Uncle Sog and Uncle Crockett knew about it.

"How did Joaquín find this place?" she asked again.

"That's what has me buffaloed," Pa admitted. "And worried as hell."

"Why would he take them?" she demanded again.

"To get back at me."

"Victorio won't hold you responsible."

"Victorio isn't the problem. He's facing bigger troubles than this from both sides of the border."

"Then—"

"If Joaquín tags me as being involved in a horse theft ring—"

"He wouldn't do that."

"I don't think so, either," Pa had agreed. "But he's determined to call my hand. A determined man is dangerous."

She thought about that, recalled Mama's departing admonition that morning. "That's what Mama meant."

"Your mama wasn't talking about Joaq—" Pa stopped

in midsentence, stared hard at Priscilla, then turned abruptly away.

It reminded her of Will, of the way he could be gentle and kind one moment, arrogant and spiteful the next.

"Men! I don't understand any of you."

Pa wheeled, his eyes flashing. "What brought that on?"

Priscilla shrugged. "I don't know." She kicked a stone into the water with the toe of her boot. "It's just that . . ." At length, she looked up at her father, shaking her head. "One minute you're sane and sensible, the next you don't make any sense at all."

"Makes perfect sense to me."

"That's what I mean. Just like Will. One minute he's friendly as can be, the next minute he acts like I have the plague or—"

"PRISCILLA!"

Her heart stilled at the fury in his voice. Pa never got angry with her, not really angry.

"I told you that man is no good. You're not to talk about him, again. You're not to see him. You can't even *want* to see him. Do you understand?"

For the second time in one day Priscilla felt a rush of tears. "How can I understand, when all you do is shout orders?" She tossed her chin defiantly. "One little kiss—"

"It isn't just the kiss; it's the man. He's no good."

"What about him is so bad?"

"Everything."

"You don't know everything about him."

"I know enough."

"Then tell me."

"I don't need to tell you anything, damnit. I'm your father. I forbid you to see William Radnor."

Priscilla couldn't believe her ears. "Forbid? When did you start forbidding me to do things? You taught me to think for myself, to make decisions, to trust my own judg-

ments about people. Now you're taking it all back, forbidding me—"

Pa had grabbed her by both shoulders then. He shook
her. The action was so unprecedented, it startled her into
silence. She stared into his angry blue eyes, her own tearing.
His anger and stubbornness fueled hers.

"I'm a grown woman, Pa. I can do whatever I please. I
can think about anyone I want to think about; I can see
anyone—"

Pa's voice softened, but his resolve remained firm. "I
don't care if you get to be a hundred and one, Priscilla
McCain, I won't have you taking up with the likes of Will
Radnor."

"And I don't care what you try to do about it, I'll take
up with the Haskels themselves if it pleases me."

The absurdity of her claim had astonished her. She ducked
her head. "Maybe not with the Haskels. But they're different.
I know why you would object to the Haskels. I know what
kind of people they are, what they're doing to us. I wouldn't
even want to take up with the Haskels, Pa. But Will— How
can you object to Will? He isn't some fly-by-night wrangler.
He makes an honest living, even if it is by working for the
Haskels. He's new in town. Newt might try to brainwash him,
but I can keep—"

"Priscilla!" Pa's eyes had narrowed to slits. His voice
was low and clear. As was his meaning when he continued.
"This subject is closed. I don't want to ever hear that man's
name again. When you return from Fort Stanton—"

"Me? I'm not going to Fort Stanton, Pa. What if the
Haskels attack Spanish Creek—?"

"I can handle the Haskels."

"But the trip will take a week or more, and—"

"You're going."

"We decided Uncle Crockett would drive the steers."

"You're going with him." When she objected further, he
added in tones he rarely used with her. "*I* decided, Priscilla.

I'm still running this dadburnt ranch. Don't you forget it again."

How could she ever forget it? she thought now, feeling her pa's arms around her, loving, protecting . . . over-protecting.

"Crockett's ready to hit the trail," he said.

"I still don't think I should go, Pa."

"You're going."

"What about Joaquín? You can't leave Mama alone with Red to go see about Joaquín—"

"Leave that to me. I still have a little sense left in this old noggin. By the time you and Crockett return, I'll have Joaquín's difficulty settled."

In her elation, Priscilla almost told him about the plan she intended to effect after Will cleared Joaquín. But she didn't. If yesterday had taught her anything, it was to keep her trump card to herself. Pa couldn't very well prepare a defense against something he didn't expect to happen. She hugged his neck. "Take care of Mama."

"I intend to, Miss Priss."

At the end of the week following Priscilla and Charlie's visit to Santa Fé, Will made his way out of town, using a crude map he had finally persuaded Newt Haskel to draw for him. He rode north along the Santa Fé Trail, turned west, coming at length to a small spread nestled among the rocks and hills east of the Río Grande.

The ride had given him ample time to think, an activity that was becoming hazardous to his mental health. He regretted coming to town under the ruse of practicing law. The job with Faust & Haskel had seemed like the answer to his dilemma when the offer was made.

But now he was stuck with Joaquín's case and he couldn't deal with Charlie until he'd represented Joaquín in a fair manner. That was his problem. His mother said his perseverance bordered on mania. No matter what the task, Will attacked it with everything he had until it was solved.

So now he had to clear Joaquín before he could settle things with Charlie. And he had to do both and get out of the territory, away from Priscilla—far away from Priscilla— before leaving her became a bigger chore than dealing with her father.

He should never have kissed her. He should never have flirted with her. The moment he learned her identity, he should have shunned her like the pox.

But he hadn't, and now she was quickly working her way into his heart, and he knew himself. He knew himself too well. Like his mother said, once he got started on something, hell pulled by four devils couldn't drag him away.

Well, not this time. Not this woman. Even if she was the first woman who'd ever lighted such an intense fire of passion inside him that all the water in all the oceans would have trouble extinguishing it.

He shouldn't have kissed her. Hell fire and damnation! He should never have kissed her. For days now the only image he'd been able to conjure in his worthless brain was an impossible dream—the dream of holding her in his arms, skin to skin, lips to lips, his body curling around hers, filling hers . . .

Fiercely, Will tore his mind away from Priscilla McCain. McCain, damnit, that was the important word. He concentrated on the scenery—or tried to.

Although majestic and beautiful, the country he rode through was rugged; Will had difficulty picturing a pureblooded horse operation in these mountains. And that's what Newt claimed the horses Joaquín stole were—pure-blooded Spanish horses.

He grinned, hearing Priscilla's sure retort. He was a greenhorn, after all. What did he know about horse raising in New Mexico Territory?

But even the horse he rode, which Carlos, the hostler,

assured him was a mountain-bred mustang, shied nervously around rockslides and pricked his ears at any distant rumble.

Arriving at his destination, Will dismounted cautiously at a ramshackle shack that hung precariously on the edge of a cliff. When Newt said the ranch was in the mountains, Will had envisioned a place like Spanish Creek—a rolling verdant valley surrounded by mountains, not a rocky cliff overlooking the river.

Back behind the shack stood an equally rundown barn and beyond that a pole corral. Between the barn and the corral a mangy wolfhound strained at a rope, setting up enough racket that Will figured the most hardened rustler should be scared off.

A large man approached Will. Of obvious Scottish ancestry with a freckled, once-fair complexion and ruddy hair tinged with gray, he wore two Colts strapped around his mammoth waist and carried a buffalo gun in a hamlike fist, all of which accentuated the man's ability—and intention, Will had no doubt—to intimidate.

"Aaron DeVries?" he questioned.

"Depends on who's askin.' "

Will introduced himself as a member of Faust & Haskel. "Newt says you raise pure-blooded Spanish horses around here."

DeVries, the rancher from whom Joaquín was supposed to have stolen the horses, glared at Will, while spitting a stream of tobacco juice off to the side. He wiped his unkempt mustache with the back of a fist. "Ain't no reason I can't raise purebloods if I take a notion."

"Looks like pretty rough country for expensive horses."

"An' it looks to me like yer new to these parts." The way the Scotsman said it, it was more like an indictment than a casual comment.

Will blanched. Hadn't Priscilla warned him not to make stupid statements? "Mind if I take a look at 'em?"

Even as he asked, Will wasn't at all sure he wanted to

set foot on the place. Certainly not in the direction of that angry hound, accompanied by its surly master. Sure enough, though, that's the way DeVries led him.

"This where you regularly keep these animals?" They had reached the muck-littered pole corral unmolested. Will rested a boot on the bottom rung and examined the six horses that stood out like cut diamonds in a second-rate mounting. Behind them now, the hound still barked, but since DeVries kicked him in the ribs on passing, his tone had changed from aggression to agony.

"You got objections?"

"To the corrals? None. This where they were taken from?"

"*Stolen* from?" DeVries corrected. "Yep. Right here."

"Were you at home?"

DeVries narrowed a dark expression on Will, who suddenly entertained the image of the Scotsman kicking him in the ribs.

"I mean, your dog would have alerted you, if you were home, that is. Were you home that night, Mr. DeVries?"

The Scotsman never missed a lick. "Maybe so, maybe no."

"When a man is accused of a crime as serious as horse stealing . . ." Will paused, perusing the horses in the corral with deliberation. "When a man's accused of stealing animals this valuable, he has a right to expect the truth—all of it."

"That half-breed ain't got no rights." DeVries spat tobacco off to the side. "He stole my horses, an' he'll hang for it."

"*If* he stole your horses, he'll hang for it."

"He stole 'em. Ask Newt."

"You have papers, I take it."

"Papers?"

"Ownership papers. Sales receipt. I'd like to see the papers."

"I didn't buy these horses, I raised 'em."

"From what?"

DeVries looked at Will as if he'd fallen out of a nest somewhere high in the sky. "You Yanks don't never git no smarter, no matter how big you git."

Will ignored the sneer. He was actually getting used to it. Dressed up in proper grammar, DeVries' snide remark would come close to Priscilla's favorite taunt. "Where did you get the original stock, Mr. DeVries?"

From the man's narrowed eyes, Will expected him to refuse to reply. He was wrong . . . again. "Rounded 'em up, like ever'body else in these parts does wild horses."

"Wild horses?"

DeVries held Will's gaze, direct, challenging. Will considered pursuing the subject, considered the consequences if he did. The idea of getting himself shot out here where nobody but Newt Haskel knew to find him wasn't an appealing proposition. And it'd be for nothing, he was certain. Aaron DeVries wouldn't be inclined to tell Will anything of value, even if the man knew it. Which Will was beginning to doubt.

"Reckon I'll be headin' back to Santa Fé, then, Mr. DeVries. Thanks for showing me around."

DeVries followed Will to his horse. Will felt the buffalo gun, handled loosely, but aimed in the general area of his spine the whole way. He hoped Aaron DeVries was surefooted.

"Newt didn't say nothin' 'bout you bein' the nosy type," DeVries commented.

Will swung up on his horse, feeling the return of a small measure of control. "Nosy?"

"Like you don't take my word for them bein' my horses."

Will shrugged. "It isn't that I don't take your word. Judge Sanders appointed me to defend a man; I'm bound by the law to consider every angle."

"Out here we see the law a mite diff'ernt. You might

oughta have Newt bone you up on our ways 'fore you run off half-cocked and start accusin' folks of lyin'. You're liable to end up gut shot and buzzard bait."

"Is that a threat, Mr. DeVries?"

"Take it any damned way you like. Tell Newt he oughta ed'jecate you next time, 'fore he sends you off."

"Count on it, Mr. DeVries. I'll certainly tell Newt every word you've said."

By the time Will reached Santa Fé the sun was setting. As it did every evening, the sunset reminded him of Spanish Creek and Priscilla. Lordy, but he seemed to have gotten himself into something he should've sidestepped. Try as he did, though, he couldn't associate Spanish Creek Ranch with Charlie McCain, not even when he mulled over the probability that Charlie had purchased that ranch with money embezzled from Will's own family. Spanish Creek seemed a world apart from the hatred he had felt for twenty-three long years—even from the promise he made his mother that long-ago night, to find the man who murdered his father and bring him to justice.

Oh, he still intended to do it. There was no question in his mind about that. He hated Charlie McCain. But Charlie's daughter was a different matter. And that worried Will.

Arriving back in town he considered going straight to his room, cleaning up, eating supper, then heading downstairs to the cantina where Newt Haskel made a nightly habit of closing up the place—before he and Jessie returned to her suite of rooms at the opposite corner of the building from the single room Will rented.

Passing the Faust & Haskel office, however, Will saw a light on in back, so he hitched his mount at the front rail and made his way around the side of the building. The sooner he got his suspicions off his chest, the better. There must be an explanation for those horses. But Newt or someone had some explaining to do, before they convinced him that Aaron DeVries raised pure-blooded Spanish horses on that rocky spread in the mountains.

Will let himself in the back door, then stood quietly at the sound of voices coming from the office beyond, Oscar's office. Oscar Haskel, Newt's brother, was senior partner in the firm. His office, running front to back along one side of the building, reflected his additional work load and stature in both size and appointments.

"You say McCain's out at Spanish Creek by himself?" Will heard Oscar question.

"Except for his wife and that feller who cain't even shoot straight." It was Newt's voice. "Charlie sent Jake and Titus Crockett off with a herd of steers for Fort Stanton. The trip'll take more'n a week, maybe longer if the weather don't hold. An' they've already been gone most of that time."

"All we need is one more day," Oscar said. "One day and we'll have Charlie McCain in his grave and Spanish Creek Ranch on our hands—all tied up with a legal seal."

"Reckon we don't need to keep that half-breed in jail, then," Newt said.

"Keep him there, in case I'm wrong. If we can't get McCain any other way, we'll figure out how to use Wounded Eagle."

Will listened, scarcely believing what he heard. His brain rushed on a pell-mell search for a safe haven.

"What about Radnor?"

"I sent him out to DeVries to—"

Before they could knowingly tip their hand, Will acted. He slammed the outer door, the sound stopping Newt's words in midsentence. Stomping across the office, Will threw open the connecting door and confronted Newt with, "What the hell do you mean sending me on a wild goose chase, Haskel?"

"Wild goose?"

"Is your hearing bad, Newt? I may be green, like everyone keeps telling me, but I'm not stupid. Aaron DeVries no more raises pure-blooded horses on that spread east of the Río Grande than I tame wild buffalo and sell 'em for circus monkeys."

"How would you—"

Oscar interrupted Newt. "You're right, Radnor. DeVries isn't the owner of those horses. It's time we brought you into our little scheme."

Newt's hand stilled on his handlebar mustache. "Now, Oscar, that's not—"

"Hush, Newt. I know what I'm doing."

Will's attention went from Newt to his brother, Oscar. Larger than Newt, more worldly in appearance and speech, Oscar was held around town to be the more intelligent of the two men. Although Will had never heard Oscar Haskel raise his voice, he instinctively knew the man would be capable of a choleric outburst, should the situation require it.

"What's this secret of yours, Oscar?"

Oscar removed a stubby cigar from his lips, contemplated the glowing tip. "Let me say . . ." His brown eyes, cold and hard, found and held Will's, warning him, before the man spoke another word, that he might be standing here in a peck of trouble. "Let's just say, it involves the reason you came to New Mexico Territory."

Will's heart leapt to his throat. He struggled to keep his face emotion-free. He forced his breathing to regulate. He stared Oscar Haskel in the eye, calling on every trick his grandfather had taught him about cross-examination. And they all failed.

Oscar Haskel smiled the smile of a victor. "To get Charlie McCain."

Will frowned, but didn't speak. Truthfully, he couldn't think of a reply. And what he wanted to do, turn and flee the room, was out of the question, given the conversation he'd overheard earlier and now Oscar's accusation.

"Don't worry, Radnor. We're after McCain, too."

"I'm listening."

"You weren't the only one who made inquiries," Oscar explained. "When you started nosing around Santa Fé, looking for a position with a law firm, we made inquiries ourselves. Philadelphia, you see, rang a bell. That old gossip regarding Charlie McCain. Or should I say, Charles Martin Kane?"

"So you hired me to help you get him?"

"More or less."

"What about Joaquín? Did you set him up?"

Oscar and Newt exchanged glances.

"Let's keep this on a need-to-know basis, Radnor. At the moment, Wounded Eagle is of no concern to you."

"Joaquín is my only concern. I've been appointed to defend him. Now it appears, against set-up charges."

"Damnit, Radnor, you aren't listening. We've just been handed a surefire way of getting McCain. Come along, and you can have the chore, or should I say the privilege, of being the one to fire the fatal shot."

"What about the two of you?"

"You want McCain dead. We want Spanish Creek Ranch. We'll all be happy."

"Killing Charlie won't guarantee you Spanish Creek Ranch. Priscilla—"

Newt interrupted Will. "Don't sound to me like he's as anxious as you made out, Oscar."

"I'm anxious, Newt. To get Charlie. Not to rush into something when I don't have all the facts."

"What'd you want to know?" Oscar spoke in a conversational tone, as though they were discussing a simple legal procedure, like drawing up a will or something. "We ride out tonight, leave in time to arrive at the ranchhouse before daybreak—couple, three hours from now. We—"

"I mean, how do you intend to claim, legally claim, Spanish Creek Ranch?"

"He's thick with Jake," Newt advised Oscar.

"All the better," Oscar replied. "She'll be safely out of the way for several days. When she returns you can have her."

Will struggled to keep his myriad emotions under control. At least they weren't planning to kill Priscilla. But what about her mother? "Thick or not," he retorted, "I demand to know how you intend to accomplish this take-over without drawing suspicion."

"Drawing suspicion?" Newt retorted. "Hell, Radnor, you are green. We're the law around here. We can do anything we damned well please."

"I see," Will replied in icy tones. "Aaron DeVries suggested I get you to educate me; I guess that about covers it." He turned to leave, even though his spine crawled at the prospect of showing his back to these men.

"Hold on a minute," Oscar called. "We're not here to split hairs. We're inviting you to go along. Can't see how it'd hurt anything. You're still after McCain, aren't you?"

Turning, Will stared hard at these men who considered themselves above the very law they had both sworn to serve. Yes, he was after Charlie McCain. But he'd never intended to go against the law to take him.

"Look at it this way," Oscar argued, "we'll provide you an opportunity for that showdown you've been hungering for, these last twenty some-odd years; while we're at it, we'll take ourselves a ranch we've been after for nearly as long. You win, we win. Where're you going to find a better deal?" Standing, Oscar Haskel withdrew the cigar from his mouth and extended his right hand to Will. "What'd you say? Are you in . . . or out?"

Will stared at the hand, his heart in his throat. Contradictory emotions fought for control. Hatred for Charlie McCain versus dedication to the law; admiration for Charlie McCain versus hatred for these lawless bastards. But above and beyond every other consideration was his commitment to the law. Two, three hours, Oscar'd said. Time for . . . what?

Taking Oscar's hand, Will watched an expression of relief light the older man's face. "Where do we meet?"

"The boys are gatherin' here." Oscar checked his pocket watch. "Two hours."

Will wanted to ask what boys, how many boys, but he didn't dare. "Wait for me." He nodded to Newt and left the room. He'd walked halfway to the plaza before he remembered his horse hitched outside the law office. Time. Wasted time.

Retrieving the animal, he rode around the plaza, hitched the horse behind the cantina, then rushed around the side, entering from the front, like any other paying customer. He stopped inside the door, searching for Jessie Laredo.

"Will!" she hailed through the smoke.

He made his way toward her, forcing his feet to saunter not run. Reaching Jessie, he grabbed her around the waist, drew her to him, and swung her around the room.

"You're in a good mood tonight, *querido*." Her laughter stopped when he began to whisper in her ear.

"Keep laughing," he warned. "I need your help. Can you keep a secret?"

"I love secrets."

When he prompted, she agreed, "Sure I can keep a secret . . . for you."

"Even from Newt?"

Her expression grew wary. *"Sí."*

"Especially from Newt," he reiterated.

"What is it, Will? What's happened?"

"I need a fresh horse."

"That's easy." Her voice, though, was soft with uncertainty. "Is there trouble?"

"Depends on whose side you're on. Meet me upstairs as soon as you can get away without drawing suspicion." When she arrived, he related the conversation he'd overheard and the one he'd been party to. "I'm asking you again, Jess. Whose side are you on?" Will held his breath, praying he hadn't misjudged the situation.

A mournfulness etched lines on Jessie's face. "For me, there's never been any doubt, Will, not where Charlie's concerned." She looked at him with the certainty of a fortune-teller. "You've decided, too. I can see it in your eyes."

"I've always known, Jess. Like I told you, I'm on the side of the law."

"The law!"

"Not Santa Fé style," Will corrected. "Now, listen close. When they ask you about me, and they will, tell them I came in happy as a lark. Lead them up here and act surprised that I'm not in my room."

Jessie patted his back. "Don't worry about me, Will. I'm much more experienced, in certain fields, than you."

A full moon lit the night, and for that Will was grateful—he supposed. Of course, if the Haskels came along too soon, they'd have no trouble picking him off in such a spotlight. With every passing mile he considered himself the eternal fool for riding to Spanish Creek to warn Charlie.

Oscar was right. This was the opportunity he'd waited a lifetime to find. The opportunity to get Charlie McCain. And here he was riding to the man's aid.

He tried to dispel the suspicion that his actions were driven by his affection for Priscilla. And affection, after all, was all it could be considered. A few simple kisses and here he was rejecting the opportunity he'd awaited for twenty-three years.

A few kisses and his brain had turned to mush.

He whipped up the horse and rode hard. Oscar had said two hours. Perhaps they would spend another half hour or so waiting for him. He'd left Jessie with instructions to send his own horse to the livery by Jorge, the errand boy who had performed the service on several occasions. He'd told Jessie to answer no questions, unless Newt or Oscar turned mean.

Jessie had laughed. "Mean? You don't know mean, compared to what I've seen in my lifctime. For a chance to help Charlie, I can endure a little slapping around."

"It wouldn't help Charlie," Will had objected. "If they find out I've ridden to alert him, they might change their plans. If a showdown's to come, let it come now."

He was thinking about Priscilla. And Jessie knew it. She tousled his head, like she would a boy's, then kissed his lips like she would an ardent lover's.

"That's for Priscilla," she said. "Since she isn't here to do it herself."

His horse was winded and the moon was on the wane by the time Will reached the hills overlooking Spanish Creek headquarters. He studied the house in the fading moonlight. Sensuously built, even the house reminded him, not of Charlie McCain, his archrival, but of Priscilla.

Priscilla, who was cocky and arrogant instead of coy and proper. Priscilla, whose kisses taunted him with promises that kept him awake nights.

Priscilla, who was on his mind much too often. He kicked his mount and galloped down the hillside, intent on his mission to alert the man he had come to destroy.

The law, he argued. The law. Man must not put himself above the law. *Charles Martin Kane did when he murdered my father.*

But that was no reason for him to make the same mistake, Will argued. He would uphold the law. He prayed that was the reason he had come to Spanish Creek on a mission that, if it accomplished nothing else, surely set him at odds with the law, Santa Fé style.

Dismounting at the hitching rail, Will watched moonbeams glance off the medieval suit of armor. He recalled the welcoming smile on Kate McCain's face the night she opened the door for him, unaware until it was too late who he was. He wondered why they hadn't told Priscilla. Perhaps by now, they had.

His foot had barely touched the bottom step when he heard a shotgun cock. He peered into the impenetrable blackness.

"So you've come at last," Charlie said from the shadows.

"I've come, Charlie, but not for you."

"Well, you haven't come for her. She's gone."

"I know. The Haskels are coming."

For a moment silence pervaded the coolness of night.

"Haskels?" Charlie asked tentatively.

"Newt, Oscar, and 'the boys,' whoever they are. I don't even know how many."

"Half a dozen or more," Charlie commented. "So what's your hand in this game? You bring their ultimatum? Sign over Spanish Creek or—"

"I'm here to help you defend your property, sir."

"In the name of Heaven," Charlie whispered. "You expect me to believe that?"

"In the name of the law. My grandfather taught me well, Charlie. He taught me that for society to advance, no man can put himself above the law."

"Old Mr. William," Charlie mused. "Yes, that was his line. You couldn't have had a better teacher, son."

"Unless it had been my father."

Six

The Haskels waited until sunup to attack Spanish Creek Ranch, and by that time the tenuous truce Will and Charlie had hastily put together had begun to crumble.

"Well, if you've come to help me defend this ranch, we'd better get to work," Charlie had barked after Will reassured him he intended to put off their own showdown until he'd cleared Joaquín.

"Humph! With the Haskels running the show, you'll never get that boy freed. I'll have to do it myself." Charlie had eyed Will resolutely. "I promised Priscilla I'd have things settled by the time she returns from Fort Stanton, and I aim to do it."

Will stared hard at the obstinate old man. He knew what he was thinking. Well, he thought the same thing. The sooner he cleared Joaquín and resolved his differences with Charlie, the sooner he could get out of this territory. The sooner he could get away from Priscilla. "The sooner the better," he swore.

After setting Red Avery to watch from the center cupola atop the barn and Kate to cooking in the kitchen, Charlie and Will took up vigil from opposite ends of the veranda. Before them in the distance loomed the everpresent wall of blue mountains. Overhead the deep blue sky twinkled with stars; some looked close enough for a man to reach up and grab a handful.

"For a man on the run, you certainly aren't set up to defend yourself," Will commented.

"I'm not on the run, damnit."

A gentle evening breeze mingled with the scents of Spanish Creek—piñon, Kate McCain's roses, and Priscilla, always, Priscilla.

"Miss Laredo says you're one of the few ranchers along the Pecos who owns his own place fair and square," Will commented, changing the subject. If he intended to help Charlie defend his property, he'd have to keep his mind off the past. He wasn't fighting for *Charlie,* his brain rejected. He was fighting for law and order.

"I do."

"How do you account for that?"

"I don't have to account for it."

"I'm not nosy, just curious. Spanish land grants would have been issued on this place, too."

"I agree, but no record exists, not that I've been able to locate."

"What about the deed? Who was the original owner?"

"There's no record of a deed ever being issued on this place, not in Santa Fé. When the Haskels decided to take it over, I'm sure they checked down in Old Mexico. If they'd found anything, I'd've been the first to hear it."

"Who did you buy the land from?"

"The government. Their surveyors came out, set the metes and bounds."

"That's curious, since property on all sides is known to have been granted."

"It's gaps like this that always intrigue lawyers like us," Charlie agreed. "I figure it has something to do with the canyon."

"The canyon?"

"There's a canyon on the place, at the headwaters of the creek . . ." Charlie's words drifted off. He eyed Will sharply. "It's not common knowledge," he growled.

"Who would I tell?"

Finally Charlie resumed his discourse, encouraged, Will decided, by the darkness that isolated them—and by the fact that he had come to Charlie's aid against the Haskels. Will recalled Priscilla's claim that everyone was after Spanish Creek Ranch. Well, Charlie knew beyond a doubt that wasn't the reason Will was here.

Resuming the story, Charlie motioned with his head toward the house behind them. "That suit of armor. Found it in the canyon, along with other artifacts that belonged to a party of armed Spaniards."

"You mean a fort?"

"More like a camp. Ambushed, died of hunger, pestilence, what have you. Way I figure it, if those were the fellers who held the land grant, they died right there."

"What about heirs?"

"Don't reckon there are any."

Kate brought coffee. The eastern sky began to lighten and still no sign of the Haskels.

"They know I've come to help you, Charlie. That's why they're so late. If they come now, they'll be ready for war."

"You claim to be that hot a shot?"

"Yes, sir, I am."

"Priscilla says you're fair."

Will smiled to himself, recalling how his marksmanship had piqued her pride. "More than fair. I've won my share of trophies."

"Trophies, huh?"

"More than you, those of yours I know about, anyway."

"You set out to outshoot me for a purpose, I assume."

"A lawyer doesn't assume, Charlie. But you're right. I had . . . uh, have a purpose."

Charlie sat silently for a long time. Then he surprised Will with, "What'd Ann have to say about that?"

"Mother? She didn't like it. But when she saw I was dead set, she gave up trying to dissuade me."

Charlie's voice lost its petulance. "She learned that early, son. You always did attack a chore with everything you could muster. Your persistence bordered on mania, even when you were a tyke. Everybody always complimented your folks on their tenacious little son. I can hear Ann now. 'Easy for you to say. You don't have to live with him. William and I call it stubbornness.' "

Will laughed. "I'll admit I was a regular pain in the ass most of the time."

"Oh, I wouldn't say that. You provided us all with more than enough entertainment. Why, I remember one evening over at your house, just a casual affair for twenty or so, not the usual two hundred for seated dinners your mother could throw at the drop of a hat."

Will groaned. "Those boring affairs."

"The night I'm thinking of was far from boring, thanks to you. You'd been working on growing tadpoles in quart jars, not for school or anything, just a hankering that came from that overworked little brain of yours. But you wouldn't keep 'em out in the carriage house, no, sir. Your tadpoles were going to be raised in the kitchen by the hearth."

"Lordy! Mother must have had a fit!"

Charlie laughed softly. "Not a big enough fit, as things turned out. No sooner'd we set down to dinner—humm . . . oxtail soup, yes, I think that was the first course that particular evening—no sooner had we dipped spoons into Ann's fragrant, steamin' soup, than you rushed into the room and whispered frantically in your father's ear. I can see it yet. Ann reprimanding you from the far end of that ten-foot mahogany table, admonishing you not to interrupt her guests, not to whisper in public, to run upstairs where you belonged, and all the while, your father's eyes started to bug from his head. He scanned the table. His attention lingered on each soup bowl in turn, beginning and ending with his own, then he turned and whispered something to you, and you very reluctantly left the table."

"I don't remember that. How old was I?"

"Six, five maybe, no more'n six, though."

"Who ate my tadpoles?"

Charlie laughed. "Not I, nor your father. Neither of us ever had the nerve to quiz anyone else, not even your mother."

"Especially not my mother," Will said.

The wind died down toward morning, stilling the leaves on the piñon and cottonwoods. Behind them in the east, the white glow of approaching morning backlighted a Western sky that took on the dark, glossy sheen of black velvet.

"Your mother still alive?" Charlie questioned from the shadows.

"She died a year back." *Before I could make good my promise.* Picking up his box of shells, Will moved off down the veranda toward the steps. *Enough of this!* Enough reminiscing. He wasn't here to listen to Charlie talk about old times. Old times with his father, Charlie's best friend. His father, whom Charlie had murdered in cold blood.

Will shivered and headed for the barn.

"See anything?" Charlie called.

"No. Sit tight. I'll check on Avery."

By the time he found Red Avery asleep in the cupola and wakened him with a kick to the rear, a faint glow had begun to nudge up over the mountains. Daybreak.

He returned to the house, his eyes searching the horizon. How would they come? Galloping over the crest, full speed ahead? Probably not. They were, after all, Western men. Indian fighters. They would know a quiet way to sneak in and attack the place when their prey least expected them.

While their prey dredged up old memories and became weak with remorse over what had gone before, and with dread over what would follow after.

The fight itself, Will did not dread, even though he had shot at men instead of targets only once before, and that recently, protecting one of the two people Charlie professed to love most, his daughter. The irony of the situation puzzled Will—that he would defend first Charlie's daughter, now Charlie himself, when in fact he had come to New Mexico Territory to destroy this man who murdered his father.

Law and order. "No man can be allowed to put himself above the law, Will," his old grandfather had instructed time and again. "As an officer of the court, it'll be your duty to stop anarchy in its tracks."

Funny, Will thought now. As many times as he'd heard his grandfather make that statement, he'd never envisioned stopping anarchy as shooting lawmen while defending his enemy. But it was beginning to look like that's what he would be called upon to do.

By the time he returned to the veranda, Will had forced himself to shake off the lethargy brought on by Charlie's reminiscing. "If they're coming, they'll come soon," he predicted.

"That's the way I figure it, too." Charlie turned a cold eye on him. "You're not lyin' about putting aside our own trouble for the time being?"

"No."

"I don't mind tellin' you, son, it's a creepy feeling, thinkin' I'll have to watch my back while I'm fightin' off Haskels."

"You won't have to watch your back."

Charlie turned his eyes to the road.

"It's an eye for an eye, Charlie. I'm not here to destroy your whole family, which is close to what will happen if the Haskels take this ranch."

"Humph! Priscilla's father for yours, is that it? I don't mean to boast, son, but killin' me'll pretty much destroy Priscilla's life, and Kate's, too." He eyed Will sharply. "Not that I have to tell you that."

No, Will thought, *you don't have to tell me that.* After twenty-three years, the pain he'd felt standing over his father's body was still acute, the memory still fresh. But Charlie's words echoed a concern that Will hadn't been able to set aside for days now. Like ripples in a pond, his actions would reach out and devour everyone around Charlie McCain. The way Charlie's actions had destroyed those around Will's father. Will steeled his mind against such thoughts, calling on the anger that had been his constant companion for as long as he could recall. "Don't lay the blame on me."

Kate came to the veranda bearing more coffee and a tray of sweet breads. She hadn't spoken a word to Will since he arrived, but now she said, "Joaquín didn't steal those horses, Mr. Radnor."

Will sipped the coffee, thanked her. "That's my understanding, too."

"When will he be released?"

"They're still charging him, Mrs. McCain. They're not about to let him out of jail, until—"

"Until they take Spanish Creek," Charlie interrupted. "And that's not going to happen in their lifetime."

"I admire your confidence," Will returned, "but it may be misplaced."

"I promised Priscilla I'd have Joaquín out of jail by the time she returns," Charlie vowed for the second time. Will took the point.

"It'll be over before she returns," he promised. "All of it. And I'll be gone."

Racket from the barn interrupted whatever response Charlie had started to make. A crowbar banging on a milk pail. Avery's signal.

Here they come, Will thought. He took a sip of cold coffee to wet his dry throat, then dried the palm of his right hand on his pants leg.

"Get back in the house, sweetheart." Charlie's voice was calm, tender even, yet commanding, nonetheless. It took Will by surprise. His own would be two octaves higher than usual, he was sure, if he were able to utter any sound above a croak.

Silently, he and Charlie watched dark forms top the mountain and proceed down the hillside into the valley, like spilled ink spreading over the grass that glistened in the first glow of the rising sun. A beautiful, breathtaking sight, awesome.

The men had ridden to within fifty yards of the veranda before they became distinct figures, six men on horseback riding steadily toward the ranchhouse. Will gripped his rifle and watched from the shadows. Oscar Haskel held up his left hand to halt his companions. As one they drew rein.

"MCCAIN!" Oscar bellowed. "Get your hide out here."

When Charlie reached for his walking stick, Will moved it aside. Charlie's shoulders bowed.

"Damn you—"

"Sit tight." Will was already on his feet. He stepped out of the shadows onto the steps.

"You damned traitor," Oscar Haskel accused. "Step aside or get yourself shot."

Will shifted his leveled rifle into view. "Ride away now and there'll be no trouble."

"You're the trouble we're fixin' to put a stop to," Newt threatened from beside his brother. He reached for his holster.

Will sidestepped into the shadows and fired. Once, twice, three times, four. Levering shells into the chamber between shots, he didn't stop until he'd fired six rounds, perfectly placed. When he finished, six Stetsons lay in the dust, and six bareheaded men sat stunned.

"You damned stuntman," Oscar stuttered.

"Hell, it's that feller from the stage," a strained voice croaked.

"You should've shot him when you had the chance, Slim." Oscar Haskel fixed Will with a murderous glare, designed, Will supposed, to intimidate. "This isn't your fight, Radnor. Move aside."

"As an officer of the court, it's my fight anytime a man takes the law into his own hands. Charlie says he owns this land fair and square. If you doubt it take him to court and show your proof."

"That ain't the way it works out here," Newt responded.

"It's the way it works everywhere," Will countered. "Among civilized men."

"You cain't speak for Charlie—"

"Then I'll speak for myself, Newt." Charlie had hobbled into the light. "Get off my land, Oscar Haskel, and take your bloodsuckin' scum with you."

"You aren't gettin' rid of us that easy, McCain. We're the law."

"The law! You dang-blasted, lily-livered—"

The man called Slim went for his gun. Will fired into the ground in front of his horse. The horse nickered, reared, and pitched Slim, who lived up to his name in build, back over his rump.

Oscar held up his hand again. "That's it for now, boys. Pick up your bonnets, an' let's head back to town." The tone of Oscar Haskel's voice left no doubt that the fight was far from over, making his parting threat unnecessary. "We'll be back, McCain. Put that in your cud an' chew it while we're gone."

Will and Charlie stood side by side, watching them go.

"That was mighty fancy shootin', son. What you got in them veins, ribbons o' steel?"

Will's insides still shook from the encounter. He started to tell Charlie that this was the first time he'd ever faced men with guns at such close range, so close he could see the color of their eyes, so close he would have no chance against their guns. The thought of it left him weak and quaking. He felt the need to talk about it, and a man like Charlie, who had survived in this wild country for over twenty years, would understand. But he couldn't talk to Charlie. Charlie had killed his father in cold blood. He certainly couldn't talk to Charlie.

Suddenly anguish returned, the old anguish, along with the determination that had driven Will for twenty-three years. Charlie had memories? Well he had memories, too, and they rushed back now, flooding him with agony—memories of finding his father, dead and clutching Charlie's pistol, memories of the blood and the tears and the promise he'd made his mother. He turned on Charlie.

"I'm not your son, Charles Kane. You'd do well not to forget that." Storming to the barn, Will relieved Red Avery, whose bloodless face testified to the archaeologist's own anxieties.

"That was some shooting," Red said with enthusiasm. "Glad you're on our side."

"I'm not on your side," Will hissed. Saddling his horse with angry pulls and shoves, he led the animal from the barn. At the door he turned back to the stunned Red. "Tell Charlie I've gone back to Santa Fé."

He had just stepped into the saddle, however, when two riders topped the far hill and galloped into the valley. Will took one look, dismounted, and turned his horse toward the barn. "Stable him, Avery." He slapped the horse on its rump. "Then get to your post. They're coming back."

Will dodged from one tree to another, making his way to the house, where Kate and Charlie had come onto the veranda. Will stopped on the bottom step, turned, and faced the oncoming riders. But when he lifted his rifle, Charlie swung his walking stick and knocked it away from his face.

"What the—"

"Tryin' to save your hide," Charlie quipped. "Miss Priss'd likely react a bit different from those Haskel fellers if you shot the hat off her head."

Will's mouth dropped open. He watched Priscilla and another rider draw near. Priscilla slid off her horse, tossed her reins over the hitching rail. Her eyes held Will's for a moment before she turned to her parents. When she looked back at him, Will could read her concern, the alarm in her eyes.

"You three look about as wore out as a pot of Uncle Sog's sonofabitch stew."

She strode toward the veranda as she talked, and without realizing it, Will walked, too. Toward her. They stopped within inches of each other. She reached up and removed her hat, wiping her brow with her sleeve, a habit he'd become accustomed to out here, performed by men. But it didn't look masculine, not when Priscilla McCain did it.

His breath came short. Her lips parted, stayed that way, beckoning him. Her worried blue eyes searched his.

"Haskels," was the only word he could get out. But for the life of him, he couldn't concentrate on the Haskels. He'd intended to be long gone by the time Priscilla returned. He'd promised Charlie. And himself. Gone from Spanish Creek. Gone from Santa Fé. Gone, even, from New Mexico Territory.

He heard the sound of shuffling and realized Charlie was hobbling up behind him. He moved a few steps aside, recalling Charlie's penchant for using his walking stick to move aside any and everything he damned well pleased.

"We run 'em off," Charlie was saying. "Oscar Haskel brought his scum out here, thinkin' to take the place. Will, here, came in time to warn us."

Priscilla's eyes came back to Will's. Her lips, still parted, curved now in a smile. She didn't say anything, and Will realized suddenly that was highly unlike her.

"Priscilla!" Kate rushed forward. "We're so glad you're here. It was terrible, worrying that you might tangle with those outlaws on the way home."

"Well," Priscilla said at last. Will could tell her mouth was dry. He had the distinct impression that it wasn't from trail dust. "Well." He watched her swallow. "I didn't,

Mama." Her face relaxed then, and her eyes twinkled. "Sorry I missed the fun."

Will's heart throbbed in his throat. He couldn't move; he couldn't talk. He wished he had his horse's reins in hand, because surely, *surely,* he would climb aboard and ride away from here.

"Wasn't much fun to it," Charlie barked. "Except the part where Will shot off their hats."

"Shot off their hats?" Priscilla rolled her eyes, mocking. "What were you aimin' for, greenhorn? Their heads?"

Will tried to think of a retort, but his brain was mush. Must be the lost sleep. *Surely* it was the lost sleep.

"Come, darling." Kate reached for Priscilla's arm. "Let's go inside. I'll fix breakfast. You, too, Mr. Radnor. The least we can do is offer you a meal. Let Crockett put away Sargeant, Priscilla."

Will watched Priscilla grip the reins in a gloved fist. His eyes strayed to the man who stood behind her. And above her. Reaching around Priscilla, he offered Will his hand. "Titus Crockett here. Don't reckon we were properly introduced that day in the brandin' pen."

Will shook the man's hand. "Will Radnor."

But when Crockett reached for Priscilla's horse, she held the reins. "I'll rub him down, Uncle Crockett. You're every bit as tired as I am." She smiled sweetly at her mother—that smile that could get her any damned thing she wanted, Will recalled.

"I'll be along in a minute, Mama." Without so much as a side glance Will's way, she strode off toward the barn, leading Sargeant.

Will fell into step beside her. Charlie exploded.

"Stay away from my daughter, Will Radnor!"

Will turned, studied his furious adversary. "You wouldn't want her to walk into a barn full of Haskels, would you, Charlie?"

"Crockett can—"

"I'll check things out. Go on back inside and rest up."

They walked side by side without touching, but the air was so charged between them, Will felt like they were touching.

Red Avery met them at the door, wide-eyed. "Thought you said there were Haskels coming."

"Sorry to've alarmed you, Avery. It was only Miss Priss here and Crockett." Contrary to what he expected, Priscilla didn't respond to that.

"How did the drive go?" Avery asked.

"Not a hitch." Stopping briefly, she untied her saddle bags and handed them to Red. "This is the government gold. Take it to Pa, will you, Red? Mama's fixing breakfast. Tell her we'll be along in a minute."

She wanted them to be alone. It was a crazy notion, a stupid one, but they walked the length of the barn and it was all that sang in Will's ears. He couldn't shake it.

Truthfully, he didn't try. But he tried to try, he argued.

Priscilla entered the stall. He recalled the last time, tried to dredge some sort of joviality, but his brain refused to cooperate. Must be the lack of sleep. Then, out of frustration, he tried to talk. As it turned out, she tried to talk at the same time.

"Tell me about—"

Their eyes sought, held. She flipped the stirrup over her saddle, loosened the cinch, like last time.

But nothing was like last time. And she knew it, too. A warning screamed through his head and down his spine. *Run Will Radnor. Run like hell. What the devil kind of game are you playing with this woman?*

He leaned against the stall, kicked pieces of hay with the toe of his boot, tried to imagine himself saying, *Glad you're home, Miss McCain. I'll be goin' now.*

"What did Pa mean, you shot off their hats?"

He glanced up. A mistake, for her blue eyes were trained on him. "Just that," he managed. Then without warning the dam broke. Words tumbled out. "I'd never shot at men that close before. It was . . . it was unnerving, even in the early morning light. To be honest with you, the only other time I'd ever shot at a man was from the top of that stagecoach. Targets. That's what I shoot at. Targets."

"Pa does, too. Or did. He said he was quite a shot in his younger days." When Priscilla lifted the saddle from Sargeant's back, Will removed the saddle blanket—like before, he thought.

Not like before. "Likely he still is." Nothing's like before, his brain cried.

"I'm surprised he let you get a shot off."

"He didn't have much choice."

She turned to accept the saddle blanket, frowned, not understanding. Their hands touched briefly, before she turned away to drape the blanket over the stall.

"I took his walking stick away." Will busied himself with the bridle.

Priscilla laughed. She turned to him, held his gaze. His fingers fumbled with the buckle.

She sobered. "You came to warn us?"

"To warn them." He turned back to Sargeant, concentrated on working the bridle over his ears. "Haskel knew you and Crockett were gone. That's why he decided to act today."

"How'd you find out?"

"Overheard Oscar and Newt talking."

"And you got here ahead of them?"

He handed her the bridle. She took it. Again they touched briefly, but that was enough. He felt like lightning had struck his hand. What had it felt like to her?

"What about Joaquín?" she was asking. "Is he still in jail?"

"Yeah. They're framing him . . . to get at your pa."

"Blast those Haskels!"

Will grinned. Serious as the subject was, he grinned. But

he tried to make up for it with a serious question. "You care a lot about him, don't you?"

"Pa or Joaquín?"

Will's throat constricted. "Both."

She nodded.

"You believe the rumors?"

"Not really. But I can't be certain."

"What if they were . . . true, I mean?"

"He'd be my brother."

"What's wrong with that?"

"I'd have to share Spanish Creek Ranch." She looked up. "I don't mean it that way. If he were my brother, I'd want to share it with him. But . . . but if he isn't . . . I mean . . . I feel so guilty about how his life has turned out. He has nothing." Her eyes begged Will to understand.

And he did. Not about Joaquín. About himself. About his feelings. And hers. Even though these feelings were misplaced and unwanted, he found himself skirting her horse, stepping toward her. When she was within reach, he caught her around the waist and pulled her to him. Their lips met eagerly. He felt her arms around his neck, on his skin, in his hair.

When they stopped for air, she pulled back. "Thank you for coming to help Pa defend the ranch."

He stared into her earnest blue eyes.

"Spanish Creek means everything in the world to me, Will. I'd die if we lost it. Pa—"

Will stopped her words with his lips. He kissed her long and wet. Even through her leather vest, he could feel her breasts. He wrapped his arms around her shoulders and molded her body to his. And at this moment, nothing else in the world mattered, nothing, except the sense of healing that washed over him. As on an ocean wave, the morning's fear was swept away, to be replaced by gentle peace and sweet, fiery passion.

Behind them Sargeant nickered. Priscilla pulled away.

She grinned, sheepish. Lifting a hand, she brushed hair back from his temple, then traced a finger across his lips. When she paused, he drew her finger into his mouth. Her eyes smoldered.

"Sleeping with steers is about as dirty a job as sleeping with horses," she whispered.

He grinned. "I can tell." But somehow he didn't mind at all. "You smell like a cowboy."

"I am a cowboy." Will watched a grin spread across her lovely face. She enchanted him. Then she laughed, and he knew he'd die a happy man, if he could hear that sound once a day, every day for the rest of his life.

"That's what I set out to be," she was explaining, "a cowboy. Back when I was ten or so, I told Pa I didn't want to try to be a lady, I wanted to be a cowboy."

"That's when you demanded to be called Jake?"

"That's when. Mama was so beautiful, and Pa was so much in love with her—I knew I could never match up. I decided to become something I could be good at."

Will stroked strands of blond hair around her ears. He watched her eyes turn to a deep fiery shade of blue at his touch, and he knew something she would be good at—very good at. "You more than match up . . . Miss Priss."

She grimaced. "That was the day I found the pistol."

"The pistol?"

"Like yours. A Colt Pocket Dragoon, isn't that what you called it?"

Will's heart stood still. He managed to nod.

"I found one sort of like it in an old trunk here in the barn. So one night I set up targets, and at dawn the next morning I sneaked out of the house in my nightgown, determined to learn to shoot."

Will listened, pensive, now.

"I know, it wasn't very ladylike. Pa was furious."

Will held her in arms that seemed turned to stone. He watched her face take on a puzzled expression.

"I guess Pa was right. I should have learned to be a lady."

Will's heart constricted. He pulled her to his chest. He wanted to ask about the gun. He wanted to see the trunk.

He never wanted to see or hear of either again. "You've learned just about everything you need to know," he murmured against her hair, thinking of all the magical things he could teach her. "You're as perfect as a man could ever want."

"PRISCILLA MCCAIN!" Kate's voice cut through his besotted senses. Will jumped away from Priscilla like he'd been shot. He watched Priscilla's expression echo his own surprise.

"Mama!"

Kate stopped not two feet from the stall. Will moved back a couple of steps, watching, wary. Kate McCain was furious. He could tell that with one look. Her usually creamy complexion was dappled with red splotches; her eyes darted from Priscilla to Will and back to Priscilla.

"Get to the house," she ordered Priscilla in a voice that trembled with an obvious effort to control her fury.

Priscilla's face, too, was splotched with red, embarrassment, he knew.

"You, Mr. Radnor, are to stay in the bunkhouse. Red will bring your breakfast."

"I'll be on my way—"

"No, you won't," Kate returned. All graciousness was gone from her voice. "Charlie says since you came to help, you'd best stay until we know the Haskels aren't coming back tonight." She looked to Priscilla. "I agreed, as long as you stay in the bunkhouse—and away from my daughter."

"Mama! How dare you?" When she reached for Will, he moved aside. "Will came all this way—"

"Get to the house, Priscilla."

"I'm a grown—"

"And I'm still your mama. I told you this man . . ."

he's . . . There can be nothing between you and this man, Priscilla."

When Priscilla turned her stricken expression on him again, Will ducked his head and mumbled, "She's right, Miss Priss."

"Right?"

He glanced up; she had looked away. Her gaze flitted around the stall. Her movements were jerky, angry.

"Go with your mother. I'll finish here."

"How dare you—"

"Go on," he encouraged. Her eyes narrowed on him, and he realized he was probably in for a tongue-lashing, he and her mother, both. He decided Kate knew it, too, for she turned to him with, "Will you stay?"

"A while."

"I expect you to keep away from Priscilla."

"I will." He meant it, too, even though he knew ahead of time, it would be one difficult task.

Priscilla moved between them. "I don't know what's got into you, Mama, or into Pa, either. Will came to help us save the ranch. If he were as terrible as you make out, why would he risk his own life?"

"I don't know why he came to help," Kate replied shortly. "But it changes nothing." Taking Priscilla by the arm, she attempted to pull her out of the stall. Without warning Priscilla jerked free and threw herself into Will's arms.

His hands came up, touched her gently, then with concentrated effort, he dropped his arms to his sides. "Listen to your mother, Priscilla."

Her eyes begged him, and he felt like a traitor—exactly what he would be if he touched her now.

"Why . . . how . . . you're agreeing . . ." Priscilla's eyes relayed the confusion she was unable to put into words. "She's being rude and unfair, Will, and you're agreeing with her?"

"Mr. Radnor understands, Priscilla. Now, go to the house."

"How could he understand? I don't even understand." She turned to Will, imploring, "How could you?"

It took every ounce of determination Will could muster to stand cold and impassive while Priscilla practically begged him to come to her aid—to *their* aid.

"Take her word for it, cowboy." Turning he picked up the comb and began to curry Sargeant's coat. He heard shuffling. At length, footsteps headed back up the aisle. He could almost hear Priscilla's anger. He felt her hurt, for he hurt, too. But he'd better get used to it, he told himself angrily. Once he finished the job he'd come to do, she'd be even more hurt.

Ripples in a pond . . .

Charlie was right. Will knew what it was like. He'd known when he came to New Mexico Territory that destroying Charlie would destroy everyone around him.

But back then he hadn't known Priscilla.

Seven

Priscilla didn't see Will again until much later. Not that she wouldn't have sneaked off to the bunkhouse to apologize for the abominable way her parents were acting, if it would have done any good. She wouldn't have hesitated to see Will—if he'd been around.

She'd told her mother so on the way back to the house, adding in a stern voice, "I've never known you to treat anyone so rudely, Mama."

Kate's brown gaze captured Priscilla's momentarily, before her eyes darted to the barn. "We told you from the beginning, darling, that man's no good."

Priscilla stopped on the veranda. "He came to help us save ranch."

"I'm not talking about the ranch."

"I know what you're talking about. So does he. You embarrassed me, Mama."

"I'd rather you be embarrassed than—" Kate's words trailed off on a high, shrill note. Priscilla noticed for the first time how pale and unkempt her mother was, proof of the harrying, sleepless night for those protecting Spanish Creek.

But was it the harrying night that prompted Mama to attack her like a washerwoman? Or was it finding Priscilla in the arms of the very man she'd forbidden her to so much as speak to? Likely, a combination of the two, Priscilla decided.

She wondered whether all mothers reacted so irrationally at the prospect of losing their daughters. That thought surprised Priscilla. Such concerns were out of place in this situation. She would never leave Spanish Creek. And Will Radnor was certainly no rancher.

Except, thoughts of him had kept her awake nights on the trail. And seeing him here today, at her home, helping Pa defend the ranch . . . Priscilla warmed just thinking about his touch, his kiss. "Please give Will a chance, Mama."

Kate caught her daughter's face in her hands. "Oh, darling, I'm sorry you've grown close—"

Priscilla pulled away. "I'm not a child, Mama. I'm a woman, now." Her body fairly glowed when she spoke the words. "For the first time in my life I want to be a woman. A lady. Like you. Pa loves you, and I want . . ." Hesitating to put such intimate thoughts into words, Priscilla pressed her lips together.

"It can't be, Priscilla. You and Will Radnor can never—"

"You'll change your mind when you know him."

"I know him. Men like him, anyway. I won't change my mind. Neither will your papa. We're your parents. You'll just have to trust us . . . for a while."

Anger swept away the last vestige of Priscilla's joy at returning home to find Will here. Anger . . . and despair. She hated quarreling with Mama. She and Pa had their quarrels from time to time. Mama said it came from being so much alike. But Mama was always in control, always a lady. Quarreling with Mama never failed to leave Priscilla feeling inept and childish.

Perturbed by her own feelings as much as by her mother's obstinate rejection of Will Radnor, she turned and stomped across the veranda. Before she'd gone more than a few steps, however, the front door burst open and Uncle Crockett strode through. "I'm taking Radnor up into the hills. We'll keep watch."

"Wonderful," Kate responded.

"I'm coming, too."

"No, you're not," Kate objected.

"Just him an' me, Jake," Uncle Crockett explained. "Your pa wants you to fill him in on our trip to Fort Stanton."

It was a ploy to keep them apart, Priscilla knew. But what choice did she have, except to go along? Inside the house, Pa was nowhere around.

"Your papa's resting," Kate explained. "You need rest, too, darling. After lunch you can go over the trip with him."

Priscilla used the time to her advantage, bathing, washing her hair, selecting a clean pair of chamois britches and a silk shirt. She polished her boots, buffed her nails, and brushed her hair until it shone. All the while, she made plans.

If Will spent the day in the hills, tired as he was, he couldn't return to Santa Fé until at least tomorrow. She'd see him tonight.

Tonight. For some elusive reason, well beyond her ability to comprehend, her body flushed with the thought. She wished for petticoats and put on her lacy camisole, instead, recalling Jessie's approval of it.

She wished for a dress with billowing skirts and ruffles like she'd seen on the Mexican dancers in Santa Fé, but she wouldn't know how to act in such a dress, even if she owned one.

It wasn't that she didn't have a single dress. Three hung in her closet. Mama had made them and hung them there. But Priscilla had never touched them, except in searching for lost shirts or britches. She took one out now and held it against her.

Standing before the looking glass she tried to envision how she would look in it. Made of heavy navy blue broadcloth, the gown was fashioned with long fitted sleeves that ended with pristine white piqué cuffs, and a neckline which would surely strangle her when she swallowed. Although the bodice was fitted to the waist and would reveal the outline of her figure, Priscilla's body objected. Recalling

Will's hands on her back, on her waist, her skin craved freedom. Her loose silk shirt touched her sensuously, like a soft wind in early spring, like Will's hands.

The thought startled her. She'd never considered that a man might put his hands on her naked body. Why should Will's embrace have created such unchaste sensations? No answer came to mind, but a strange idea did, the idea that her body was wise beyond her experience.

And the possibility of learning such wildly sensuous lessons in Will's arms eased even her anger at her obstinate parents. She would bring them around. One way or another. She always did.

At lunch Pa was still in a stormy mood. Priscilla knew it had something to do with Will following her to the barn. Mama wasn't any happier. She'd hoped to persuade them to invite Will to supper, but the odds on that were looking slim.

Of course, Mama noticed her silk shirt. All she did was lift her eyebrows, but Priscilla knew the look of disapproval well. After lunch her mother led the way to the library. Priscilla followed at Pa's pace.

"Damned nuisance, this walking stick."

"How much longer will you need it?"

"Rest of my life, accordin' to your mama."

Priscilla grinned at his petulance. He'd never been one to sit around. "Not that long, Pa."

"I'm fixin' to throw the dadburnt thing clear into Old Mexico."

Without thinking, Priscilla responded with a cheery, "I heard Will took it away from you." One of the things she'd always loved about Pa was his ability to laugh at himself. He never took himself seriously, therefore he never took offense, a trait she had thankfully inherited. It had allowed her to function in a world where nice girls grew up to be ladies and were expected to dress and comport themselves as such. But when Pa spoke, she discovered, that the humor of this particular situation had been lost on him.

He stopped short in his tracks, jabbing his walking stick in the direction of Santa Fé. "I told you, Miss Priss. I never want to hear that man's name on your lips again."

Tears rushed to Priscilla's eyes. She stared aghast, stunned as much by her own reaction as by Pa's harsh words. She wiped her face furiously with the back of her hand. She never cried. Never. Wordlessly, she stalked off, leaving Pa to hobble after.

A moody silence enveloped the library. Mama sat behind the desk, ledger opened before her; Pa took an easy chair, grumbling about throwing his walking stick away. Priscilla pulled a ladder-back chair up to the opposite side of the desk. She dumped the first sack of gold coins onto the surface and proceeded to count.

"Didn't you count that at Fort Stanton?" Pa barked.

"Of course." She continued to recount the money.

"Five hundred dollars?" Pa quizzed.

Priscilla nodded, counting in stacks of ten-dollar gold pieces.

"That should put us in the clear for taxes."

"For this year," Mama said.

"Other than that," Pa asked, "how'd the drive go, Jake?" Priscilla didn't miss his attempt to make amends. "Any problem out of Holbert's Santa Fé boys?"

"No trouble. Uncle Crockett could keep a sidewinder in line. You should have seen them, though, when a couple of Victorio's braves rode into camp the second night out. I thought those cowboys would turn tail and run for cover when I asked the Apaches to sit at the fire and share our meal."

Charlie grunted. He should have laughed. Generally he loved hearing such a tale.

"I had a steer cut out for them to take back to the ranchería," she continued. "They got fired up over Joaquín.

Wanted to ride into town and break him out of jail. I told them Wi—"

Priscilla stopped with Will's name on her tongue, conditioned now to the choleric response it drew from her parents. "I told them Joaquín had a lawyer, and we would keep them informed how things came out."

"That's all we need," Charlie groused. "Victorio's braves charging into Santa Fé on the warpath."

"They won't," Kate predicted. "Victorio is too busy keeping his people out of the army's way. None of his braves would dare take off on a tangent right now."

The money was all counted. Priscilla resacked it, then rose and began storing it in the safe. Her mind played idly with the coming night, and how she could slip out of the house to see Will.

Suddenly the front door burst open and the situation was taken out of her hands. Footsteps sounded in the foyer. After a curt knock, the library door opened to Uncle Crockett and Will, who propelled a ragamuffin boy about twelve or so into the room by a hand to his frail shoulder.

Charlie tried to rise, failed to make it, and slammed his walking stick against the floor. Kate rose and came around the desk. Priscilla had to concentrate on standing still, else she would have rushed to Will's side.

His eyes held hers for one brief, wonderful moment, before his attention turned to her pa.

"Jessie sent the kid," Uncle Crockett explained.

"Tell Mister McCain what you told us, Jorge." Will encouraged him in a gentle voice. His hand rested lightly on the boy's shoulder. Priscilla wondered how her parents could consider such a man no good.

"They're gonna break Wounded Eagle outta jail." The boy's eyes were round as the ten-dollar gold pieces Priscilla had locked away and just as bright.

"Joaquín?" Kate sank back against the desk.

A stunned silence followed. Charlie tried again to rise and made it this time.

Priscilla crossed the room without thinking. She knelt before the child, with Will's nearness burning into her flesh. She resisted the urge to look at him. "Who, Jorge? Who's going to break Joaquín out of jail?"

"The Haskels."

All eyes stared at the child.

"Haskels?" Charlie snorted. "Humph! They're the ones who put him in there."

"Maybe this is their way of releasing him without admitting they don't have a case," Kate reasoned.

"They're planning to lynch him." Will's voice was quiet, steady.

"Lynch him?" Priscilla cried.

"Why in tarnation would they do that?" Charlie barked.

"Tell Mr. McCain exactly what Jessie said," Will encouraged the boy.

Jorge squared his slender shoulders. *"Señorita* Jessie, she say I should come an' tell you, pronto. The Haskels are gonna break Joaquín outta jail so they can break Charlie McCain."

"Break Charlie . . ." Kate's words were muffled by her gasp.

Priscilla raised eyes to Will who stared at her with a strangely passionate expression. Not the kind of passion she felt when he held her and kissed her. This was passion of a different kind—wild and furious and desperate. As if transmitted to her through his eyes, that passion fired hers.

Will dragged his gaze away from Priscilla. "Tell them, Jorge, in exactly the words you told us."

"Señorita Jessie, she say *Señor* Newt told her. He's the sheriff." The boy paused as if waiting to be certain this much was understood.

"Go on, boy," Charlie barked. "We know who the sheriff is, damn his hide."

"Señorita Jessie say *Señor* Newt say if they break Joaquín outta jail and lynch him . . ." Jorge's eyes traveled up to Will. "That's hangin', ain't it?"

Will nodded. "Go on."

"Señor Newt say if they lynch him till he's dead, it will . . . it will break Charlie McCain, then they can take the ranch. *Señorita* Jessie, she say she don't want you broke, *Señor* McCain."

Silence hung as though suspended from the vigas overhead. It created a buffer between Priscilla and her parents' wrath. The boy's claim put things in perspective; at this moment, everything else was secondary. Rising to her feet, she grasped Will's arm. "What are you going to do?"

Will looked down at her hand. He stared at it so long, Priscilla began to feel heat rising through his sleeve. Around them pandemonium broke out.

"Humph! They'll never get away with a stunt like that."

"They plan on blamin' it on Victorio and his braves," Uncle Crockett explained.

"This is absolutely ridiculous."

"Hell, Kate, every damned thing the Haskels do is ridiculous—or worse."

"How can we believe this boy?"

Priscilla heard Mama's strident voice and looked to see her staring, not at the child she accused of lying, but at Priscilla's hand still clutching Will's arm.

"He's telling the truth, Mrs. McCain," Will responded. "I know Jorge. He lives behind the cantina, runs errands for Jessie, and for me, too, time to time. She sent him, you can be sure of that."

"But what if he mis—"

"He got the message right, too. The Haskels could pull it off, outrageous as the stunt sounds to civilized people."

Priscilla watched a strange sort of acknowledgment pass between Will and her pa.

"Whether it will accomplish their end," Will continued,

"breaking Charlie . . ." Will dropped his gaze to the boy before finishing. ". . . only Charlie knows."

"How 'bout it, Crockett?" Charlie quizzed. "You believe this cock 'n bull?"

"Yeah, I do. And you do, too."

Charlie struck his walking stick against the floor. "Humph! I believe it. Can't afford not to, which is what they're bankin' on. Newt Haskel didn't accidentally let those plans slip to Jessie. He told her on purpose. They're countin' on me stormin' in and raisin' a ruckus." He studied Will. "How much time do we have?"

"Couple of days, maybe. According to what Newt told Jessie, Oscar's gone somewhere down south, and they're waiting for him to return."

Charlie slumped back to his chair, muttering, "Dad-blasted sorry scoundrels. Sorriest excuse for human beings on God's green earth." He raised stricken eyes to Kate. "But what in hell can a crippled old man do to stop them?"

Kate slid to her knees beside her husband. She pressed her lips against his arm briefly, then rested her head there.

Will stepped back. "I'll think of something, Charlie. Joaquín's my client."

Priscilla watched Will leave the room with purposeful strides. Silence, heavy and ominous, fell once more over the occupants of the library. Through a haze she saw Uncle Crockett run knobby fingers through his salt-and-pepper hair. She stared at his stubby forefinger, recalling stupidly how he had gotten it caught in a rope one day when they were rounding up cattle. Pulled the end off clean at the joint. Priscilla had been no more than twelve at the time. Why did she recall such a thing at this moment?

She turned back to Pa. He held his head in his hands and stared down at his cracked boots. Mama covered one of his hands with her own.

Priscilla glanced back to the open door. The boy, Jorge,

had disappeared. Followed Will outside, likely. He'd said he
would think of something. But what?

Racing from the room, she rushed to the veranda in time
to see Will toss the boy onto the back of a saddled horse
and send him on his way. He turned to catch up his own
reins.

"Will!"

He stopped, reins gathered. His eyes held hers. She had
no idea what was on his mind.

She reached him, grasping his sleeve, like in the library.
"What're you going to do?"

His eyes, solemn, serious, traveled over her face slowly,
feature by feature. She wondered what he was thinking.
"Talk to them, I guess," he said finally. "Try to reason—"

"Reason? With Oscar Haskel? Or Newt? You might as
well try to reason with a fence post."

"Yeah." His free hand came up, cupped her jaw in the
briefest of contact; his fingers gently traced her face. She
felt the fine hairs on her cheek rise. "I'm sorry, Miss Priss.
I'll do the best—"

"We'll have to beat 'em to it."

His hand stilled. "What?"

"Break him out of jail. We'll have to do it before the
Haskels. You said we have time. A couple of days."

"Jailbreaking is against the law, Priscilla."

"Well, so is murder, greenhorn, and the Haskels have
already admitted they intend to murder him."

"I'll find another way."

"There isn't another way."

"I've never heard of such harebrained tomfoolery."

"It'll work. We can—"

"*We* won't do anything. Do you hear me? Whatever is
done, I'll do."

"You'll need help."

"Not yours." Will stared hard at her. The passion in his
eyes was for her, now. She thrilled to it . . . until he spoke.

"Damnation! Why didn't your parents raise you like a girl?"

His words struck Priscilla like a steer horn to the gut. She ducked her head to hide her hurt. "Well, they didn't. So you can quit wishing for the impossible. We have more important things to worry about." She felt him touch her cheek, shooting fiery tingles down her spine.

He lifted her face with two fingers beneath her chin. When she refused to look at him, he planted two soft kisses there, one to each eye. "You're loco, you know that, cowboy?"

His soft tones eased her wounded pride, but his earlier accusation left her self-conscious. She pursed her lips and resisted opening her eyes.

"You're asking me to break a prisoner out of jail, Priscilla."

At the change of subject, she jumped back into the fray. "He's innocent."

"He's in jail."

"He's innocent."

"I'm an officer of the court," Will argued. "I can't go around taking the law into my own hands."

"The Haskels do."

"That would make me no better than they are. No, no, no. A thousand times, no."

"I suppose you have a better idea. Not a stupid one, like reasoning with them. We can't let them hang Joaquín."

"*I*, Priscilla," he corrected in firm tones, then softer, added, "I won't let them hang him. I'll go to Judge Sanders."

"Blast it all, Will Radnor. Sanders is in Oscar Haskel's pocket. They're using you to run roughshod over my pa, and you're letting—"

He grabbed both her shoulders, drew her close, held her tightly. "I'll do my best for Joaquín. I told you that. I mean it." He kissed her then. Rougher than he ever had, quicker than he ever had. Releasing her abruptly, he stepped into the saddle and pulled the reins around.

She figured he was mad. Well, let him be. "I'm coming—"

He looked back at that. "Sit tight, Miss Priss. I'll let you know when it's over."

"I'm coming, damnit."

A wry smile flitted across his face. "Your mama's right. You can't get tangled up with me. There's no future in it."

Her breath caught in her throat. *Tangled up?* Embarrassment flooded her, turned to chagrin, then to fury. "Don't flatter yourself. It's Joaquín I'm worried about. I certainly don't intend to leave his safety to a stupid greenhorn like you."

He looked her solidly in the face, as though he were accepting a challenge from a stranger. "And I certainly don't intend to leave the law to a trigger-happy cowboy like you."

Will felt her wrath burn into his back when he rode away from the ranchhouse. What tomfoolery! Break a man out of jail? Him? William Penn Radnor IV, who had hated crime and violence since the day he was ten years old and discovered his father's murdered body? And who had devised this ignoble plan?

The daughter of his father's murderer, which proved the point. He had to get Joaquín cleared and his business with Charlie settled and get the hell out of New Mexico Territory.

He could read the headlines now: *HEIR OF PRESTIGIOUS PHILADELPHIA LAW FAMILY HUNG FOR CONSPIRING WITH NEW MEXICO'S FEMALE VERSION OF BILLY THE KID.* Hell fire and damnation! He was even beginning to curse like her.

What a woman! What a wild and crazy woman. She was everything his brain rejected . . . everything his heart desired. He stopped short of thinking about the myriad of magical things his body wanted from Miss Jake McCain.

Instead he turned his attention to the problem of preventing the Haskels from lynching his client. Priscilla was right about the judge. He'd never go against the Haskels. Certainly not to side with someone new in town, someone who had no proof of Joaquín's innocence, someone who had gone over to the enemy, as Oscar Haskel would surely have informed him by now.

But if he couldn't depend on Judge Sanders for help, who? Priscilla was right again. He couldn't do this alone. The thought sent a chill down his spine.

He could see himself sneaking into the darkened jail. Even if he could get the keys, even if he could arrange for the jail to be empty, even if the jailbreak were accomplished without fanfare, even if everything else worked, Joaquín would undoubtedly balk at leaving the safety of the jail in the company of a man employed by Faust & Haskel.

An unfriendly cuss, Joaquín. And defensive. If he wouldn't listen to Charlie or Priscilla, he certainly wouldn't listen to a greenhorn like himself.

Although Will had slept a couple of hours under a tree earlier in the day while Crockett kept watch, by the time he reached Santa Fé he was feeling the effects of his sleepless night. He'd ridden back to town at a slower gait than usual, his mind occupied with keeping Joaquín safe—and Priscilla out of his hair and off his mind. When he entered the dusty main street, the plaza was coming to life again after siesta. He left his horse at the livery, still pondering the question: To whom could he turn for help? It was beginning to look more and more like he was about to lose a client.

Priscilla's lovely face popped to mind. And he was about to let Priscilla down. Somehow that troubled him more than thoughts of losing Joaquín. And that, in turn, troubled him even more.

He recalled her pensive expression when she related her fears of never measuring up to her mother. His heart ached for the little girl who had decided to become a cowboy in self-defense. She'd obviously done well by her decision. She was a damned fine cowhand, by all accounts.

But what a lady she'd become, too! And dang his hide, he'd better free Joaquín and get out of New Mexico Territory before she realized he thought so.

Will took the stairs at the back of the cantina more determined than ever to cut short his stay here. Shadows of cottonwood limbs danced over the worn wooden steps. Will had climbed halfway to the top before he noticed Jessie.

She'd started down, but remained poised on the second step. Then it came to him. *Jessie.* Of course. That's who could help.

"Hey, Jess, I need to talk to you. Private."

"I know."

"Jorge returned safe and sound?"

She nodded. "Wait for me in your room, Will."

Jessie, he thought. Yes, Jessie was the one person who might be able to help. She was friendly with the Haskels. And she'd already proved her loyalty to Charlie.

Lost in plans, Will opened the door to his room. His brain skidded to a halt. "Hell fire and damnation! What're you doin' here?"

Priscilla turned from the open set of French doors. She'd obviously watched him cross the plaza. Her smile was the smile of an angel, and heaven help him, but the sight of her answered his question for both of them. He swallowed against a suddenly dry throat.

"How'd you get here so quick?"

"I don't mosey along when I have someplace to go, greenhorn."

Someplace to go. With a crazy leap his mind's eye pictured the bed—off to his left, to her right, close, too damned close. "Damnit all, Priscilla. Get out of here."

But he didn't move from where he stood in the doorway, and she stood stock still. The setting sun fanned its golden rays around her like she was one of those statues of the saints he'd seen in the cathedral across the plaza.

But she wasn't a saint, and neither was he, and what he was thinking would see him in hell.

"I'm going with you, Will. Jessie's agreed to help us. She's gone to take care of a few matters. As soon as she gets back—"

"What's wrong with your hearing?" he snapped. Striding toward her, his only intention was to get her out of harm's way, even if it meant setting her bodily on her horse and sending her back to Spanish Creek. "Out. Out you go."

"When I told Jessie our plan, she agreed, Will. There's no other way."

He took hold of her shoulders. *"We* don't have a plan—"

For some reason, she lowered her voice to a whisper. "Jessie agreed—" He found himself whispering back.

"I'm not doing it, Priscilla."

"There's no other way." She looked up at him with eyes as doleful as any he'd ever seen. His hands tightened on her shoulders.

"Please, Will. We can't let them kill Joaquín. What if . . . I mean, if the gossip turns out to be true, they're right. It would break Pa. Help me, Will."

At some point he stopped listening to her words and heard only her voice, her pleading, her vulnerability. And he knew he would do whatever it took to set her world aright . . .

Before he tore it apart for good.

It wasn't her begging that got him, Will reasoned. He couldn't abide women who used feminine wiles to get their way. But Priscilla McCain wouldn't know a feminine wile if it slapped her in the face. When Priscilla stooped to begging, it would be for something important—like a man's life. A man who could well be her brother.

He looked away . . . for his own good. And for hers. But his palms began to move over her silk shirt. He felt her skin warm beneath his touch. He tried not to look at her again, for to do so would be to surrender, but he wasn't that strong a man. Unable to stop himself, he pulled her to him. Their lips met with an eagerness born of fear—the fear of never holding each other again.

He pulled her closer. She came readily. Her hands skimmed his neck, spiraling shafts of fire down his spine, directly to the source. He groaned.

His lips opened, his tongue delved, and he knew if he had a hundred years with this woman, it wouldn't be enough. He felt her flip his hat to the floor. He felt her fingers weave through his hair; he pulled her body to his.

Only then did his hands leave her shoulders. Tugging her shirt loose, he ran his palms inside, up her ribs, feeling the lace that had been but a hint through the pale silkiness of her shirt. He recalled what Jessie had said.

Holding her around the rib cage, he pushed her back and stared into her liquid blue eyes. His thumbs traced half circles beneath her breasts. Her eyes registered a mixture of surprise and passion. A heady combination.

"No corset, Miss Priss?"

She grinned. Under other circumstances, it might have been considered a sickly grin. But he recognized it. Her muscles were so tight with pent-up passion she could hardly move. He recognized it, because he felt the same way.

His hands moved up and forward. He palmed her breasts, felt her nipples push against him, separated by a thin layer of lace. He felt his own body probe for relief. He knew she could feel it against her belly.

He wondered what she thought about it. Her reaction was to pull his head forward, his lips to hers. Her lips moved urgently over his; her breasts pressed into his palms. Her supple body melted against him.

He dropped his hands. They caught on her gun butts. His

brain made an about face. Abruptly, he released her and stepped back. She looked at him, her eyes alight with confusion and passion.

"Damnation, Priscilla. This is getting out of hand."

The way she looked away, he could tell she misunderstood. Pulling her face back to his, he kissed her forehead. "It has nothing to do with you. It's just—Your mama's right."

"You don't like—"

"Liking has nothing to do with it." His eyes devoured her swollen, red lips. "I like it better than just about anything I've ever done."

"Then—"

In desperation he moved around her. Standing in the open French doors, he gripped a doorframe in each hand and stared between his arms into the ancient plaza, while ancient emotions raged inside him. Passion, and something much softer and more dangerous, vied with a hatred he had lived with all his life.

He felt her hand, placed gently on his back, just above his belt. "I know how hard this is, Will. I know how much the law means to you."

Damnation, she misread everything. No, he misrepresented everything.

"But it's the only way to save Joaquín."

He felt her close beside him, so close her breath blew softly against his shoulder.

At length he turned. Her hand slid off his back, and he reached for it. Taking both her hands, he held them, while he walked her backward, seating her in the chair. He knelt before her. "I thought about it all the way to town," he admitted. "I couldn't come up with another way, either. But I decided to talk to Jessie. The way she feels about your family, I'm sure she'll help. Maybe she has enough influence with Newt to save Joaquín."

Priscilla tipped her chin in an expression he'd come to

recognize as one of defiance. "I looked over the jail on my way in. We can—"

Will gritted his teeth to gain control before he continued. "Hold it right there, cowboy. There's no *we* in this party. How many times do I have to tell you? It's *me*. All the way. Me."

"You can't do this alone."

"I may not do it at all."

"You don't listen very well, either." Her voice was soft, dangerous. He looked down at their clasped hands and tried to grip his runaway emotions.

"There's no other way, Will. It has to be done, and you need my help, because you don't know the country."

"I'm not a complete washout," he snapped. "Even if I were foolish enough to break him out of jail—or try to—I can find my way to Spanish Creek."

"We can't take him to Spanish Creek," she cried.

That brought his head up. He held her startled gaze. He knew what was coming.

"I told you about stupid ideas, greenhorn." But she smiled when she said it, and he looked quickly away. "We can't draw the Haskels to Spanish Creek. Mama's there. And Pa isn't well enough to fend them off. Uncle Crockett wouldn't—"

"Hell, Sherman's army wouldn't be enough to fend them off, if we . . . if I . . ." Will's words stumbled to a halt. Priscilla grinned. She didn't say "I told you so." He wasn't even sure she thought it.

Priscilla wasn't like that. But she was pleased as Punch that he'd slipped. Lordy, if this woman wasn't a pain. Cocksure of herself. He glared back at her, but all he felt was passion, pure and undiluted.

"So, Miss Jake McCain, where does an ol' outlaw like yourself take a man once she's broken him out of jail?"

She laughed. He fought the urge to kiss her. Rising

abruptly, he turned to the open doors. "That wasn't meant as a compliment. Hell, I can't even insult you."

"You didn't try very hard."

He looked down at her, shaking his head. "Most folks I know would be highly offended to be called an outlaw."

"Like Pa says, if a man knows his own worth, it doesn't make any difference what others call him."

Will pursed his lips to suppress a grin.

"Besides, I know you didn't mean it."

Will averted his gaze.

"You're just a little aggravated with me for being right."

"You're not right," he whispered on a sigh. Fortunately Miss Jake McCain was still naive in the ways of passion. He wished she were as incapable of stirring his.

"We'll take him to Victorio," she was saying.

The idea was disconcerting. "They'd never allow—"

"They trust Pa," she interrupted. "We'll be perfectly safe."

"Sure. Perfectly safe. I've heard what Apaches do to white men. They may never allow *me* to leave, but *we'll* be perfectly safe."

She came up behind him while he spoke, laying a hand on his arm in a way that jangled his already jangled nerve endings. When he spoke, his tone was intentionally gruff.

"I told you there isn't a *we* in this charade."

"Yes, there is."

She said it with such conviction that he didn't question her meaning. Her meaning didn't matter. He took her in his arms before he could steel himself against such foolishness. And although he closed his lids against her sparkling blue eyes, her voice sang merrily through his senses.

"You need me, Will Radnor."

Lordy, did he ever.

Eight

Before Jessie returned, Will managed to come up with one final argument to counter Priscilla's outrageous proposal and her own involvement in it—an argument he figured was a foolproof way to convince her, if not of the folly of her plan, at least to return to the ranch and leave Joaquín's welfare in his hands.

"You intend to ride off into the night and leave Spanish Creek to Charlie?" he quizzed. "You know as well as I do, the Haskels will head straight for the ranch the instant Joaquín turns up missing." *If they don't hound us out of town,* he worried. "Charlie'll need you."

She cocked her head, as though she were the cutest thing this side of heaven, and Will was pretty sure she was. "I'm not the stupid member of this team."

He grinned in spite of himself.

"I've done some planning, too, greenhorn."

"On something other than how to turn me into an outlaw?"

"You won't be an outlaw."

"I beg to differ. Breaking the law puts a man on the outside of it, hence he becomes an outlaw."

"The Haskels are breaking the law," she explained in exaggerated tones. "We're helping right things. Pa says laws are made to serve man, not man to serve laws."

Her statement broke the spell she had woven around his brain, for Will had heard those words before, at least a thousand times. He'd learned them from the same source he supposed Charlie had—from his grandfather in the offices of Radnor & Radnor, formerly Radnor, Radnor, & Kane in Philadelphia, the City of Brotherly Love. And that realization unsettled Will. For with it came another, even more unwelcome possibility: Could he be falling in love with Charlie McCain's daughter?

If that were happening, Lord help them both, for their shared past was so horrendous no amount of time or depth of feeling could erase it. If that were happening, his only recourse would be to distance himself from this woman.

"We have an outlaw on our side," she was saying.

"Bully for us."

"Don't go gettin' cantankerous, Will. I'll be there to protect you."

"Thanks a lot. Who're you teaming me up with now, Billy the Kid?"

"Someone even better. Someone who knows my parents. I thought of him on the way to town. There's this outlaw—I think he's a bank robber, or maybe his specialty is robbing stages, I'm not sure. No one talks about him much. But I remember Pa saying that Bart would never refuse to help them."

"Bart who?"

She shrugged. "Jessie knows." Her eyes danced. "She's gone to send him a telegram even as we speak."

"A telegram? This is getting more bizarre by the minute. How do you send a telegram to an outlaw?"

"I told you, Will. I don't know the details. I only know what I know."

"Which isn't a hell of a lot."

"It's enough. Jessie swears she knows how to contact Bart. She thought it was a good idea."

"She would," Will mumbled.

"By the time the Haskels gather their wits and get to the

ranch, Bart will be there to help Pa and Uncle Crockett. Jessie said he'll probably bring some friends."

"Probably isn't good enough."

"Don't worry so much. Bart will come. Jessie said he vowed to come to Mama's aid—I suppose she meant Mama's and Pa's aid—no matter where or when. It concerns something that happened before I was born—in California, Jessie said. Funny, I'm finding out more things about my parents all the time. I didn't know they'd ever been to California."

Delighting in her prattle, Will's brain cleared when she mentioned California, at least enough for him to recall the newspaper clipping that had alerted him to Charlie McCain. Absently, he sank to the same chair where he'd seated Priscilla earlier. California. Now he remembered. Three people were mentioned in that article. Kate, Charlie, and another man. Bart, the outlaw? Likely. By that time, Charlie had been on the run for a while, himself. He would have had plenty of time to take up with other outlaws.

"That's not much to go on," he commented. "What else do you know about it?"

She shook her head.

"Yet, you're willing to leave your mother and father in the Haskels' line of fire and go traipsing off across the country—"

She cocked her head again, stopping his words with thoughts run amuck. "I wouldn't leave Spanish Creek undefended for anything in the world, but if the gossip is true, Joaquín's death would devastate Pa. And even if it isn't true, we can't let them murder him." She changed suddenly, from serious to cocky. "I'm coming with you. I can't let some greenhorn lawyer break a man who might be my brother out of jail and head straight for the enemy's camp and . . . and get them both killed."

Her concern was touching. He didn't tell her so. Instead,

he rested his elbows on his knees and buried his face in his hands. At her touch, he flinched.

She knelt before him, as he had done before her earlier, and she took his hands, completely unnerving him, oblivious to the fact, he knew. "Bart will come. Jessie says he owes my parents a debt that can never be repaid."

Will peered up at her serious, innocent expression. She had no idea what Bart owed her parents. Actually, he didn't know, either. But if Bart came to Spanish Creek, she'd learn. Saying they made it back from Victorio's camp. Then who would be devastated?

"Speaking of Jessie," he said suddenly, "she was the one who helped me slip out of town ahead of the Haskels the other night. If she helps again, she'll be putting herself in danger. Besides that, the Haskels aren't likely to trust her, again."

"I told you not to worry, Will. They don't know she helped you before. I asked her about that. She said you told her to act surprised when they came looking for you and found you gone. She did and they believed her. So stop worrying."

"Even so, I don't like involving her."

"She wants to help."

"Why?"

Priscilla dropped his hands like they'd come straight from the coals. She made a chore of rising and crossing to the French doors. He studied the side of her face. Was that a blush on her sun-kissed skin? Or was her face still flushed with passion? His body was, and he knew the sensation would stay with him for a long time. Lord help him, Will thought, it was true. He'd come to destroy her father and he'd fallen in love with her.

Distance. He had to put distance between himself and this woman. In a physical effort to reinforce his decision, Will rose and positioned himself stoically at the opposite end of the double set of doors. He followed Priscilla's gaze into the plaza, where the sunset was beginning to turn the silvery cottonwoods a fiery red with reflected light.

An old hunger came back to him, a yearning for life to have been different. For a time after his father's death, he'd gone to sleep every night with that wish upon his lips. Then his grandfather had put a stop to it, saying, "There're times we can't control what happens in life, Will. We have to make the best of things. And we can never go back. That's the challenge—to take bad things and make something good out of them."

Since then he'd followed a straight and narrow path, determined to honor his pledge to his mother by finding his father's murderer, and that path had led to something good, possibly the best thing he'd ever found—or ever would find. But there was no way on earth the evil that had gone before them could be erased. Despair stirred inside him at the knowledge that six feet away stood a woman he could love for life, and enjoy loving . . . if things had been different.

His despair turned to resentment, leaving him restless, edgy. For years now his father had been but a memory, a cold and lifeless memory. He could no longer recall what it had been like to sit on his knee or hear his voice or feel his arms around him.

But he could hear Priscilla's voice, her teasing, her bewitching laughter; he could feel her arms around him, her body against his, alive and warm and real. She was filled with so much exuberance and passion he knew she could heal his ancient wounds. If things had been different, she could have. If she weren't Charlie McCain's daughter.

But she was Charlie's daughter.

He felt her turn toward him, and when he looked, his heart lurched at that cocky smirk; it had become so familiar, so quickly.

"Better oil your guns, greenhorn. We might get a chance at that rematch before we get home again."

Will groaned. But for the life of him, he couldn't shake

his anticipation, not even with the knowledge of how dangerous this scheme would be for Priscilla. Or with the control it would take to curb his feelings for her in the days ahead. He knew things would work out better if he could keep their relationship strictly business, man to man.

Which, if he kept his eyes and hands off her, might not be impossible. Hell, he'd pit the two of them against any ten marksmen in the territory. "All right, cowboy, have it your way. But don't let me catch you wastin' bullets."

Jessie arrived then, and the rest of the day passed in a blur of activity. "I sent the telegram, Priscilla. And arranged for three of Carlos' best horses. It's too risky to take your own. You're to pick them up in half an hour. It'll be good an' dark by then. There'll be a sleeping bag and a sack of food tied behind each saddle."

"None of which we'll need unless we get out of town alive," Will snapped.

"I've taken care of that," Jessie told him. "While I was sending the telegram, I ran into old man Monroe and his two sons. You know them, Priscilla." She turned to Will. "The Haskels took all but a hundred-acre stretch of Monroe range a couple of years back, and they're ready to help put a stop to the terror. They agreed to hang around the cantina until it's dark, disappear for a few minutes, then ride hell-bent-for-leather north toward their spread. Folks'll report three riders tearing out of town to the north. That should buy you several hours."

"Wonderful," Priscilla exclaimed.

"Not wonderful," Will groused. "We're not headed for a Sunday afternoon picnic."

"I know that, Will." Priscilla rolled her eyes. "If you can't come up with a little enthusiasm, I may decide not to take you along."

It took an extra second for her words to sink in. *"You* may decide not to take *me* along?"

"Well, I . . ."

"You spent the better part of a day convincing me to become an outlaw, now you're letting me off the hook? What the hell am I supposed to do, sit around town and read about you in the newspaper? Identify your body at the morgue? Carry the news to your parents? Attend your funeral?"

Priscilla laughed. "I knew you were just itchin' to get in on the fun."

Will sighed. Jessie tied up a few loose ends.

"I'll ride out to Spanish Creek and tell Kate and Charlie what's going on."

"Thanks." Priscilla grimaced. "They're going to be mad as the dickens."

"I'll reassure them, *chica*."

"Tell them it was the only way to save Joaquín."

"I will."

"Tell them not to worry, that Will's—" She stopped short. They would worry; there was no stopping that. More so, since she would be with Will. But what choice did she have? Pa wasn't well enough to handle the situation. This was the only way—her best judgment.

Suddenly it was time to go. Jessie sent Priscilla to fetch the horses.

"Will and I'll wait until the alleys are dark," she said. "You know exactly where to meet Priscilla, Will?"

"I know." His gaze found Priscilla's. She grinned.

"Be careful, greenhorn."

For a moment he felt lost in her. For a moment he wanted to call the whole thing off—the *whole* thing—everything, except Priscilla. "You, too," he said before turning away.

He stared out the window until she had time to get well away from the cantina. Then he turned serious eyes to Jessie. "What's your stake in this?"

She held his troubled gaze. "It's an awfully long story, and not very interesting. Self-pity never is after so many years have passed. I want Priscilla to be happy. Leave it at that."

"Then you'd better get ready to pick up the pieces, because you've misjudged this situation—mightily misjudged it."

Jessie patted his arm. "I don't think so. I'm pretty good at assessing matters of the heart."

"Maybe when you have all the facts," he retorted. "That aside, this is a dangerous, harebrained scheme, and you should have talked her out of it."

"Did you try to talk her out of it?"

"Of course."

Jessie smiled, her point made. "Wait till you know her a little better. There's no talking Priscilla out of anything. She's like Charlie. Two peas in a pod."

Will didn't tell her that was the wrong thing to say. Or the right thing, maybe, for it brought him back to the task at hand—his task. Distancing himself from Charlie's daughter. And keeping them both alive.

Jessie was the next to leave, with a satchel slung over her shoulder and a jug of port wine under her arm. Will waited the specified thirty minutes, giving her time to lull Newt with the spiked wine and whatever seductive tricks she'd packed in that bag. He wondered a bit uneasily what sort of degenerate behavior he was fixing to walk in on; whatever it was, Jessie would be good at it.

Priscilla would be, too, at seduction, that is. No, he rebuked, Jake McCain was a cocky, self-assured female cowboy. That was all she would be to him. All she *could* be to him.

Crossing the plaza, he went over his lines, as instructed by Jessie, knowing full well that once he stepped inside that jailhouse, he would be doomed to carry out Priscilla's harebrained scheme.

Jake's harebrained scheme, he corrected. Priscilla McCain existed only behind a barricade in a distant corner of his brain. Someday, perhaps, he would be able to exorcise even her memory. For at no time would it ever become a welcome memory. It was never pleasant to think back on what might have been. He'd known that before he arrived in this god-forsaken territory.

At his knock, deliberately aggressive, Jessie answered the door. Will entered, removed his hat and looked Newt Haskel squarely in the face. It was the first time he'd seen the man since their encounter at Spanish Creek.

"What're you doin' locking up the jailhouse, Haskel?"

Newt jumped up at sight of Will, knocking over his chair. His face glowed like the setting sun. "When'd you crawl out from under that rock, Yank?"

Will took in the situation. It wasn't anything like what he'd expected, except for the whiskey glasses. Instead of entering a love nest, Will found himself in a schoolroom. Slate, chalk, and books were scattered over the sheriff's desk.

Neither did Jessie resemble an ordinary schoolmarm, not the ones they had back East. Her hair hung loose over bared shoulders; her breasts bulged above the low cut of her blouse. Jessie Laredo, he thought, every schoolboy's fantasy schoolmarm.

From the looks of things, Jessie was teaching Newt Haskel to read and write—or having a go at it, and Newt looked about as embarrassed over the whole thing as a man caught with his britches down, which was closer to what Will had expected. He suppressed a grin.

"Sorry to barge in. I need to see my client."

"You ain't got no client here." Newt tossed a handful of wanted posters over the slate. "Nor no business—"

"I don't want trouble, Newt. The court appointed me to represent Joaquín. Not ten minutes ago, Judge Sanders advised me to see about getting a confession out of him. Said he'd go easier—"

"Won't do no good now," Newt snapped. If Will had doubted the Haskels' plans for Joaquín, Newt's expression would have convinced him. "Get on out of here, Yank. Go on back to Spanish Creek and wallow with your kind."

"I didn't come here to—"

"Newt," Jessie purred just loud enough for Will to hear, "let him see the boy." She had righted Newt's chair and gently eased the sheriff back into it. With her lips so close to Newt's ear Will felt the skin at the back of his own neck twitch, she whispered, "When he's gone, we'll lock the door and not answer it again."

Newt squinted at Will, unwilling to back down from the confrontation, yet obviously eager to be rid of Will's presence.

When Jessie began to fumble with Newt's britches, Will shifted his gaze to the desk. He studied a tattered edition of *McGuffy's First Eclectic Reader.*

"Here, Radnor." Jessie jangled a ring of keys impatiently. "Take 'em and be quick about it. Can't you see you've interrupted something important?"

Will lunged for the keys, admonishing himself to slow down, to act normal, to take it easy. He'd barely turned his back to the pair, when Jessie called. "Take a lantern."

He picked up one of two lighted lanterns in the room and headed for the separating hallway. Behind him he heard Jessie whisper something; Newt groaned.

All in the line of duty, Will thought. But somehow even faith in Jessie's expertise wasn't enough to still the trembling in his gut. After unlocking the door that separated the front room from the jail cells in the back, he strode down the short hallway, calling, "Joaquín?" He wanted Newt to hear his aggressiveness. The next few minutes would be tricky, what with his own inexperience in things shady, and Joaquín's penchant for being disagreeable.

"It's Will Radnor, I need to talk to you. Get over here."

"So talk. I'm not deaf."

"A lawyer's conversation with his client should be confidential. I don't intend to shout my . . ." Turning his back to the outer room, Will lowered his voice. ". . . good news.

Remember what Priscilla told you the other day? What she said I could do for you—and you doubted it?" He lowered his voice even further. "Get the hell over here, so we won't get ourselves shot and leave her out there holding the damned horses." While he spoke, he glanced toward the back, looking for the door Jessie had instructed him to unbar while he had the lantern. It was behind the last cell. Somewhere . . .

Like a panther in the night, Joaquín appeared suddenly, soundlessly on the other side of the bars. Will's first indication of his presence was the man's foul breath in his face. He drew back a few inches. His neck hairs prickled.

"Sit tight," he whispered.

"What the hell's goin' on?" Joaquín's high-pitched whisper revealed something in addition to his combative words.

"Take it easy." Will kept his tone low, even, as if soothing a spooked horse. "I'll be right back." Taking the lantern, he tiptoed toward the back door, wishing he were as nimble-footed as Joaquín. The light wasn't nearly good enough, but he found the door, and the wooden bar. Slowly, in contrast to his thrashing heart, he lifted the bar, then as quietly as possible set it aside. Steeled against the squawking of rusty hinges or the creaking of old wood, he tested the door, opening it but a couple of inches. Joaquín could force the rest, if need be. He returned to the cell.

"This for real, white eyes?"

"Unfortunately, yes."

"Why?"

"It's a long story," he echoed Jessie. "Priscilla and I will tell you later. There's not much time, so listen good."

In the flickering light, Will watched Joaquín's usually emotionless face harden into a mask of suspicion. "It's a trick. You're gonna shoot me when I open that door."

"No."

"Why should I believe you?"

"You can't afford not to. The Haskels are planning a necktie party, just for you."

Joaquín fell silent, and Will instructed him. "I'll leave by the front way." Speaking, he fumbled now with the keys, trying to keep them from banging against each other. "Wait until you hear me leave the building. Jessie's in there with Newt. She'll make sure you won't be heard leaving by the back way, if you're quiet about it."

The first key didn't work, but the second one did. "Sit tight," he warned. "Wait until you hear Jessie bar the front door. She'll count to a hundred after that, then make some kind of racket to cover any noise you make . . . if it isn't much."

"I don't make noise, white eyes." But Joaquín's braggadocio was expressed in a subdued tone. Will detected a tremor, and in this the two men found a common thread of need and mistrust.

"You're doing this for her," Joaquín accused.

"You're my client, damnit. I'm doing it to preserve the law." Will turned toward the front room. Unlocking the separating door, he called in a loud voice, "I'll be back bright and early tomorrow, Joaquín. With pen and paper. If I don't get some cooperation, I'm through. Judge Sanders can find himself another jackass lawyer."

Reentering the front room, Will gaped at Jessie, who reclined across Newt's lap with her back to the jail cells, obscuring not only Newt's vision but a good deal of the sound that would come from that room. The schoolbooks had been packed away.

Newt's shirt was unbuttoned. Jessie's blouse was drawn off her shoulder on the far side. The position of Newt's hand and mouth, didn't leave much to the imagination.

Will tossed the key ring to the desk, where it landed with a loud clang. Jessie sprang up at the sound, adjusting her clothing. Newt's eyes were half-closed, from the spiked whiskey as much as from passion, Will imagined . . . he hoped.

"Get th' 'ell outta . . ."

"I'm going. I'm going."

Pulling the outside door closed behind him, Will waited on the step until he heard the heavy beam slam into place, barring the door from the inside. Then he made his way around the side of the jail and into a fantasy world of lacy piñon shadows, his heart in his throat.

Priscilla waited back in the shadows behind the jail, disguised, at Jessie's instructions, in serape and sombrero. She held the reins to three saddled horses. Although she was aware of the necessity to keep from drawing attention, she couldn't stand still.

Darkness had fallen over the town. Dogs barked in the distance. Yellow lamplight played from distant windows. When she saw the back door of the jail open a crack, she jumped, then settled down to worry about what might have taken place.

She knew the plans, yet she couldn't recall opening and closing the door being part of them. What was that greenhorn doing? Had he changed the plan and gotten himself caught? Was he at this minute being locked in the cell with Joaquín? The thought brought a smile. That'd be like two cougars caught in the same trap.

More than likely, Will was having a hard time convincing Joaquín to come out. She'd told them he would. But neither Jessie nor Will would listen.

"Will's going in," Jessie declared.

Will agreed with her. "I go in or I don't go at all." She liked the way he'd held his ground. Even after her earlier outburst about not allowing him to come along, he hadn't backed down.

He could see right through her. She knew that. And she liked it. She liked to tease him and get him riled.

But more than that, she liked to kiss him. She liked being in his arms. She liked his hands on her. Her body flushed when she thought about the way he'd touched her breasts. She felt her nipples thrust against her camisole, as though begging for more.

She knew the facts about mating. Growing up on a ranch, one learned such things at an early age. And her parents had been intimate around her. At least she'd thought they had been. They'd freely kissed and embraced.

But she'd never suspected the rest. The touching, the feverish, liquid heat that spread through her body, the aching in her loins, the yearning that traced its way from head to foot, throbbing, pumping life, glorious life through her veins. Again, she realized that her body had been prepared for such intimacies far beyond her experience and knowledge.

Was there more to learn? Surely. The realization that she would learn it from Will Radnor set her pores on fire and her heart to singing.

If he lived through her foolhardy scheme, she admonished, worried now, lest he be arrested along with Joaquín. He was too smart for that, she argued. Way too smart. He could take care of himself, and her, too, she had a feeling. If he lived through her harebrained scheme.

Finally, at long last, a figure rounded the corner of the jailhouse. She recognized him. A thrill raced through her. He'd made it.

It was hard, feeling like she did, to keep her mind on the business at hand. All she really wanted was to fling herself in his arms and kiss him. She wanted to feel his body probing sensually against hers. She knew what that meant. But she had never imagined it would feel so good, so right.

She wanted to tell him that. She wanted to ask him what

else she had in store and demand that he teach her now, tonight, here, beneath the piñons. But she didn't.

"How'd it go?" she whispered, handing him a serape and sombrero like her own.

"We'll see."

"He believed you?"

"He didn't want to. I told him he didn't have a choice, that if he didn't come out, you'd be caught out here holding the horses. That seemed to reach him."

When Will held up the serape, looking for the top, she took hold of it and slipped it over his head. Her hands rested on his shoulders, with the tacit excuse of pulling his shirt collar through. She felt his muscles quiver and wondered whether it was from her touch or from his encounter with Newt and Joaquín.

"You're learning, Will Radnor," she teased. "For a greenhorn, you've got possibilities."

He studied her a moment, but, as was often the case, she couldn't begin to guess what was on his mind. She hoped he was thinking about kissing her. She suspected she shouldn't be so bold as to kiss him—unless worse came to worst.

"Thanks," he mumbled, finally. Stepping aside, he ducked his head and fitted the sombrero on it. He pulled the chin strap tight. It hid his eyes, so she couldn't tell whether he was looking at her.

"What happened in there?"

"I unlocked the back door and Joaquín's cell. I told him not to leave the cell until Jessie sets up a racket in the other room."

"What kind of racket?"

Will busied himself with his saddle. He flipped the stirrup over the seat and tugged on the cinch, tightening it.

"What were they doing?" she demanded, a little louder this time. "Jessie and Newt."

"Sh, Pri—*Jake.* Someone might hear you."

"There's no one around, *Radnor.*" Jake? Not Miss Jake. Not even Miss Priss, which she hated. Not Priscilla, which he pronounced with a Yankee twang that had begun to sing melodiously through her senses.

"So, what were they doing? Jessie said she could keep Newt occupied—"

"Leave it alone," Will snapped. Turning, he leaned back against the saddle, arms folded over his serape, eyes trained on the back door of the jail.

She followed his line of vision. "Let's see. She took a satchel . . . filled with what? . . . and liquor. She wore that low-cut—"

"Cut it out," Will whispered under his breath.

Heavens, he was uptight. No wonder. What he went through in that jail would have been unnerving to anyone. But she recalled Pa's claim that a nervous man was a dangerous man, to others as well as to himself.

So, Priscilla decided, in the line of duty, she should try to lighten Will's mood. "Let me guess," she began boldly, aided by the darkness that enveloped them and by her newfound obsession with all matters sexual. "There's no bed in the front room . . . They were in the front room, weren't they?"

Silence.

"Front room. No bed." She turned to Will's stoic profile. "I'm not sure about this, Will. Do you always need a bed?"

With an audible gasp, he turned his face to her, tilted now, so the moon caught his expression beneath the wide brim of the sombrero. He glared at her. "Cut it out." After a moment, during which the shock she felt at his harshness registered in his own eyes, he turned abruptly back to the jail.

"No, I guess you don't always need a bed." She watched his profile for a reaction, but he remained stiff and mute. "*Yes* would have been an easy answer, but for some reason you must be reluctant to discuss intimate—"

"Cut it out, Jake. I'm trying real hard to forget you're a woman. So give me a break."

The silence almost suffocated her. The silence and his harsh tone . . . and his words. Forget? Why would he want to forget? She'd seen passion in his eyes. She'd felt it in his touch, in his body. Now he wanted to forget it? Why, when she wanted to remember and experience and . . . The thought of what this meant flooded her with embarrassment.

And hurt. And anger. How could she have allowed herself to submit to the passion of the moment? She'd known from the first he was a man of mercurial mood swings. He was ill-tempered and rude and despicable. Her parents were obviously right.

His voice pierced the stillness. His tone could have come from a stranger. She wished it had. Then she realized what he was saying.

"Here he comes." Turning, Will caught her around the waist, lifting her to her saddle. "Get going. Ride one block east, then out of town. Joaquín will take this street. I'll go—"

"I know the plan."

"Then ride."

She stared at the crown of his sombrero. "You expect Joaquín to follow your instructions?"

"His weapons are on your horse."

Mutely she handed him the third serape and sombrero.

Taking them, he tipped his hat with a finger to the brim. Like a native, she thought sadly. Before Joaquín reached them, Will slapped the rump of her horse. "Ride, Jake."

Nine

Priscilla was the first to arrive at the grove of oak trees southwest of town, their designated meeting place. She'd ridden faster than was good for her horse, hoping the wind in her face would cool her off and lessen the acute sense of betrayal that had begun to compound the hurt of Will's rejection. What she needed was anger, but at the moment she was too confused to be mad.

She wasn't worried about the Haskels following them out of town, she assured herself. Jessie's plan had been well laid.

Running into Mr. Monroe and his sons, who'd agreed to strike a trail to the north, had clearly been a stroke of luck put to good use.

No, Priscilla wasn't worried. Certainly not as worried as Will. He'd been against her scheme from the beginning, but she had forced him to acknowledge that her plan was the only way to save Joaquín's life. She was still convinced she was right.

But look what being right had cost her. She'd traded Joaquín's life for Will's respect. She'd do it again, of course. A man's life was more important than anything else. Without one's life, nothing could be accomplished. Nothing.

And it was beginning to look like nothing was going to be accomplished in her own life. Will's harsh words screamed through her memory with the raucous tones of a mockingbird who'd spent his life living among hawks. Mocking. Taunting. Embarrassing.

I'm trying real hard to forget you're a woman.

To forget? How could he say such a thing? Why did he want to forget? The memory of his kisses teased her with soft yearning. The gentleness of his touch. The tender heat of his body against hers. Forget all that? She wanted to remember it forever. She wanted to experience it again. All of it and more. She wanted him to teach her more.

And he wanted to forget it ever happened. That's what he meant. His reason, though unstated, was obvious. She wasn't feminine enough to suit him. She might have the body of a woman, but she wasn't a lady. Blast it all. She wasn't a lady.

She was a cowboy. She trailed horse herds and roped calves and branded steers. She even cursed like a man. He'd told her so himself.

And certainly she didn't dress like a lady. The idea of girding up in corsets and high-necked, tight-bodiced gowns made her gasp for breath, just thinking about it. She'd worn britches and shirts and boots all her life. To Mama's consternation, to be sure.

Since the Haskel trouble began, she'd started buckling on guns and carrying a Winchester. She was an expert marksman. As good as that blasted greenhorn.

But lately she'd tried to change. Her loose silk shirt whispered against her skin, reminding her of her meager attempt to dress like a lady. One silk shirt and one lace camisole obviously hadn't done the trick.

So what would turn her into a lady? In the darkness Priscilla tried to call forth images of her mother, who was the finest lady she'd ever known. She considered every detail, from Mama's soft voice to her delicate constitution to her sensuous silhouette.

Oh, Mama! Why didn't I listen to you? What should I do now? What she'd like do was crawl under a boulder and hide for the next thousand years. Will's rejection hurt. Beyond that, it humiliated her. For he had rejected the very thing she craved. And she'd had no compunction about showing him how much she craved it.

Kissing him back. She felt again the heady thrill of his tongue on his lips, in her mouth.

Playing her fingers through his hair. She felt his heated skin, the muscle twitches, the way he had drawn her near and nearer, pressing their bodies together, fitting them together.

She remembered. How well she remembered. And she wanted it again. No, she wanted to die of embarrassment. But more than that, she wanted to know how to act when he rode up to this oak grove in the next few minutes. She wanted to know how a lady would act. Why had she been so stubborn? Why had she resisted learning the very things she needed to know for her own happiness?

She checked the sky overhead. The big dipper had swung low. He would be here soon.

Surely. Unless . . .

By the time Will and Joaquín galloped into view, Priscilla was fit to be tied. She hadn't realized she'd been worried about them until they topped the hill. Seeing them, concern for herself vanished, and she knew it had been but a smokescreen for her deeper worry. Will and Joaquín. Facing the Haskels alone. She had imagined them in jail. She'd imagined them lying by the roadside shot through the back. She'd imagined their horses stepping in varmint holes . . .

"I'd almost given up on you." In her relief, she forgot to restrain her enthusiasm.

Will stepped from the saddle. His eyes roamed over her, searching. "Have any trouble?" Even though his tone was brittle, she took the question as a sign he'd been worried, too.

"No trouble." She smiled. "We did it, Will. I told you it'd work. We did it!"

"Don't speak so fast."

"The worst is over," she assured him.

"The worst is far from over." He glanced back toward town. When his gaze returned to her, his eyes were hard as flint. "Where I come from ladies get excited over the latest fashions, not over breaking prisoners out of jail."

His tone was caustic, as it had been earlier in town. It sliced through Priscilla's emotions as surely as if he'd used Uncle Sog's meat cleaver. Hurt and fury poured from her wounded spirit. She struggled to suppress her hurt, to allow her fury to emerge. When she spoke it was with icy control. "Then that should make it real easy for you to forget I'm a woman, greenhorn."

Will spun away, but not before she saw the dismay in his expression. "We can't dillydally around here till daylight, waiting for the Haskels to catch up." He looked at Joaquín. "Which way do we go?"

Will's harshness added much needed fuel to Priscilla's anger, giving her strength to fight back. "The Haskels are chasing Mr. Monroe and his sons."

"You know that?"

"Yes."

"You *saw* them?"

"No, I didn't see them." He was right, blast him. But she'd be damned if she'd say so.

"The Monroes?" Joaquín, too, had dismounted, and like Will, held his reins in hand. "What's ol' man Monroe got to do with this?"

"Jessie saw them in town this afternoon," Priscilla explained. "They agreed to ride out of town after dark, giving folks an eyeful of three riders headed north."

"*¡Madre de Dios!* Did you alert the whole damned country?" Pivoting with sure-footed ease, Joaquín started to remount. "I'm gettin' out of here."

Will grabbed his arm. Joaquín tensed. Priscilla jumped between them.

"Will," she warned. Unarmed though he was, Joaquín was still as dangerous as any of Victorio's braves. Rage flared between the two men.

Will's voice, low but clear, traveled over Priscilla's head from behind. "We broke the law to save your hide, Joaquín, not to mention the danger we put ourselves in. You're sticking with us until we reach Victorio's."

"Victorio's?"

"They won't follow us there," Priscilla explained. "It'll be the safest place. Maybe the only safe place."

"I can get to the ranchería by myself." He glared at Priscilla. "I don't need you or any white-eyes lawyer to save my hide."

"Then we should have left you in jail," Will hissed. "They were fixin' to break you out and lynch you."

"Says who?"

"Newt told Jessie," Priscilla said.

"The Haskels are mean, not dumb. Why the hell would they do something stupid like that?"

"They figured killing you would be the easiest way to break Charlie McCain."

"Like hell." Joaquín staggered backward, obviously stunned by Will's claim.

"They think killing you would cause Pa so much distress he'd quit fighting them over—"

"Spanish Creek," Joaquín spat.

"Spanish Creek," Priscilla repeated.

Distress flashed across Joaquín's face, before his features turned to stone. "Like hell it'd break Charlie. He'd probably pay them to do it. That'd free his conscience, once and for all."

Priscilla felt Will tense behind her. His voice was cold, emotionless. "I don't like it any better than you do, Joaquín, but for the time being, we stick together."

Tense seconds ticked past. Will dropped his hand. Joaquín stepped away. But for the longest time Priscilla couldn't move. She stood gazing off into the night, clenching and unclenching her fists, concentrating on getting a grip on her emotions, forcing her hurt into the deep recesses of her heart, submerging it with anger. Finally she strode to her saddled horse.

"Mount up, girls," she barked in her best imitation of Uncle Crockett calling cowboys to horse. "Time's wastin'. The Haskels won't be fooled for long." Stepping into the saddle, she spurred her mount. The horse reared, then pitched forward into the night.

"We'll ride south," Joaquín called.

"No," she hollered over her shoulder. "We'll cross the Río Grande, then turn south. That way, if the Haskels pick up our trail, we won't lead them to Victorio." Behind her she heard the men set out. When one of them came abreast, she steeled herself to look straight ahead.

"Break a horse's leg, they'll catch you for sure." Joaquín kept pace. When she didn't respond, he added, "I don't know what burr's between you and that white-eyes lawyer, but if you run your horse to ground, don't expect me to hang around and face a noose."

She turned a stony face to him. Joaquín, her childhood friend. Joaquín, possibly her brother. She'd broken the law to set him free, yet somehow all she felt was pain, for in doing it, she had ruined any chance she might have had with Will Radnor.

Will heard Joaquín's comment from behind the two riders. Priscilla didn't respond, but he knew the answer. Hell, he'd deliberately antagonized her, pushed her away. Of course she didn't understand.

But he couldn't explain—yet. Soon enough she would know, and she would hate him. So she might as well start hating him now.

She led them on a wild race through the night, as though they were being pursued by the devil, and Will followed like he had good sense. Joaquín was right, she risked breaking a horse's leg. So did they, following her. Hell, he didn't even need to follow her.

He shouldn't follow her. She and Joaquín could take care of themselves. He should let them go on to the ranchería, while he headed back to Spanish Creek and had it out with Charlie. He could have his business with Charlie finished and be gone from the territory by the time she returned to the ranch.

He should.

But he didn't. He told himself he couldn't leave his client to outrun the law by himself. But of course that wasn't the reason he spurred his winded horse and kept up with the mindless pace set by Miss Jake McCain.

Even now when he knew all was over between them, over before it had begun, his heart was heavy. Now, when he should be worrying about how to prove Joaquín's innocence before a crooked judge—saying they escaped capture and hanging and he managed to get in and out of Victorio's ranchería with his scalp intact—now, after he'd finally found the strength to check their rampaging emotions, even now all he could think about was holding her in his arms, feeling her body against his, tasting her sweetness—

The last thought elicited a sardonic chuckle. Sweetness and Priscilla McCain shouldn't fit in the same sentence. But they did. Even when she rode in wild revenge through the dark night, she was somehow the sweetest thing he'd ever known. And he followed her like he had good sense.

Hours later with the moon hidden behind heavy clouds, they reached the Río Grande. Priscilla plunged in at a speed more suitable for a shallow mountain stream. Joaquín drew up on the bank.

"There's a safer place to cross downstream," he called after her. Already she was two horse lengths into the raging water. Joaquín turned his mount south. "You'll get yourself killed," he called.

Without hesitating, Will passed Joaquín and spurred his

horse into the river behind Priscilla. The horse struggled against the current. Water rushed over his legs and swept between his body and the horse's neck. He tightened his hold on the reins and wondered at his sanity.

Hell fire. He didn't need to prove his prowess to this cocky madwoman. Nevertheless he kicked his horse, guiding the swimming animal to the upstream side of Priscilla. "Did you break him out of jail, so you can kill him on the ride to safety?"

She turned stony eyes on him. "If you're not man enough to cross here, go downstream."

Will spurred his mount ahead of hers. Gaining the other bank, he kept going. By the time he heard her horse scramble up the embankment, he was disappearing into the foliage. She called to him in acid tones.

"If you're going with us, you're headed the wrong way, greenhorn."

The sky was black with the last hours of night when Joaquín caught up with them. "We should stop for a while."

"Later," was the only answer she gave.

Will followed her and Joaquín brought up the rear, grumbling to himself. "I don't know what the hell you did to rile her, white eyes, but you'd better set it straight before she kills us all, herself included."

Although the idea was unsettling, Will declined the suggestion to make up with Priscilla. By the time the sun peeked over the top of the nearest mountain range, she appeared to have settled down. When they came to a clearing nestled back in the foothills, she drew rein.

"Why don't we rest awhile?" She even smiled at him, which, Will realized later, should have been a warning. "You haven't gotten much sleep the last few nights."

"More like none," he replied.

She'd already dismounted beneath a rocky overhang and had begun to unsaddle her horse. "We'll divide up the housekeeping chores." She tossed a canvas bag to Will. "After you stake your horse, carry some water for coffee. Joaquín can build a fire, while I see what Jessie sent for nourishment."

Will dismounted and pulled the saddle off his tired mount. Considering the situation, he realized Priscilla had been thinking of the horses when she stopped to rest. They would never outrun a posse if they wore out their horses.

Taking the bag, he headed for the river. Joaquín gathered firewood, and by the time Will returned, the place had taken on the look of a real camp. He noticed three bedrolls, spaced for privacy, back against the wall of the hill.

Priscilla had a skillet out and was stirring something over the fire Joaquín had built. "Smells good," he commented. "What is it?"

"I wouldn't know. I'm not much of a hand at cooking." She pursed her lips and glared into the skillet, additional signals that things weren't as harmonious as they seemed.

She dished up the food and slapped a tin plate in his hands. He took it and began to eat the green chile stew. Joaquín accepted the next plate. The three of them sat silently around the fire. Finally Will decided to attempt to bring things back to normal. Whatever the hell that was.

"How far to Victorio's?"

"If the trip's getting too hard for you, Radnor, you don't have to come the rest of the way." Priscilla's tone reminded him of summer grapes that hadn't ripened yet. "You can ride back and help Pa defend Spanish Creek."

The tongue-lashing was unexpected, and while he recovered, Joaquín jumped in with his favorite topic.

"Since when did Charlie need help with anything?"

"Since his daughter started breaking prisoners out of jail."

Priscilla glowered from Joaquín to Will. Rising, she didn't even try to keep the scorn from her voice. "If you get sleepy, there'll be coffee on the fire, Joaquín. Wake me for second watch."

"I—" Will began.

"You think we could sleep while some greenhorn kept watch?"

Will stared her down, or attempted to.

Joaquín evidently felt the need to placate her. "I got all the sleep I need for a month of Sundays in that jail cell. You two catch some shuteye. We'll ride out in a couple of hours."

Will was still smarting over Priscilla's rebuff, understandable, though it was. That's why he was so slow at picking up the signals, he reasoned later, when he crawled into his bedroll and tried to go to sleep. The damned thing was thin as last year's socks and it lay on top of a slab of solid rock. Some campsite she'd found. If he didn't know better—

Sitting up, he peered through the juniper shrubbery that separated his bedroll from Priscilla's. She was sitting on her pallet, staring his way. And then and there he knew he'd been set up.

Resisting the temptation to move his bed, he smiled as sweetly as she was doing, and called, "Night, Jake."

"Sleep tight, Radnor," she returned, in that innocently sweet voice that would get her anything—almost.

Will flopped to his side, visions of those blue eyes dancing in his mind—until he hit rock. For a minute he thought his hipbone had cracked. This damned rock was hard as steel. He tossed and turned, as carefully as possible, and by the time Joaquín called them to saddle up a few hours later, Will knew he was black and blue. Fortunately Miss Cowboy Jake McCain couldn't see the damage she'd wrought.

But it was a lesson well learned, he vowed, as he followed Priscilla on another hell-bent ride which lasted the better part of the day and into the following night. An hour or so past dark she decided to stop again. And he took charge. Choosing his own sleeping spot, he laid his bedroll away from the camp she was busy setting. He didn't dare comment, for fear of what she would try next.

As before, she made coffee and heated the food—this time it was only tortillas and goat cheese. They sat spaced around the campfire and ate without talking, until Priscilla broke the silence.

"I hope Bart's gotten to the ranch by now."

"You'd better," Will replied. "The Haskels surely have."

"Bart Ellisor?" Joaquín questioned. "What's he got to do with this?"

Priscilla explained, finishing with, "Something happened between Pa and Bart a long time ago. Jessie said Bart promised to come to Pa's aid anytime he was needed. I hope he meant it."

"Something happened between Charlie and a lot of people," Joaquín retorted.

Will rose, cleaned his plate with a handful of grass, and wrapped up in his blankets. Lordy, he could sleep a week. The cold, hard ground had never felt so soft. He slept till sunup, when Priscilla began banging on the skillet with a vengeance that would raise the dead.

He sat up, rubbed fists to his eyes.

"Ready for coffee?" she asked.

"More'n ready." By feel rather than sight, he located his boots and stomped into first the right, then the left. But his toes had barely wriggled into the left boot when he felt something inside. Without thinking, he kicked the boot a good ten feet.

"Something wrong?" Priscilla asked.

Will's heart pounded in his ears so loudly he could hardly hear her words. But her solicitous tone told the tale. He glared at her.

"Only a greenhorn steps into his boots without shaking 'em out. Never can tell what crawlin' critters have found a home overnight. Pa says it has something to do with smelly feet."

"Or spiteful companions," Will mumbled, hobbling over

to pick up his boot. He shook it out. The dried skin of a sidewinder fell to the ground.

"Well, what d' you know. Even vacated snake skins crawl around here."

Priscilla didn't meet his eye when she handed him a cup of coffee. He took it with skepticism. Priscilla McCain contrite? He might be a greenhorn, but he hadn't been born yesterday.

"Thanks." He held the cup in his palm, letting the hot tin warm him. His heart rate began to slow. He sipped the coffee.

His eyes flew to Priscilla. She stood her ground, perusing him in an innocent fashion. "Too strong?"

Damnation. Never mind the Haskels behind him and the Apaches ahead, Will entertained the unsettling notion that he might not survive the wrath of this woman. "No, no. An eye-opener. Just what the ol' body needs after a hard sleep." Deliberately he took another swallow and almost choked on the fine granules. He'd never tasted coffee so muddy.

"I'm not much of a hand at cooking," she explained. "Uncle Sog taught me. It's camp coffee. If you're not up to it—"

Will stomped into his other boot, then hobbled to the fire, where he lowered himself by increments to a nearby boulder. He'd never been so sore in his life, and there was no way on earth he'd be able to disguise that fact from an ol' cowhand like Jake McCain.

He watched her pour herself a cup of coffee. She eyed him over the brim, as though waiting to see if he was man enough to drink the same thing she did. Will drained the cup and wiped his mouth with the back of his hand.

Joaquín came up then. When he picked up the coffeepot, Priscilla reached for it, but too late. Joaquín had already filled his cup.

Will didn't notice the grimace on Priscilla's face until

Joaquín took a swig of coffee. Of a sudden he opened his mouth and spewed the hot liquid over the clearing. The fire sputtered. Will wiped drops off his face.

"Sonofabitch, Jake," Joaquín cursed, "what'd you put in this coffee?"

Will eyed Priscilla. She smiled that sweet, innocent smile that was beginning to leave him cold inside. "I couldn't slip and display culinary skills, Joaquín. It might remind Will I'm a woman."

Will held her angry gaze, noting the hurt beneath it, feeling about as low as that sidewinder that'd mysteriously turned up in the toe of his boot.

"Well, you damned sure didn't have to make my coffee with mud, too." Joaquín tossed the cup to the ground and started kicking dirt on the fire. "I don't know what's eatin' you, Jake, but if you don't settle down, I'm ridin' off an' leavin' you two to fight it out between you."

By nightfall two days later, they had covered what Joaquín estimated to be most of the distance to Victorio's ranchería, almost every mile of the way in silence. When they stopped for the night, Will untied his bedroll. He was dead tired; he ached all over, inside and out. What hard riding hadn't done to his body, seeing the hurt he'd caused Priscilla had done to his soul. "I'll take care of my own things," was all he said.

They sat around the campfire in silent contention. Will chewed the stale tortillas and drank coffee. Thankfully it was fresh and tasted more of river water than of mud.

"We'll reach the ranchería by midmorning tomorrow," Joaquín offered.

"Do we just ride in?" Will asked.

"Not unless you want to get shot. They've had us in their sights all day. Sometime tomorrow they'll meet us, see what we want, and if they approve they'll take us in."

"Why shouldn't they approve?" Will asked.

"If we're followed, we would lead the Haskels to them," Joaquín explained.

"I doubt if the Haskels will waste their time with us, not since they practically admitted setting you up. My guess is they're already at Spanish Creek." He looked to Priscilla. "With luck Bart has arrived to help Charlie defend the place."

"I'm sure he has. Jessie was certain he'd receive the message."

You can't be sure of anything, Will thought, except that by the time this is all over, I'm going to have hurt you worse than either of us would have ever thought possible. The idea of it left him as edgy as a riled grizzly bear.

Joaquín, as usual, didn't pass up an opportunity to slam Charlie. "When did Charlie McCain start needin' help? He's outlaw enough for ten Bart Ellisors."

Will cautioned himself to let it pass. Joaquín's hatred for Charlie wasn't, after all, what had him rankled. But suddenly he was fresh out of control. He tossed the dregs of his coffee into the fire. "I'm sick and tired of your belly-aching about Charlie, Joaquín. You're a grown man. When're you going to start taking responsibility for yourself? Even if Charlie is your father, so what? As I recall, you rejected his help." Rising to his feet, Will added. "Be glad he's still alive. Mine isn't." He left the fire, tossing over his shoulder, "I'm takin' first watch."

Priscilla watched him go. Her heart ached with the turmoil that man had put her through. Yet she felt strangely sorry for him. His own father dead? She wondered when he had died, and how. How old had Will been at the time? She couldn't imagine growing up without a father, without Charlie McCain as her father. Her heart beat painfully at the thought. And with sympathy for Will. And with a measure of guilt. She'd given him a real hard time.

Not that he hadn't deserved it. Some of it. Rejecting her like he'd done. But it wasn't really her, he'd rejected. Just their romantic relationship. He didn't seem to dislike her, not really. He just saw her for what she was, for what she'd set out to become, a cowboy. Even if she wasn't his type of woman, that shouldn't keep them from being friends. Unless she'd already ruined that with her foolish pranks.

Joaquín refilled the coffeepot with water and she added grounds. While it boiled she cleaned the skillet, plates, and utensils and set them aside for the morning meal. When the coffee was ready, she poured two cups and carried them out to the ledge where Will kept watch.

He turned at her approach.

"Brought you some coffee."

He didn't respond or make a move, so she sat beside him, and handed him a cup. He took it. She watched him stare into the contents.

"It's coffee," she said quietly. "Nothing else."

He took a small sip, as if to assure himself. But still he didn't respond. He stared out into the blackness, toward the north from where the Haskels would come. If they came.

"I'm sorry, Will. I've been hard on you, and . . . I mean, I didn't know. Do you want to talk about it?"

"Talk about what?"

"Your father. What happened?"

Her question startled him. Hot coffee sloshed out of the cup, over his hand. He ignored it. Turning his attention to the blackness, he stared at it, seeing her face, her blue eyes as they surely looked, feeling her beside him, warm and sensual.

Hearing her, her genuine concern. With surprise he realized that he knew her well by now. Well enough to distinguish between her true nature and the false front she erected to hide her hurt. He knew her well, and she was good at listening when a man needed to talk. He'd found that out more than once.

"I've acted really dumb," she was saying. "I was . . . I don't know why I've been so horrible to you. But you can talk to me. We can be friends." She paused, then added in her sweet, soft voice, "Man to man."

The idea was ludicrous. It startled him even more than her earlier offer. Friends? Maybe. Man to man? He turned to her, could just make out her features in the pale light. Moonlight played around her hair, giving her the effect of a halo. He grinned. No halo for impish Miss Jake McCain. But what he wouldn't give to lay her down on a soft feather mattress and spread that golden hair over a plump pillow . . . or even here, on a fragrant patch of grass—

Brusquely he turned away. He squeezed the tin cup so tightly he felt it bend beneath the pressure.

"We can—"

"No, Miss Priss, there's no way on God's green earth we can be friends, man to man." And at that moment, their fathers had nothing to do with it.

Jessie shrank into the corner of her room. Her tongue licked at the salty blood dripping from the corner of her mouth, while she considered her chance of slipping through the French doors to the balcony and shinnying down the support column before Newt could catch her.

With Newt lumbering toward her, the chance was slim. On the other hand—

She moved, still eyeing him. She grabbed the iron knob and Newt grabbed her. His fist clamped around her arm, cutting into her flesh. She struggled; he held on. Like she was no more than a fish on a line, he pulled her toward him. Her slippers slid across the tile floor quite against her volition. She was powerless to stop him.

"What you take me for, Jess? Dumb? You think I'm no more'n a dumb-ass simpleton. Always knew you were sweet on Charlie McCain, jes' never figgered you for a fool stunt like that."

"You're hurting my arm, Newt."

"It's more'n your arm'll hurt when I'm finished." The anger in his eyes clouded with some softer emotion, which he quickly extinguished.

"Don't do this," she begged. "Please—"

"You made me look dumb, Jess. Real dumb. Sittin' there with you on my lap and those schoolbooks spread all over the place, while that Yankee lawyer broke my prisoner out of jail."

By this time he had pulled her to eye level. She choked back a gag at his whiskey-soured breath. This wasn't, after all, the first time she'd been manhandled by a drunk and abusive man.

She'd lived through her husband's rampages, and even through the beating she received when he discovered that she'd alerted Charlie to his murderous ways. Yes, she'd lived through the pain and anguish before.

Tears stung her eyes. That had been long ago. She'd forgotten the terror. She'd been young and idealistic then, and, yes, probably a little bit in love with Charlie. Not that he'd ever known it. She hadn't realized it herself until it was too late. After he returned to Santa Fé a married man, she couldn't reveal such a thing.

She respected Charlie. And she respected Kate. And in the final analysis, she hadn't been able to let the Haskels destroy him, whether or not he had fathered Joaquín.

Jessie had her doubts about that. Charlie was a one-woman man. And Jessie had known enough men to recognize that trait. But Kate had been sick after Priscilla's birth. Sick for a long time. And Nalin lived with them. Having recently delivered a baby boy herself, Nalin nursed Priscilla during the time it took Kate to recover. So anything could have happened in those days at Spanish Creek.

But Jessie, for one, wasn't about to start passing judgment. No, she had her own sins to answer for. She had no place condemning others.

"We got old man Monroe," Newt was saying, "but Oscar

took a bullet from one of his bastard sons." Holding her by her long black hair, he slapped her hard across the face, then back the other way. She slumped and he turned loose, dropping her to the floor like an armload of firewood.

"Hear that, Jess? My brother took a bullet because of your sneakin' ways. An' I ain't even heard you say you're sorry." He kicked her in the side.

"I'm sorry . . ." she whimpered.

"Say it again."

"I'm sorry . . ."

"For what, Jess? What're you sorry for?" He kicked her again.

Curling herself for what meager protection that could afford, she whimpered and hated herself for being so weak.

"For what?" Newt demanded. "Say you're sorry for helpin' Charlie McCain and I might let up."

She remained silent; the room became a darkened blur behind her closed eyelids.

"Say it, Jess. Say you're sorry you helped Charlie. That you got my brother shot up helping Charlie. That you helped a prisoner escape." He kicked her again.

"We could hang you for that, Jess. You aided a prisoner—"

"Joaquín isn't guilty of anything, Newt."

"Maybe, maybe not, but you surely are. Guilty as sin. Leadin' me on, lettin' me believe you cared. I should've suspected, but you know what, Jess? I believed you." His voice took on an incredulous tone. "I believed you, goddamnit." He kicked her.

She scooted away, trying to hide herself beneath the table where his boots wouldn't carry as much thrust. The fringe from her table scarf whispered against her bruised face. "I cared," she whispered.

"About Charlie, damn his soul. Not about me."

"About you."

"You made me look dumb, Jess. Know that? Dumb. Real

dumb. An' that's real funny, you know, 'cause you're the dumb one. Goin' aroun' town like a big businesswoman with your cantina and your haulin' company. An' you got it all by rattin' on your husband. I should've known better'n to get mixed up with a woman who'd ratted on her husband. Got him killed, that's what you done."

"He—"

"Well, you ain't gonna do the same to me. I found you out. An' in time, too. Wanna know what I'm doin' about it?" He kicked at her, the toe of his boot landing with a vicious thud against the small of her back.

"We've got 'em on the run, Jess. Yessiree. On the run. Slim an' the boys are headed out to Charlie's right now, but that ain't all, Jess. Oscar thought it up, after he got hit. That little gal o' Charlie's is in on it. I figured that out real quick. She and that Yankee lawyer are real thick. Well, we're onto 'em."

Priscilla? Jessie stirred. She knew she needed to get up. To fight Newt. To plan. To help Priscilla. But the room was spinning, and she wasn't sure how many more blows she could take from Newt's boot without passing out.

"That'll get Charlie, don't'cha think? Quicker'n lynchin' that half-breed son o' his. Charlie sets store by that little gal, even though no man in the territory can figure out why."

His voice lowered, became conversational, his tone inquisitive. "What man'd want a gal like that for a daughter? Why, she looks more like a man, and if you can't tell the diff'ernce . . . I reckon she'd be a plumb embarrassment to most men. Oh, well, that's Charlie's business." He laughed. "And works to our favor. The trail might be cold, but we'll catch them two. They'll head for Spanish Creek one o' these days, an' when they do, we'll be awaitin'. That little gal won't stay away from home too long. We've got all the time in the world, Jess. Time an' patience, that's all it'll take to catch 'em. An' to break Charlie McCain."

He kicked Jessie again, so hard she tasted blood when she bit her lip to keep from crying out. Blackness swirled around her. She heard him mumble something about one for good measure.

Pain streaked through her, burning trails along her skin and piercing into her body like the blades of a hundred jagged knives, erupting from her mouth in a gush of sour venom.

After that she didn't hear anything for the longest time. Finally the plinking of Lupe's piano drifted up the stairs from the cantina, washed over her like gentle waves, soothing, cooling the burning in her stomach.

She had to get up. She had to warn Charlie. She had to help Priscilla. But she was cold. So cold.

With feeble fingers she caught the fringe on her satin table scarf and, after a series of weak jerks, pulled it down on top of her. China and glass clattered to the floor and shattered all around. Then the world turned black and warm and still.

Ten

Heat shimmered from the rocky canyon walls and glinted off Priscilla's saddlehorn. She followed Joaquín, who followed a nameless Apache through the narrow, winding corridor of red and gray stone. Turning in the saddle, she looked behind her through the dust and undulating heat waves to Will, and behind him to the two Apaches, also nameless, who brought up the rear.

Will had been astonished to learn that the Apaches did not call one another by name. One of the few times he had intentionally spoken to Priscilla since her fruitless attempt to mend their relationship had come after the three Apache braves arrived at their camp that morning.

With their arrival Joaquín became a different man, assuming command in a quiet, yet authoritative manner.

"The vedette have watched us a day and a half," he translated for Priscilla and Will. "We are not followed. My brother, José Colorado, remains in the foothills, keeping watch."

More talk in the Apache language. Again Joaquín translated. "They will take us in, now."

"In where?" Will questioned.

Joaquín's expression was stolid, yet Priscilla heard pride in his voice. "Victorio's ranchería. They await us."

Once they were mounted, Joaquín dictated the order in which they would ride. The brave who'd done the talking, the vedette, or guard, Joaquín explained, would go first.

Followed by himself, Priscilla, then Will, with the other braves bringing up the rear.

"We're prisoners?" Will questioned.

"No. Keep your weapons. But do not touch them."

They mounted while the braves sat their ponies. "What are their names?" Will had asked then.

"Their names will not be spoken," Joaquín replied.

"Not spoken?" Will turned to Priscilla, eyebrows raised in question.

"Apaches never call each other by name. Superstition. They believe it brings bad luck."

He had smiled at that, a wry sort of smile that gave her the impression he was thinking about something else. But a smile of any sort was rare these days, coming from Will Radnor.

An hour later they still rode single file through the innards of the overlapping mountains. Priscilla had never been to Victorio's ranchería, and anticipation muted some of her distress over Will's behavior—or, more precisely, over how to deal with the fact that she was beginning to care deeply for a man who had no interest in her. Not even as a friend, judging by the brusque way he'd halted her overtures the evening before.

He was a strange one, Will Radnor. Strange and bothersome, to use a word her mother favored.

I'm trying real hard to forget you're a woman. She'd learned one thing about Will Radnor—once he set his mind to something, he worked at it day and night. Turning in the saddle, she caught him looking at her, but no sooner had their eyes made contact, than he turned away, staring instead toward the red and gray striated cliffs that rose to either side of them like a festive layer cake, part strawberry, part vanilla. There was nothing festive, however, in Will's somber mood. He hadn't been looking at her, she realized, but through her. Something weighed on his mind.

And it must be heavy, to preoccupy him on a journey

such as this. Even though visiting Victorio's ranchería had been a childhood dream of hers, Priscilla still felt her heart quicken as they traveled deeper and deeper into the mountains, further and further from civilization, as she knew it.

After an hour of winding their way through the mountain, they arrived without warning. Coming down out of a pass, they skirted a boulder the size of a large building, and there it was—Victorio's ranchería, sitting in the lee of a high mountain valley. A swiftly flowing stream ran in front of the village. Half-clothed brown-skinned children played along its bank, squealing and splashing. At sight of the riders, they hushed, as though on command, and rushed to hide behind their mothers' skirts, as children have done the world over. The women rose from their washing and stepped back, creating a wide aisle through which the procession passed. Vedettes, with red headbands waving in the breeze, scrambled down from their rocky posts.

Priscilla took it all in. Several dozen brush and hide wickiups were scattered along the length of the valley, most of them beneath stands of oak and sycamore. Thin tendrils of gray smoke rose from cooking fires in front of each hut. Up in the hills, smoke sifted through pines and cottonwoods.

The silence was eerie—the only sounds, the plodding of their horses' hooves and the thrashing of her heart. She didn't recognize a single person. Not one.

Work and play stopped as the column advanced. Men and women alike stood in their tracks, watching as solemnly as if the flag were passing in review. She wondered what Will thought of it all. She wanted to turn in her saddle and look at him, but she didn't.

A dog raced out and nipped at her horse's legs. A woman kicked it, eliciting a yelp. Tail between its legs, the creature slunk off toward a wickiup.

Priscilla had begun to wonder whether anyone would speak to them, when a woman stepped out of the crowd.

She was very brown and very wrinkled and when she smiled it was to reveal toothless gums. Her hair hung loose in long silver-streaked strands from a center part to her shoulders. She wore a long black cotton skirt topped by a worn deerskin shirt.

Not until she reached them, did Priscilla recognize her—Nalin. It must be, although Priscilla knew Joaquín's mother to be no older than her own, this woman looked haggard and ancient. But when she saw Priscilla, her black eyes glowed with welcome.

Then a man stepped out of the crowd. No taller than Joaquín, he wore the dress of the other men, white man's britches tucked into knee-high, cuffed moccasins. His heavy cotton shirt was belted with a wide leather belt; the familiar strip of red flannel was tied around his forehead, holding back his shoulder-length black hair. When he stopped, the procession halted, too. The man's eyes focused first on Joaquín, then took them all in, each in turn.

Joaquín turned to Priscilla. "It's him."

Victorio. She relayed the information to Will. He nodded. Instinctively she knew she would have known the war chief without being told who he was. Broad of cheek with fine aquiline features, he carried himself like a leader, aloof but in charge.

Following Joaquín's lead, Priscilla and Will dismounted. The reticent Apaches inched forward. Then suddenly everyone began talking at once. Several of the younger men greeted Joaquín; the brave who led them in spoke with Victorio.

Nalin came through the crowd. She took Priscilla's hands in her own, which felt like rough-side-out leather. "It has been a long time, daughter of my friend."

"Too long, mother," Priscilla replied respectfully.

Victorio was issuing orders in Apache. Beside her, Joaquín translated. "You are to go with my mother."

"What about Will?"

"He follows the men."

"What—"

"They won't harm your white eyes, Jake. They know he helped free me."

My white eyes? She hoped Will hadn't heard that. She relayed the rest of the message, adding, "They speak Spanish. They may not want you to know it, but they do. If you need anything tell them in Spanish."

Will listened, as stolid in manner as Victorio, himself. "Thanks," he mumbled.

Before she could say more, the crowd began to disperse. Two braves led Will toward the river. Victorio threw an arm around Joaquín's shoulders and drew him up one side of the hill. Nalin took Priscilla's hand and led her away.

They skirted a clearing, barren except for a huge pile of brush in the center. The sight brought to mind the tales of horror that circulated in Santa Fé about the Apaches' brutal treatment of their captives. Will had heard at least some of those tales. He must be terrified.

She knew she would be, if she hadn't known Nalin all her life. Even so, she was a little nervous and chided herself for it. She'd met several of Victorio's braves on the trail or when they came to the ranch for meat. But she'd always been in the company of Pa or Uncle Crockett or Uncle Sog, or all three. She'd never felt quite so alone as at this moment. Will would surely be more anxious than she.

Nalin led her midway up the rocky hillside to the last wickiup in the encampment. Below them children resumed their play, laughing and squealing, while birds sang from high in the trees. Women returned to their cook fires; men sat cross-legged in front of their wickiups, repairing harnesses, cleaning rifles.

Before entering the wickiup, Nalin dipped water from a hide-lined hollow in the earth and offered it to Priscilla. Drinking, Priscilla noticed several other hide-lined hollows filled with various foodstuffs—piñon nuts, mesquite beans, and similar dried objects, many of which Priscilla couldn't identify. Hide sacks, and others made of canvas and stamped with the insignia of the United States Army had been filled and were propped against the wickiup.

"We prepare to break camp." Nalin glanced back down the hillside. Following her gaze Priscilla noticed filled sacks beside other wickiups. "We must go before the soldiers begin their fall campaign."

Priscilla's breath caught at the suggestion. She knew what Nalin meant—before the soldiers attacked the ranchería. "When will you go?"

"When our chief has no more hope for peace, we will go." Speaking, Nalin lighted a clay vessel containing oil. The flame sent fingers of light flickering around the tidy room, highlighting furs spread in one corner for sleeping. Several sizes of clay vessels sat around the walls, which were unexpectedly covered with a hide liner that had aged to a soft brown. Figures were painted on the liner in earth tones, varying from red to gold to black. The drawings encircled the room, like scenes painted on an ancient vessel.

"My husband's work," Nalin explained. "He was historian of the *cihéne*. He painted scenes of importance to The People."

Priscilla perused the drawings—braves on horseback galloped around the walls, both man and beast painted for war; herds of horses raced from a canyon gorge; a woman . . . Intrigued, Priscilla moved closer to examine the figure of a woman with white skin and a thick blond braid hanging down her back.

"Your mother," Nalin said.

Mama? How could that be? Moving on, Priscilla studied each scene in turn, all depicting the blond-headed woman— alone, standing or working, scraping a hide, digging a—

"The grave of your mother's mother."

My grandmother? Except for the fact they were no longer alive, Priscilla knew nothing about either of her grandmothers. In the next scene, the same blond-haired woman was joined by a man; in another they were embracing.

"Your father."

Pa? She walked on, coming to the depiction of a second white-skinned man.

"Your mother's kin, I believe, although he was a man much feared and was not spoken of by your parents."

In the final painting the blond-haired woman, the woman Nalin claimed to be Mama, wore a sensual doeskin shift embroidered with beads and hung with tiny bells.

A hazy sense of recognition dispelled some of Priscilla's disbelief. She had seen that garment—or one very nearly like it—in her mother's wardrobe. This one was painted the light brown of doeskin. The dress Priscilla had seen was aged to a rich copper hue.

Until now she'd scrutinized the paintings without fully accepting Nalin's claim that they depicted her parents. Mama had no connection with this village. Not that Priscilla knew of.

For years, though, she had known that both her parents were held in high esteem by Victorio and the *cihéne.* Hadn't Pa told her only recently that he'd known Nalin's husband?

"These things really happened?"

"They are the history of The People. My husband was historian."

As though obsessed, Priscilla studied each scene a second time, and a third. At her questions Nalin revealed a strange tale that bore more resemblance to fable than to fact, a tale about a stranded covered wagon and Mama having been lost in a snowstorm and the *cihéne* rescuing both Mama and Pa.

Nalin stroked a hand down the length of Priscilla's heavy blond braid.

"I wear it like Mama does."

"Hair the color of gold comes from the Great Spirit," Nalin claimed. "Your mother's hair brought good fortune to my wickiup." The old woman led Priscilla to the last drawing, which depicted an Apache woman large with child.

"My firstborn," Nalin said. "He will succeed our warrior chief one day."

Not Joaquín, Priscilla knew, but a man she had known also as a child. José Colorado he was called, the child of Nalin's husband, who had died before the babe was born.

"I was unable to bear children," Nalin explained, "until I touched the hair of your mother. Before the next full moon I conceived."

The reverence in Nalin's voice left no doubt that the woman believed her own tales, even if Priscilla found them a bit too strange to digest. But they filled her with questions to take home.

"Your mother was a brave woman." Again Nalin stroked Priscilla's hair. "You are like her, bringing my son to safety at great risk to yourself."

Priscilla thought of Will, of his rejection, of his reasons. "I wish I were like her in other ways."

"The Great Spirit would not have given you this hair, *niña,* if He had not also given you wisdom and courage. Come, it is time to bathe yourself; we must attend council tonight and support this son you saved from the white man's death."

"Joa—?" Priscilla closed her lips over the name. "Why does your son need our support?"

Nalin was busy laying out clothing and readying Priscilla's bath. "In the morning you will go to the river with the other women," Nalin was saying. "Today there is not time. Bathe and dress while I get you some food."

Before Nalin left the wickiup, Priscilla called to her. "The man who was with us, where is he?"

"Your young man is well cared for. He, too, had a hand in saving my son's life. He will be shown our gratitude."

* * *

Across the camp Will wasn't sure whether he was being killed with kindness or parboiled for dinner. Certainly he hadn't expected to find himself undressed, sitting on heated rocks in a sweat lodge full of naked Apache men. Nevertheless, here he was, and the steam that sizzled from the red-hot rocks—and the ceremonial chanting—actually succeeded in relaxing him.

From time to time one of the naked men ladled water over the stones. First one, then another of the men chanted in a language that to Will's uninitiated ears sounded like a mixture of grunts, groans, and heavy breathing. He was furnished with a clay jar filled with something that tasted like weak beer.

No one spoke to him, so he had no idea what was going on. And although Priscilla had said the men spoke Spanish, he wasn't sure he wanted to ask any questions.

Before he was shepherded to the sweat lodge, a squaw had brought him clean clothing—heavy duck britches which he could have bought in Santa Fé, a calico shirt, and a strip of red cloth; he assumed he was expected to tie it around his head. His first real surprise had come upon arriving at this lodge, where his companion—it helped not to think of the man as a guard—instructed him by sign to strip and sit.

So, here he sat, lulled by the steam, the liquor, and the chanting into a welcome state of semiconsciousness. He judged a couple of hours passed, before he was instructed—again by sign—to follow the naked men down to the river, where they plunged their weakened bodies into the frigid water that ran off snow from higher altitudes. He would never have believed a man could survive such barbaric treatment.

He wasn't, after all, an outdoorsman. He'd been raised in the city. But at this moment, Philadelphia seemed as far away as the moon on a cloudy night. He recalled telling Priscilla that Santa Fé seemed like a foreign country. Well Victorio's ranchería was definitely on another planet. Everything was foreign, well, almost. Fortunately he recognized the men's bodies as being similar to his own. Lord help him, if they hadn't been. If he could be thankful for anything, he supposed it would be that in stripping before this group of naked men, he was assured that, different planet or not, he was in the company of similarly built beings. For what that was worth.

And Priscilla was here somewhere. He hadn't seen her since arriving, but he'd had a lot of time to think about her. He wondered while dressing whether the other men had sat on those steaming rocks and fantasized about being with their women.

Their women. That thought was more of a jolt than his plunge into the icy mountain stream. Living proof that he hadn't been successful in his bid to exorcise Priscilla from his brain. All he'd done was hurt her, confuse her. He hadn't even made her angry for very long.

He doubted she could stay angry very long, not with that open, teasing temperament of hers. Oh, she could act snippy all right, snippy as any society woman he'd ever known, but like everything else Priscilla did, she put her own brand on it. And for some reason, which he knew could hold formidable consequences for both of them, he found even her snippiness enchanting.

By the time he dressed and followed the men toward a bonfire that glowed in the center of the village, Will's stomach was growling. He hadn't eaten in so long he decided it wouldn't be too difficult to put out of mind the unsavory tales he'd heard concerning the Apache diet—as long as he didn't look too closely at the dogs or ponies, which were reputed to be among their favorite entrées.

But, arriving in the central clearing, Will was disappointed to find—not supper waiting around the bonfire, but—a council of sorts in progress. A number of older men, elders he supposed, were seated in a circle around a fire, whose flames had died down to smoldering coals. Briefly he wondered whether these people hadn't sweated enough of the devil out of themselves in the sweat lodge. Then he saw Victorio.

The chief sat on a bright red trader's blanket, obviously the place of honor. Led around the outside of the circle, Will took a seat at the designated spot, directly across the fire from the war chief.

Although in the growing darkness he was unable to see faces beyond the second row of men, he could make out figures of women and children grouped in a larger circle around the perimeter.

Then Joaquín entered the circle, and the gathering fell quiet. Will's head cleared suddenly. Fear had a way of doing that, he thought. Accompanied by vedettes, one to each side, Joaquín walked in straight-backed solemnity, stopping two or three feet in front of Victorio. Every man in the circle trained his eyes on the war chief.

At first Will thought they intended to honor Joaquín, but their continued silence alarmed him. A *tribunal?* My God, had he saved his client from the Haskels only to have him tried by a harsher court? One which operated by laws he didn't know and in a language he could neither speak nor understand?

Will recalled Joaquín scoffing at the suggestion that he be tried by a jury of his peers in Santa Fé. Well, it looked like that was exactly what was happening in this remote corner of the world. And here he, Joaquín's appointed lawyer, sat powerless.

They speak Spanish, Priscilla had claimed. Well, they weren't speaking it now. Turning to the man at his side, Will tried, asking in Spanish, *"¿Qué pasa?"*

The man shook his head. Sign language, Will decided, for a refusal to communicate with white eyes.

He glanced around the gathering, searching for he knew not what—other than courage, which he felt mighty short of at the moment. Finally, he realized he had no recourse.

With more trepidation than he could recall ever feeling before—did they draw and quarter a man for approaching the chief at such a time?—Will rose and made his way toward Victorio. Just in time he remembered not to call the chief's name.

"If this is to be a trial," he said in Spanish, "I am his lawyer."

"Lawyer?"

"I speak for him—"

"I know the duties of a lawyer, white eyes. But your court has no jurisdiction here. This man's crime must be judged by our laws."

"Crime? What is his crime?"

"He stole the horses."

Will's eyes widened. "No. Ask him. The horses belong to . . . uh, to no one. They were unbranded."

Victorio's lips looked chiseled from the stone of the mountain. "You did not listen. Your laws and ours are different. You do not recognize our laws. We do not recognize yours. Branded or unbranded, it is of no matter to us."

"A brand means they belong to someone. These horses were unbranded. He couldn't steal them, because they belonged to no one."

"Who told you that?"

Will swallowed and began again. "The horses were unbranded—"

"Listen with your head. Brands have no meaning to us. The horses belong to the *cihéne*—The People—and to our friend at Spanish Creek."

"To Charlie?"

Victorio nodded in stoic confirmation. "He does not own them in the sense that white eyes own property," the chief explained. "That is not the way of The People. We gave him the right to use the horses."

"How—?"

"The man before us is one of you and one of us," Victorio cut in, obviously finished with the discussion. "He stole from The People. He stole from our friend. We cannot allow either. Take your seat and speak no more."

Dejected, Will turned to Joaquín, who glared his displeasure. Will lifted his eyes heavenward, thinking—or trying to. When he lowered his head, it was to look directly at Priscilla, although he didn't recognize her at first.

She had come to stand beyond Victorio, at the edge of the clearing. Without breaking eye contact, she moved toward Will, slowly, gracefully, as if she were gliding through the late-afternoon haze and the dreamlike trance this place had cast over him.

He tried to keep his attention on Joaquín, but his brain was filled with Priscilla. His first conscious thought was that he couldn't call her Jake anymore. Not in that getup. Her golden hair hung loose. Interspersed with streamers of beads and tiny silver bells, it fanned about her shoulders and blew gently in the breeze.

Her shoulders. He took in her costume, then, a beaded doeskin shift that draped sensuously over her curves, made the more sensuous by the slow steady way she walked toward him, as though she were a little unsure of herself, a little self-conscious. The dress was soft, the color of fresh cream, and he could practically smell it, taste it, feel it against his skin. He clenched his fists at the thought of it, the softness—of the shift, of Priscilla.

His mind raced back to the day they met. To the feel of her when he'd caught her around the waist, steadying her when the stagecoach lurched forward, knocking her off balance.

He grinned. She'd never admit it, of course, that she'd been thrown off balance. Priscilla was like that. Cocksure of herself.

Or she had been. His eyes returned to hers. He saw them swimming in shimmering liquid—tears. He felt tears well in his own eyes, hot and burning.

She had been sure of herself. Until he came along and

turned her perfect world upside down. And she didn't even know why. But soon she would.

Too soon.

As if she'd been drawn to his side by their mutual needs she reached him, stopped, standing tall and proud. She held him, tethered, though separated by several inches of charged air. Then she reached out and put a hand on his arm, although it felt more like a band of steel straight from the fire.

"We can't interfere, Will." She spoke in English.

He tore his gaze from hers. Looked at Joaquín. At Victorio.

"Come with me," Priscilla urged.

Glancing down, he stared at her hand on his arm, thinking stupidly that her fingernails were clean. Funny, the way unimportant details like that interfered with the important things. With who she was. Who she really was. A woman who could touch his arm and pull his heart right out of his body.

"Come, Will. I want to show you something."

With her hand holding his, she led him through the circle of silent Apaches. Halfway up the hill, his brain began to clear. He turned, looked back at the gathering. "Joaquín," he said, trying to speak around the driest throat he'd ever had.

"He'll be all right."

"They think he stole Charlie's horses."

"He'll be all right. They'll just punish him a little, that's all."

Later it was funny. Hilarious. That he could turn his back and walk away from a client, leaving him surrounded by wild Indians who were going to *punish him a little*.

Later it was funny. But at the moment, he was lost in the essence and the promise and the overwhelming sense of unreality that had been creeping up on him ever since they arrived at this camp.

Overwhelming, yes. Yet invigorating. This ranchería was another world, another planet. In another world anything was possible.

His damp hand slipped inside hers. She tightened her grip and led him with purposeful strides toward a wickiup at the far edge of the camp.

"This is Nalin's home," she explained.

He glanced down the hill, toward the ceremony that was out of sight now.

"Joaquín will be all right," Priscilla assured him. "They're grateful to us for saving him."

"What will they do?"

She shrugged.

"I'm his lawyer."

"Not here."

"This is a New Mexico Territory, a United States—"

"No. We left New Mexico two days ago. Besides, this is Victorio's territory. Joaquín will be all right. Their laws are fair. Pa says—"

"Charlie." Reality returned in small increments at the name. "Will he follow me everywhere?"

Priscilla laughed. "Pa is a hero to these people."

She'd dropped his hand when they entered the wickiup, and he now rammed one balled fist into the other, struggling for balance, sanity, something.

"Pa—"

"Leave it alone, Priscilla. Everyone in the world doesn't have to like Charlie . . . or even approve of him."

"What a terrible thing to say!" She moved away. He followed, stopping in the center of the wickiup. "I know what's bothering you," she said, "but I had no choice."

She skimmed her hands down her shift. He clenched his own, lest they reach out and grab her.

"It was Nalin's doing," she was saying. "Look around. This is what I wanted to show you. Nalin says these drawings are of my parents." Her hands went to her hair. She sifted fingers through its length, setting the little bells to jingling. Will's nerves joined in, as if in concert. "They believe blond hair is sacred, a gift from the Great Spirit. I couldn't refuse to wear the dress, even though I knew you'd be angry."

She wasn't making sense now. "Angry?"

"That I've dressed like a woman. That I—"

"Hus . . . sh." The word hissed out on ragged breath.

"What?"

He could tell he'd startled her. He held her gaze until he felt like he was drowning in her. The room began to spin. He felt steam rise, and thought of the sweat lodge. Another world. A strange, yet somehow wonderful world. Another world, where anything was possible. Anything.

Except resistance.

"Lordy, Priscilla, I . . ." He inhaled deep drafts of heady, sweet-smelling air, trying to clear his senses. But her eyes held his, curious, waiting. Lordy, he was waiting, too. Had been for so long now. He expelled his breath in one great puff.

". . . I'm dog-tired of fightin' you, Miss Priss." He watched her eyes widen by degrees, those startling blue eyes. He loved how they sparkled when she laughed. But he hadn't given her much to laugh about lately.

He recalled wondering whether they burned blue fire when she made love. And at that moment he knew, if he burned in the eternal fires of hell for it, he could resist her no longer. He lifted his arms. "Come here."

He watched her come, tentatively. The bells in her hair and on her dress tinkled when she moved across the room, softly, like summer wind singing through oak leaves. Although part of him cried to rush to meet her, he resisted. He stood still, arms outstretched, savoring every sensation, storing it away, like a squirrel stores nuts, for nourishment in the long and desolate life ahead.

Then she was in his arms. Suddenly life returned to his

limbs. He crushed her to him, buried his face in her hair. How long he'd waited to see it down, to feel it. He nuzzled his face in her hair, against her neck.

Then they were kissing. Their lips merged, sealed as by fire, forming a channel for their breath, their tongues. As on a river of dreams, life passed back and forth from one to the other, giving and taking, soft and wet, and hot, so very hot.

Then, for no discernible reason, as though life had become too perfect, reality intruded. Charlie McCain, that son of a bitch! He'd taken Will's father, now he was destined to take the one and only love of his life. With hands that were rougher than he intended, Will drew their faces apart. He stared deeply into her eyes, searching, questioning. His heart beat with heavy, anguished throbs. His breath came in short gasps. He watched worry cloud the passion in her eyes.

"You have to understand something." Their lips touched lightly when he spoke. He couldn't move any further away; it was as if to do so would tear the life out of him. "This is all we'll have. This time. When we return to the ranch, this . . . us . . . it'll all be over."

"Oh, no, Will."

He nodded.

"I'll change. I will, I promise. I'll become a lady. I'll wear ribbons and bonnets and gowns and . . ."

He stared aghast, wondering why she was carrying on about clothing at time like this.

". . . even a corset."

His hands left her face. He skimmed her body, though to do so set him on fire. He'd heard about Indian tribes where a man was required to walk on live coals to prove his manhood. Well, he would pass that test with flying colors. Anyone who could stand this close to Priscilla and not melt wouldn't blink an eye at live coals.

A corset? He kissed her again, wet and deep. He was

drowning and he never wanted to come up for air. But he did. He stroked her breasts, feeling her nipples thrust against his palms. A corset?

"Don't you dare," he mumbled into her mouth. Once more he claimed her lips and felt himself consumed by desire.

She pulled back, her eyes questioning. "But you want me to be—"

"I want you just the way you are, cowboy."

"But—"

"Wanting you and having you are two different things. You have to understand. This . . ." He pulled her closer, molded her curves to his pleading body. "This is all we have."

"No, Will. I can persuade my parents—"

"Damnation, Priscilla. For once, just shut up and listen. This is ALL. Either we proceed on those terms, or we don't—"

She stopped him with her lips. A forceful kiss that defied him to deny their passion one moment longer. He'd been right about the dress, it was soft, soft and sensuous, and from the feel of her when he swept his hands from her shoulders to her buttocks, it was all she wore.

The very thought called forth a demand for speed from his long-denied body, which he quickly rejected with the dismal truth that this would certainly be their one and only time together.

Lifting his lips, he watched her eyes smolder. "How long do you think we have?" His palms slipped up her sides, lifting the shift along with them.

"After they deal with Joaquín, they'll beseech the Great Spirit to protect them against the soldiers. It's a ceremony with dancing and chants. Nalin said it'll take a while."

Will tried to worry about Joaquín; he tried to worry about Victorio and his people; but he could only rejoice in their gift to him: time. His hands moved past her shoulders, releasing her dress, cupping her face. Caressing her with his gaze, he laved her face with kisses, until he felt her shudder against him.

"On the other hand, greenhorn . . ." Speaking, she took his hand and led him across the wickiup. ". . . we don't have all night."

That was all it took. But he couldn't stop kissing her. Slanting his lips across hers, he let his tongue dip and delve. His emotions ran amuck. While his mind played with the dangers inherent in what they were about, his hands busied themselves with more important matters, like working the soft doeskin up her thighs, scrunching it around her hips.

His first touch of her bare, heated skin sent a tremor racing the length of his frame. He clutched her buttocks in his palms, pulled her to him, molded her against him, savoring, demanding, anxious.

"Oh, Will!" She wriggled against him, angling backward for better fit, while her hands gripped his shoulders, and her fingers dug into his flesh. "I keep wanting . . . something . . ."

"I know, love." Talking, he stripped the garment further upward, baring her breasts. His palms covered them. They were hot and full and heavy with need. "I want it, too." His thumbs strummed her nipples. He gazed into her eyes, watching the blue flame take hold. "You . . . all of you . . . that's what I want."

He was lost in her now, floating on the musky sweet air, swimming in the liquid blue heat of her eyes, drowning in the heady, insistent want of her. Aided by the drums and chanting that filtered to them from the clearing below, his heart pounded to the erratic cadence of hers. His brain demanded haste; his heart insisted on restraint. For once his heart was right. But right, as usual, was not easy.

Standing breathless beneath his fondling hands, Priscilla felt emboldened, powerful. She clasped her hands behind Will's neck, drawing his face to hers. When he was close enough, she traced the outline of his lips with her tongue, then ran it across the crease. His lips opened, she boldly dipped inside. When he caught her tongue and began to suckle, her legs grew weak.

He worked to ease the doeskin shift over her shoulders; she helped, wriggling her head through the opening. He tossed it aside without taking his eyes from her body. Grasping her solidly by the shoulders, his gaze traveled up her body and down, lingering here and there.

Priscilla knew she must glow brighter than the meager flame in Nalin's oil lamp, yet she reveled in Will's perusal. For he wore an expression of wonder, like he'd never seen a woman's body before.

Before she could ask him, his hands skimmed over her chest. He lifted her breasts, held them cupped in his palms. They felt so heavy, she thought surely they must have doubled in size. When she looked, he dipped his head and ran his tongue over one nipple, spearing desire in the form of hot liquid straight through her.

"Oh, Will . . ." She clutched his head, threaded her fingers through his thick hair. He took her nipple in his mouth and began to suckle. She felt like he'd ignited a flame inside her.

Then he lifted his face, and she felt bereft. "Don't stop."

His lips possessed hers; his hands skimmed downward, spanned her waist, fanned over her belly, inched lower, oh, so much lower. He cupped her; the heel of his hand ground into the curly patch of hair. His fingers slipped into her wetness and she felt the world spin around her. When he withdrew his hand, she protested again.

". . . not enough time . . ." he was saying. Clasping her buttocks in both hands, he lifted her until her legs locked around his hips. Unsteadily, he bent his knees and lowered her to the floor, depositing her in the middle of a giant black bear pelt. But when she tried to draw him down with her, he pulled back, disentangling himself.

"Wait . . ." His voice was husky; she could tell his mouth was dry. In the dim light she watched the vein in his neck throb. He worked studiously, accompanied by the distant drums and the little bells in her hair, as he fanned it in drifts about her head. He stretched her arms out to either side, then sat back on his heels and looked at her with such reverence she felt like a deity.

But a deity with no control over her body or her life. "Will . . . please . . ."

His eyes returned to hers. She held out her arms. "Come here," she whispered. Before complying he stripped his shirt over his head, then began unbuttoning his britches, holding her in his gaze, all the while.

She watched, mesmerized, as he unclothed himself, revealing more of a man than she'd ever imagined seeing, and every bit of it was wonderful. By the time he struggled out of his britches and moved toward her, she knew this was the only man she would ever look upon. In her entire life, the only man for her.

Her fingers touched his rippling muscles, traced them down their rigid length, through the brown pelt of hair on his chest, past his darker nipples, down to his slender waist. In spite of all her attempts not to, she couldn't keep herself from looking further. His arousal was big, hard. She'd never imagined . . .

Glancing back at his face, she found a grin on his lips. "Ready to call it off?"

She knew he was teasing, by the sound of his voice, but mostly by the way he moved over her with obvious determination.

She wanted to tease him back, but she couldn't, her mouth wouldn't form the words, so she shook her head. Moving her hands around his waist, she tugged until he dipped toward her, nudging her belly with his arousal.

Again she wanted to tease him, but again she was unable to, stopped this time by the grim look in his eyes.

"It's going to hurt, cowboy."

She tugged him closer. "No . . ."

"Yes, just a little."

But she thought of the days just past, of his rejection, of the horrible thing he'd said to her. "The worst is over."

If he heard her words, he ignored their meaning, for while she spoke, he slipped a hand between them, slid it over her abdomen, into her wetness. This time he didn't stop with tender strokes, but delved inside, deep inside, deeper. Her breath came short, her pulse began to race. Fiery heat spread like a range fire over her skin. His eyes delved into hers, while his fingers plunged, again and again and again. Until, at length, her hips began to rise to the thrusts, involuntarily.

She wasn't at first aware of her movements, but when she realized what she was doing, she knew it was right, good, wonderful . . . yet, she knew there was more. It was like the time just before sunrise, when the sun inched upward toward the horizon; any minute it would shower her with the brilliant light of another miraculous day.

"Hurry . . ." she sighed. "Please, hurry."

Suddenly it wasn't his fingers that probed, but his body. She felt his arousal, hard and large and hot against her.

Her eyes flew to Will's.

"It'll hurt," he said again. "Just for a moment."

She nodded, breathless now. What if he was right? He felt so big, so hard, what if . . .

He scooped her in his arms, rested his forearms on the pelt beneath them, lowered his lips, took hers, and thrust. Tentatively at first, then hard, fast . . . deep.

She flinched. He held her tighter. Finally, she realized she was holding her breath. She released it, feeling him inside her. Deep inside her. Joining with her. Like they were one. He was hers. And she was his.

She drew their faces a few inches apart. She held his

gaze. He loved her. *Will Radnor loved her.* She could see it in his eyes.

"You all right?" he asked.

"Oh, yes, Will, yes. It's wonderful. Wonderful. I never imagined it would be . . ."

Again, while she spoke, he began to move, slowly at first, then faster and faster. It surprised her. She'd thought it was all over. Not that she'd wanted it to be over. She hadn't, she'd wanted more, but . . .

Then she was moving with him, meeting his plunges by lifting her hips, over and over and over. She squinched her eyes closed. Suddenly the sun peeked over the horizon; it moved steadily now, faster and higher . . .

Until it exploded in a brilliant array of color in her head.

When he felt her climax, Will allowed his own release. It came hot and fast. So fast. Too fast. In a matter of seconds it was over. He collapsed on top of her, rolled to his side, cradled her in his arms.

And her words came back to him. *The worst is over.* No, he thought, *the best is over. The worst is yet to come.*

Eleven

"I like the way you finally answered my question."

Will propped himself on an elbow. Drawing closer he snuggled against Priscilla's side, felt her skin, as soft and silky as the bear pelt on which they lay. "What question's that?"

Idly he traced an index finger over her face, feature by feature. The meager light from the oil lamp cast them in shadow.

Priscilla wriggled against him. "That you don't need a bed."

"All I need is you, cowboy." And he meant it. Lordy, how he meant it. But reality pounded at the door he had closed against it in his brain. He felt her breath catch and knew she'd heard the longing in his voice. His finger trailed down her neck, across her chest.

"You're sure?" she whispered.

"Positive."

"I mean sure about me . . . about the way I . . ."

"If you did anything better, I'd think you were an angel sent to transport me to heaven." His hand closed over one tender breast, stroking it gently, as though it were the finest jewel. His body sprang to life. "And I'm far from ready to leave this earth."

"But Will, if it isn't the way I dress and act, what is it?"

His face hovered above her. Their lips brushed when she spoke. Their breath mingled, sweet and hot. A sudden, incredible feeling took hold of him, the feeling that everything would work out, after all.

How could it not? She was an angel, a princess, everything he'd ever desired, and more. She was things he'd never dreamed of a woman being. One of his mother's favorite quotes popped to mind, "The Lord works in mysterious ways, His wonders to perform."

But their way wasn't mysterious; it was treacherous. Horrendous. Disastrous. Even if they remained forever inside this strange and foreign world of the Apache, even if they never left this wickiup, things couldn't work out for them, because in his heart he knew the truth.

And this was one truth that would not set him free. This was one truth that would destroy the precious bit of heaven he held in his arms.

"Let's not ruin tonight, Miss Priss." He drew her close and loved her with a passion made hotter by the fact that the embers were about to be extinguished for all time.

José Colorado returned to the ranchería the following day, bringing the word Priscilla had anxiously awaited, until Will made his devastating announcement that their relationship *had* to end once they returned to Spanish Creek.

She didn't believe that, couldn't believe it. But Will did. She had no idea what lay behind his assertion, since he refused to give one substantial reason for such a horrendous turn of events. Every reason she thought of, he denied.

"You're married!" she had whispered, when he rose from their pallet the night before, dressed, and prepared to leave the wickiup. The idea had come to her suddenly and it was devastating.

The council was breaking up. Sounds of chanting and dancing ebbed. Even then, Priscilla hadn't wanted Will to leave, but he insisted.

"This was too special, cowboy. These people may operate

by different laws, but I won't tarnish your name by allowing them to catch us together."

She knew it was best. "No telling what Nalin would think. Pa says Victorio's Mimbreños practice monogamy."

"Strange, isn't it?" Will questioned. "Considering the gossip about Nalin and Charlie."

"Pa might have told me that to keep me from believing the gossip."

"But you do believe it, don't you?"

"I don't actually believe it; I just . . . I'm afraid to disbelieve it."

"Yet you've loved your father though it all. Even if he was unfaithful to your mother . . ."

"Oh, Will, I know it's hard to understand. Perhaps if Mama had reacted differently—you know, hurt, angry, but . . ."

"But what?"

"I don't know. I could never truly believe—"

"That Charlie could do anything wrong," he finished. "You hold Charlie up like a god of some sort."

Will was right; she couldn't deny that. But couched as an accusation, his claim put her on the defensive. "Pa's human," she acknowledged. "He does wrong things. We've had our share of arguments."

"I don't mean arguments. I mean sins, crimes."

"Pa?"

"See? You'd never believe ill of Charlie. You'll always take his side, even when the opposition proves right."

"I'll stand up for Pa, if that's what you mean. Of course, I will. To the ends of the earth. What difference does that make?"

Will's eyes probed to the very heart of her. An expression of melancholy, almost primitive in its intensity, turned his features to stone. She didn't know this man . . . this stranger. Even after the intimacies they'd shared, she didn't know him. And that angered her.

"You'll never understand. I thought you were like him, but you aren't. He's forthright, honest. But you, one minute you're loving, the next you're cold and distant. And you expect me to take it all in stride, to understand something you won't even try to explain. Well, I guess I've figured it out. What does your wife think about all this? Where is she? Did you leave her behind? Run off and . . . and abandon her, like you intend to abandon me?"

Will had grabbed her arms, then. He jerked her to him with fierce, angry movements. "I'm not married. I've never been married. After this, I—" He kissed Priscilla, hard, rough, demanding. Desperate.

When he looked at her again, she watched moisture glaze his eyes and pool in the corners by his nose. "Since I can't have you, Miss Priss, I'll never marry anyone."

His words stunned her. She hadn't realized he'd released her, until suddenly he was leaving the wickiup.

Since he can't have me? "Who said you can't have me?" she called after him. "You haven't even bothered to ask. Don't I have any say . . ."

He kept walking. She watched him disappear into a womb of darkness. "Ask me," she cried, a whisper now, though the demand screamed angrily in her head. In her heart.

Priscilla dressed, but by the time Nalin returned to the wickiup, she was still so shaken, she didn't think to ask about Joaquín, until she realized that Nalin was solemnly performing some ritual. Priscilla's heart leapt to her throat.

"What happened?"

Nalin had begun to untie the wickiup liner. Her eyes were on some distant scene.

"What punishment did your son receive?"

Nalin's expression lightened. "He is to accompany The People."

"It's settled?"

"Sí. As soon as the son of my husband returns, we will set out."

"For Tres Castillos," Priscilla whispered, as though to speak the destination aloud might further curse this band of displaced people.

"For Tres Castillos," Nalin agreed. "The *cihéne* have too few young men left to fight the white eyes. Both my sons are needed to go with us into the danger."

"But I thought you were fleeing to Mexico for safety."

"From the Americans, *sí.* But who can say what wickedness the *Nakaiyi* have in store for us."

The Mexicans, Priscilla thought, recalling the tales Pa had told about bounties. Several Mexican states paid bounties for Apache scalps: one to two hundred pesos for a brave, half that for a woman, and half again for a child. The stories were horrendous. Apache prisoners brought even higher prices, for they could be used as slaves. Yes, Mexico would be a place of last resort, a much-feared place for an Apache.

A hushed mood fell as a pall over the two women. During the next few hours Nalin dismantled the wickiup from the inside, packing hides and skins and cooking vessels. Priscilla helped as best she could.

"How far to Tres Castillos?" she asked once.

"Five suns, I am told. It is a place I have never been and would not go now except for our chief's foresight." She left the skins on the ground for sleeping. The last thing before retiring, she enlisted Priscilla's help in rolling the hide liner that carried not only the history of The People, but of Priscilla's people, too. When it was done, she presented it to Priscilla with solemn ceremony. "This is for you, daughter of my friend."

"Oh, no—"

"It is your history, *niña.*"

Priscilla stared at the heavy roll of hide. Then she studied the somber woman whose life was so linked with her own.

She wondered what the paintings on the hide really meant. She still had trouble understanding what had prompted them. Whether fact or fable, however, they had been recorded by the Apache historian.

"We will keep it safe for you," she told Nalin. "And for your children."

Impatience to return to Spanish Creek built inside Priscilla, as her mind filled with a multitude of questions to ask her mother. But returning home had a gloomy side, too. She sobered, recalling Will's insistence that their relationship, such as it was, would end when they arrived back at the ranch.

Suddenly she felt like she'd been awakened from a dream, to find herself in the real world, where everyone seemed bent on keeping secrets from her. The bits and snatches she had learned about her parents these last few weeks were like a few pieces of a large puzzle. A puzzle she hadn't even known existed until Joaquín's arrest—and Will's arrival. Will, too, kept secrets—the most damaging of all, because whatever drove him threatened to separate them forever.

One thing Will hadn't kept secret—his feelings for her. Those he couldn't have hidden under a ten-gallon Stetson. She had seen love in his eyes, felt it in his touch. But was love enough?

That night, lying on the same soft bearskin where she and Will had lain together, Priscilla tried in vain to luxuriate in the wonder of their lovemaking, but her joy was dulled by an overwhelming sense of loss.

Loss for something she'd never really possessed. She wondered what it would be like to really lose someone. To be married and have that person die. To be a mother and have your child leave.

She thought about Will, whose father had died. Had the loss of his father hurt so badly, he couldn't allow himself to love again, not even a woman? She had no answers, only questions. Something was holding him back, and for the first time since she met him, she understood that it had nothing to do with her.

Yet her sense of relief was hollow, for in the end, if he wouldn't discuss the situation, she had no way of fighting it.

During the long night, when concern for Victorio's poor displaced people, or worry over losing Spanish Creek to the Haskels should have occupied her mind, Priscilla could think only of Will. She tried to convince herself she was better off without him, but that was the most difficult of all. Impossible. At least for the time being.

Sometime during the sleepless nighttime hours, hope emerged the victor. If Will's anguish sprang from some hurt in the past, she might, given time, be able to help free him to love again.

And that's exactly what she had been given—time. Since Victorio had ordered Joaquín to travel to Mexico with The People, she and Will would have several days alone on the trip back to Spanish Creek.

And what wonders couldn't a woman perform with several uninterrupted days in the mountains? Will couldn't run off and leave her. For one thing, he wouldn't know where to go. He was, after all, basically a greenhorn. And for another, he was too much a gentleman to leave her alone to fend for herself.

Priscilla awoke to a din of activity the following morning. Nalin had already arisen and was outside dismantling the wickiup. Pulling on her britches and shirt, Priscilla stomped into her boots and peeked out the doorway. All down the hillside, the camp bustled with women at work breaking camp.

"Lucky I woke up," she teased Nalin. "You might have taken the roof down over my head."

"We take only the hide and skins," Nalin explained. "When we leave camp, we burn the frames."

"Burn the frames?" Priscilla stared around in amazement.

"We can leave no lodging for evil spirits." Nalin spoke as if her statement held all the logic in the world, and indeed, it did, for the *cihéne*.

Shouts erupted from the clearing below. A vedette scrambled from his post; a rider splashed across the river. Nalin perked up.

"My son. My first born has returned."

José Colorado. "Surely the Haskels didn't follow us here," Priscilla worried.

Nalin was quick to read the mood of those below. "All is well. If he carried a warning, there would be silence and much action, instead of greetings."

Then Priscilla spied Will working his way up the hill through the gathering crowd. Her pulse raced at the sight of him. Memories of their night in each other's arms brought warmth to her cheeks and a swelling of passion in the lower regions of her body. Her heart filled to bursting with joy, and she knew suddenly that no matter how many years they had together, she would be as smitten on the last day as she was at this moment.

A battle unrelated to the Haskels loomed ahead of her, that was for certain, but it was a battle worth fighting. Already she had made plans.

Will kept his eyes on her until he came close enough for her to read his expression, then he turned his attention to Nalin, addressing her in Spanish. "Your son says the way is clear for us to leave."

"When?" Priscilla asked.

"As soon as you're ready." Still Will didn't look at her, a fact that dismayed her. They were still several days away from Spanish Creek. He'd said nothing about ignoring her before they arrived. She opened her mouth to tell him so, but he interrupted, speaking in English.

"Joaquín is drawing me a map."

"A map? I know how to get to Spanish Creek."

Will looked at her then, rather, he looked toward her. He didn't make eye contact. She fought down her concern by reminding herself that this kind of behavior was nothing new from Will Radnor.

"We can't go straight in," he was saying. "José Colorado counted a dozen men camped in the hills west and south of the ranchhouse."

Priscilla blanched.

Will's expression softened, but still he didn't meet her eye. "It's all right. He didn't see activity. Said they appeared to be standing guard."

"They're waiting for us."

"Looks like it."

"I wonder if Bart made it."

Will shrugged. Nalin spoke to Priscilla in Spanish. "Tell your man to bring the horse. I will lash the history behind your saddle."

Her man. Priscilla's cheeks burned. She trained her eyes on the rolled piece of hide, hoping Will hadn't understood. But of course he had. He spoke Spanish like a native.

"What're we hauling back?"

She nudged the hide with her boot. "This."

His eyes darted to the wickiup, then back. "It'll slow us down."

That was all it took to snap the short leash her anger was hitched to. "How could you suggest leaving such a . . . such a . . ." At last, his eyes held hers. Her insides fluttered, like she'd eaten butterflies for breakfast or some fool thing. "It's important."

He brought the horses without further argument, but Nalin insisted on lashing the hide to Priscilla's horse, by herself. While they watched the old woman work, with fingers made awkward by years of toil, a change came over Will.

"This might not be such a bad place to live, after all,"

he quipped in English. "I wouldn't mind having my responsibilities limited to hunting and making war."

Priscilla figured he was trying to make amends, but she had no intention of letting him off so easily. "Then it's fortunate you've decided not to marry, greenhorn. I don't know many women who would readily take on the life of a workhorse. Unless you're interested in taking an Apache wife."

Speaking, she watched his jaws tighten. A muscle in his neck twitched. Good. The more she prodded him with his true feelings for her, the better.

For no matter how hard he tried, Will Radnor could never convince her that he didn't feel something deep and passionate and wonderful—for her. Not after last night. Strange, how that one night of lovemaking had already begun to change her. She felt stronger, somehow, more mature, wiser. Pray God she was, for it would take all that and more to break through the barrier Will was so good at erecting between them.

Once the hide was lashed to Nalin's liking, the old woman hurried inside and returned with a pack which she handed Priscilla. "Food for your journey. Stop at the river and fill your canteens."

Priscilla hugged her. "Thank you, Mother. Be careful on your journey to Mexico."

Nalin stroked Priscilla's blond hair. "Once your mother's hair brought good fortune to my wickiup. Your hair will bring good fortune to us now."

Priscilla stepped into her saddle. *"Vaya con Dios."*

Nalin pressed her lips over toothless gums and stared stoically as first Will, then Priscilla, turned their mounts and headed down the hill.

At the bottom, Joaquín came forward. He handed Will a map drawn on ledger paper. Together they went over the details, then Will folded the paper and stuffed it in his shirt pocket.

"Priscilla can help me decipher this," he said. "She knows this country a damned sight better than I do."

Joaquín extended his hand. *"Gracias,* white eyes. If I ever need a lawyer—"

"You'll need a lawyer when you return to New Mexico."

"Maybe I will stay south of the border." But he looked at Priscilla when he said it, and she could see in his eyes where his heart was, even before he spoke the words. "Take care of Spanish Creek, Jake."

"Come home when you can," she whispered. But that was the wrong thing to say, she saw immediately, for the new Joaquín wasn't more than skin deep. At her words, his eyes narrowed, his shoulders bowed, and he glanced sharply away.

"Adios," Will said, and Priscilla nudged her mount behind his.

"Vaya con Dios," she called to Joaquín.

Are you my brother? her heart cried.

Will spread over a boulder the map Joaquín had drawn. Rays from the setting sun splashed across the sky like a spilled vat of molten copper. In the glare he could barely see the map. But that wasn't the reason he'd come out here, away from the camp Priscilla was busily setting.

They'd ridden all day in amicable, yet distant companionship, if there was such a thing, he thought. He'd found it relatively easy to keep their conversation neutral while they were on horseback. But when they stopped for the night, the first sight of her on the ground, within reach, sent him off to the edge of the precipice for safety. If he kept his distance, he'd be all right. And he had to keep his distance.

Two days, three at the most, they'd be back at Spanish Creek. Two to three days hence, he would confront Charlie. Two to three days and he would be out of Priscilla's life.

The hopelessness that had haunted him all day, gnawed at his gut. Truth be known, it'd worried him like a saddle burr ever since he left Priscilla alone in the wickiup the night before. He'd tried to squash it with firm resolve; when that hadn't worked, he'd tried to close off every thought of her, dispel every image that drifted through his brain like steam from that infernal Apache sweat lodge.

Later, he could think about her, he assured himself. Later, he could recall their night together. Later, with the safety of distance. Get back to Philadelphia, then it would be safe to think about her. But until then—

"Will?"

He jumped.

She laughed. "Don't worry, I won't shove you over the edge."

He glanced downward, toward the bottomless canyon floor. In his present state it wouldn't take much. "When did you gain a conscience where greenhorns are concerned?"

She laughed again. But instead of the retort he would have received a few days ago, she squatted on her heels beside him and turned her attention to the map. Obviously she wasn't as affected by his presence as he was by hers, for while he was trying to gain control of his brain, she studied the map.

"What's this?"

Joaquín's ink drawings swam before Will's eyes; his mind was on the woman by his side. He flattened his palms on the warm boulder and held them there, silently defying himself to lose control.

"Billy the Kid's hideout," he responded.

"Billy the Kid? Why would Joaquín think—" Then quickly, as if she'd just thought of the answer, she added, "To show off in front of his white-eyes lawyer, I suppose."

Will grunted. He'd almost laughed at her cynicism. But he knew her well, and to laugh with her was to lose himself.

"Joaquín doesn't trust the Haskels. He thought we might need those outlaws' help if the Haskels come—"

"They won't."

Will stared out over the distant vista. He was beginning to wish they hadn't stopped for the night. It had been his idea. The terrain they traveled was unfamiliar, and they couldn't afford to break a horse's leg or take off down the wrong canyon.

"I haven't been around long enough to say what the Haskels will do," he admitted. "If they're guarding the ranch—"

"If they're guarding the ranch, they haven't taken it," she cut in, rising to her feet. "I knew Pa could hold out. He's used to dealing with unsavory characters. And if Bart's arrived . . ."

While she talked, Will turned his attention to the map, struggling to concentrate on the trail Joaquín had drawn for them to take the next day.

"Supper's ready, Will."

His heart contracted. "Go ahead. I think I'll . . . I'll just sit here awhile."

He heard her leave. At least he thought he did. He heard the jangle of her spurs. But suddenly her hands touched him from behind. She clasped his shoulders; her thumbs anchored like hot tongs at the base of his neck. He shuddered.

"I'm glad we have a few days alone, Will."

He tightened his shoulders, but instead of moving her hands, she began to massage him.

"I told you, Priscilla—"

"I know. I understand. But we can be friends, you'll see. In the next two days I'll show you—"

"I told you, Priscilla—"

"I don't mean friends like . . . well, like I suggested before." Now she was kneading his shoulders. "Man to man.

That was foolish. I didn't understand what you meant until last night."

When he attempted to shrug off her hands, she moved them higher, encasing his neck with strong fingers, massaging his neck, running her fingers behind his ears. *Like she knew what she was doing,* he thought. She didn't, of course. She couldn't. But if she didn't stop . . .

She didn't stop. She kept right on massaging his taut, tired muscles and talking in that damned seductive voice of hers.

"With you living in Santa Fé," she was saying, "and me at Spanish Creek, we have to learn to control our emotions. The way I see it, by the time we get home we'll be the best of friends. Comfortable with each—"

"I'm not staying in Santa Fé."

Her hands stilled on his head. He felt her fingers grip his scalp. He envisioned her face tightening, too. Suddenly she turned him lose and sank to her knees beside him. When she spoke, her lighthearted tone gave no hint of distress.

"That's even better. Where will you go?"

"Back to Philadelphia."

"Philadelphia? Wonderful." Together they stared at the reflected glory of the coppery sunset. "All the way to Philadelphia. Surely we can be friends from that distance. You can write me."

"Pris—"

"And I'll write you. I'll probably marry Red before the year's out. Mama's getting anxious to have grandchildren running around the house. And Pa's anxious, too." She said it with the tone you'd use to relate the market price for cattle. "So you see, there's nothing to keep us from being friends."

Will held his tongue.

"I like you so much, Will. I want us to be friends." She laughed. That soft, seductive laughter, like she didn't have a care in the world. It trilled down his spine and made a fist in his gut. "Never thought I'd be saying all this about a greenhorn." She placed a hand on his sleeve. An innocent gesture in itself, but if he'd needed reminding that he couldn't be friends with Priscilla McCain, that was dead proof. His pulse skyrocketed.

"For a greenhorn, you've come a long way, Will—"

He rose, shrugging off her hands. "Let's go eat. What've you fixed for supper, fried rattlesnake?"

She rose, dusted off her britches with both hands. And she laughed again. This time it settled around his heart and squeezed real hard. "See," she said. "I knew we could be friends."

"Friends don't feed friends coffee made with dirt," he commented halfway through the meal, which, fortunately Nalin had prepared for them: ground corn cakes, roasted acorns and piñon nuts, and some sort of dried meat—he attempted to occupy his mind by trying to identify it. Of course, he wasn't successful. Thinking about dried dog meat couldn't hold a candle to thinking about Priscilla.

She cocked her head and perused him in silence. "Out here the number of tricks you play on a man is a measure of how much you like him."

There she goes again, he thought, man to man. But although she sat on the other side of the campfire, she still fired his blood. He knew she always would, even after she learned to hate him.

Priscilla had spread their bedrolls back off the cliff under the protection of a grove of liveoaks. Will perused them, wondering how he could sleep so close, yet keep his distance. Not over a foot separated the blankets, but he supposed he should be grateful for that much space.

He finished eating and carried water for coffee, while she put away the food and banked the fire. Time to retire. His racing heart told him he was in for a sleepless night, fighting back his need for Priscilla.

"There's no snake skin in it, if that's what you're wondering." She'd already taken off her boots. Now she knelt on her bedroll and began fussing with the covers.

So, he thought, *she's particular about the way her covers are turned down.* To take his mind off the difficulty, he lifted one corner of his own bedroll, wishing he had the gumption to move it to the other side of the clearing . . . or to the other side of the mountain. "Humm, grass. We should have worked out this friendship earlier."

She snuggled down and pulled the blanket up to her shoulders, as though oblivious to his presence. White moonlight sprinkled through the oak leaves and dotted their bedrolls. It glistened from Priscilla's hair like gold coins, and for a moment Will was lost in the desire to cuddle up next to her and bury his face in it. She seemed totally unaffected.

" 'Night, Will. Blow out the light, when you come to bed."

He laughed, captivated by this new, playful Priscilla. "I could try, Miss Priss, but I'm afraid Charlie's the one who hangs the moon for you." He took off his boots and crawled into his bedroll.

She didn't reply, and after a while he figured she'd fallen to sleep. He tried to settle down, but before he succeeded, she spoke, right in his ear, so near he was certain she'd crawled under the covers with him. Before he could stop himself, he rolled his head toward her. She was still in her bedroll, but had risen on an elbow. Her chin rested in an open palm. She was staring down at him with big, hollow eyes.

"I need to talk to you about something, Will."

Her plaintive tone alarmed him. "What is it?"

"Last night."

He blinked in a false effort to hear her better.

"I haven't had a chance to tell you how I felt—"

"No, Pris—"

"It was . . ." Her voice was softly seductive, and he

knew he couldn't discuss their night in the wickiup and remain sane.

"Priscilla, we can't talk about last night."

"But Will, I—"

"Priscilla—"

"Maybe it'd be easier if you called me Jake."

"Lordy! Priscilla . . . Jake . . . it doesn't matter what I call you, we can't talk about it."

"It was my first time, Will. I need to talk about it."

Sighing, he rolled his head away, stared into the star-studded sky, feeling like a lummox. Had he gone from lover to father in one fell swoop? But damnit, he had taken her innocence, knowing things could never work out between them. Didn't he owe her something—consolation, at least? Wasn't she entitled to something from him? If no more than a sympathetic ear?

He rose on an elbow and looked at her across the narrow space. He'd thought her closer, somehow, and when he found her further away, he was gripped by an irrepressible need to pull her close—to hold her and comfort her, he told himself.

Just in time, he resisted. "Shoot, cowboy. I'll listen." *But don't ask me to say I'm sorry,* he thought, surprising himself.

"Well, it was . . . wonderful."

His heart lodged in his throat. Thankfully, for anything he might have been tempted to reply would've gotten him—both of them—in deep trouble.

"But, well . . ."

"But what?"

"Well, I was . . . not exactly frightened . . . but, I mean, I know it would have been more wonderful if it hadn't been the first time. I mean, if I'd known what was going on, I could have . . . I mean, I could have helped you enjoy it more."

Air whooshed from Will's lungs, leaving him breathless

and a little dizzy. "There's no way I could have enjoyed it more."

"Oh, I'm sure there is. I've thought about it all day, and if we could try it again—"

"No."

"If we could try it again, I'd—"

"No!"

"Just once more."

"NO!"

"I just thought—"

"Well, stop thinking."

"I can't. It's all I can think about."

Will groaned.

"All day. That's all. If we could do it again, I'd be able to enjoy it, too."

"I thought you said—"

"I did. I enjoyed it . . . more than anything I've ever done. It was better than learning to ride a horse, or learning to shoot, even better than the first time Pa let me help mark calves."

Somewhere in her tirade, Will flopped to his back and covered his face with an arm to hide the grin he couldn't keep from his lips. "That's pretty stiff competition, cowboy. I'm glad I managed to pull out ahead."

"Oh, you were more than ahead. But I guess it's like learning anything else, once you get the hang of it, you get better and bet—"

"Pris . . . cil . . . la." By the time the warning left his lips, Will had levered himself eye to eye with her again. "I told you, there's no future for us."

"And I told you I'm going to marry Red Avery."

Even though she'd said the same thing earlier, the idea stunned Will. Without realizing it, he sat up on the bedroll. He looked her square in the face. "That simple-minded, overeducated archaeologist? Why, he's the most worthless thing I've ever seen on a ranch. If he's half as worthless on a . . . in other ways—"

"That's why I need you tonight, Will." She had risen to her knees and held the blanket tightly beneath her chin. She seemed closer, somehow. "What if he is? I'll be condemned to a life of—"

"There're other solutions. Did it ever occur to you not to marry him?" His words were spoken hastily. His eyes bore into hers. But she just smiled.

"Well, I have to marry someone, Will."

He glared at her.

"And since you won't have me, you could at least help me . . ." Her words drifted off. "Please."

"No. It's out of the question. No. After we get to the ranch, it's all over—"

"I understand."

"There's no future for us—"

"All I'm asking is for tonight."

Their gazes locked. He couldn't see the blue of her eyes; they looked black as a midnight sky. But her teeth glistened in the moonlight, and he knew the smile. The smile that had captivated him from the very first day he'd met her. The smile that he knew was designed to get her any damn thing she wanted.

Not that she was cunning or deceitful. Not Priscilla. Like she'd said of her father, she was forthright and honest. For in the end wasn't she asking of him the very thing he thought he couldn't live without?

"No strings?" he whispered.

She shook her head.

"No future?"

"No future."

"No tears or heartache?"

She stared at him a long time before replying, and he thought he saw her smile waver. "Why would my heart ache, Will, when you've given me so much joy?"

Why, indeed? For the same reason his would. For a past that had haunted him for twenty-three years, a past that she, by a stroke of very bad luck, happened to share. There would be heartache, no question about it.

But wouldn't there be anyway? They might as well take something good away from this miserable experience. Not good, wonderful.

"If you're sure . . ."

Before the words left his mouth, she had scrambled out of her bedroll and into his. She snuggled against him, nude as the day she was born. His hands touched her soft skin gingerly, as though to really touch her would hurt.

But at that moment he wasn't sure which one of them he was more worried about hurting, Priscilla or himself.

"You're sleeping in all your clothes," she accused. Her hands were already busy working his shirt up his chest.

"Protection," he mumbled.

The shirt cleared his head. He flung it aside, while her hands nestled in his chest hair and her fingers began to work magic with his dwindling reticence.

"Protection?" she was asking. "The Haskels are far behind. And regardless of what you thought the outcome would be, we escaped Victorio's ranchería unscathed."

Her fingers touched the top button on his britches the same time his did. He squeezed them, loving her, knowing he shouldn't, couldn't.

"Unscathed?" No, he thought, they hadn't escaped unscathed, certainly not Priscilla. Together they unbuttoned the fly. "It appears to me we did a lot of damage.

"Damage?" She snuggled against him, while he kicked his britches off his ankles. Her arms went around his trunk, she held him, caressed his back. He felt her breasts burrow into his chest, felt her legs twine around his, her curly patch of hair rubbed against his abdomen just above his own. He felt her throb against him, felt himself probe for relief, for satisfaction, for love. He snuggled his face in her hair and knew he was in heaven.

"Thank you for agreeing, Will," she was saying. Her hands found his hips, rested there, cupping his hipbones in her palms. "There's so much I want to know, to do, and last night I was too shy . . ."

Will nudged her face up, covered her lips with a wet suckling kiss. "You, shy, Miss Priss?"

"Well, it was my first time, and . . . there're so many things I want to know." While she spoke, her hands traveled around in front of him, settled below his ribs, in the hollow above his stomach.

"Like what?" Drawing her back, Will kissed traces down her neck, across her chest. His hands found her breasts. He lifted them, fondled them, stroked their nipples with his thumbs.

She shuddered. "Like this." Her voice wisped out.

"What?" He took a nipple in his mouth; she arched against him.

"This. How does my body know to do things I never even imagined . . . I'd be doing?"

He groaned, delighted by her breathless prattle, aroused by her open, free nature. Sliding a hand down her abdomen, he found her wet. His fingers slipped back and forth. "How 'bout this? You're wet . . . and . . . ready . . ."

"Oh, yes, I am. Isn't that . . ." Her hands moved. She found his arousal, held it. Squeezed it. ". . . the most amazing thing?"

He felt himself expand in her hands. "Amazing . . ." His lips nibbled their way up her chest. From below, his fingers slipped inside her. She wrapped a leg around his hip, opening . . . for him.

"Oh, Will, I never knew anything in the world could be so wonderful."

He shifted her to her back, moved over her, fitting his

length upon her own, gently, barely touching. She wriggled beneath him.

"But you knew, didn't you?"

He kissed her face, letting her prattle, loving it, recording it.

"You've done this so much, it must be—"

"What?" He drew his face back, frowned at her.

"You've done this—"

The idea was ludicrous. "I've never done this."

"But—"

"Not *this*. The motions, some of them. But not this. Nothing . . . has ever been . . . like this." While he spoke, he guided his arousal into her, sank deep, feeling himself throb against the walls of her body.

"We fit. Isn't that amazing?"

"That's the way we were made, love."

"I know, but—" She stopped suddenly. Her voice changed. "Do you mind that I'm so curious?"

He started moving. She lifted her hips to meet him. "Mind? Lordy, Priscilla, there's nothing about you that I mind. Nothing I would change. Nothing." *Except that you're Charlie McCain's daughter.* Which, was, after all, the only thing that really mattered.

He kissed her then; stopping her words, loving her and damning himself for it. She wrapped her legs around him, riding to the crest, thrust for thrust, *like she knew what she was doing,* he thought. And she did. Lordy, did she ever.

The end came soon, too soon. The moment she cried his name, he emptied himself into her. They lay together, clutching each other, spent, empty. But instead of the elation that should have filled the void, distress rushed in.

"Oh, Will, isn't it the most wonderful thing? A miracle?"

"Humm . . . The Man Upstairs planned it that way."

She held him tight, pressed her face into the hollow of his shoulder and mumbled. "He made you just for me, Will Radnor."

Will's arms tightened, holding her as if it were the last time. "No, Priscilla, He made you just for me." And that was the cruelest trick of all.

The following day was idyllic by any standards. Will rode beside her, companionably, pretending for Priscilla's sake, that the road they followed was a straight path to happiness. Although such a thing was impossible, he was able, with effort, to block out the trouble that awaited them at the end of the trail.

In genuine friendship and affection, they merged themselves with the summer landscape, with the spacious sky overhead, with the towering mountains that rose around them, with the song of bird and the scent of pine and the feel of soft, dry air.

"Oh, Will," she said once, "we *are* the very best of friends. I knew we would be."

He grinned at her, trying valiantly to hide the love and desire that welled inside him. "Tell me, how do you figure that, cowboy? If I recall correctly we spent the first part of our relationship at each other's throats."

She laughed, sending music and magic soaring through his senses. "You give as good as you take, Will Radnor." After a while, she added, "We have so much in common. That's a startling fact, you being a greenhorn and all."

He grunted. "Just how long is the sentence for being a greenhorn?"

She glanced at him, opened her mouth to respond, then stopped. It was as if the sky had dimmed. Will recalled experiencing such a feeling once before. But this time her smile returned, radiant as ever. She laughed.

"I guess forever. If you were to come back from Philadelphia, you'd just have to start all over."

He turned away, stared down the trail that wound through

the forested mountains ahead of them. "Then I don't guess it'd pay a man to return."

"Jessie! What happened?" Kate rushed to the hitching rail where Jessie Laredo sat slumped in her saddle.

Charlie hobbled after her, eyes and rifle trained on the foothills in the distance. "Careful, sweetheart. Those hills are crawlin' with Haskels."

Kate reached Jessie. "Let me help you."

Charlie joined them, saying, "Hell, Jess, I'm surprised Oscar let you through."

". . . had to warn you, Charlie." But it was Kate whose eyes she sought. "And to tell you . . . Priscilla's all right."

"Priscilla," Kate sighed. "Thank God." When Jessie wavered, Kate reached for her. "Let's get you in the house, then you can tell us all about it."

By this time Charlie had seen Jessie's battered face. "Crockett!" He waved his walking stick in the direction of the barn. "Come help Kate get Jessie to the house."

Jessie practically fell from the saddle into Titus Crockett's arms. With Kate hurrying ahead and Charlie hobbling behind, Crockett carried her up the steps and into the cool interior of the house.

"Take her to the first bedroom on the right," Kate instructed. "I'll find the medicine kit."

By the time Kate returned, Crockett had stretched Jessie out on the four-poster. Charlie was sitting beside her, while Jessie tried to talk.

Kate immediately started to bathe the woman's battered face. "I'll be as tender as I can, Jessie."

"She says Newt did this."

"Oh, dear, no." Kate stared in horror.

"She helped those dadburnt kids break Joaquín out of jail, an' this's what she got for it."

Kate's hand stilled on Jessie's face.

"I had to, Kate. Newt and his brother were fixin' to lynch Joaquín."

"Will said he'd think of something, damn his hide."

"It was Priscilla's idea, Charlie. You know your daughter. Once she gets a bee in her bonnet—"

Charlie huffed and puffed. Kate muttered, "I know . . . I know . . ."

"For the life of me, I couldn't think of a better way," Jessie said. "Neither could Will—"

"Priscilla's with Will Radnor?" Kate's voice quivered.

In halting words, Jessie explained how she had tricked Newt, how Will set the stage, and how he and Priscilla set out with Joaquín for Victorio's ranchería. "Between them, Will and Priscilla are more than a match for Oscar's bunch."

"What'd'ya mean?" Charlie barked. "Oscar's scum are camped on my doorstep. Long as those kids . . ."

"Not all the Haskel guns are trained on Spanish Creek." Jessie gingerly touched her swollen cheek. "Newt took great pleasure in telling me that they'd sent men after Priscilla. I'm sure that's the reason they let me get through. They wanted you to know."

Charlie's walking stick clattered to the tile floor. His face went white; Kate sat so still Jessie thought she might collapse.

"Will's a good man," Jessie insisted. "He'll take care of her."

"Humph!" Retrieving his walking stick, Charlie rose with more agility than Jessie had seen in him since the shooting. He clomped to the window.

"I don't know what you have against Will Radnor, Charlie. He's a fine young man. Priscilla could do a lot worse. And it's plain to see they're smitten—"

"My daughter is not *smitten* with a Radnor," Charlie barked.

"Nothing can come of it, Jessie," Kate said. "It's a terrible situation. But if he can protect her, get her home safely . . ." Kate closed her eyes as if in prayer. "Right now, that's all I ask."

A fist jammed in his pocket, Charlie glared morosely out the window. Jessie watched him. Then she recalled the telegram.

"Has Bart arrived yet?"

Kate's eyes flew to Jessie. Charlie turned from the window like he'd been blown around by an angry wind. They responded in unison.

"Bart?"

"Bart Ellisor," Jessie said. "It was Priscilla's idea to contact him. She wasn't about to go off and leave Spanish Creek undefended. She remembered you saying that Bart had promised to come to your aid any time you called. I nosed around Newt's office, found a recent poster, and telegraphed a personal advertisement to the *Tucson Gazette.*" She smiled, then winced when pain shot from her jaw in every direction. "It worked. I received a telegram from him two days ago saying he was on his way."

"Bart?"

Charlie hobbled to Kate's side. He pulled her head against his hip and stroked her hair. "Don't think about it, sweetheart. We have plenty else to worry over right now."

Jessie looked from Charlie's stricken face, to Kate's, which was white as newfallen snow. A tremor of foreboding crept up her pain-wracked neck. *What had she done, sending for Bart Ellisor?* Priscilla had thought her parents would welcome Bart's help. To Jessie's mind, they should. But now . . .

"First things first," Charlie was saying. "Until I get Priscilla back—"

"What're you saying?" Kate's voice betrayed her anxiety.

"Hell, sweetheart, I can't let her fend for herself with the Haskels on her trail."

"Will Radnor is—"

"That's another thing has me worried. What if this is Will's way of getting to me?"

"Oh, no."

"Will?" Jessie searched each troubled face.

"Crockett!" Charlie barked. "Get in here an' let's talk about how you're gonna defend these women while I'm gone."

Jessie watched Kate's shoulders slump. She seemed to age before their very eyes. Jessie felt her own strength ebb. "You can't go after them, Charlie. That's what they're countin' on."

"She's my daughter, Jess." He tightened his hold on Kate. *"Our* daughter. I'd face the old devil himself to protect her."

Twelve

By the time they stopped to camp the second evening, an understanding of sorts, unspoken though it was, had developed between Priscilla and Will. Call it friendship, call it whatever she wanted, it had suffused Will the whole day. Like life-giving rays from the sun above, Priscilla's presence warmed him, invigorated him, and he managed with little difficulty to push aside the not-so-distant future and concentrate on the one promising night ahead.

"You're downright congenial when you get your way about things, cowboy," he teased. "What happens when someone crosses you?"

"Like who?" Priscilla filled the coffeepot.

He settled on the single bedroll she had spread on a bed of pine needles while he carried water from the little mountain stream nearby. He removed first one boot, then the other. "Charlie. Your mama. Red Avery."

At his mention of Avery, Priscilla's hands froze in midair. She turned, glared at him, silently taking him to task.

"Oh, I forgot," Will said innocently. "Avery's a spineless—"

She glanced away.

"Is that why you're marrying him? So you can lead him around by a ring in his nose?"

Priscilla made a chore of settling the coffeepot into the banked coals. "I thought I taught you not to ask stupid questions."

He laughed, drawing her attention again.

She cocked her head and smiled, suddenly oozing sweetness. "You left out someone."

"Who?"

"Yourself."

She might as well have kicked him in the gut.

"You asked how I react when someone crosses me. What would happen if you crossed me, greenhorn?"

"As I recall, we've locked horns a few times."

She grinned, smug. "You haven't scratched the surface of my wrath, Radnor." Her expression grew radiant, but her next words eclipsed her sunny smile. "Lucky for you, you're going back to Philadelphia, so you'll never know how downright ornery I can get."

"Lucky for me." But he didn't feel the least bit lucky. This time he was the first to look away.

Then his luck changed.

"Will?" She turned an incandescent smile on him—that same ol' smile that left him short of breath and taut with wanting her. Instead of waiting for a response, she rushed toward him eagerly. When she was within reach, she threw her arms around him with such vigor he toppled backwards.

Lying atop him, she kissed him, open-mouthed and wet. When he began to respond, she lifted her head. She tugged seductively at a lock of hair that had fallen over his forehead; her fingers blazed a trail of passion down his body. He wrapped his arms around her, pressing her closer, holding her tightly, as though to prevent her moving—*or leaving*.

He reveled in the feel of her—every long, lithe inch of her—stretched out on top of him. His body sprang to life, reminding him of the sunrise they had watched together that morning. Like the morning sky, his body began to glow from the inside out with a fiery expectancy.

"Oh, Will, aren't we lucky? We have another night together. One more night. In each other's arms . . . to do . . . all those wonderful things."

She kissed him between phrases, then capped off her assault with, "I love it all. The way your lips feel against mine, the way our skin seems to fuse together, the way your hair feels between my fingers, the way your tongue traces wet trails causing me to shiver, the way you can be hard and demanding and gentle all at the same time, the way—"

"Pri . . . cil . . . la . . ." He drew out the warning.

Her prattling stopped, hung in the air between them. She caught her bottom lip between her teeth, a grin showing nonetheless, as though she were waiting for an announcement of great magnitude.

"Shut up and kiss me, before your confounded babbling drives me screaming over that cliff yonder."

Then of a sudden, while he gazed into the most sincere and loving pair of blue eyes ever to come from the palette of the Lord Above, Will Radnor saw the light. He watched her wet her lips with her tongue, a slow, sensual invitation.

He'd been set up. Every beat of his heart thrust his chest against her breasts. He'd been set up by the most unlikely of predators, a guileless girl who, before she met him, had wanted nothing more out of life than to be a cowboy.

No doubt about it. He'd been set up. But holding her like this, with her lilting voice trebling down his spine and her curves fitting his body to perfection, he was incapable of dredging up the will to object.

By the time they were disrobed and lying in each other's arms again, Will had decided the best ploy was to make the most of the situation. Her words thudded through his brain—*one more night.* Tomorrow they would arrive at Spanish Creek. Tomorrow their fantasy would end. Tomorrow he would drop off the edge of the world into oblivion.

The astronomers of old had been right—the world was flat; it consisted on only one thing—Priscilla. And once she was gone, oblivion.

So he loved her like tomorrow would never come, drawing forth her passion, her sweetness, taking every drop of her, leaving nothing for tomorrow, for someone else.

And she loved him like it was the beginning. She curled around him like a kitten, explored his body with the sultry inquisitiveness of the new, playful Priscilla. Priscilla, the seductress; Priscilla, the woman, who had found the mate of her choice and set out to conquer him against odds even she did not know.

And in the end she was the one who succeeded. For even with the truth pounding on the door of reality, Will could not think about tomorrow. Not with Priscilla in his arms, her lips on his body, his body filling hers. For Will, there were no tomorrows, only tonight, only Priscilla.

He lay awake long after she had fallen asleep in his arms, pondering this unwelcome development. Somewhere between Santa Fé and this isolated mountaintop, Priscilla McCain had become the very thing she had resisted so long and so vigorously—a woman. A woman who had found the mate she wanted. Will knew her well enough to see it now. He should have seen it earlier.

Priscilla had tackled this challenge the same way she tackled everything that mattered to her—giving all, withholding nothing, boldly pursuing her goal. It was in her makeup. It was one of the reasons he loved her so much.

Determining that she could never please her father as a daughter, she decided to become a cowboy, and she had succeeded. Jake McCain was the best damned cowboy in New Mexico Territory.

And now she had set out to catch a mate. Trouble was, she'd already caught him, days ago, weeks ago. He didn't know when it had happened, just that it had happened, likely the first time he saw her in that stagecoach, ready to climb on top and take her chances defending it against outlaws. She could have done it, too. She hadn't needed his help.

He grinned. Hell, she certainly hadn't wanted his help. Will shifted a little, careful not to awaken her. His smile faded, as the certainty gnawed and clawed deep inside him, struggling to free itself. His fears before leaving Santa Fé had been realized—he loved her; Lordy, how he loved her. Lying here with her in his arms, still flushed from their lovemaking, he faced that wonderful, terrible fact: He loved Priscilla McCain, daughter of the man who murdered his father. With a certainty that sprang from some ancient truth, he knew, also, that she was the only woman he would ever love. And as hard as he had tried to submerge that love beneath the hatred he'd lived with and nurtured for twenty-three years, the joy of loving her would not be denied.

He struggled to resist the overwhelming urge to awaken her and tell her so. To tell her the truth. The truth. That he loved her and hated her father. That he had come to New Mexico to destroy her father. To plead with her to understand, to help him work things out so that Charlie McCain wouldn't succeed in taking another loved one from him.

It could be done.

It could be done, if she loved him more than she loved Charlie. But Priscilla would never love anyone as much as she loved Charlie. Likely no one would ever come close. The best a man could hope for was the knowledge that her love for her father was a different kind of love than it was for him. That, and the fact that Priscilla had an enormous wellspring of love from which a man could draw.

Nestled against his side, fitting with a sureness that in itself told the tale, her arms twined around him, she clung like the ancient ivy that grew up the red brick walls in the City of Brotherly Love.

Somewhere out in the darkness a coyote called. Here in the clearing he smelled the sweet clean scents of the mountains, the fir, the piñon from their fire, and the heady aroma of Priscilla and their lovemaking. He inhaled deeply, as if to consume her by scent.

Then from somewhere near the far side of the moon came memories, unbidden, unwanted, a stream of memories, chilling the love-fire that had burned so brightly inside him. Memories of his father, lying on the red carpet with his life's blood pooling darkly beneath him; memories of his father's cold, lifeless eyes; of the pistol clutched in his father's hand; of the empty pistol case in Charles Kane's office.

Memories of his mother's tears, so poignant he could feel them yet, scalding in their intensity, ceasing only with his youthful promise to avenge his father's death.

Memories of Priscilla the day she saw his pistol. That damned Colt revolver.

Will's breathing deepened, became labored. His heart grew heavy with the awful, sickening truth of the matter. It couldn't be done. Her mother had said it first. It couldn't be. In despair, he buried his face in Priscilla's golden hair, and he cried.

Priscilla felt the warm rays of the rising sun touch her face, but she resisted opening her eyes. The evening before came back in gentle waves of slow, poignant joy. She stretched an arm toward Will, but found his place vacant. Disappointment. Today would be her last chance to prove to him how much he needed her.

" 'Morning, cowboy."

Opening her eyes, Priscilla frowned, seeing Will fully dressed. He knelt beside her, handed her a cup of coffee. Steam wafted from the hot liquid. Following the steam, her gaze locked with his. He wore that same old somber expression.

She bolted to a sitting position, then belatedly grabbed the edge of the blanket and covered her breasts. Her eyes never left his.

"Drink up, so we can hit the trail," he was saying.

As if it were a condemned prisoner's last drink, she lifted the cup to her lips and sipped.

"How far'd you say to Spanish Creek?"

"Midafternoon." The word fell from her lips like a boulder and sounded hollow when it hit the cool morning air.

Will's gaze held hers. "Priscilla, there's something I need to tell you. I thought about it all night—"

Oh, Lord, that bad?

"—and I can't see any other way. I don't think it's wise to tell you, but . . ." His words trailed off. He took her cup and set it aside. With the tenderest of movements, he grasped her by the shoulders and lifted her toward him. She watched him earnestly, fearing the unknown, even when his lips descended to hers. He kissed her.

Briefly. "I decided to be selfish. To tell you. Because if you know, maybe . . . maybe that'll make a difference . . . later."

"Oh, Will." Her breath came short. "Just say it, please. Get it over with."

He grinned, a smile that brought relief to his grave expression, even though it never reached his eyes.

"Okay. Here goes—"

A series of rifle shots tore through the stillness.

Will gripped her shoulders tighter. "Priscilla, I—"

Another volley of shots stopped him. This time they sounded closer.

Priscilla kissed him, soundly, quickly, as he had kissed her. "I love you, Will Radnor, so don't worry about a thing. Whatever it is, we'll work it out later." Oblivious to her naked state, she dropped the blanket and began pulling on her clothing. "If we don't get shot, first," she added, stomping into her boots.

Will stared, stunned by the interruption as much as by the ninety-degree shift in Priscilla. Hell, she'd gone from seductress to cowboy in less than a second. He grinned in spite of himself. "You forgot to shake out your boots, cowboy."

"There're some things worse than snakes in your boots, greenhorn." Suddenly she was all business. "Grab your rifle."

"Victorio promised to keep the Haskels off our tail," Will reminded her. "Those are probably hunters."

"Probably can get you killed."

She had a point. Somehow he felt relieved. Had the Lord Above intervened to stop his vain declaration of love?

Another volley of shots erupted, this one longer. Three, four, he counted five shots, echoing back and forth across the canyon. Priscilla had already scooted closer to the cliff edge, intent now on only one thing, protection.

Will agreed that the shots had come from the east, across the canyon, the trail they would have been riding only minutes later. But Priscilla was right. It didn't pay to take anything for granted. "I'll check behind us, to be sure."

By the time he returned, creeping bent over so as not to offer a target, she had stamped out the fire and covered it with earth. "In case they've been too busy up to now to see our smoke," she explained. "Are the horses all right?"

"Humm." In silent accord Will took up watch from the left side of the camp, Priscilla from the right, lying on their stomachs, their guns trained across the canyon.

"Think it's Indians?"

"I don't know." After a minute she asked, "Aren't we close to that hideout of Billy the Kid's?"

Will nodded.

Rifle fire crackled again, volleying back and forth in the distance.

"Sounds like one against several," Will commented.

"Humm."

"Who?" Neither of them had the answer.

The sun climbed higher. Sweat trickled down Will's neck and seeped beneath his shirt. Half a foot or so away, a line of ants busily carried food to their home; insects droned in the morning stillness.

Across the way the battle erupted again. Many more shots this time, uncountable in the rapidity with which they were fired.

"They're closing in," Will observed.

"We've gotta do something."

"Do something? What the hell—"

"Go to his aid."

"Whose aid?"

"Whoever's in trouble."

"Who?" he demanded.

Priscilla turned her attention from the distant canyon. "I don't know, Will."

"That's my point. We might be going to the aid of some outlaw or some—"

"Well, I'm finding out." She scooted back from the ledge.

"What the hell are you doing?"

"I'll saddle the horses. Keep your eyes peeled. Try to pinpoint his position so we won't lose time searching for him."

While she issued orders, Will rose. Reaching her, he pulled her around. "You pinpoint his position. I'll saddle the horses."

She frowned. "Since when have you been better at saddling horses than I am, greenhorn?"

In spite of the situation, he grinned at her cocky attitude. "Since I fell in love with you, cowboy." The words tumbled out of their own volition. Hadn't he decided not to tell her? He watched her assimilate the shocking pronouncement. Her eyes grew round; they sparkled. If he'd needed confirmation of his feelings for this woman, or hers for him, here it was, in living color. He realized suddenly that his wish list was simple. He wouldn't require much to keep him the happiest man in the world. Looking into Priscilla's sparkling blue eyes every morning for the rest of his life would be all the prize he'd ever want or need.

Rifle fire broke out again, startling him into action. "Get down, damnit. And stay down while I saddle the horses."

In the end, he had to push her down, for she stood frozen

to the spot, staring at him. Hell fire and damnation, he shouldn't have told her. Now she would expect, rightfully, all the accoutrements that went along with such a declaration—commitment, marriage, children—none of which he would be able to give. None of which she would want, after they returned to Spanish Creek.

The rifle volleys continued. "Well, get busy, greenhorn," she snapped. "We can't stand around looking sappy while someone gets himself gut shot."

In spite of the situation, Will couldn't suppress a grin. "Right." Turning toward the thicket where they'd tethered the horses, he swooped up the bedroll without breaking stride.

"Be careful back there," she called. "I don't want you catchin' a bullet, now that life's gettin' interesting."

It had worked! Her plan had worked. Priscilla took up her post, while inside she felt like any minute she might explode from the sheer joy of being alive and in love—and having that love returned. He'd said it! He'd said it!

What she'd really like right this minute was to ride off in the opposite direction. Ride until they were out of sight and sound of any other human being, whether they were shooting at each other or not. Ride until she and Will were as alone as they had been mere moments ago.

Ride to some secluded, romantic site, with soft grass and maybe a creek trickling down the mountain, and birds, yes, birds singing from the trees, a private place where they could take off all their clothes and lie in each other's arms and make love—after she demanded that he say it again. And again. And maybe even again.

Words mushroomed in her head. Questions: How did he know and when had he realized it and why had he fought loving her so long and hard? Questions, whose answers she would have been frightened to hear only hours ago. Now she longed to hear them.

Will whistled, drawing her attention. When she turned he

held the reins of both their horses, saddled and packed. She scooted toward him. She wanted to throw herself in his arms and demand he tell her again. Yet, something inside her wanted to savor that magical declaration a while longer. Something inside her begged to resist touching him, talking about it—about them—to revel in anticipation of later. To allow that anticipation to build and build throughout the day until by the time they finally came together it would've become real. Right now, it felt more like a dream. For a split second, she entertained the notion that he hadn't said the words at all. That she had wanted to hear them so badly, her imagination had taken charge of her senses.

But the look in his eyes revealed the truth. He loved her. He didn't seem very comfortable with the fact, but he loved her. That was all right. She could make him comfortable with it later. For now she was content knowing that she had succeeded beyond all her expectations.

By a stroke of sheer luck, she had performed some ancient, magical miracle and Will Radnor had fallen in love with her. The realization empowered her in a way that was unexpected. Rather than feeling driven by some inner force that shouted, *HURRY! HURRY! HURRY!* she was content to sit back and allow herself to savor her success. She had time, now. They had time. Time for everything.

Later they could resolve whatever remained unresolved, because Will Radnor loved her. He had admitted it. Right out loud.

By the time they worked their way around the hillside, crossing the canyon by a narrow gorge overgrown with juniper, the afternoon was well under way.

"He's on top of this hill," she whispered.

Will nodded. "We'll stake the horses in that thicket over there." Dismounting, he handed her his reins, then rifled in his saddlebags for shells, which he dropped into his pockets. "Sit tight, Miss Priss. I'll be right back."

She caught his sleeve. "Not on your life, greenhorn."

"It's your life I'm worried about."

"So it's a draw. I'm worried about yours. We go together."

"Now, Pris—"

"Don't Priscilla me. This calls for our best judgment, and I'm the one familiar with the country."

He glanced to the top of the hill. "I hardly think there's a chance I can get lost in the next hundred feet."

Rifle shots crackled above them. "We're wasting time."

"Then stay with the damned horses. I'll be—"

"Like hell, I will. Maybe I shouldn't have worked so hard to make you fall in love with me. Maybe I don't want to be hitched for life to someone who's going to treat me like a . . . like a *lady.*"

"Damnation, Priscilla." Will extended his hands in appeal.

She swept past him, dropping the reins of both her horse and his into his outstretched hands. "The name's Jake."

She'd reached the crest by the time she heard him scramble up behind her. She turned a silencing frown to him, but waited for him to catch up.

"He's right up there," she whispered. "Twenty, thirty yards, I'd say." She grabbed a handful of rock and started to swing up.

Will caught her. He hauled her down beside him. "For God's sake, Priscilla," he whispered. "One sound and he'll shoot you. He probably isn't expecting Annie Oakley to come to his rescue."

She huffed. He was right, of course. "Any suggestions?"

He held her gaze, as if to say, *You need me, whether you're willing to admit it or not.* "We'll have to disarm him, before we break the news that we're friends. If it turns out we are friends." Will glanced around. "You take the right, I'll take left."

"Okay."

"Go slow, now. And remember we're on the same team.

No competition. I'll give you the glory, so there's no need to try to prove you're the better man."

"Will!"

He touched a finger to his lips. "I'll count to three. We move out together."

She nodded.

"One. Two." Their gazes locked. She felt his love pour into her, his love and concern. "Quietly," he reminded her.

"You, too, greenhorn."

He winked. "Three."

Within seconds they were looking at each other from opposite sides of the boulder. Breaking eye contact, they scanned the area ahead of them. Priscilla focused her attention on the figure of a man in the brush. As in slow motion she heard Will's rifle cock.

The figure swerved at the sound, turning toward Will. *Joaquín!* "It's me," she called. ". . . and Will. We've come to help."

After a tense moment, Joaquín relaxed. The surprise on his face briefly mirrored welcome, then turned to indifference.

"Who's got you pinned down?" Will asked.

"Haskels," came the reply. "José Colorado brought word. I rode all night to find you. I'd almost given up."

"How many are out there?" Will asked.

"Three. José watched them for a whole day, before he was sure. They didn't come from town, but from Spanish Creek.

"Spanish Creek?" Priscilla cried.

"We knew they were there," Will reminded her.

"I hope Bart's arrived."

Joaquín squinted off in the direction of the attackers. "Don't worry your pretty blue eyes, little Miss Priss. Charlie'll hold onto Spanish Creek for you."

Any response Will or Priscilla might have made to

Joaquín's familiar cynicism was checked when the hillside on which they stood suddenly flew apart.

The sounds came afterward, shots whining through the stillness. Priscilla was scarcely aware of the barrage before Joaquín landed on top of her, forcing her to the ground. Will hit her from the other side. They collapsed in a heap on the rocky ground.

Before the dust settled, Priscilla was struggling to free herself from the avalanche of concerned men.

"Hey, the enemy's out there."

The two men stared at each other, Joaquín with a harsh expression that defied Will to question his right to protect Priscilla; Will with equal possessiveness.

When bullets again ripped through the shrubbery that served as their only cover now, Will scooted back. "We'd better get busy defending ourselves or we'll be the ones needing the help of an old outlaw."

That statement proved prophetic, Priscilla thought later, for after a couple of hours spent exchanging fire, the Haskels showed no sign of giving up. From all indications, they were dug in for the long haul.

"Oscar must want us pretty bad," Will commented. Priscilla had taken one corner of the cliff, Joaquín the middle, and Will the opposite side.

"I don't think it's Oscar, so much as it is Newt," Priscilla argued. "We made him look real bad. Especially you, Will, and Joaquín, slipping out of the jail while he was . . . uh, what did you say they were doing, Will?"

Will glanced her way at that, and she held his gaze for heated moments. A rifle shot splintered a branch in front of Joaquín.

"Hey, you, two. If you're not going to pay attention, get out of my way."

Priscilla scanned the opposite cliff and fired. A yelp splintered the air.

"You hit one, cowboy."

"They're moving." Joaquín reloaded as he spoke.

"Moving?" Priscilla peered into the growing shadow. "Which way?"

Will fired. A rifle flew into the air, then fell to the ground.

"That one was off to the right of their original position, by a good fifty yards," Joaquín observed.

Priscilla concentrated, searching the distant hillside for a color out of place, movement, a bird flushed out of its nest.

Will suddenly fired once, twice, three times.

"Now who's wasting bullets?"

He glanced at her. "I never waste bullets."

"So what were you shooting at?"

"They've fanned out. That one was off to the left."

Hair bristled on Priscilla's neck.

"We've gotta get out of here," Will told Joaquín. "Which way's safest?"

Joaquín didn't respond for long minutes. He drew a bead with a steady hand, then started firing. He sprayed the canyon from the point at which Will had last, to where Priscilla had hit someone.

With his shots still ringing down the canyon, he replied, "There's no safe way."

"Well, we dang sure can't stay here and wait for them to come after us." Will looked pointedly at Priscilla. "Not with Priscilla along."

His concern heated a trail down Priscilla's spine.

"I'm not that coldhearted, white eyes."

"Then damnit, find us a way out."

Shots rang out again, blasting dirt and bits of rock into them. Lifting her rifle, Priscilla returned the fire. "They'll know we're gone, the minute we stop returning their fire."

"Won't take 'em long to figure it out," Joaquín agreed.

In answer to another round from the canyon, Will fired a round.

"They're blocking the trail we need to take," Priscilla said. "We'll never make it out."

"Yes, we will," Will told her.

Joaquín agreed with Priscilla. "Not to Spanish Creek."

"Then where?" Will demanded. "You know this area better than they do." He added, less heatedly, "Surely."

Joaquín scowled at Will. "Surely I know something better than you, white eyes."

"We don't have time for your cynicism, Joaquín. It's up to us, you and me, to get Priscilla out of this alive." He glared at Joaquín. "Even if we don't."

"Will!"

"He's right, Jake. Now you've got two men to fight for you. If you'd known that would happen don't reckon you'd've been so hungry to become the best shot in the territory. But of course that's not the reason you did it. Couldn't leave Charlie McCain without a son—just to prove who owns Spanish Creek."

"Where can we go?" Will interrupted.

Joaquín eyed him. "You an' Jake finished with your shootin' match?"

Will glared back at him. "We're finished."

"Then we'll go."

"Where's your horse?"

"Shot out from under me."

"Damnation." Will cast his eyes heavenward. "What else is going to go wrong?" A second later, he added, "Take Priscilla's horse. She'll double with me."

Joaquín shrugged. "It's your rain dance."

"Let's get out of here before they turn it into a necktie party."

But Joaquín had the last say. "Go ahead. I'll keep 'em busy while you two get the horses ready."

Priscilla followed Will down the steep slope. Behind her she heard Joaquín fire repeatedly into the canyon. The sun was beginning to set. It was time they got out of here. Her spine tensed at the thought of being caught by Haskels before they reached home.

As it turned out, they didn't go home. Not that night. Will and Priscilla were already mounted when Joaquín skidded into the thicket where they waited. He took one look at Priscilla's horse with the buffalo hide lashed behind the saddle. "What's this? You taking up wickiup building?"

"It's your mother's liner."

His eyes narrowed.

"I'm taking it to Spanish Creek for safekeeping."

Joaquín stood so still a bee lighted on his nose, then quickly darted away. After an intense moment, he ducked his head.

He didn't say anything. He didn't have to. She knew what he was thinking. It was his history, too. Or it should be.

Will nudged his horse into line behind Joaquín. They rode silently, tensed against an attack from behind. Priscilla sat in front of Will, shielded by his body. She settled back, leaned against him—the man she loved. The man who loved her. He'd said so. She was hard-put not to enjoy being in his arms, even under such grave circumstances.

After they had traveled a distance, Will kicked his mount up beside Joaquín's. "Where're we headed?"

"I think we can make it to the Kid's."

"Billy the Kid?" Priscilla questioned.

Joaquín turned her way, but in the shadows she couldn't make out his expression. Of course, he only had one expression: cynical. When he laughed it surprised her.

"You don't believe the gossip, do you, Jake?"

"That you ride with Billy the Kid?" she asked. "No."

After a while he responded, "You're right. I don't. But I know him. He hates the Haskels worse'n Charlie does. We can hole up there until we think of something better."

"How much trouble'll we have protecting Priscilla from those outlaws?" Will wanted to know.

Joaquín studied Priscilla with an emotionless expression. "Leave that to me."

The way Will's arms tightened around her, Priscilla had the distinct feeling that he didn't intend to leave anything to Joaquín. But neither did he come up with an alternate destination, and an hour later they arrived at a mountain fortress that reminded Priscilla of Victorio's ranchería.

"They have us in their sights," Joaquín told them. "When they approach us, leave the talking to me."

"Be sure you make it clear that Priscilla is not to be touched."

Joaquín didn't respond, but a dozen or so yards further, he held up his hand, halting the procession. With a slow steady hand, he lifted his hat from his head three times, then whistled in imitation of some sort of bird.

A similar whistle returned to them, almost like an echo from the mountain itself.

Joaquín whistled again, this time a bit differently.

"Joaquín!" Rocks slid down the hillside ahead of a man who scrambled toward them. "How goes it?"

"Oscar Haskel's men're on our tail."

"How far?"

"Two, maybe three miles."

The guard studied Will and Priscilla in the gathering darkness.

"They're okay," Joaquín assured him. "This here's Will Radnor, the white-eyes lawyer who broke me outta jail, right out from under ol' Newt's nose. And the woman's . . . uh, that's Jake McCain . . . my sister."

Thirteen

Sister. Priscilla hadn't paid much attention to Will's concern for her safety in the outlaw camp, until they were confronted by the coarse, heavily armed guard. Ruffian, she corrected. Will must have sensed her alarm, for his arms had tightened protectively around her.

Then Joaquín made his astonishing claim. *Sister.* Suddenly, the armed guard took on a whole different character; she saw the world from a new perspective. Joaquín would protect her. And Will.

With Will's arms around her, they followed the guard's lead through the gathering darkness. *Sister.* He'd said it to protect her, and, of course, she didn't need protection. But at the moment, none of that mattered.

At the moment she basked in a sense of belonging, of camaraderie, of family. Not that she'd ever lacked family, not that she'd ever considered herself alone. But suddenly she felt whole, somehow. And secure—even riding into the camp of a notorious outlaw like Billy the Kid.

She had Joaquín—who called her, Sister. She leaned her head back against Will's chest. And she had Will. At this moment, that was all she needed.

Ten minutes later they arrived at a frame shack that had definitely seen better days. Weathered by time and the elements, the building canted to one side, betraying a foundation that was as unstable as the rest of the structure looked. The windows were devoid of glass, but some kind of canvas had been tacked across the holes; it left more area open to insects than it covered, however. Dim light glowed from within, giving the effect of a lantern burning somewhere further inside the building.

They were ordered to keep their seats. The guard bounded up the rickety steps. When he opened the door, a shaft of light showed a porch that only the nimble-footed— or slow-witted, Priscilla thought—would tread.

But one sight of the man who stepped through the doorway and approached them erased all thoughts of rickety porches. Small in stature, swaggering with arrogance, Billy the Kid was the spitting image of his wanted posters.

"Joaquín, *amigo*. Heard 'bout your trouble up in Santa Fé. Figured them Haskel bastards'd put out your lights by now."

"They figured to," Joaquín responded easily. "Took a turn at me again today. We left 'em shootin' at an empty hillside over on Turkey Canyon."

"Turkey Canyon?" The Kid looked off into the darkness, the way they'd come. "What's that, five miles, six?"

"Somethin' like it."

The Kid turned his attention to Will and Priscilla. He didn't speak. Joaquín introduced them. "That's Will Radnor, my lawyer."

"The other?"

"Jake McCain."

The Kid squinted at Priscilla, as if deciding whether he should believe Joaquín. "Charlie's daughter? What'd you do, take her for a hostage?"

"She was in on it, helped get me out of town."

"Sonofabitch, what'd'ya know?" The Kid perused them with his small-pupiled eyes, as infamous as his stature. If his size fooled a man, the saying went, those eyes made it crystal clear—this man was touchy as a rattler, and it'd pay a feller to step lightly while in his presence.

"Might as well climb down," he invited. "Wilbur here'll

take your weapons. All except Joaquín's," the last for the benefit of a string-bean shaped ruffian who ambled toward them, slack-jointed.

Suddenly Priscilla felt Will's arms slip from around her. The reins dropped in her lap. She didn't dare look down, but she felt his hands hover near her hips. Before she could think of a way to intervene, he spoke. "I'm not giving up my gun." His tone was thankfully low, for Joaquín's ears only. But, in the stillness, the Kid either heard or understood the situation. "Not with the Haskels coming up behind us," Will added, like a true greenhorn, Priscilla worried.

"I'll vouch for 'em, Kid," Joaquín offered quickly.

By this time a crowd had gathered on the rickety porch. Fanned out to either side of the Kid, four men, all of whom looked as coarse and tough as the guard who'd led them in, and Wilbur, who slouched nearby, ready to take their guns. In the dim light emitting from the ramshackle house, Priscilla could tell each man there had eyes only for her.

She shuddered involuntarily, watching Billy the Kid consider the situation.

Will obviously didn't know when it was best to keep his mouth shut, for he whispered to Joaquín again. "I'm not goin' in there unarmed, not with those men ogling Priscilla."

"I'll watch out for her, white eyes." Then, in a louder voice, Joaquín addressed the crowd. "Jake McCain's my sister and any of you *cabrónes* who looks at her crooked'll answer to me."

The ogling switched to Joaquín and turned menacing. A sickening premonition dispelled the last traces of Priscilla's earlier pleasure. She had to do something, but what? Without another thought, she swung a leg high over the saddle-horn and jumped to the ground, rifle in hand.

She glared from one man to the next. "I can defend myself, Joaquín." Will jumped to the ground behind her.

Priscilla didn't dare turn around to look at him. Her attention focused on Billy the Kid; she felt her stomach go weak. Before she lost her nerve completely, she added, "Any man here who doubts it, bring your rifle and we'll settle up."

"I'm backing her," Will announced.

"Won't be any need—" the Kid started to say.

Joaquín slid off his horse and stood beside them. "You men have always treated me fair, but if push comes to shove, for the record, I'm on Jake's side, too."

The screen door slammed. Another, taller man crossed to stand amicably beside Billy the Kid. "Miss McCain can count me on her team, as well."

Priscilla's gaze found the speaker. A shiver raced down her spine. If ever a man looked out of place, this tall, gray-haired, fastidiously dressed man looked it here. A stiff white collar ringed his neck above a black suit. His coloring was dark, here in the dim yellow light, at least. His carefully styled gray hair sparkled with cleanliness.

"Who's he?" Will whispered from behind.

She shrugged.

Billy the Kid slapped the newcomer on the shoulder. Even though the little outlaw had to stretch to reach the taller man's shoulder, it in no way diminished Billy the Kid's stature. "Seems you're properly chaperoned here in our den of thieves, Miss McCain. I'll trust you to keep your troops under control."

The Kid's invitation to come inside, weapons and all, had barely left his lips when he turned to those on the porch and shouted. "You heathens keep your hands to you'selves."

Later, sitting across a scarred wooden table, eating green-chile stew from chipped enamel bowls, Will whispered in Priscilla's ear, "He should have included *eyes* in those orders." The men kept their distance, remaining far enough away from Priscilla that they couldn't be accused of touching her, but their eyes were glued to her.

All except the older man who had offered his protection. He sat apart in a darkened corner, neither participating in the card game in progress around a dirty mattress, nor joining the new arrivals at the table.

In fact only Billy the Kid sat at the table with Priscilla, Will, and Joaquín. He and Joaquín talked back and forth, Joaquín catching him up on their activities since leaving Santa Fé.

"Victorio pulled out for Tres Castillos."

"He's one tough hombre," the Kid observed. "Should've stayed and fought it out."

"He'll have fight enough to keep him busy south of the border," Joaquín predicted.

The Kid looked pensive. "If anyone was ever hounded more'n me, it's them redskins."

"I thought you were supposed to go to Tres Castillos," Priscilla told Joaquín at a lull in the conversation.

He stuffed half a biscuit in his mouth. Without looking at her, he spoke around his mouthful. "When José Colorado brought word that the hills were crawling with Haskels, Victorio sent me to find you and Radnor."

"And we found you instead," she replied. Even in this hovel filled with outlaws, Priscilla felt her joy return. What a memorable day this had been! Will told her he loved her; Joaquín called her, Sister. And here she sat, between the two of them. Her hand slipped to the bench beside her. Will covered it with his own, squeezed, reassuring. *He loved her.* He'd said it!

Across the table, the Kid rolled a cigarette. Joaquín took out the makin's and started his own. From the far corner a lighted cigarette winked when the stranger drew on it. The man who'd come to her aid. "Who's the man in the corner?" she asked.

The Kid's hands stilled on the tobacco-filled wrapper.

"That question's out of line, Jake," Joaquín cautioned.

Billy the Kid's shoulders relaxed a bit. "This place might not look like much to you, ma'am, but it's the only safe place most of us have. A man on the run can always find shelter here. If we questioned everyone who approached—"

"You questioned us."

Joaquín tensed and Will cleared his throat.

Billy the Kid laughed. "You're made out to be a real fine shot, Miss McCain, but no man's ever called you an outlaw."

"I understand." Priscilla stared into the darkened corner. "But—he sounded like he knew me."

"New Mexico's a small territory," the Kid said. "Any man in these parts is likely to know the name McCain. Most men know of you."

Priscilla left it at that. When Billy the Kid rose to leave the table, Will stopped him.

"We have our bedrolls. Any problem with us taking them out under the trees?"

"None, lawyer. Clem'll be out there standin' guard."

"A trusting soul," Priscilla quipped after they retrieved their bedrolls from the barn where one of the Kid's men had unsaddled and rubbed down their horses.

"Trusting souls don't live long in this neighborhood," Will returned.

They walked silently away from the house, each carrying a load of bedding. Beyond the circle of house light, Will put an arm around her shoulders and drew her close.

"That was a damned stupid thing you did back there, Priscilla." His voice didn't censure, but she bristled, nonetheless.

"It wasn't stupid. It was necessary. Pa says a man has to establish a base of strength early in a conflict."

"I doubt Charlie intended for you to confront half a dozen armed outlaws. Jumping off your horse with your rifle cocked; don't you know you're supposed to take things slow and easy around men like that? Isn't that the phrase they use?"

"Well, it worked. Pa says a man—"

"If you're not careful, cowboy, Charlie's philosophies'll end up getting you killed."

She leaned into him. "You were there, Will. And Joaquín. I don't see what the fuss is about."

"You wouldn't. For a woman as bent on seduction as you've been the last few days, you turned back into a hardened cowboy real quick."

Priscilla felt her cheeks flush. "Seduction?"

He chuckled. "You're something else. I've never known a woman who's better at hiding her bag of feminine tricks. I'll have to admit, when you decided to play seductress you took me by surprise."

Although his tone indicated he was teasing, she cringed. "Did you mind?"

"Mind? Hell, I ate it up and begged for more. Or didn't you notice? Of course, all that play-acting wasn't necessary."

"Play-acting? I wasn't—"

"I know." His husky voice sent desire spiraling down her spine. He drew her to a halt, tossed the bedroll to the ground, and studied her beneath the pale moonlight. "Not even the Lord Above could put two separate people in skin as soft and tight as yours. You're no seductress, Priscilla McCain, but you're one hell of a woman."

She glowed. Basking in his teasing, she dropped her armful of bedding on top of his.

"What I'm wonderin',' " he was asking, "is where you learned the art of seduction? That's one thing I'll have a hard time believing you learned from ol' Charlie."

She laughed at the idea, then kissed him lightly on the lips and felt a groan rumble from his chest.

"I don't know where I learned it," she admitted. "It surprised me, too. It must be something women are born with, like . . . like a sixth sense or something."

He hugged her close. Slanting his lips across hers, he kissed her long and deep. When they drew apart, she said,

"It's strange. From almost the first day I met you I experienced all kinds of unusual sensations. They confused me. I didn't understand them. Actually, they embarrassed me."

"Embarrassed you?"

"I felt giddy and hot; my head seemed to spin every time I was around you; I had trouble thinking straight. Do you know what I mean?"

He nipped her nose with a wet kiss. "I know, cowboy."

"It's like I told you. From the beginning I had the strangest feeling that my body knew things my brain hadn't learned yet. I began to worry. I wanted to ask Mama, but . . . well, I couldn't . . ." Her words drifted off; she grew pensive, recalling her parents' disapproval of Will. "I thought about asking Jessie, but I never got up the nerve."

"So you learned it on your own?" His voice was soft, tender, admiring, even.

"Pa says desperation tests a man's abilities and finds him prepared or wanting."

"Desperation, huh?"

Bending toward her, Will stopped short of kissing her. This time he pulled her tight and buried his lips in her hair. When he turned her loose, it was with a purpose.

"We'd best get our bedroll laid before those outlaws start howling at the moon." The site where they had stopped was a hundred yards or so from the house. "This okay?"

She grinned, thinking of home. Home, where her persuasive skills would be tested again, this time against her parents. She was anxious to return, to put the trouble with the Haskels behind them, to present Will's case to her parents.

"It isn't Spanish Creek," she responded, "but I guess it'll do." Curious, she watched him stomp the ground with a bootheel.

"What are you doing?"

"Checking the bedrock. That rocky hill you put me on the first night out of Santa Fé nearly cracked my bones."

She laughed. "You took it in stride, greenhorn."

He continued stomping his heel to the ground. "I learned young that if you let someone know they're getting under your skin, they tend to burrow deeper."

She watched him reach for a bedroll, and spread it on his place of choice. He topped it with the other roll of bedding. She smiled, pleased. "So, I'm under your skin, am I, greenhorn?"

"I guess you could say that."

It wasn't the way he'd put it earlier in the day when he declared his love for her. Words she had savored time and again through the turmoil that followed. It seemed like a year ago, now, so much had happened since he made that startling confession of love. "Tell me again."

"You get under my skin."

"Not that." She touched his shoulder, drawing his attention. When he straightened, she moved into his arms. "What you said this morning—your reason for wanting to saddle the horses."

Although his face was in shadow, she could feel his eyes penetrating the darkness, driving into her. He didn't move a muscle, except for one hand, which he lifted slowly and with infinite tenderness stroked her face.

"I spoke out of turn," he said in a quiet, husky voice that stopped her heart. Or was it his words that stopped her heart?

Out of turn? She stifled her distress, tried to clear her head. To think. To reason. *Out of turn?* He couldn't mean it.

Only moments ago he had teased and flirted with her. Even now he caressed her with tenderness. And before . . . all those times before . . . those wonderful times. He was a passionate and gentle lover, yet, here he was, on the verge of denying it all, yet again.

"I should never have said—" he was saying.

"Stop."

His hand poised where it was, a finger at one corner of her lips.

"You said it, Will." She braced herself, daring her voice to tremble. "You said it, and it's done. I won't let you take it back."

Moving away, she knelt and began to smooth out the wrinkles in the bedrolls. With difficulty, she managed to use studied movements, to resist the urge to fling it all in his face.

Will knelt beside her, placed a hand on her shoulders. She flinched.

"I'm sorry, cowboy."

She fought back tears. But for some reason she couldn't keep her mouth shut. "Don't lie and say you didn't mean it, Will." His hands gripped her shoulders. "I know you meant it. Maybe you didn't mean to say it, but you feel it. You love me, damnit."

Even as she berated him, she knew it was the wrong thing to do. But she couldn't keep her blasted mouth shut. "I love you, too. But I'm not at all sure I want to live the rest of my life with a man who possesses such a mercurial temperament."

Will dropped his hands from her shoulders. She heard him sigh heavily, then finally crawl into the bedroll. After a lengthy silence he spoke through tight jaws. "I never asked you to live the rest of your life with me."

"Good." She remained on her knees, as still as a frightened hare. "Because if you had, I would have refused." She knelt so long, her legs began to ache. But it was nothing like the ache in her heart. She'd lost him, and she didn't even know why. And she certainly didn't know what to do about it.

"Priscilla?"

He sounded contrite. She didn't respond.

"Come to bed, cowboy."

Cowboy? Who was this man, who could tell her he loved her and show it in so many ways it must be true, yet who in the next breath denied it and everything he did and felt?

Who was he, this Will Radnor who set her on fire and abolished all hope from her soul at one and the same time? This man who could break her heart and then blithely call her to bed?

"Come on," he urged.

Feeling his hand grope in the darkness, she shifted away from him. After he stilled, she fumbled around, found one corner of the cover, and eased herself down. But just when she thought for sure he'd gone to sleep and left her awake to protect herself against that houseful of lusting outlaws, he spoke again.

"I'm sorry, Priscilla."

She didn't dare move. He was too close. His voice came from somewhere very near her shoulder. She wished for two bedrolls. But wishing didn't count for much at the moment.

"You're right." She heard him sigh. "You usually are, of course."

"Don't try to placate me, greenhorn."

"I'm not trying anything, except to be honest with you, and maybe with myself, for a change. You're right about it all. I love you. But I didn't mean to say it."

Distracted from her anguish by the sound of his own, she turned to find him as near as she'd thought. In the darkness she could barely make out his form—his broad shoulders, the curve of his head. But she didn't need to see him. She could feel him, his breath, his heat . . . his agony.

Lifting a hand, she touched his cheek, and the next thing she knew she was in his arms. He held her close, stroking her back, breathing his warm sweet breath into her hair. She snuggled against him, holding him with a death grip, and wished they didn't have their clothes on.

"How long do you think we'll stay here?" she whispered.

"Forever, I wish."

* * *

Miracle of miracles, they left for Spanish Creek the following day. Early the next morning Will and Priscilla folded their bedrolls and carried them to the barn. Joaquín met them there, accompanied by the mysterious stranger who had pledged his help to Priscilla the evening before, then promptly disappeared into the shadows.

Joaquín exhibited uncustomarily high spirits. "Jake, this is the man you've been expecting."

The tall stranger, who looked close to Pa's age, Priscilla thought, bowed, a formal gesture that further separated him from the ruffians who inhabited this outlaw hideout. "Bart Ellisor, Miss McCain."

"Mr. Ellisor!" Taken by surprise, she didn't think to curb her tone. "You're supposed to be helping Pa defend Spanish Creek. Didn't Jessie make that clear?"

"Jessie left no doubt, young lady, but my travel options are, shall we say, limited. I couldn't very well take a stage. Authorities from Texas to California would have loved that." He grinned then, relieving some of her anxiety. "Goes with the work."

"But Pa . . ." She cast Will a worried glance.

"Charlie'll make out," Will assured her.

"What's wrong with Charlie?" Bart asked.

"He was injured in a fight with the Haskels—"

"Kate's alone at Spanish Creek?"

"Except for an aging foreman and a less-than-worthless archaeologist," Will furnished.

"That settles it." Bart turned to Joaquín. "Tell Mr. Bonney we will accept his offer."

"What offer?" Priscilla wanted to know.

"Mr. Bonney offered us his help in escaping the Haskels. His men will create a diversion, while we leave by another route."

"Oh, thank goodness." Priscilla turned radiant eyes to Will. "We're going home." He scowled. She knew what he was thinking. "After we secure Spanish Creek—" she began.

"How does the Kid intend to perform this miracle?" Will interrupted, speaking to Bart.

"The man called Clem is out locating the Haskels' position," Bart explained. "When he returns, Mr. Bonney will take his men into the hills to engage them in a skirmish. Meanwhile, we'll head south, work our way east, then north. It'll take longer to reach Spanish Creek, but we should have safe sailing."

"We'll do it!" Priscilla looked up to find Bart Ellisor favoring her with a wistful expression.

"Did anyone ever tell you how much you favor your mother? Except for Charlie's eyes, of course."

Clem rode in then, preventing further discussion. But Priscilla's brain overflowed with questions about this handsome, mysterious stranger and his connection to her parents. Obviously, they had known one another well, yet her parents rarely spoke his name.

Leaving the hideout in the wake of Billy the Kid's gang, Joaquín led them through the mountains by a southern route. Hours later they turned east, as planned. The mood was serious—Priscilla's spine tingled a good part of it—and afforded little opportunity for conversation. By mutual, if undeclared, consent they ate their noon meal—hardtack and jerky, washed down with flat canteen water—in the saddle. It was well after sundown before they stopped for anything other than to rest and water the horses—their destination, an isolated patch of grass beside a spring on the eastern side of the mountain range they had worked all day to cross.

"No fire," Joaquín ordered, after they'd unsaddled their horses. So they sat beside the spring, eating more hardtack and jerked meat. This time, though, they had plenty of icy sweet water from the spring. When no one seemed ready to retire, Bart pulled out a bottle of rye whiskey and splashed a measure into each cup. Before she finished her drink, Priscilla felt the weariness of the day's ride slough away, leaving her relaxed and a bit mellow. Finally, she found the courage to ask a question that had bedeviled her all day.

"How long have you known my parents, Mr. Ellisor?"

"A while, Miss McCain. A while."

She studied him by the dim light of the moon, wondering why he would evade her question, since he and her parents were obviously old friends. The nature of his work, probably. Before she could decide whether—and if so, how—to question him further, Will changed the subject.

"I've been thinking about your case, Joaquín."

Joaquín glanced up. His eyes were hard. Since leaving the Kid's hideout, his cynicism had deepened, a fact that disappointed Priscilla. She knew it had a lot to do with their destination—Spanish Creek.

"I may've found a way to clear you," Will was telling Joaquín. "Victorio claims those horses belong to The People and to Charlie. If that's true, maybe I can work out a deal."

"No deals for me, white eyes."

"Sit tight and hear me out. I need a little more information, like why the horses are unbranded, which, by the way, will work in our favor, if things go as planned."

"Things never go as planned."

Priscilla spoke up. "The horses are unbranded because they're . . . well, The People consider them sacred."

"How does Charlie fit into all this?"

"Victorio gave him use of the horses. For some reason he trusted Pa not to abuse the privilege. No one was to ever speak of them. That's all I know."

"Then how can Charlie prove he owns them?"

"He can't."

Will persisted, but Priscilla shrugged, uneasy about revealing in front of Bart the secret that had been kept for generations.

Then Bart himself joined the conversation. "I may be able to shed some light. Victorio gave Charlie the horses, trusting him to use them only in times of need, in repayment for Charlie's help in that Rodrigo Suárez affair."

"What affair?" Priscilla wanted to know.

"It happened after Kate and Charlie were stranded in that snowstorm."

"Snowstorm—" Suddenly Priscilla recalled Nalin's tale and the drawings on the wickiup liner.

Bart cocked his head, obviously as hesitant to discuss the past with Priscilla, as she had been with him. "If you haven't been told all this, I'm not the man to—"

"I'm sure it was an oversight, Mr. Ellisor." She scrambled to piece together the story Nalin had told her only days earlier. "I mean, I know my parents were lost in a snowstorm and Victorio's people found them and saved their lives."

"*Our* lives," Bart commented, half to himself.

Priscilla's breath caught. Details of Nalin's story bombarded her. "You're the other man!"

Bart held her gaze across the distance.

"The other man in the drawings," she explained. "I have it. That's what that roll of hide is. The wickiup liner where Nalin's husband recorded the story."

"The story?" Clouded with ominous overtones, Bart's reply sent a shiver down Priscilla's spine. "Part of it, perhaps."

Her curiosity won out. "What's the rest?"

Instead of responding, Bart took a long drink from his cup, then pointedly refilled it, this time with straight rye whiskey.

Will refilled his own cup. "If you can shed some light on Charlie's ownership of the horses, Mr. Ellisor, I'd appreciate it. Joaquín here's been charged with stealing some of them. If I can prove they belong to Charlie McCain, that'll go a long way toward clearing him."

"Oh, they belong to Charlie, all right. It happened a few months after the snowstorm. You know how Apaches are, they don't set prisoners free, not white men, at least. But

Victorio and his band were being harassed by a group of unsavory white traders, and I happened to have the good fortune of killing a couple of them. Since I'd done them that service, they patched me up and freed me."

Pausing, he drank, his mind trained on some distant memory; again Priscilla sensed something ominous, or, at the least, melancholy.

Bart turned his attention to Priscilla. "Your mother pleaded Charlie's case with ol' Victorio, and they set him free, too, on the condition that he bring them the ringleader of their enemies."

"Rodrigo Suárez," Priscilla whispered, "Jessie's husband." She was mesmerized by the tale now, and by the way Pa's and Nalin's and Bart Ellisor's memories dovetailed. Again, she was filled to brimming with questions. How could she have spent nineteen years with her parents and remain so ignorant of their past?

"Jessie Laredo's husband," Bart confirmed. "To make a long story short, Victorio repaid your father by giving him limited use of some horses that had inhabited a canyon somewhere in New Mexico, undetected by any white man since the time of the Spanish explorers."

"Spanish Creek Canyon," Priscilla acknowledged.

Shrugging, Bart refilled his cup. Priscilla began to wonder how a drunk gentleman outlaw would act. But Bart Ellisor didn't show signs of inebriation. Likely his kind imbibed strong liquor with more frequency than others.

"As soon as we reach Spanish Creek," Will was saying, "I'll talk to Charlie. With his help we may be able to wrap this thing up."

But Priscilla's questions were a long way from being wrapped up. "You said you've known my parents a long time, Mr. Ellisor?" He had sidestepped the question once, so she quizzed him tentatively. She hated to prod an outlaw of his caliber, especially after her blunder at Billy the Kid's hideout.

"Indeed, I have Miss McCain. And it would give me great pleasure if you addressed me by my given name, Bart."

She smiled at his formal request. "Of course . . . Bart. I'll be happy to, if you'll call me Priscilla."

"Priscilla, a beautiful name, for a beautiful woman, if I may be so bold."

"Or you can call her Jake," Joaquín offered. "Most folks do."

"Jake?"

That seemed to amuse him, so the tale followed, told by Joaquín, Priscilla, and even Will. As the discussion progressed, Joaquín lost some of his cynicism, and Priscilla was delighted to learn that Will recalled a good deal of the story. Then she remembered the pistol.

"The pistol that started it all," she reminded Will, "the one I shot at those tin cans. That was the pistol I found in Pa's trunk, the one similar to yours."

"The pistol . . ." Will's voice drifted off. He stared out into the black of night.

"I found it in an old trunk in the barn," she explained to Bart. Then turning to Will, she added, "The day we left on the cattle drive, I looked for it, but it was gone." She shrugged. "Pa doesn't even remember it; that's how long ago it was. So I'm probably wrong. It may not have been like yours, after all."

Will held her gaze. "Like I told you, Miss Priss, you're usually right." It was the kind of teasing thing he generally said, accompanied by a broad smile. This time he didn't smile, in fact, he didn't even sound lighthearted. But of course they'd put in a hard day's ride.

"I'm ready to turn in," she told the group. "It's been a long day."

"We have a couple more ahead of us." Joaquín rose and headed for the far side of the spring. "I'll take first watch."

"Wake me for second," Bart offered. But his eyes were

on Will. Priscilla suddenly realized that he was frowning at Will, as if he were disturbed about something.

"Will Radnor," Bart mused. "Wouldn't happen to be from Philadelphia?"

She watched Will stiffen. His response was curt. "That's right."

"William Penn Radnor." Bart enunciated each syllable. "Knew a man by that name, a lawyer, like yourself—heard about him, rather," he corrected. "Wouldn't happen to be kin of yours?"

Will studied the outlaw for such a long time, Priscilla decided he wasn't going to reply. Something hard and large thudded in the pit of her stomach. She watched Will extend his hand to Bart, in a strange, wary sort of way, as if the two men were only now being introduced. "William Penn Radnor IV, Mr. Ellisor."

He emphasized *Mr. Ellisor* in a way that gave no hint of familiarity, and Bart did not offer the courtesy he had extended to Priscilla only moments earlier.

"Your father?" she whispered. "Bart knows—knew—your father?"

"So it seems."

Priscilla looked from one man to the other. They glared at each other like two bulls squaring off in a pasture. She wouldn't have been surprised to see their feet pawing the earth.

"Well," she said too blithely, "isn't that a coincidence?"

Bart was the first to recover. He turned to Priscilla with a thin-lipped smile. "Coincidence? Scratch the surface of a coincidence, Priscilla, and nine times out of ten, you'll uncover a well-devised design." Rising, he took her hand, bent over it, and brushed his lips across her skin in a gentlemanly salute. "At least that's been my experience."

Fourteen

By the time they arrived back at Spanish Creek two days later, Priscilla had learned a sad fact of life: Love and commitment don't always go hand in hand.

Will loved her. He had admitted as much. But he was a long way from being committed to her. Blast him. In admitting he loved her, he had also admitted that he hadn't intended to tell her so.

Blast him! One side of her wanted to hate him, argued convincingly for that end. But another side felt sad and lonely and very much in sympathy with this man who rode for the most part now, aloof.

Since Bart's challenge—that's what it had sounded like, Priscilla realized—Will had withdrawn into the indifference she'd had to wheedle him out of time after time during their short-lived relationship.

Was another try worth the effort? she wondered. Certainly, before she went to all the trouble of lifting his spirits yet again, she should face the fact that Will Radnor's personality needed a drastic overhaul. Bart startled her out of her reverie.

"What did Charlie and Kate have to say about you riding off into the mountains with Will Radnor?" He spoke from her side, where he had stationed himself as a symbolic guardian since his and Will's run-in. Actually, it probably wasn't symbolic, given his occupation.

That thought worried her. "I left without telling them,"

she admitted a bit uneasily. "Jessie offered to ride out to the ranch and break the news."

"You struck out on your own? How long have you known Radnor?"

His question skirted some unnamed difficulty and raised Priscilla's already tested hackles. "If you have something to say about Will, say it."

Bart didn't reply immediately. They rode across a long valley and up a grassy hillside in silence. Finally he approached the same topic from a different angle. "Your mother's probably fit to be tied, and your father, too."

"You're right about that."

"Why'd you do it?"

"There wasn't a choice, Bart. The Haskels were about to lynch Joaquín—"

"Why didn't you leave his rescue to Radnor?"

The idea stunned her. "To a greenhorn?"

Bart's left eyebrow shot up. She grinned, sheepish.

"You'll understand, once we get to the ranch. I wasn't reared in a conventional manner."

He laughed at that. "Anytime a girl as pretty as you can convince her father to turn her into a cowboy, no, I wouldn't say she was reared in the conventional mores of the day."

"Pa didn't raise me to be a cowboy. Truth known, he fought it every step of the way. Until . . ."

"Until?"

"Until he realized I'd managed to become what I set out to become, a real help to him on Spanish Creek."

"And your mother? How does she feel about it?"

"She tried to turn me into a lady, but, as you see, she didn't get very far."

"On the contrary, Priscilla. You're a lady of the first caliber—lovely, well-mannered, considerate, charming . . ." He studied Will, who rode just beyond earshot. ". . . with poor judgement where men are concerned, like many a lady I've known."

Priscilla felt her face flush. Bart, too? she thought. What was this obvious flaw in Will Radnor which everyone but she herself seemed to notice. Or did everyone else look at him and see a city-slicker and look at her and see a cowboy, and assume they were unsuited to each other? Was she the only person who looked beneath the surface and glimpsed the man Will really was? The man she loved.

Lamely, she changed the subject. "You sound as if you've known my parents a long time."

"I have. A long time."

"How did . . . I mean, if you don't mind my asking, how did you meet?"

He stared into space for a while. When he spoke again, it was quietly. "I'm your mother's stepbrother."

"Stepbrother!"

He nodded.

"I didn't even know. Why haven't I heard this before? You're . . . you're my . . . my uncle."

"Not necessarily. One isn't required to claim step relations."

"How absurd." Priscilla laughed. "We're certainly not in a position to be choosy. I mean . . ." She stopped, abashed at her bad manners; he'd barely finished commending her deportment, and she—

"You mean you're in such dire need of relations, even a washed-up old outlaw might have a chance?"

"More than a chance. Besides, you're not washed-up. You're not even old. I'd guess you and Pa are about the same age."

"Near enough."

"Oh, this is wonderful! Mama'll be so happy!"

"I wouldn't count on it," Bart responded under his breath.

Priscilla was sure she hadn't heard right. A stepbrother was a brother. And an uncle. She'd gone through life without an extended family; now a real uncle had showed up.

Not that Uncle Sog and Uncle Crockett would count less, now that she'd found a real uncle, but . . . *A real uncle.*

She glanced to Will, eager to share her happiness. He was looking at her, staring, rather. He looked apprehensive, then she realized that it was just his habit of staring through her, rather than looking at her.

Will was the first to turn away. One of the many knots that had tied his stomach as tight as a hangman's noose relaxed. She didn't know . . . yet.

He'd listened to the drifting inflections of Priscilla's and Bart's conversation with a goodly measure of dread. Bart Ellisor knew. He knew what had happened to Will's father, he knew who was responsible, and he knew why Will had come to New Mexico Territory. Will had seen it all in the outlaw's expression the first night out.

And every time Bart had caught his attention since. *Stay away from Priscilla,* the outlaw seemed to shout. You can't use her to accomplish your destructive ends.

It was a silent, unspoken warning. But Will hadn't needed even that much. Bart's probing had brought home the magnitude of his mission. No longer was he able to hide the ugly truth beneath his passion for Priscilla. And that fact fueled him with an urgency to be done with the dastardly deed and leave the country.

All day he had wrestled with an inner debate—he should ride ahead, reach the ranch first, finish his own business, and be gone.

On the other hand, he owed Joaquín his expertise. But that was a shallow excuse; there was no denying the truth. Even though Priscilla would soon look at him with loathing and anguish, instead of pleasuring him with beckoning glances like the one he'd just received, he couldn't leave her.

Not until he was forced to. For, damn his hide, in some small part of his stupid brain, he held out hope. Hope that there was a way, a future for them. A future filled with happiness and love. Her laughter trilled down his spine.

"Will! There it is!" She had sprinted to his side and now kept pace.

He followed the line of her outstretched arm. They'd come upon Spanish Creek headquarters from the northeast, the rear. The path down the mountainside was thickly populated with fir and aspen. When he reined his horse to a halt, Priscilla drew up beside him.

"Joaquín has already scouted the trail," she reminded him. "No Haskels on this side."

He looked at her, a mistake.

"I have the most exciting news, Will." She glanced over her shoulder to where Bart trailed twenty or thirty yards behind. "He's my uncle."

"What?"

"Bart Ellisor. He's Mama's stepbrother."

"And you didn't know it?"

She shook her head, pensive for a moment. "I hope it isn't because Mama and Pa are ashamed of his occupation." Her joy bubbled forth again, contagious even in Will's melancholy state. "Wait till they see him," she cried. "They'll be so surprised. Now it all makes sense. Of course, he would pledge to come to Mama's aid. He's kinfolk."

Will listened with half an ear. The other one, and his entire head, buzzed with something much less wonderful— losing this magnificent woman. As if she understood, she caught his cheek in her palm.

"Don't be sad, Will. I know Bart's questions reminded you of your father's death. I know it still hurts. But just wait. As soon as we run the Haskels off Spanish Creek, I'm going to sit Pa down, and Mama, too, and tell them about us. It won't be anytime before they'll love you, too. We'll be so happy. All of us. You'll have a family, then. They'll be your—"

He stopped her the only way he knew how, with his lips.

Disregarding her self-proclaimed outlaw uncle who approached them from the rear, Will reached over, clasped Priscilla behind the neck, and pulled her face to his.

Their lips met eagerly. He kissed her in frantic haste, desperately trying to put all his love and passion and desire into this one last embrace. For that's what it would be, if his plans worked out.

When finally he relaxed his hold on her neck and they drew apart, she had tears in her eyes. He did, too. He could feel their sting.

"Don't worry, Will. One of these days I'm going to succeed in my major mission in life."

He stared through her, hearing her words, knowing only that he was about to succeed in his major mission in life, and it didn't feel anything like it was supposed to.

"Aren't you curious what it is?"

He tried to grin. "What is it, cowboy?"

"To love every last trace of sadness out of you."

He held her gaze, delved deeply into her sparkling blue eyes. As if from a different world, he heard horses approach from either side. Joaquín and Bart. If only it were a different world, he thought. In a different world Priscilla McCain would have no trouble realizing her major mission in life.

"Ready to ride?" Joaquín questioned into the charged hush that had fallen between them. Gaining their attention, he added, "I'll lead the way. Stay close."

Will turned stony eyes to the adobe buildings in the distance. Steeled against what lay ahead, he fell in behind Joaquín. Priscilla came next; Bart pulled up the rear.

Titus Crockett was the first to see them. Once he recognized Joaquín, he hailed the house, and Kate and Jessie came running.

Priscilla hurried ahead. Joaquín followed her. Will and Bart fell behind.

"Don't seem too anxious to get there," Bart commented.

Will studied him hard, letting all the fury inside him meld into a core of fiery anger. "Neither do you, *Uncle* Bart."

Will turned back to the welcoming party, scanned the scene, looking for Charlie, but he was nowhere around. Likely looking for his walking stick, Will thought with a surprising spurt of lightheartedness, which was quelled by a high-pitched scream. Then Priscilla's voice cried, "Mama!"

Tensed against a danger he couldn't immediately locate, Will watched Priscilla run. He saw someone stagger. *Kate.* Jessie reached her first. Then Priscilla.

Will jumped from his horse and ran toward her. At closer range, he noted Kate's white, pasty complexion; she stared past him, her eyes blazing, as though she were witnessing the end of the world. He started to turn around, but her next cry stopped him in his tracks.

"YOU! Stay away from my daughter."

Will's heart thudded to a standstill. If he hadn't been looking at her, he wouldn't have recognized Kate McCain's voice. Strident, harsh, harsher even than when she caught Priscilla in his arms in the barn. That was the first time she'd ordered him to stay away from Priscilla.

Now she was screaming it at him. He felt weak. He knew he deserved her wrath. He should never have agreed to help Priscilla break Joaquín out of jail; he should never have agreed to go with her to Victorio's camp. He should never have looked twice at Priscilla. Moving aside, he glanced around for Charlie. Suddenly he realized that Red Avery was missing, too. Likely gone rock hunting even with the enemy about. Will's spirits rose involuntarily. Less than worthless—

"Get away! Stay away! Stay away from my daughter!"

Will turned back to Kate. With a start, he realized she wasn't screaming at him, after all. Turning, he saw Bart Ellisor, not over three feet behind him, standing stock still, staring at Kate. Not exactly humble, but certainly not threatening. While Will was still struggling to make sense of things, he heard Priscilla's plea.

"Mama, it's Bart. Your brother."

"NO!" Kate's scream, primeval in tone and intensity, rent the stillness. As the sound died away, she began to crumble.

As though captured in a nightmare, Will reacted. He reached Priscilla, took her shoulders, tried to move around her. Kate's head dropped. Before Will could get hold of her, Titus Crockett had moved Jessie aside and scooped Kate in his arms.

"Mama?" Priscilla was almost crying now.

"Carry her inside," Jessie was instructing. "Here let me get the door. Down the hall . . . The bedroom . . ."

Priscilla gripped Will's hand in a tight fist. He held on, while she pulled him through the door and into the cavernous interior of the cool adobe house.

"What is it?" he asked.

"I don't know."

They reached the bedroom. Will stopped in the doorway. Priscilla released him and rushed to her mother's side. He watched her kneel on the striped Navajo throw rug, reach for her mother's hand, lay her cheek against it.

Jessie moved toward him, carrying a water pitcher. She shook her head sadly, as if he were supposed to know what the hell was going on.

"Where's Charlie?" he asked.

Jessie's stricken expression caused Will's own knees to go weak.

"They've got him. Newt and Oscar."

In two steps Will reached Priscilla. Bending close, he took her by the shoulders and whispered against her ear. "I'll be right back, cowboy." When he felt her tremble, he took a chance and kissed her cheek for reassurance.

Out in the kitchen Jessie was pumping water to fill the clay pitcher. Words stuck in Will's throat. He stared at her, silently demanding an explanation.

"They're calling it an arrest."

"Arrest? How? When? For God's sake, why?"

Jessie set the pitcher on the table. She ran slender fingers around its mouth, staring through Will as if she were looking at something long gone and far away.

"Newt told me their plans," she said. "After he . . ." She lifted her hand and tenderly touched the large blue and yellow bruise beneath her right eye. Will's stomach turned at the sight of her battered face, evidence of Newt Haskel's brutality.

"That sonofabitch—"

Jessie continued as if he hadn't spoken. "They were going into the mountains after you and Priscilla. You know Charlie. Nothing would do but for him to ride out and find Priscilla."

Tipping his head back, Will stared at the ancient ceiling—pole vigas interspersed with rows of latillas. "And they caught him?"

"*Sí.* My guess is that's what they planned all along. They knew Charlie would ride to hell and back for Priscilla."

"How do you know they didn't just kill him?"

"Newt came in under a white flag to tell us they had Charlie, said he *arrested* him for masterminding the jail break."

"Masterminding! Hell fire, Jess, Charlie didn't even know about it until it was over."

"What does that matter? To a Haskel, I mean. The end justifies the means, Will. I thought you'd learned that by now."

"I should have." He let his eyes travel over her battered face. "Looks like you've learned it, too."

"It took me a bit longer. Guess I'm thicker-skulled than most." She smiled, rueful. "Fortunately, I suppose, else he'd have succeeded in kicking out what few brains I have."

Will crossed to the door, unable to look at Jessie's healing wounds, the price she'd paid for Joaquín's freedom. Balling a fist he thrust it into his opposite palm, again and again and again. "I hope Joaquín's satisfied."

"It wasn't Joaquín's fault."

"Nothing's ever anybody's fault. If folks could learn to live and let live, to take what life hands out and try to make something better out of it, instead of always tearing down, destroying—"

"Is that why you came to Spanish Creek, Will? To live and let live, to forgive and put the past behind you?"

By the time Jessie finished, Will had turned and was staring at her, wide-eyed. "She told you?"

"That, and a whole lot more," Jessie acknowledged.

Will's heart filled with infinite sadness. "Now you know how futile your matchmaking efforts were."

"Now I know. But you and Priscilla aren't the only ones hurt. Kate McCain has enough on her plate right now to test the mettle of a saint. First Priscilla runs off to the mountains with a Radnor, then Charlie's captured by the Haskels, and now Bart Ellisor rides in with her daughter."

"What's the story on Bart?"

Jessie picked up the water pitcher. "That one isn't mine to tell."

"I don't even want to hear it. Right now all I'm worried about is telling Priscilla—"

"Telling me what?"

Lifting his stricken gaze, he found hers. She stood in the doorway. He could tell she'd been crying and was even now fighting to restrain more tears.

Without one thought wasted on either the past or the future, Will crossed the room and took her in his arms. Priscilla needed him. That was all. Plain and simple. But when he tried to draw her close, to cradle her head against his shoulder, she pulled away.

"Tell me what, Will? What's happened to Pa?"

Priscilla clutched Will's arms at the wrists. She felt his pulse beat against her fingers, saw it throb in the vein in his neck. His gaze bore steadily into hers, increasing her fear. "What, Will?"

"He's in jail . . ." Turning a raised eyebrow to Jessie for confirmation, Will added, ". . . in Santa Fé?"

Jessie nodded.

"Jail?" Priscilla turned to Jessie, too. "I don't understand."

"The Haskels live by the law of the barbarian, *chica*. The end justifies the means."

Somewhere in the distant reaches of her brain, Priscilla saw the cuts and bruises on Jessie's face. They didn't look right; something was wrong. Panic grew like yeast inside her. She thought her body might explode. She visualized parts of herself flying around the kitchen, her head, her arms, her heart.

"They claim Charlie masterminded Joaquín's escape," Jessie repeated for Priscilla.

"Masterminded?" The word whooshed through Priscilla's lips.

"They're holding him, in Newt's words, until he signs papers transferring ownership of Spanish Creek to them, or until hell freezes over, whichever comes first.' "

Priscilla heard the words. Gradually they came into focus; it was like seeing a tree on the crest of a distant hill, then riding toward it, bringing the image into sharper and sharper focus. Her mind cleared. She stepped back from Will.

"I'm going after him." Her voice was steady. She noticed, because her body still trembled inside. "They'll regret the day they ever heard of Spanish Creek Ranch."

"That isn't the answer, cowboy."

"No?" She looked at Jessie again, suddenly realizing what her brain had seen the first time—Jessie's battered face. "Newt's revenge?"

Jessie's hand went to her face. "It's nothing—"

"Nothing! When are you—when is everybody—going to

wake up? After they kill us all? Nothing? They stole our cattle, drove off our cowboys, shot Pa, beat you up. They threatened to lynch Joaquín, and now they've *arrested* Pa. Nothing? How much more will it take . . ."

"Priscilla?" Will reached for her, but she swerved aside. Her eyes scanned the room, the walls. She felt like a caged animal.

"I'm going after Pa, Will. Are you riding with me?"

"That isn't the way," he repeated.

Her breath came so short it momentarily choked her. For one brief moment, she gazed into Will's eyes and wanted to throw herself in his arms. But the Haskels had Pa.

Despair flooded her. "Those bastards have taken the last thing they're going to take from me. Get your gun, Will. Ride with me."

This time when he reached for her he grabbed her arms and held on. "Calm down, Priscilla. Let's discuss—"

"Then don't come." She jerked free. "I'll go—"

"Damnit, no you won't go. Not alone. Not with me. Not with anyone else." His voice lowered, became a plea, soft and gentle. "They've got Charlie. All they need is you, and it'll all be over. Charlie'll sign those papers quicker'n you can shoot a petal off a sunflower blossom, if he knows they have you."

"Will's right, *chica*. Charlie was livid when he saw how Newt treated me. If it were you . . ."

Priscilla couldn't believe her ears. "All right. You don't have to help. I don't need you, anyway." She fixed a dagger glare on Will, her chin thrust into the air. "Uncle Bart will help." Turning, she stomped through the back door.

The door hadn't finished slamming, when a shrill cry broke out behind Will. He turned to see Kate clutching the door facing, her eyes wild.

"Stop her, Mr. Radnor. Stop her, please."

Will struggled to grasp the situation.

"Don't let her go near that man."

Will's eyes flared. "Who, Mrs. McCain?"

"Bart Ellisor. Don't let Priscilla—keep him away from my daughter."

Will looked to Jessie, who nodded. "Go after her, Will. I'll help Kate back to bed."

Will sprinted across the clearing that separated the house from the barn, imagining Haskel bullets flying in all directions. But that was nothing compared to the turmoil inside him. What the hell was going on? Whatever Bart Ellisor was guilty of must be pretty damned bad, for it had suddenly raised his standing with Kate McCain—and he knew she hadn't forgotten why he had come to Spanish Creek. She'd told Jessie about it.

By the time Will reached the tack room, where Joaquín and Bart were hunkered on a stack of feed sacks, Priscilla was already presenting her case to Bart.

"Where's Red?" she was asking. "He'll go, too."

"Red lit out," Crockett said. "Right after they took your pa. Guess he couldn't stand the heat."

Red Avery was gone. Will tried to dredge up some sort of joy over that development, but the peril they faced was much more threatening than the disappearance of a less-than-worthless archaeologist, even if Priscilla had threatened to marry the no-account . . .

Stepping behind her, Will took Priscilla by the shoulders and held her against her initial struggle to free herself. "Listen to me, Priscilla. I have an idea. You may reject it. But I'd appreciate you taking time to listen."

"There isn't time, greenhorn." Fury sounded in every syllable.

"There's always time to consider a better plan." He didn't actually agree with that, but it had been the first thing that came to mind. Law school hadn't prepared him for dealing with hurt and determined women, especially not with a woman he loved so much he'd throw himself on a loaded cannon to save her from harm. Which, he decided, wasn't far from what was required here. "I'll go."

Her fury evaporated. "Oh, Will—"

"Alone."

Fury returned. She jerked to free herself, but he held fast. "Listen. Just listen."

"Won't hurt to listen, Priscilla," Bart put in. "I've never had much luck with an operation when I started out half-cocked."

Will felt her stiffen, but he tugged her around to face him, anyway. Her eyes were red and they brimmed with tears waiting to be shed. But that didn't dim their determination.

When he relaxed his hold, she shook free. But she stood her ground. "I'm waiting," she said. "But not for long."

"I'm the only person here the Haskels will deal with."

"What makes you special?"

"I'm a lawyer. A good one. And they know it, they hired me. They're breaking the law right and left, and I can call them on it in technical terms that might carry some weight."

"That sounds like a greenhorn—stupid."

"Maybe, but it's true. If you ride out there, they'll capture you. Kidnap you." Despair and fear welled inside Will. "Damnit, Priscilla, you saw what Newt did to Jessie, and he's been sleeping with her for a year."

Priscilla crossed her arms, clasped them with the opposite hands. Will covered her hands with his.

"Trying to hide your fear? You can't do it, cowboy, and it's justified. Those are madmen out there."

"They have Pa. I'm going after him."

"Another jailbreak?"

She glared, neither agreeing or denying.

"After you break him out of jail, then what? Another race into the mountains?"

She tilted her chin.

"While you're gone, saying you make it that far, they'll take Spanish Creek. Sure as shootin'."

"You have all the answers?"

"No." His admission surprised her enough that her guard dropped, exposing the terror beneath her bravado. "But if I ride out there under a white flag, same way Newt came here, I may be able to get some answers."

"They won't turn him loose just because you tell them to."

"I know."

Bart made a show of rising, dusting off his britches. "I've had my fingers in enough spoiled pies to know what kind of fellers we're dealing with here. Radnor's idea is worth a try."

Will slid his hands up her arms; he clasped them behind her neck, forming a support for her to lean against. He felt her muscles, tight as a coiled rattler.

"I could ride with you," she said.

Pursing his lips, he shook his head. "Your mama's had enough to worry about lately. Stay with her. She needs you more than Charlie does, right now."

She neither spoke nor moved, but he felt her muscles sag against his hands. He stared at her, loving her, hurting for her. Tears gathered in the corners of her eyes and brimmed. Just before they spilled over, he brought her to his chest, cradled her like a baby.

"Come on, Joaquín." Bart's voice was gruff. "Let's go saddle up a cayuse for Radnor."

Her tears came then, pouring from her eyes, soaking his shirt front. He held her tight, crooning softly, "It'll be all right. We'll work it out. It'll be all right."

"Oh, Will, I was so wrong."

"There, there."

"It isn't Spanish Creek I love, it's Pa. And now he's in jail, and they might . . . lynch him . . . for something I did—"

"Not for anything you did. They'd have gotten Charlie, one way or another. And if we hadn't gotten Joaquín out of that jail, they'd have lynched him. I know that now."

"But . . ." Her sobbing became erratic. "I just hope Pa knows . . . it's not Spanish Creek . . . it's him . . ."

"He knows."

"But I've never told him. What if he . . . We have to save him. He can't . . . I'd want to die if anything happened to Pa. Help me, please."

Will's arms tightened around her. His heart felt like it might actually break. He knew it would if he turned her loose—*when* he turned her loose. He buried his face in her hair and wished he could stand this way forever, holding her, loving her. "I'll do my best, cowboy."

Bart brought Will's horse, and he stepped astride.

Crockett scared up a salt sack he'd tied to a limb. "Wave it high," he admonished.

"Take it slow," Bart cautioned.

Will looked down at Priscilla.

"Please, Will . . ."

"Run to the house," he said. "Stay close to your mother."

She stared at him, her eyes red, her face swollen. She seemed about to fall apart. He wanted desperately to hold her a while longer, to take her to the house and tuck her in bed and sit beside her until she remembered that she was a strong woman; until she realized that her world would still turn without Spanish Creek, without her father, without himself.

Riding away from the adobe ranchhouse, Will tried to slough off his apprehension. Priscilla would be all right. All he had to do was pull a piece of magic out of the air and save Charlie McCain, then Priscilla would be all right.

He recalled thinking not too long ago that a man would have a hard time living up to Charlie's image in Priscilla's mind. Now she'd said as much. Which was just as well, since he could never have her anyway.

But when he rode away from that barn with her pleas for him to save her father ringing in his ears, Will couldn't keep from wishing that she'd shown a tiny bit of concern for his own safety.

"Those are the demands, Oscar. Take 'em or leave 'em."

"I think we'll leave 'em, Yank."

Will had ridden a mile or so up the western mountainside before he came upon the Haskel camp. His skin fairly crawled with the images of their brutality fresh in his mind. He didn't recognize the man who stepped in front of his horse, and the interloper didn't introduce himself.

"I've come to bargain with Oscar Haskel."

The man leered, revealing a mouthful of tobacco-stained teeth. "He'll bargain, that's fer shore." Without asking permission, the guard took hold of Will's reins and led the horse behind some brush.

It was a setup that bespoke permanency, Will noticed immediately. The Haskels weren't skirmishing, they'd come to win the war. Two pitched tents, a plank table with long benches to either side, rifles stacked around trees—he guessed a couple, three dozen of them. Oscar had dug in and was loaded for out-and-out war. Visions of Priscilla charging into this camp set his temper on edge.

Will sat his horse, trying to regain his cool. Oscar Haskel bent his head and stepped through the opening of one of the tents. His left arm was in a sling, but that didn't seem to slow him down. He didn't ask Will to step down, and Will wasn't sure he'd be inclined to do so if invited.

"Joey here says you've come to bargain."

"That's right."

"Well, now, there isn't much left to bargain with, way I see it. Spanish Creek . . ." Oscar paused and looked from side to side, as if to establish the fact that he had already taken some of Charlie's range. "Spanish Creek belongs to me. Charlie went to a lot of trouble to break that half-breed out of jail—"

"Charlie had nothing to do with that jailbreak." Will glared at Oscar. No, he thought again, being short an arm hadn't slowed the man down. Hell, the way Oscar operated, he could afford to have both arms in slings. Oscar Haskel paid men to do his shooting for him.

"What proof do you have?" Oscar demanded.

"A man is innocent until proven guilty, Oscar. What proof do *you* have?" Will fully expected Oscar to boast that he needed no proof. But he didn't. That was more Newt's style. Will glanced around. "Where's Newt?"

"Newt? Gone to town. That little *señorita* of his turned on him, but he's found another. You know Newt, can't stay away from the women. Never saw a woman who could keep him satisfied more'n—"

"I've come on business."

Oscar Haskel stopped talking. With a generous amount of disdain, he stuffed the cigar back in his mouth. "Business? What business?"

"I've brought an ultimatum." Will suppressed a grin at Oscar's surprise, but he reminded himself it was only surprise, not surrender.

"As an officer of the courts of the Territory of New Mexico, I'm drawing up papers that charge you and Newt with various crimes: two counts of false imprisonment; two counts of harassment; and Newt with one count of assault with intent to commit murder."

"Murder? Newt didn't murder anyone."

"Have you had a good look at Miss Laredo's face?"

Oscar chomped on his cigar.

"I don't doubt the injuries extend to other parts of her body, but her face is evidence enough."

"Ol' Newt may have kicked that bitch around, but he never set out to murder her."

"No? Well, the charge will be filed and Newt can explain for himself."

"Listen here, Yank. I've had about all I intend to take of your high-prancin' city ways. I told you before and I'm tellin' you again—one last time—we do things differently out here."

"And I'm telling you again and for the last time, Oscar, New Mexico Territory belongs to the United States and is bound by the laws of the land." In a sudden gesture of bravado, Will waved his fist at Oscar Haskel. "If Charlie McCain isn't sitting at his own kitchen table by noon tomorrow—in good health—I'm riding into Santa Fé to file the charges as outlined."

"File 'em, Yank. File 'em. See what good it does."

Futility swept over Will, but he didn't let it show. "It'll do some good, Oscar. Maybe not the first time, but I won't give up. You can kill Charlie, you can take this damned ranch, but the only way you can stop me now is to shoot me in the back when I ride out of here." The thought crossed Will's mind that he was beginning to sound a lot like Priscilla. Maybe that's what it took to live around such lawless men.

Oscar removed the cigar from his mouth again. "That half-breed, Wounded Eagle, ride in with you?"

Will glared without responding.

"Reckon that means he did. When Newt gets back, he'll be comin' in after him."

Will pulled the reins against his horse's neck.

"You're a fool, Radnor, you know that? A fool. Risking your life for a little piece of land that doesn't even belong to you."

Suddenly Will had had enough. He turned a harsh eye on the arrogant man. "I'm not risking my life for a little piece of land, Oscar. I'm risking it for a great, big piece— the United States of America."

Oscar Haskel frowned, showing Will his unbounded ignorance.

"Unless we're willing to risk all for the law of the land anytime and everywhere it's threatened, we won't have a country to risk our lives for. Law and order, Haskel. You took an oath to uphold it, same as I did."

Fifteen

Priscilla stood in the clearing and watched Will ride away. Behind her Bart lounged in the shadow of the barn door.

"Do what Radnor suggested," he said. "Run to the house."

Priscilla's eyes remained fastened on Will's disappearing figure. "Do you think he can do it?"

"Radnor? Who knows? Like he said, it's worth a try."

"Mama hates him." When Bart didn't comment, she turned around.

"Likely she has her reasons," he observed. "Mamas usually do."

"There is no reason. How could there be? She's only known him a few weeks. Of course, he's a greenhorn, but he's shaping up real nice. He worked for the Haskels when he first came to town." This idea cheered her. "He should have proved by now which side he's on. If he can persuade Oscar Haskel to set Pa free—"

"Priscilla. Your mother needs you at the house."

Priscilla followed Bart's line of vision to where her mother stood in the back door staring toward them. From the distance Priscilla couldn't read her expression, but she was obviously distraught. Those blasted Haskels!

"Come with me, Bart. She needs us both."

"Right now all she needs is you—and to know that her little girl is safe."

"But you're—"

"I'll help Joaquín and Crockett keep watch. With Charlie gone, that'll ease Kate's mind a lot more than having me underfoot."

"You're so understanding." She watched him glance again toward the back door where Mama waited.

"I've had a lot of years to learn, honey."

His tone was pensive. Without thinking, Priscilla threw her arms around his neck. He flinched when she touched him, and when she kissed his cheek, he drew back as if she'd put a branding iron to him. "I'm so glad we found you. And that you're my uncle."

He remained unresponsive. She knew she'd embarrassed him. An old outlaw like him, having a girl throw her arms around him and kiss him in broad open daylight. But blast it, he was her uncle.

"Give us time," she told him. "Pretty soon you'll be so comfortable around us, you'll never want to leave." She recalled promising Will a family. From the sound of things Bart Ellisor needed one, too. "We're your family, Uncle Bart."

"I gave up families a long time ago, honey."

"No—"

"I'm better off this way, so you don't go tryin' to change things."

From the kitchen door Kate watched Priscilla stare after Will Radnor. She saw her turn back toward the barn. Kate's stomach bunched in knots. She gripped the doorframe with a tight fist. She was on the verge of calling out, when Priscilla threw her arms around a shadowy figure, drawing him into the light. *Bart Ellisor.*

Kate's knees started to buckle. She tightened her grip. Her daughter in the arms of Bart Ellisor! How much more could she take and remain sane? First, Priscilla had run off to the mountains with Will Radnor, then the Haskels abducted Charlie, now Priscilla in the arms of . . . of that demon.

Strengthened by fear for Priscilla, Kate hurried down the walk. Priscilla turned suddenly and hailed her.

"Coming, Mama."

Kate caught her breath. Her life sped by. The only life she had ever allowed herself to recall. Her life here at Spanish Creek with her family—Charlie and Priscilla.

When Priscilla ran toward the house, Kate saw her as the little tomboy she'd despaired of ever growing to womanhood. Britches and boots and crooked pigtails. Not even washing her mouth out with soap had stopped Priscilla's occasional bout of cursing.

She couldn't count the number of times in the last few years when she'd tried to get Priscilla into a corset and petticoats. She still hadn't succeeded, but her daughter's sudden fancy for lacy camisoles and silk shirts had been sign enough that Priscilla knew what she wanted.

And what Priscilla wanted, she usually got. They hadn't exactly spoiled her, but there hadn't been any reason to deny her the freedom she thrived on out here at the ranch.

And what joy that little girl had brought her! Pure joy for nineteen years, joy enough to erase much of the despicable past and give Kate herself a second chance at happiness.

Deep inside she'd always known boots and britches wouldn't be enough for Priscilla. Beautiful, passionate, and idealistic as only the young can be, Priscilla had been destined to find a man. A man who would change her, show her the joys of being a woman.

But never would Kate have believed, not in all her many visions of that day, that when it arrived, it would be so ghastly. Of all the men in the world, Priscilla had fallen in love with Will Radnor. And as if that weren't enough, she'd brought Bart Ellisor back into their lives.

"Mama, you shouldn't be out here." Reaching Kate, Priscilla threw an arm around her shoulders and turned her toward the house. "Joaquín and Uncle Bart will keep watch."

Kate's feet ground to a halt. "That man is *not* your uncle."

"He said—"

"He can claim to be God, Priscilla, but he is *not* related to you."

"But . . . Why would he lie?"

Kate drew a shaky breath. Without fully realizing it, she allowed Priscilla to guide her back to the kitchen. As from afar, she heard voices.

"I'll help you get her to bed, Priscilla."

"I'll do it, Jessie. Why don't you fix her some tea? You'll find violet leaves in the right-hand cupboard. That should relax her." Kate felt Priscilla's arms around her shoulders. "Will's gone to try to talk some sense into Oscar Haskel, Mama."

Kate barely heard her. She felt helpless, yet somehow full of strength. Like a mother cougar in the mountains surrounding Spanish Creek, her one thought was to protect her daughter. "That man! Stay away from him, Priscilla."

Priscilla sighed audibly. "Don't worry about that now, Mama."

"I have to. You don't know—"

"I know Will's helping us get Pa back. That's the important thing. We'll get him back. Then everything will be fine."

"Nothing will be fine!" Kate pulled away. She scanned the kitchen. The walls seemed to move, to fall inward. Any minute they would crush her. She shielded her head with her arms.

Priscilla tried to pry them down. "Let me help you back to bed. I'm sure you haven't had any rest since Pa's been gone and even before . . . since I pulled that terrible stunt."

Kate peered through her arms. "What stunt, Priscilla?"

"Breaking Joaquín out of jail." She tugged again at her mother's arms. "I didn't mean to worry you, Mama."

As from a distance, Kate heard her little girl's voice, begging for something. Priscilla rarely begged. She usually got her way without it.

"I didn't realize how worried you would be," Priscilla was saying. "I thought it was the only way to save Joaquín's life. And you did want that, didn't you, Mama?"

Kate stared vacantly, trying to grasp Priscilla's words, to understand. What was happening to her child? To her world?

"I didn't know Pa would come after me. I didn't know they'd arrest him. I thought Bart would get here to help him defend Spanish Creek."

Bart. Bart Ellisor. And Priscilla. Bart and Priscilla. Alone together.

"How long?" Kate demanded.

"How long for what?"

"How long were you out there together?"

"Mama, I'm trying to be patient—and to understand. I'm sorry I worried you, but nothing bad happened to me in the mountains. Nothing bad at all."

"You were with *him*. That's bad . . ."

"Blast it all, Mama!" Priscilla was almost shouting. Priscilla never shouted, not at her. Sometimes at Charlie, but never at her. "I'm home and I'm safe, but Pa's out there. It's Pa we should be worrying about."

"Your father would die if . . ."

"Hush. Just hush. I'm in love with Will Radnor, and he's in love with me. There's nothing you or Pa can do to change that. Right now I'm too worried about Pa to talk about it." Kate felt Priscilla tug harder on her arm. "Come to bed, Mama. Jessie's making you some violet tea—"

Kate jerked away. "I won't drink it. I won't let you put me to sleep. I have to protect you from that . . . from that man!"

"For heaven's sake, Mama, Will isn't even here. There's nothing to protect me from—"

"Not from Will Radnor. From Bart."

Priscilla turned her loose. With the small bit of sanity left Kate, she watched her daughter's face contort in disgust. *Good,* she thought. *Good, she sees Bart for what he is.* But Priscilla's next words were angry. Almost hateful.

"Oh, Mama, how could you even think such a thing? You raised me. You loved me. Don't you know me? How could you accuse me of . . . of . . . such indecency?"

Kate heard Priscilla's angry pleas. Her hurt. But the truth was heavy, overwhelmingly painful. Her poor baby. "It isn't you, Priscilla. It's them . . . it's Bart."

"That's disgusting!" Priscilla was shouting at her. Really shouting this time. "Go ahead, imagine me with all the men in the world. I don't care. All I care about is Pa. And I'll do whatever it takes to free him. Even if it means giving up Spanish Creek."

As though a whirlwind had blown up and swept her off, Priscilla swirled away. Kate reached for her, but too late. The back door was already slamming.

"Here, Kate." Jessie placed a steaming cup on the table. She pulled out a chair and guided Kate to it. "Sit down and drink this. I'll go after her."

Kate sat, suddenly weak. It was the fear. Tears brimmed in her eyes. When Jessie left, she would cry. When Jessie left . . .

Jessie didn't leave. "Kate, I may be speaking out of line, but . . . I mean, I never had a daughter. Actually, I never had a mother, not one who was strong enough to fight for me. But the way I see it, you need to explain things to Priscilla."

The suggestion brought Kate's head up with a snap. "What?"

"Explain things. Everything. About Will Radnor. And about Bart."

"No." Kate stared aghast. "Never!"

"She needs to know, Kate. She deserves the truth."

"No."

"Don't you understand how hurt she'll be? When this is all over, even if Will manages to get Charlie back, everything will come to a head. There's no other way, now. And it's Priscilla who'll be hurt the most."

Kate inhaled, finding the horror of Jessie's words somehow soothing. That was reality. Priscilla, her daughter, whom she would protect at all costs, to herself or even to Charlie.

She stared into the steaming cup of tea that was supposed to put her to sleep. To sleep, when she must remain awake and in possession of all her faculties in order to protect Priscilla. Especially with Charlie gone. He would expect her to protect Priscilla. She tried the tea, a sip, then a larger swallow.

"She needs you," Jessie was saying. "More than she needs Charlie." Jessie patted Kate's arm. "Men aren't always good at understanding broken hearts. Oh, they suffer them, same as women, but they tend to go out and kick a fence post a few times or chop some wood. After they work out the rawness, they put the rest of their pain into some locked corner of their brains. Women are different. Priscilla will carry her hurt over Will Radnor to her grave. You know that, Kate."

Kate's eyes at last focused on the woman across the table.

"You know that," Jessie repeated directly to Kate's face. "So do I. Priscilla needs you. Now, because you're both scared to death for Charlie. Later, because she will have been denied the love of her life."

"I didn't mean . . ."

"No one could have prevented this," Jessie was saying. "No one. But now it's done, and you alone can hold her and console her and show her that regardless of how life treats her, she can go on. You'll be her example, Kate. An example she's going to need. But you can't be anything to her until you tell her the truth."

Kate held Jessie's piercing gaze. She allowed Jessie's words to take form and meaning. Jessie was right. Priscilla needed and deserved the truth. Her tears began to flow. She made no attempt to halt them. They poured down her face, dripped onto the table. She watched one splash into her cup of tea. Deep inside Kate, truth and shame squared off, and the winner was her fear for her beloved daughter.

"Come, Kate. Let me help you to bed. Then I'll find Priscilla."

Kate squared her shoulders against an overpowering weight. She stared at the far wall, seeing nothing but a mesmerizing gray haze. And her own mother.

Her own mother who could never talk, never share, so Kate had never been allowed to heal. Not until Charlie. Memories rushed back to her, displayed in vivid color against that misty gray haze. It had happened not long after her mother married Bart's father. A few months, maybe. She'd been fifteen, Bart eighteen. And on a lazy summer day while their parents were in town, Bart Ellisor . . . Bart Ellisor lured her . . . into the barn . . .

Kate dropped her head to the table. Tears poured forth . . . into the barn and . . . raped her.

"I'll bring Priscilla to your room," Jessie was saying.

Kate looked up. She tried to focus on Jessie, but all she could see was a fuzzy, undulating form. Arms tingling with weakness, she struggled to free herself from Jessie's hold.

"Come, Kate."

"NO!" She was as out of breath as if she had climbed Wheeler Peak. "No. I can't . . . please. I can't."

Jessie's grip relaxed. She felt Jessie's hand, soothing on her head. Inside her, everything turned black. At last, she knew how her own mother had felt. Weak, not from lack of love or understanding, but weak, sick and weak, from fear, not for herself, but for her daughter.

* * *

Will found Priscilla in the barn, hunkered in a corner of Sargeant's stall, sobbing into her drawn-up knees.

His heart stopped beating. *They'd told her. Kate had told her . . . about him.*

Stiff with apprehension, he managed to kneel before her. Threading fingers through her hair on either side of her head, he lifted her face to his. Gently, he kissed her, first her forehead, then her lips, expecting her to withdraw in disgust at any moment.

"Pa? Did you . . . Did they listen?"

"I gave Oscar until noon tomorrow to release him."

Her eyes searched his for answers he didn't have. "Don't ask me if they'll do it, Miss Priss. We'll just have to wait and see."

When tears brimmed in her eyes again, he pulled her to his chest. "Come here, cowboy." Lifting her until they were both on their knees, he snugged her against him. "I haven't had a hug in way too long." He felt her chest rise and fall, tremulously. "Try not to worry so much, love. If this doesn't work, we'll find another way."

"I know, but Mama . . ."

"How is she?"

"Terrible. I think she's losing her mind. She . . . she told me . . . she believes . . ."

Damnation! Kate had told her. For a minute Will had thought otherwise. Fear worked its debilitating havoc inside him. He felt physically sick and sick at heart. He sat on his heels and held Priscilla. His heart thrashed so violently, it choked in his throat, and he had trouble speaking. When he managed to, they were the hardest words he'd ever tried to utter. "I'm sorry, Priscilla. I'm . . . so sorry. I wanted . . . no, that's wrong. I didn't want to, but since you had to find out, I wanted to be the one to tell you."

"You? How did you know?"

"I . . . What are you talking about?"

"How Mama feels about Bart."

"Bart?" Will closed his eyes. A wave of relief washed over him. He kissed her softly, for reassurance—for himself as much as for her. Relief? Short-lived, at best. "What about Bart, love?"

"Oh, Will, it's terrible. Mama thinks I've been . . ." In the dimly lit stall, Will watched splotches of red blossom on Priscilla's cheeks. ". . . that we've, Bart and I . . . I mean, she thinks I've been with him . . ."

Embarrassed, she might be, but Will could tell she was even more distressed and confused. She stared him right in the eye, finishing with, "She thinks I've been with him, like . . . like us."

"Damn!"

"Why would she think that?"

"I don't know."

"She says Bart isn't my uncle. She said, 'He can claim to be God, Priscilla, but he is not related to you.'"

"Your mother's under a lot of stress."

"I didn't realize how much she would worry about me being in the mountains . . ." She shrugged. "With *two* men. I'm surprised she didn't include Joaquín in it."

Will nipped soft kisses over her face. He hadn't intended to kiss her, not ever again. He'd promised himself he wouldn't hold her, that he wouldn't even touch her.

But she needed him now. *And who would she have later?* His guilty conscience needled him. *Who? After you've finished destroying her world?* But that was later, this was now.

She needed him now. He eased them down until they were lying face to face in the sweet-smelling hay. And he needed her. Lordy, how he needed her. "You weren't with *two* men."

She snuggled against him, disturbing and pleasing and arousing all at the same time. She was good at that. Better than anyone ever had been before or ever would be again. Priscilla was all things to him, lover, companion, partner, competitor, even. Priscilla was perfect, for him, anyway.

As if to confirm it, his lips angled over hers in perfect union; he snugged her softness into the hard contours of his frame. No one had ever felt as good against him. No one ever would. Yes, Priscilla was perfect in every way but one—she was Charlie McCain's daughter.

When their kisses deepened and their need grew, he drew back. "Not here, love."

"Where?"

"I don't know." He nipped her nose with his lips, and grinned. "You live here, I don't."

"One day you will."

The idea fitted. Somehow, damnit, it fitted. He feigned chagrin. "Is that so? You have my life all planned, huh?"

She smiled that damned smile. "All of it, greenhorn. We'll start by convincing Pa that you're . . ."

As his lips covered hers, halting her impossible dream, at least halting her expression of it, he realized that he'd done this before. It seemed to be the only way he had of keeping Priscilla quiet. And oh such a sweet, delicious way to quell the bitter, repulsive truth.

"RIDERS COMING!"

Bart's alarm resounded from the guard post in the center cupola on the barn roof.

Priscilla and Will rose as one.

"Pa?"

Will raced to the adjoining stall, where he jerked his rifle from his saddle scabbard. "Wait and see." He scrambled up the ladder leading to the loft. By the time he reached the second ladder, the one that led to the cupola where Bart was on duty, Priscilla had caught up with him. Bart apprised them of the situation in curt shouts.

"They aren't friends, that much is certain. Three of 'em.

Ridin' wary. Comin' from the north. Must have learned it from us heathens."

Before Will could stop her, Priscilla tugged his rifle from his hand and scrambled up the ladder.

Gaining the cupola, she called down. "It's Newt."

"Is Charlie with him?" Will followed, wedging himself into the tight space between Priscilla and Bart. No sign of Charlie McCain.

Joaquín and Crockett stood at the foot of the ladder, while the three in the cupola watched three riders pick their way through the trees, emerging finally into the clearing behind the cluster of adobe outbuildings. They were headed for the house. When they were within earshot, Priscilla shouted to them.

"Where's my pa, Newt Haskel?"

The sheriff drew rein. "Exactly where he's gonna stay, Jake. In jail."

"Oscar agreed to turn him loose."

Newt hooted loudly. "We ain't gonna turn no one loose, Jake. We've come to arrest us another outlaw."

"You'll get no one here."

She watched Newt speak to the men on either side of him. They tugged at their reins and started to fan out.

"Stay where you are," she ordered,

They pulled rein.

"Send out that half-breed outlaw and we'll be on our way."

"Joaquín is no outlaw, Newt. You're the outlaws." Her words hadn't died away before she lifted Will's rifle and fired a warning shot.

"Priscilla!" Will jerked on the rifle. She wrenched it, keeping control.

"Priscilla, damnit, don't—"

"Turn loose, greenhorn." She elbowed him in the ribs and raised the rifle to her face again.

He'd have to give Newt credit, Will thought, the man

held his ground. "Send him out, Jake. We know he's around here someplace. Send him out, or we're comin' in."

Priscilla fired. Once, twice, three times. Will lost count. He couldn't take his eyes off her. He dared not look at Newt and his cohorts. Her expression was one he knew well, cocky. Surely—

The gunfire died away; the shrill neighs of frightened horses filled the air. Will chanced a look. All three riders fought to control their mounts and keep their seats while their horses reared and pitched. No reins. She'd shot the damned reins!

He looked back at her. With two fingers she tipped the brim of an imaginary Stetson. Cocky. The smile was there, too. That smile that won him over every time. Damn! Her world might be falling apart, but her pluck and spirit shone through. This time when he reached for the rifle, she let him take it.

"Party's over, Newt," he called down. "Next time's for blood."

"You won't get away with this."

"Tell Oscar I expect him to honor our agreement. Charlie McCain is to be sitting at his kitchen table by noon tomorrow. If he isn't, we're coming after you." Will watched anger flush the face of the man below.

"You'll pay hell comin' after the law, Radnor."

"You've had about all the chances the law allows," Will returned. "Now get out of here."

While those in the cupola watched, Newt and his cronies conferred, then, following the sheriff's lead, they filed back up the hillside they had descended so confidently only a few short minutes before.

Priscilla broke the silence. "Let's see, greenhorn, Stetsons are larger targets, so three sets of reins should count more than six Stetsons."

At her teasing, Will turned to see that playful smile. Innocence personified, he thought. "I'll consider it."

"You aren't ready to concede?"

"Not by a long shot. But you might be able to change my mind. What's your best offer?"

"You two are crazy," Bart broke in.

"Maybe." Unable to resist, Will took Priscilla in his arms and kissed her. As his lips descended, he grinned, "But it sure beats the heck out of almost anything else for fun, doesn't it, cowboy?"

"No sane man calls that fun," Bart groused. "This thing's far from over. There's trouble ahead, Radnor, in case you forgot. What're you planning to do about that?"

Will lifted his lips. His hands slipped from Priscilla's back to her arms, which he gripped. He couldn't turn her loose. It was as if by holding her, touching her, he could retain control, when he knew and Bart knew there was no chance for such a thing.

Finally he looked away from Priscilla's blue eyes, off toward Santa Fé, where Charlie was in jail. Maybe he should go in now, today, and have it out.

Priscilla slipped an arm around his waist. It felt good, so good. He recalled her mother's wild imagination. Jealousy speared through his gut. He couldn't stand to think about Priscilla in another man's arms—be it Bart or anyone else.

"Those fellows are out for blood," Bart observed.

Will pushed Priscilla toward the ladder, knowing that was what Bart was after, separating him and Priscilla. Hell, whether he was a relation or not, he surely acted like one.

"They're not out for blood, Bart." Priscilla stepped onto the ladder. "They're after land, and they can have it, if that's what it takes to get Pa home safe and sound."

Sixteen

"I could have told you they wouldn't turn Pa loose." Priscilla, along with everyone else at Spanish Creek, had spent the morning awaiting the arrival of Charlie McCain. Kate sat in a chair on the front veranda. She stared silently toward the far blue mountains, her lips pursed as if to stifle her numerous fears. Jessie scurried back and forth from the kitchen bringing coffee and prattling in an obvious attempt to keep spirits up.

Joaquín, Crockett, and Bart took turns watching from the cupola, while Will roamed from barn to house, house to barn. Jessie's prattling heightened his jitters.

Priscilla paced. Her bootheels thudded against the tiled veranda; her spurs jangled incessantly.

It was well past noon, before any of them moved from their appointed posts. Then Priscilla stopped her pacing. That was the first indication Will had of her intentions.

The next thing he knew, she hurled her accusation at him, adding, "Only a greenhorn would try to reason with Oscar Haskel." She bounded off the veranda and headed for the barn.

Will caught her by an arm, bringing her up short. She glared at his hand.

"Come with me, or not," she spat.

"You aren't going anywhere."

"We tried it your way. I could have told you it wouldn't work."

"So, we try something else."

When she pulled to free herself, he held on. "Something else," he repeated. "Not something old, like riding into Santa Fé half-cocked. If you won't believe me, listen to Bart. He told you that approach wouldn't work, and he should know—"

"Turn me loose, greenhorn."

Bart had arrived by now, followed by Joaquín and Crockett. Will struggled to think of a new angle, even while he acknowledged to himself that Priscilla was right. Yes, he'd known it all along, so why the hell hadn't he come up with another plan?

Because there wasn't any, he thought, certainly not another acceptable plan. His fight now was to keep Priscilla from riding into that pack of wolves. That's what they were waiting for. He might have been wrong about them releasing Charlie, but he'd bet his life on the rest. Oscar Haskel was sitting out there waiting for Priscilla to ride into his snare.

Crockett spoke up. "Will made it clear as Wheeler Peak on a sunny day. If Charlie wasn't sittin' at his own kitchen table by dinnertime today, we'd ride in an' get him."

Jessie called for attention from the veranda. "No sense discussing it out here in full sight of Oscar's guns. Come on in the kitchen." She took Kate by the arm. "Let's go feed these hungry men, Kate. Priscilla, I need your help."

Tossing a final glare Will's way, Priscilla followed Jessie and her mother into the kitchen.

Will sighed. He hadn't won the battle, not by a long shot, but Jessie's quick thinking had bought him time. Entering the kitchen, he hung back, allowing the others to take their places: Joaquín and Crockett sat at one end of the long oak table, Priscilla at the opposite, where she waited, stony-faced, biding her time, he knew, until she could saddle Sargeant and ride, heedless of her own welfare, after the men who had kidnaped her beloved Charlie.

He crossed and took the seat to her right. Bart remained standing. He lounged just inside the back door, as though awaiting an invitation to enter the house. Will was tempted, but stopped short. Whether Bart stood or sat was none of his concern. Not that Bart was being ignored. Jessie hovered over the old outlaw with a doting manner that gave Will cause for thought.

Kate McCain didn't sit at the table, either. But once inside the kitchen, the familiarity of serving dinner seemed to relax her. She and Priscilla hadn't spoken to each other all morning that Will had noticed. But Kate seemingly in charge of her faculties, began dishing up the pozole she had warming on the back of the stove.

As much as could be expected for a woman whose husband was in jail, whose ranch was threatened, and whose daughter had fallen in love with the wrong man, Will thought.

Priscilla had told him about it the evening before when they sat on the veranda, listening to the wind in the cottonwoods, listening to their feelings; the latter were louder; they droned in Will's ears like a hive full of angry honey bees.

"I told her we're in love and there's nothing she or Pa can do to change it."

"You shouldn't have."

"But it's true, Will. And it's growing as fast as Uncle Sog's sourdough starter. Pretty soon, it'll spill over, plain as day for everyone to see."

"We can't let that happen." Will had paused. He tried to swallow the lump in his throat, then finished lamely, "Not for a while."

"Well, you'll have to help suppress it," she had countered. "Kissing me in front of Bart didn't help."

"I know. I . . . I couldn't stop myself."

"That's what I mean. We're in love. And it's . . . it should be wonderful. As soon as Pa's safe, you'll see. This whole ranch will ring with laughter and joy."

He couldn't burst her bubble. It was all she had to keep her mind off her father, and off her mother, and off a dozen other things she didn't even know to worry about right now. He tried to lighten the mood. "So, what are your plans for me, cowboy? You intend to turn me into another Charlie McCain?"

"Will!" He could tell he'd gotten her dander up, as Charlie would've said. She rose, but instead of stomping off— Priscilla wasn't one to leave the scene of an argument—she came and knelt beside his chair, taking his hands in hers.

"I don't want another Charlie McCain. I already have one. I want a William Penn Radnor IV."

That gave him pause.

She laughed. "Sounds pretty highfalutin for a girl who doesn't even wear dresses."

"Sure does." But what he thought was, *Sounds too damned good.*

"I'll make the handle fit," she promised.

Lordy, she was wonderful. Delightful. He could see them now, weathering every storm, side by side. With Priscilla to keep their spirits afloat, there was nothing they couldn't do.

But he couldn't see them together, not in the future. So he did what he usually did to check his guilty conscience, he kissed her.

Once, tenderly, almost chastely, except for a couple of exchanges of tongues and a wet and glorious finale. "Time to hit the sack, cowboy. Tomorrow promises to be a full day."

That reminded her of Charlie, and he spent a few minutes reassuring her. He didn't know what to expect any more than she did, but whatever came, they'd tackle it.

Together.

Which was what they were doing now, he thought, seated

around the kitchen table like they all liked each other. "That's what I said, all right," Will responded to Crockett's earlier statement. "Any ideas how we can go about it and not get our necks stretched?"

"Same way we did Joaquín, greenhorn."

Everyone in the room stared at Priscilla. "That stunt won't work twice," Joaquín objected. "Newt may be stupid, but Oscar sure as hell isn't."

Jessie agreed. "It'll take more diversion than me teaching Newt to read."

"Than you doing what?" Bart questioned.

"Poor Newt," she mused, "Oscar's always giving him a hard time about not knowing how to read. He's been trying to get me to teach him, but on the sly. He didn't want Oscar finding out. I used it against him."

"Sounds to me like it was for a good cause, Jess." Bart's voice was soft. Will noticed how the old outlaw looked at Jessie, with a lot of pride and something else. And Jessie was grinning like a schoolgirl. Their relationship wasn't quite as hot as his and Priscilla's, but from the looks of things, it was getting there.

Will glanced around the kitchen. Kate was in the corner grinding corn for masa. "We'll have to come up with a good reason for going in," he said. "A real good reason."

No one had a ready answer.

"As I see it, our problem is twofold, getting Charlie out of jail is the first step; the second step is clearing both Charlie and Joaquín."

"That last'll be harder'n springin' him from jail," Crockett predicted. "Judge Sanders is the hangin'est judge this side of the Mississip."

"There're other judges in the territory," Will said. "I'll find one."

"One who isn't in the Haskels' pocket," Priscilla added.

"One who isn't beholden to the Haskels," Will agreed. "That'll be . . ."

A sudden hush fell over the room. Will's words drifted off. The hair on the back of his neck stood on end; damn, they'd left the place unguarded for mere minutes, and—

He followed the awed stares of those across the table. Joaquín rose. Priscilla followed him.

Kate rushed toward the door, drying her hands on her apron. "Nalin!"

Will stood. He saw the old woman, although he wouldn't have recognized her without Kate's calling her by name. She had entered the kitchen as silently as a ghost and stood in the doorway, her face a withered mask. Long, gray-streaked hair flew in tangles around her leathery face and shoulders. Her calico shift was dirty and caked with red mud. It hung limp and tattered from her bony frame. Kate was the first to reach her.

"Come in." Kate took her arm. "Come in, Nalin. We thought you were in Mexico with Victorio."

Will watched the drama unfold. Joaquín took one of his mother's arms, Kate took the other. They edged her gently toward the chair Priscilla had vacated.

Will moved to the door; he peered outside, toward the Haskel's camp. All was still. Bart came up behind him.

"What's going on?"

"She's Joaquín's mother. When we left the ranchería, she and Victorio's Mimbreños were headed for Mexico."

"Looks like she didn't make it."

Behind them, Nalin began to talk. She spoke in Spanish, with lapses into Apache, intermixed with a keening that set Will's teeth on edge.

"We are no more, The People. We are no more."

Joaquín squatted beside her chair, holding her by a frail arm. "Victorio . . ."

"He is dead. Murdered at Tres Castillos."

The silence in the room became palpable.

"José Colorado?" Joaquín asked.

"Your brother escaped, and maybe a dozen more. Many others are prisoners of the *Nakaiyes*."

"Where are they, those who escaped?" Kate's voice was controlled now, respectful. Will thought of the wickiup liner, of the reverence in which Kate McCain was held by Victorio's people.

"Scattered to the mountains," the old woman replied. "The People are no more." Her words gave way to another round of keening. Will glanced from one person to the next. Kate was on her knees beside Nalin. Priscilla had moved across the table and sat staring at the old woman's masklike face.

"My hair . . ." Priscilla touched her head. Tears brimmed in her eyes. "It didn't help."

"Sí, niña," Nalin responded. "I prayed for the Great Spirit to bring me here."

When Will saw tears roll down Priscilla's cheeks, he could stand it no longer. He crossed the room, squatted on his heels beside her chair, and took her hands in his.

"You walked here, *Mamá?*" Joaquín asked. "Alone?"

Nalin turned her attention to her son. Lifting a leathery hand she placed it on top of his head, as if bestowing a benediction. "The Great Spirit answered my prayer. He did not let me die before I saw you again, *hijo.*"

Again silence hung in the air, heavy as the scent of piñon on a damp day. When Crockett cleared his throat, Will blinked back his own tears. If ever a person needed a show of dedication from a parent, it was Joaquín.

"Our chief is dead. The People are no more. I am free to reveal the truth."

The group gasped as if in unison. Kate recovered first.

"We'll leave you and Joaquín—"

"No. You must all hear and understand. I have kept silent to protect The People. Now they are gone. I can tell my son the truth." She turned her full attention on Joaquín. "I know you have suffered, *hijo*. I could have relieved your suffering many years ago. But the truth would have brought ruin to The People, for your father was a powerful man."

Will's grip tightened on Priscilla's hand. Nalin spat the word *powerful* with venom.

"The name of your father is Oran Darnell."

The name stunned Will. Surely he had misheard.

"He is an old man now, if he is still alive. When he came to this territory he was a powerful man in the government of the white eyes."

No, Will hadn't misheard. Senator Oran Darnell. Father of the present Senator Darnell, he thought. The present senator wasn't much older than Will.

"I remember," Kate was saying. "I remember when he was here. A group of senators came to the territory on a hunting excursion. They stayed up at the old Burgwin site. It was after Priscilla was born and I was so sick. You were here, taking care of me."

Nalin nodded. *"Sí,* my friend."

Priscilla had jumped to her feet. Will rose, too, wondering what to expect. Her gaze was trained on Joaquín. She seemed poised to leap across the table.

Nalin spoke again. "Do you understand, *hijo?* My lips were sealed."

Joaquín's face revealed no emotion. He was, after all, half Apache and had taken his novitiate with the young men in Victorio's band. "It is over, *Mamá.*"

"I don't understand," Priscilla cried. "All these years I thought . . . we thought . . ."

Nalin persisted, focusing her dwindling energy on her son. "Our warriors would not have allowed my honor to go unavenged. There would have been bloodshed; the white eyes were searching for any reason to remove us from our lands. If I had told—"

"Charlie knows?" Joaquín questioned.

Priscilla gaped at him from across the table. Will could feel her anguish, could see it on her face. Her hands gripped into fists at her side. It was like a death, he thought. All these years she had believed Joaquín was her brother; only days before he had called her, Sister; now in the space of a heartbeat, it had all been taken away from her—from both of them.

"Charlie does not know," Nalin was saying. "Charlie McCain is an honorable man and a true friend of the *cihéne.* He would have avenged my honor, same as any of our brave warriors. No one would have been safe. We would have had death and destruction."

"What have we now?" Joaquín no longer concealed his bitterness. "When have we ever had anything but death and destruction from the white eyes?"

Nalin peered earnestly into Joaquín's face with what must surely be her last ounce of strength. "Please, *hijo,* say you understand."

Joaquín rose. "It is a difficult thing, understanding." For the first time he looked directly at Priscilla. Will winced at the sight of the man's blue eyes. He knew it was even more unsettling for Priscilla. He rested a hand, lightly, on her back.

"One man cannot understand the actions of another," Joaquín was saying, "any more than one man can avenge the death of another." After a long moment, he dropped his eyes to his mother. Bending, he kissed her wrinkled forehead. "You did what you had to do, *Mamá.* Now I will take you home."

"We have no home, *hijo.*"

"Then we must go and build one. We do not belong here."

"Yes!" Priscilla cried. "You do!" She reached across the table, grasping for Joaquín, but he remained stoically beyond her reach.

Kate took his arm. "Priscilla's right, Joaquín. This is your home. Nothing has changed. Nothing . . . Except . . ." Her words trailed off, her sentence unfinished. Everyone in the room with the possible exception of Bart Ellisor, knew the end of that sentence. . . . *except Charlie McCain is not your father and Spanish Creek is not your birthright.*

Will pulled Priscilla against his chest. Turning her toward him, he saw her bloodless face, the desperate way her gaze pulled away, reaching for Joaquín.

"The important thing now," Kate was saying, "is to get your mother to bed, Joaquín. She is in no condition to take one more step anywhere. I'll fix a room. Jessie, would you heat the pozole? Priscilla, come with me. Bring clean sheets for the front room."

Priscilla didn't move. She continued to stare helplessly at Joaquín.

Kate helped Nalin toward the hallway. "Come, Priscilla. Get the sheets."

Priscilla stood stock-still. Will didn't even feel her breathing. With the jerky movements of a marionette, Joaquín turned his attention from his mother back to Priscilla. They stared at each other long, hard. Will had no trouble reading the pain on Joaquín's face.

"Joaquín, I . . ." Priscilla's voice faltered. Joaquín turned abruptly toward the door.

"Joaquín, wait . . ." She moved away from Will, toward Joaquín, but the door had already slammed.

"You can talk to him later." Will turned her toward the hallway. "Your mother needs you."

"But Joaquín needs—"

"To be alone, I suspect. Run help your mother. I'll see about him."

Outside he found Joaquín standing in the shadowed eaves, rolling a smoke. He glared stoically at Will with those startling blue eyes. Again the mere sight of them struck Will like a slap to the face. They hadn't come from Charlie, after all. He imagined Joaquín examining those eyes in a looking glass, year after year, swearing that they proved Charlie was his father. How would Joaquín feel now when he looked into a looking glass and faced the fact that the man he had wanted to call him son, never would; that the ranch he had coveted for so many years would never be his?

"I have an idea, Joaquín. If it works we might be able to clear your name and free Charlie with one and the same stroke."

Joaquín scowled.

"I'll need your help. It'll take all hands and the cook for this one." He glanced toward the kitchen. "Sit tight." His sweeping glance took in Crockett and Bart Ellisor, who stood apart at the other end of the veranda. "I'll be right back."

By the time Will reached the bedroom, Kate had settled Nalin into a chair. She and Priscilla were busy making the bed. Kate glanced up at his approach; her glare stopped him in the threshold.

"We'll need privacy, Mr. Radnor."

"I'll give it to you. But first, I have an idea that might help us free Charlie."

That got Kate's attention, but even after he outlined his plan, she remained hesitant. "If it'll help Charlie and clear Joaquín, too . . . I don't know what Charlie would do. I can't . . ."

"Mama, Will's right. Pa would want us to do whatever it takes."

"But deeding the canyon . . ."

"It's just a piece of land, Mama." She smiled at Will. That distracting smile, he thought. Those damnable blue eyes. "Until they took Pa, I didn't realize the truth—it isn't the land that's important, it's the people who live on it."

"You're right, darling, but . . ."

"All I'm asking, Mrs. McCain, is for permission to draw up the papers. I'll take them to Charlie; he doesn't have to sign them."

"You think deeding the canyon to Joaquín will convince a judge that he didn't steal the horses?"

"An honest judge," Priscilla barked, reminding Will of the way Charlie responded when his dander was up. "Which Judge Sanders certainly isn't."

"There has to be an honest judge somewhere in this territory. I'll scour the countryside until—"

"You won't have to do that, Mr. Radnor. Charlie swears by Judge Anson, up at Chimayo."

"Judge Anson?"

She nodded. "But I don't understand how deeding the canyon will help. Joaquín is accused of stealing horses, not land."

"I can draw up the papers to read 'land and livestock.' It shouldn't be necessary. Those horses are as native to that piece of property as elk or bighorn sheep. But I'll add 'livestock,' if you like."

"Do that, Mr. Radnor." Kate turned her attention to the bed. Will watched her purse her lips. When she looked back at him, it was to inquire, "How will you get it to Charlie?"

"I'm an attorney. They can't deny me the right to see the prisoner."

"Those people can do anything they please."

"Santa Fé's a growing city," Will argued. "The Haskels know they have to keep up the appearance of being law-abiding officials. If they refuse, I'll threaten them with going to Governor Wallace. But that shouldn't be necessary, Oscar Haskel won't have anything to lose this time, not that he knows about."

Jessie came in with a bowl of pozole. Kate looked squarely at Will for the first time. Her expression wasn't warm, but it wasn't frigid, either. "Draw up your papers, Mr. Radnor. Take them to Charlie. Now, you'll have to excuse us."

Priscilla followed him down the hall.

"What else do you have up your sleeve, Will?"

Stopping in the dimly lit hall, he considered how best to tell her.

"I like your plan to clear Joaquín, but how will it help us free Pa from those blasted Haskels?"

Will ducked his head. He knew that convincing Priscilla to stay behind would likely be the hardest part of the job. He hedged by ignoring her use of *us*. "It'll get me inside the jail. Bart can help work out the details."

Priscilla stepped nose to nose with him. "When do we leave?"

He shook his head, brushing the tips of their noses. "This one's for the boys, Miss Priss. You sit tight—"

She held her ground. Priscilla usually did. "He's my Pa; I'm in on this one, greenhorn. I'm as good a shot as any man."

"I'll grant you that . . . with one possible exception." He took her face in his hands, felt her tensed muscles. "But you're not *any man.*"

"Then consider me one of the boys." She grinned. "That'll help you forget I'm a woman."

Their gazes delved; his brain ran amock. "I thought you knew by now . . . I've given up . . . that hopeless task." Speaking, he nudged her backwards, across the hall, through an open door, into a room, privacy.

"But since you don't seem to remember, how 'bout I show you again." Backing her against a wall, he kissed her, deep and sensuously, while his hands showed her in no uncertain terms what he thought of her feminine attributes, one by one.

Lifting his lips, he studied her in the dim light. "Had enough?"

But her arms were around his neck and she pulled his lips back to hers. "Never, greenhorn. I'll never get enough of you."

Nor he of her, he thought, weary of the whole charade. Easing back, he changed the subject.

"Are you all right . . . about Joaquín?"

She closed her eyes a minute. He felt her tremble. "I'm sad for everybody—mostly, for him, I guess. I like your idea of deeding him the canyon. Pa will, too. Now he'll have something from Spanish Creek."

"And something from The People."

"Hum, the horses. I hope it makes a difference. I keep remembering how he called me his sister. It made me feel . . . proud. Now it isn't true. And I feel so lonely. I think he does, too."

"Tell him you feel that way. Tell him relatives don't have to be by blood; they can be by choice."

It was the wrong thing to say, of course. For she immediately drew him back, kissed his lips, and replied, "By choice, like us."

They waited for dark. Joaquín scouted a trail up the north side of the mountain keeping to the densest covering of trees and underbrush. The plan was to stick together until they neared Santa Fé, then separate. Will would ride alone into town where every man on the street could see him approach the jail.

Alone. Like he already felt. He'd succeeded in talking Priscilla into staying behind. She was needed to keep Oscar Haskel from taking the ranch while they were away. And to keep up the ruse that no one had left.

"That'll be hard to do, with all of you gone." She'd rolled her eyes. "Unless Red shows up."

Although he hated to leave Priscilla alone, Will was hard-put to wish for Red Avery's return. "Saddle several horses," he suggested. "Ride yours in plain view. After a while, change clothes and pretend to be me."

She eyed him up and down, cocky. "I could pull it off a lot easier, if I had that derby of yours."

"It isn't a derby, cowboy, it's a bowler."

"Well, if I had it, I'd make a more convincing green-horn."

He wanted to kiss the smirk off her lips, but her mother came up just then, so he stepped into the saddle with a promise. "Since you're so fond of that hat, guess I'll have to give it to you one of these days."

She didn't miss a beat. "It's you I'm fond of Will Radnor. Be careful."

Kate reached them. "While you're in Chimayo, Mr. Radnor, would you look up Ol' Sog, our range cook? We haven't had word from him since Priscilla left him there with a broken leg."

"Glad to, Mrs. McCain."

"Judge Anson can point you to the doctor."

"He's the only doc in town," Priscilla put in.

Kate turned to her daughter. "I'd like a word with Mr. Radnor alone, darling."

Priscilla's smile froze. "Mama, don't—"

"Go ahead," Will interrupted.

Her gaze held his; he could see defiance build quickly. "Hold down the fort, cowboy." He tipped his hat. With an exaggerated sigh, she retraced her steps to the veranda, where he could see her standing with fists on hips, her golden hair highlighted by the pale light of the moon.

Kate didn't speak until Priscilla was out of earshot. "Thank you for helping Charlie, Mr. Radnor."

Will studied Priscilla across the distance. "I'm not doing this for Charlie."

"I know."

"Yeah, well, Charlie should be home by morning."

"What then?"

Will knew what she meant. Likely she was afraid to put it into words. Likely he'd be afraid to answer, if she did. The absurdity of him rescuing Charlie McCain went beyond all reason . . . until he considered Priscilla.

"Before Charlie gets back," he suggested, "why don't you and Priscilla sit down and have a long talk?"

"Yes. We must . . ."

"When this is over, she's going to need you."

Will watched her go cold. "That's what Jessie said."

She wasn't thinking about Charlie's trouble with the Haskels now; Will could see that. Nor even about Priscilla. She was wondering what Will intended to do to her husband.

Well, he was wondering the same thing.

"I'll tell her, Mr. Radnor." Kate stared him directly in the eye. "But only my story. You insinuated yourself into my daughter's heart. It's your job to tell her why you've done it."

Stars shone down from the black dome of sky. Will followed Joaquín up the mountain and down the backside. Bart Ellisor and Titus Crockett kept pace to either side. Each of them had a story. Joaquín, whose dream of Charlie McCain being his father had been quelled once and for all time; Bart Ellisor, who had somehow earned the wrath of the McCains and obviously regretted it. Why else would he have risked capture by authorities from Texas to California to rush to their aid?

Will wondered about Titus Crockett. What was the crusty old foreman's story? Priscilla claimed Crockett had quit as foreman of one of the largest spreads in Texas to come to New Mexico with Charlie. Why?

Will tried to concentrate on Crockett. He tried to concentrate on Joaquín and what was surely one of the biggest disappointments in a man's life. He tried to concentrate on Bart Ellisor's reasons for becoming an outlaw.

Mostly he tried to concentrate on the night ahead. On the morning, when he would enter the jail and face Newt

Haskel and, with luck, free Charlie McCain. But his mind was filled with Priscilla.

They rode through the night, their horses' hooves thundering over the earth in a dramatic rush toward a climax that Will both dreaded and was anxious to have behind him. He rode with half a mind and knew he needed to get hold of himself.

But hour after hour passed, and all he could hear was the thunder of the horses' hooves. The cadence reverberated with one word—regret. It spiraled through him, burrowing into the crevasses of his mind, into the fabric of his flesh, into the very marrow of his bones. Regret.

Joaquín warned of a landslide up ahead. They found another route.

Regret.

They arrived outside the city at precisely the appointed time. Sunrise.

Regret.

They parted ways.

"Give me fifteen minutes," he told Bart.

"I'll be there."

Regret.

Will rode down the long, winding street alone. All was still, inside his head, outside in the street. In the distance he saw a string of burros—loaded with the day's firewood—wind down the mountainside. He watched small, barefoot boys flog the animals with switches. But he heard nothing.

Except the word *regret.*

He stopped across the street, dismounted, hitched his reins over the rail. He walked toward the jail. His bootheels thudded on the packed street. His spurs jangled with each step, reminding him of how far he'd come. One month ago he wouldn't have known a spur if he'd seen one hanging on a nail. Today the sound rang with dismal familiarity. It reminded him of the Romans, of the Coliseum, of the fanfare. The sound of valor, the sound of champions, the sound of success.

The sound of spurs and boots and afterwards, what?

Regret.

Newt stood spread-eagled in the open doorway, his scarred boots wedged against each facing, his expression insolent.

"I've come to see my client, Haskel."

"You broke him out of jail, case you forgot."

"Charlie McCain."

"He cain't have no visitors. Especially not you."

Will had expected such a reaction. "Listen, Newt, we in the legal profession sometimes have to put personal animosity aside and tend to business."

Newt glared. "Make fun of me all you want, Radnor, but I ain't simple-minded."

"I didn't mean to imply you were. I want us to understand each other. You have a prisoner to protect. I respect that. I have a client to advise. He's entitled to my services, Newt, under the law. We both know that. So, like I said, let's put personal feelings aside and obey the law."

"You've gotta be plumb loco to think I'd fall for the same stunt twice." Newt glanced away, staring toward the plaza beyond the jail. Will watched embarrassment mottle his face.

"Tell you what, Newt. Come on in there with me."

Newt jerked his head around.

"Come with me. Stand beside me while I confer with my client. I don't have to allow that, of course, but under the circumstances I'll let you tag along."

When Newt still didn't move, Will edged himself through the door. After initial resistance, Newt stood back and let him into the outer office.

"Get your keys, Newt. Take me in there." Will watched Newt step outside and look around the corner of the building. In his mind's eye he pictured the grove of cottonwoods where Priscilla had waited the night they broke Joaquín out of jail. He heard her voice, her teasing . . .

"I've come alone, Newt."

"Wouldn't do you no good, if you hadn't." Newt dug in his pocket for the keys. "You won't take me for a fool twice."

"Never intended to, Newt."

Newt unlocked the door, then ushered Will inside, making a show of unsnapping the thong on his holster. "Jes' remember, I'm right here beside you. One false move an' I'll gun ya down."

Will gave him a scathing look, but said nothing. Then they were there. Before the cell. Will was reminded of the last time. Until the prisoner rose from the cot near the back and hobbled forward.

"Where's your cane, Charlie?"

Charlie's blue eyes narrowed. "Where's my daughter?"

"At Spanish Creek."

Charlie stopped in front of Will, mesmerizing him with those damned blue eyes. Will could see how Joaquín—and just about everyone else in these parts—had gotten the wrong idea.

Forty-nine years old, with stubbled chin, wiry, disheveled hair, and a head wound scabbing on his left temple, Charlie McCain was nonetheless a formidable man. Those blue eyes were hard as pressed glass.

"What're you doin' here, Radnor? Who's side'r you on, anyhow? What the hell'd you do with my daughter?"

Will barely comprehended Charlie's barked interrogation, conscious only of the man and of his own mission. Something soft and unfamiliar stirred deep inside him.

Stunned, Will stared at Charlie and wondered when he'd stopped hating this man who had been his nemesis for twenty-three years. Had it been the evening they spent reminiscing on the darkened veranda, the first time he'd gone to Charlie's aid? Was it the way Charlie had called him son—the sound ringing pleasantly in his ears even while he abhorred the speaker? Or had his love for Priscilla intervened? Had he started seeing Charlie through his daughter's eyes?

Will struggled to dredge up the old hatred; that it was hard to do, worried him. He needed that hatred, now more than ever.

"I've found a way to clear Joaquín of those horse theft charges, Charlie."

"I'm listenin'."

Will handed him the document he'd drawn up on Charlie's own Spanish Creek stationery. Charlie didn't even look at it. He continued to glower at Will. Whatever Will's new sentimentality, Charlie didn't appear to be affected by it.

"How's my daughter?" Charlie barked.

"Fine."

"What'd you mean, fine?"

"She's fine, damnit. She's at home with your wife." Will looked over at Newt. "And with all the others. They're all there. Except that worthless Avery. He took off after they kidnapped you."

"Humph!"

"Bart Ellisor is there, too."

That got Charlie's full attention. His free hand gripped the bar. "Bart? How's Kate takin' that?"

"She's fine, Charlie. Read the paper. Newt here was kind enough to let me in, but his patience is gonna run out in about two more minutes. Read it and if you agree, sign it."

Charlie scanned the document. "I can't sign this."

"Yes, you can."

"Those . . ." Charlie cast Newt a withering glance. "They don't belong to me, damnit."

"Victorio and most of his people were killed at Tres Castillos."

Charlie's face fell. "Victorio?" Life seemed to leave him. "No." He slammed a fist against the bars, then gripped them with both fists, crumpling the document. "Who's left?" His voice sounded like it had come from an old man.

"Nalin escaped. She's at Spanish Creek. She told Joaquín the truth."

"Lord have mercy!" Charlie twisted his neck, looked at his Stetson, lying on the bare mattress. He turned back to Newt, barking a command. "Get me the hell outta here."

"No way, José," Newt quipped.

"My family needs me, damnit, and you're holdin' me on some trumped-up charge. You dadburnt—"

"Charlie," Will interjected. "The paper. I only have a few minutes. Newt's patience is wearing—"

"I don't give a—"

"The paper. Are you going to sign it or not?"

Charlie finally looked Will in the eye. Will had never been good at charades, not even the parlor-game version. He stared straight into Charlie's eyes and hoped a meaningful frown would do. He dared not glance out the window or toward the back door.

"I can't do anything for you, Charlie. But Joaquín is my client. Sign that paper and I'll ride to hell and back to find an honest judge to record it." Will handed Charlie a fountain pen, which had also come from Charlie's desk at Spanish Creek.

Finally, Charlie seemed to get the message, for he took the pen, signed the paper, and thrust the whole crumpled mess back into Will's hand. "Much obliged."

Will nodded to Newt. "I'm finished." Will hadn't turned his back good, when Charlie stopped them.

"Joaquín? How's he takin' it?"

Will turned back, stepped toward Charlie. Newt was right beside him. "It's hard to tell," he replied honestly. "Disappointed, I'm sure. Who wouldn't be, to find out your father had been some whoring old congressman when you'd lived your life hoping he was Charlie McCain?"

The two men locked gazes and Will had the distinct impression of two old bull moose locking horns.

"Old congressman?" Charlie asked.

"Senator Oran Darnell. Senior, I suppose. The present Senator Darnell is about my age."

"How's Nalin?"

"Mrs. McCain's taking care of her."

"Priscilla?"

Will turned away without responding. He'd already assured Charlie that Priscilla was fine. He couldn't do that again. It might be true now, but it wouldn't be for long.

Then he saw Bart. The old outlaw had entered the jail and slipped down the hall. His face was covered with a bandanna. Over it his eyes met Will's.

"What the hell—?" Newt sputtered.

Bart had thrust a double barreled shotgun into Newt's ribs before the sheriff realized what was happening. Will slipped past.

"See ya, Charlie," Will called. Exiting the jail, he stepped into the saddle and rode. It was a full day's ride to Chimayo, and he wanted to make it by nightfall.

Seventeen

When night came Priscilla took up watch from the veranda out front. She couldn't get Will off her mind. Would his plan succeed? Could he free Pa and clear Joaquín—and keep himself alive and well in the process?

Pa's arrest had served one purpose. It had shown her how much she loved him. Not that she'd ever doubted it, but now she knew she'd put too much importance on Spanish Creek.

Oh, she loved this ranch. No question about that. She couldn't stand to think about living any place else—surviving any place else. But if it came down to choosing between Spanish Creek and Pa's safety—his life—there was no choice.

The night sky glittered with stars. Priscilla settled back and tried to stay alert and keep her mind on the Haskels who were out there plotting the end to Charlie McCain's world.

"Priscilla?" Kate walked on kitten feet across the tiled veranda floor. "Will I disturb your watch if I sit with you?"

"Of course not, Mama."

They sat in what Priscilla took for companionable silence, until she realized her mother was fidgeting. "Pa'll be all right," she soothed. "Will's plan is good. They can pull it off. Especially with Oscar and most of his men camped on our doorstep."

"I know. I . . . uh . . ."

Priscilla heard her mother draw a deep breath. "I need to talk to you, darling."

"Fine." But it wasn't fine, Priscilla thought, suddenly wary. She recognized Mama's tone; she was fixing to get another lecture about Will.

"Jessie said I had to tell you, and she's right. Mr. Radnor said it, too."

"Will?"

"He said I had to tell you before he and your papa return."

Priscilla stared out at the stars. They were fuzzy, moving—swimming in an ocean of black. For some reason, her insides grew weak—Mama's ominous tone, likely. "I'm listening."

"Don't be aggravated, darling. Please. This is . . . the most difficult thing I've ever been required to do."

"Then don't do it. I don't want to hear anything—"

"The truth. You must know the truth. Now, before your world flies apart."

"Oh, Mama, don't overdramatize. We're both worried sick about Pa, but Will's taking care—"

"Priscilla." Kate's tone—gentle, yet commanding—halted Priscilla's objections. "There is no way in the world I could overdramatize, as you call it. Part of the story belongs to your papa. I'll leave that to him and to . . ." She reached for Priscilla's hand.

Uneasiness crawled up Priscilla's spine. She shifted the rifle to the other side and took her mother's hand. It was cool, clammy. Kate gripped her tightly, finally drawing both their hands to Priscilla's knee, where she patted and stroked her daughter, as one would a child.

"Such a big girl. All grown up. Where did the years go?"

Mama should have had other children. "I don't know, Mama, but I enjoyed them, every minute of them. Now, I'm beginning to feel guilty. I should have paid more attention to you and Pa. I don't remember ever telling Pa I loved him." The words came unbidden; equally unbidden were the tears that formed in her eyes. "Or you, Mama. I've never told you how much I love you."

"I know you love me, darling. Your papa knows, too. But we haven't been honest with you. I don't mean we lied, but we've kept things from you. We had our reasons. Some of the dastardly things in our past were best forgotten. And when would we have told you? These things a child could never understand, yet we've only now realized . . . How time has slipped away. You're all grown up. You're a woman now."

Priscilla struggled to hold back tears. She *was* a woman now; she'd known that since the first time she saw Will Radnor. And she was happy about it—or she would be, once their trouble with the Haskels was over. Will had showed her that being a woman, a lady, wasn't contradictory to her nature. She loved him; he loved her. Their love was strong; it supported her even now, through Pa's arrest and Mama's strange behavior.

"Whatever it is, Mama, I don't need to know. I'll take your word. I don't expect you to tell me everything about your life. Or Pa, either . . ." Her words drifted on the soft evening breeze, for Priscilla realized suddenly that she did expect that. No matter how dreadful—but how could anything in Mama's life have been dreadful?—she needed to know. It was her life, too. In a sense, what happened to her parents, happened to her.

"I'm sorry, Mama. I didn't mean to make it difficult. I'm listening."

When Kate spoke again, it was painstakingly, as though each word was more difficult to speak than the last. "Bart Ellisor's father married my mother. I was fifteen. Bart was eighteen. One day . . ." Suddenly Mama was crying. Priscilla heard it in her voice. She turned to see moonlight glisten off the wet streaks that streamed down her face.

Slipping from her chair, Priscilla knelt beside her mother

and buried her face in her lap. Kate stroked Priscilla's hair with trembling hands. Finally, she reached in her sleeve and pulled out a handkerchief. "I'm sorry, darling. I'd never told this story to anyone except your papa until they took him away the other day and Jessie and I were here alone. She'd told us Bart was coming, and I . . . I panicked."

Priscilla lifted her face. Sitting back on her heels, she took her mother's hands. "Well, you don't have to tell it again."

"I must. Truthfully, I want to. My mother would never allow me to talk about it. It wasn't mentioned in our house, not once in ten long years. If my mother had been able to talk with me, to share with me, even to cry with me, maybe . . . maybe . . ." Kate sniffled, squared her shoulders, and continued. "One day while our parents were in town, Bart . . . Bart raped me."

A dizzying sickness washed over Priscilla. For a moment the darkness seemed alight with thousands of twinkling stars, then she realized she was squeezing her eyelids closed. She reached for her mother, drew her near. "How dreadful."

When Kate tried to continue, Priscilla stopped her. "No. Not another word. You don't have to talk about this."

Kate struggled free. She clasped Priscilla's face in both hands. "I want to, darling. You need to know. As things turned out, I should have told you long ago."

The horror of Mama's disclosure began to sink in. No wonder she'd reacted to seeing Bart with such vehemence. Tears rolled unchecked down Priscilla's face. "I brought him here, a living reminder—"

"I've recovered from the assault, darling. As much as anyone ever recovers from such a horror." Kate's voice trembled. Priscilla heard her draw a deep, determined breath. "That's the reason I fell to pieces, seeing the two of you together. Knowing you'd been in the mountains with him for days."

"Nothing happened," Priscilla assured her. "Bart was . . . he was a perfect gentleman."

"I'm sure. He's never stopped trying to make up to me for . . . what he did." Kate sighed. "That's what drove him to the outlaw trail. I know it. He wasn't a *bad* person; he was well liked in town. He made one mistake—one terrible mistake."

Priscilla couldn't stop crying. "How can you say that? After he . . . after he . . ."

"It's true. Now all he wants is my forgiveness. I've never been able to forgive him."

"That's what Pa meant. A long time ago I heard him talking about Bart—I didn't even know his last name. Pa said he was an outlaw who had pledged to come to your aid anytime, anywhere."

Kate nodded.

"I'm so sorry."

"Don't be sorry. We haven't time for that."

"But what . . . what will we do with him?"

"Do with him?"

"I mean, he's coming back, bringing Pa. He'll be here anytime. By morning, Will said. What should we do?"

"We'll do nothing, Priscilla. He came to help. We needed his help. We'll thank him for it."

"But . . . I mean, you can't stand to . . . to see him."

"Nonsense, darling. This isn't the first time I've seen Bart since . . ." Regrouping, Kate continued, "I saw him in California once, before you were born." She smiled at Priscilla. "I wished him well. That wasn't what he wanted. Like I said, he wanted, I'm sure he still wants, my forgiveness." Kate stared into the distance with pursed lips. "I don't know . . . I just don't know."

"You don't have to forgive him, Mama. Not ever. How could you?"

"Priscilla, darling, life isn't that simple. You liked Bart a lot, until now. He's personable, like you said, a gentleman.

He wrecked his whole life with one terrible mistake when he was young."

"And yours. He wrecked your life, too."

"Some of mine, yes. But I was the lucky one. I found your papa."

Priscilla squinched her lids against another rush of tears. "Pa."

Kate drew Priscilla close, squeezed her a minute, then turned her loose. Priscilla felt her stiffen. When she turned, she saw them, too, standing in the darkened barn door.

Priscilla grabbed her rifle. Kate placed a hand on her arm. The shadows took form.

"Pa." And behind him, Joaquín and Bart. When she jumped up, Kate stopped her.

"Wait here, darling."

While Priscilla watched, Kate left the veranda and ran to the arms of her husband. The door slammed; Jessie came up beside Priscilla; she paused, then hurried down the steps. Priscilla watched, stunned, as Jessie headed straight for Bart Ellisor. She didn't throw herself in his arms, but stopped in front of him, reached to place her hand on his shoulders and stood on tiptoe to kiss his lips.

Priscilla recalled the day she herself had kissed Bart on the cheek. After what her mother told her, revulsion stirred in her stomach. But it was quickly squashed by reality—her mother's pragmatic recitation of the vile act that had taken place so long ago. Mama claimed that was what drove Bart to the outlaw trail.

Priscilla had wondered—given the opportunity, she knew she would probably have asked him—what had happened to lead him astray.

The vile deed could never be excused. But Mama had recovered. Now Priscilla had to decide how she felt about it and how she would treat Bart.

While she watched from the veranda, Mama and Pa drew

apart. Mama turned to Joaquín, took both his hands. Then she turned to Bart and took his hands, too.

Priscilla cringed inside, wondering whether she could have reacted so graciously and why her mother felt it necessary. Then she thought of Will Radnor, of what he meant to her. And she knew she would shake the hands of the devil himself if he helped protect Will from harm.

Lost in thought, Priscilla didn't realize Joaquín had moved until he stood on the step below her.

"Your white-eyes lawyer got off to Chimayo, Jake."

"I wish we were with him."

"He'll make it. He's not as green as you think."

"I know." Priscilla heard her voice tremble and knew it was as much from Joaquín's attempt to reassure her, as from worry over Will. "Thank you."

He stood stock-still, his head tipped toward her. His face, what she could see of it in the waning hours of night, was expressionless. When she lifted her hand to touch him, he turned away.

"Joaquín."

He turned. Although she knew he couldn't see her any more clearly than she could see him, she somehow felt bound to him.

"I'm glad you have the canyon."

He shrugged.

"I . . . I always thought you were my brother." Again, she reached toward him. Her hand remained suspended, upturned, in the void between them. "I wish you were."

He merely grunted in response, but somehow—perhaps because she wanted to believe it—he didn't sound as cynical. When he finally spoke, it was in a subdued tone. "Even if it meant sharing Charlie McCain?"

She bit her bottom lip. "Even if it meant sharing everything."

* * *

Will found Judge Anson as agreeable as Kate had suggested. After examining the document Charlie had signed and the affidavits from Kate and Crockett stating that Charlie McCain never left the ranch on the night Joaquín broke out of jail, the judge signed papers by which the charges on both Charlie and Joaquín were dropped.

Then Will went in search of Doc Sloan, where he found Charlie's old range cook, Ol' Soggy Bottoms, recovered enough to ride back to the ranch. Using Charlie's name, Ol' Sog purchased a horse at the Chimayo livery and the two set out for Spanish Creek.

Will soon discovered the old biscuit cutter to be a talkative soul, whose favorite topic was Jake McCain.

"She's like a daughter to Crockett an' me, both. We helped raise her. An' I'd say we done a right fine job."

Will agreed, although he would rather not have discussed Priscilla's attributes for two solid days. He was on his way to destroy her world, and he didn't need anyone to make him feel more guilty than he already did.

"Best danged horsewoman in the territory. Likely the best horseman, too."

Will agreed.

"Best danged shot in the territory, man or woman."

Will agreed. He could have related the incident on the stagecoach to Ol' Sog, but he didn't. He could have offered the night he helped Charlie defend Spanish Creek as proof of his own marksmanship, but he didn't.

"Purtiest girl in the territory."

Will agreed.

"You ain't got much to say, Radnor. What's matter, cat got your tongue?"

Will shrugged.

"Or has that little gal got you tongue-tied? Seems to me it's time for her to be findin' a feller, and from what you've told me about helpin' Charlie an' Joaquín out of their fixes . . . well, it's my guess there's more to it than offerin' a neighborly hand to a man in a twister."

"Joaquín is my client," Will argued. "As for the rest, let's just say I don't like to see officers of the court playing by their own rules."

Ol' Sog spat a stream of tobacco off to the side. "Sure, son. Anything you wanna call it's fine by me."

What Will wanted to call it and what it was, were horses of two different colors. But wasn't he doing the very thing he accused the Haskels of—playing by his own rules? Sure, he'd convinced himself that when he faced Charlie, it would be by the book. But like Charlie himself had said, the statute of limitations ran out long ago. Anything Will did would have to be done with Charlie's cooperation or outside the law.

On the other hand, didn't a pledge made to his mother take precedence over everything else? For a long time now, it had. For twenty-three years, every night when he went to bed instead of saying his prayers, he recited his vow of vengeance. On his mother's grave, he had pledged again to fulfill that long-ago boyhood promise.

Then he arrived in New Mexico and met Priscilla.

By the time they slipped down the back side of the hill and approached the Spanish Creek outbuildings, Will was feeling about as low as a rattler with his belly dragging the ground.

Charlie was the first to see them. At his call the others came running. Jessie. Bart. Kate. Joaquín. Will's heart stopped. Where was she? He heard commotion from the barn. Running footsteps. Spurs. Priscilla's. He didn't look. He couldn't look. One look and he'd be lost.

Sog dismounted. Will dismounted.

"Sog!" Kate rushed past Charlie in her attempt to welcome the old cook back to the range. Charlie hobbled after. He wasn't using his walking stick. Must have thrown the thing away, Will thought, like he was always threatening. Or else left it at the jail.

The two stove-up cattlemen approached each other, clapped shoulders, then hugged in a jerky, self-conscious sort of way. Titus Crockett arrived and joined in the celebration.

Priscilla stopped beside Will. So close he could smell her familiar scent—clean air and horse sweat and the stable.

"Will?"

He glanced down at her briefly, then away. If he looked too closely, he knew he would be unable to keep his hands off her.

Charlie glared at him, as if waiting for the ax to fall. Kate, too, stared hard. Behind her, Jessie and Bart stood together, holding hands and likely their breaths, Will thought.

Priscilla embraced Sog. "Uncle Sog, we've sure missed you."

"I don't doubt it, missy. You never could get pie dough to cook up worth a darn."

Priscilla laughed. She grabbed Will's arm. "Look what your broken leg got us, Uncle Sog. I found him on that stagecoach you insisted I take."

Suddenly Will knew, if he never did another decent thing in his life, the time had come to set the record straight. Freeing himself from Priscilla, he searched his saddlebags and pulled out the signed documents. He handed them to Charlie.

"It's all here. Judge Anson signed them and recorded the deed for Joaquín. He notified Judge Sanders that he's calling in Federal agents until the Haskels draw in their hired guns and start operating by the law."

Charlie took the papers, responded with a dry, "Much obliged."

That finished, Will grabbed Priscilla by a wrist. More

curtly than he intended, he addressed her mother. "Mrs. McCain, I'd appreciate time alone with your daughter."

Without waiting for permission, he dragged Priscilla off toward the barn, not daring to so much as look her in the face. A heavy inner silence surrounded him, shutting out all external sounds except the jangling of their spurs, which provided a perverse cadence for his march toward destruction.

Priscilla skipped to keep up with Will. His behavior might be strange, but it could only mean one thing—he was as anxious to see her as she was to see him. To see, to touch, to hold. She felt downright giddy with it all.

"You did it, Will. I never doubted you could, but oh it's so nice to have Pa home. And Joaquín cleared. You even brought Uncle Sog back."

They'd reached the opposite end of the barn by this time. Will came to a sudden halt. But instead of turning toward her, he just stood there, gripping her wrist and looking out at the valley and the mountains beyond.

"You even got the Haskels off our back."

"Priscilla."

Pulling free, she threw her arms around his neck. "Most important, Will, you're back, safe and sound."

"Priscilla . . ." Reaching up, he pried her hands loose.

"Now, Mama and Pa won't have any reason—"

"Damnation, Priscilla. Just shut up and listen."

Her heart jumped to her throat, where it lodged. She stared at Will, at his eyes, until he looked away. Something was wrong. She knew that now. She felt it. Smelled it in the air.

"I should have told you this . . . a long time ago . . ." Dropping her hands he moved away. She watched him stuff his hands in his back pockets, like a native, she thought. She moved behind him and took his arm.

"Whatever it is, Will, we can work it out."

"No." He shook free, avoiding her eyes.

Fear stirred her ire. "Then tell me. Go on, get it over with."

He drew a deep breath. When he spoke, his voice lacked vitality, spirit. "Remember I told you my father was dead?"

"He isn't? Why would you tell me . . ."

"He's dead, Priscilla. That isn't the point. The point is, he was murdered."

"Murdered?" In an instant Priscilla's ire turned to pity. "When, Will? How?"

"When I was ten." Will turned toward her. His face stiff, a mask. "I found his body and . . ."

"Will, don't. You don't have to talk about it. I don't need to . . ." She felt a repeat of several nights earlier when Mama made her devastating confession. What was happening? Had she suddenly turned into Mother Confessor? They should be rejoicing, not—

"Please, Priscilla, just listen. Let me finish before I lose my nerve."

"I'm sorry. Go ahead."

"My father was a lawyer in Philadelphia. One night when he was working late, my mother sent me into his office building to get him." Will inhaled, gazed off toward the horizon. Priscilla could only imagine what horrors he was seeing. But when she reached a sympathetic hand to touch him, he jerked away.

"He was dead. Lying on the floor of his office, a bullet hole in his chest."

"Oh, Will—"

"He had a gun in his hand." Will glanced at her again. "Remember that day down by the river in Santa Fé, the day I caught you shooting at that sunflower blossom?"

"After you'd ignored me in town?"

He grinned, a wry, unhappy sort of recognition. "Remember the pistol I used that day?"

"Of course."

"That pistol was clutched in my father's hand."

"Oh, Will. Maybe you shouldn't have kept it. I mean . . . the memories are so painful——"

"The police took it. They said it would help them find the killer."

"Did it?"

"No. They never found him. A few years ago, they returned the pistol to me. But it didn't really belong to me. Or to my father. It belonged to my father's law partner. It was one of a matched pair."

Priscilla was at a loss for words. She wanted to console him, but he had shied away three times now. She wanted to tell him it wasn't healthy to carry around so much hurt for such a long——

"That night, the night I found my father's body, I made a promise to my mother. I vowed that if the police didn't find my father's murderer, I would."

Priscilla's eyebrows shot up. For some reason the hair on her neck stood on end. She held her breath, waiting.

"That's why I've come to New Mexico Territory."

Priscilla's mouth went dry. "Revenge? Revenge will ruin your life, Will. Revenge——"

"Tell me about it." His tone was bitter. "But damnit, Priscilla, I promised my mother. I owe it to my father's memory. And there's the law. My father's partner shot him in cold blood and he's gotten away with murder all these years. That's what will ruin a person's life."

"If the police knew who he was, why didn't they arrest the man years ago?"

"They didn't know. Not for sure. My grandfather refused to press charges. The . . . uh, the murderer left town, changed his name, changed his occupation, raised a family, became a model citizen."

"That doesn't seem possible, does it? A murderer becoming a regular person. How did you find him?"

"A newspaper clipping from a trial in California. When my grandfather died, I found it among his papers."

"Your grandfather knew?"

Will nodded. "All along. He was . . . well, you would've had to know him. Grandfather was a grand old gentleman, of the old school, like they say. Neither he nor my grandmother would have considered dragging the family name through a public trial. I understand, in a way. My father was dead. Nothing could bring him back. But, you see, my father's partner embezzled money from the firm. We suppose . . . *I* suppose . . . my father found him out, the partner killed him, then fled with the money. A sordid thing like that . . . well, it wouldn't have been acceptable in Philadelphia society."

"Society? Society is more important than bringing a murderer to justice?"

"In my grandparents' day, yes. There were only three times when it was considered proper for a person to have his name in the newspaper: when he was born, when he married, and when he died."

"Sounds rather pompous and stuffy to me."

Will grinned, another sad sort of grin, filled with something she read as longing. "To you it would, Miss Priss."

She held his gaze for a long time. "So, you've come to New Mexico to find your father's killer. Is that what you're trying to tell me? That your mission of vengeance is what you've claimed all along will keep us apart?"

"In a manner of speaking."

"You intend to go out and get yourself killed to right a family wrong? Is this one of those feuds that continues generation after generation? Will your children—"

"Priscilla, that isn't all. I mean, that isn't right. I don't intend to get anybody killed."

"Then what do you plan to do with this murderer-turned-model-citizen?"

"I'll take him back to Philadelphia."

"But it happened so long ago."

"Statute of limitations has run out," he agreed. "But I intend to take him back, close the records, and make him face the consequences, whatever they turn out to be."

Relief and pride mingled and swept over Priscilla, bringing a return of hope. "I should have known you wouldn't seek blood for blood. You're not like that, Will. You're fair. I've never known anyone who believes in upholding the law more than you do. But what if he won't go with you? What if he starts shooting?" Her fear for him returned. "I couldn't stand to lose you. Your father's dead. But I'm alive. I love you . . . I . . ."

"Priscilla, there's more . . . the worst."

"What could be worse?"

"The murderer's identity."

"Oh?" She felt like Sargeant had kicked her in the gut for absolutely no reason, out of the clear blue sky.

"His name was Charles Martin Kane. He changed it to . . ."

Fear turned to horror. It swirled in ugly black circles in her head. She barely heard Will speak her father's name. But she knew he'd said it.

". . . Charlie McCain."

Priscilla clutched at a stall to stabilize her suddenly spinning equilibrium. "No," she finally managed.

Will nodded. His face was stiff, his eyes relentless.

"If this is some miserable joke . . . If you're trying to pay me back for all those tricks I pulled on you on the trail . . ."

Will caught her arm. When she looked, he was staring at his hand on her arm. She felt like he'd caught her in a vise and was pulling her downward in a spiral toward oblivion.

"It isn't a joke, Priscilla. It's true."

"No." She struggled to breathe. "No."

"I wish . . . Lordy, I wish it weren't . . . but it is. I'm sorry, cowboy."

"Sorry?" Her voice quivered, releasing each sound on a different octave. She jerked to free herself. Then she was running. Through the corral. Over the fence. Across the meadow. Running. Gasping for breath.

Will found her in a secluded glen beside a narrow mountain stream a hundred yards or so from the barn. She was lying on the ground and he could tell from the distance that she was sobbing.

He knelt beside her. When he tried to stroke her hair, she rolled away and sat up, fighting mad. She jumped to her feet. He rose, too. They stared at each other, Will in despair, Priscilla in anger.

"If you don't love me, greenhorn, all you have to do is say so. You don't have to make up some horrible lie about my pa."

"It isn't a lie, Priscilla. Lord knows how desperately I wish it were."

"Then you're as stupid as I first thought. Pa, a murderer? How could you even think such a thing? You've seen him, talked to him; for God's sake, you even saved his life and rescued him from jail. Now you're calling him a murderer. Is that why you went to Chimayo? To check up on Pa?"

"No, but it's the reason I came to New Mexico, to find Charlie McCain."

He watched her expression go wild. He wanted to hold her, but he dared not even try.

"You've known this all along?"

He nodded.

"Does he . . . does he know you're accusing him—"

Will nodded again. "Your mother does, too."

"They couldn't."

"They do. Charlie and I discussed it the first time we met."

They fell silent. Will could see her remember his first trip to Spanish Creek. Lordy, he remembered it, too—the fiery sunset burning in her golden hair, the peppery humor in her teasing, the blazing passion in her eyes. He remembered it well. He always would.

"You came about Joaquín," she objected. "You helped in the branding pen. You were so angry, so rough . . ."

"That was why. I introduced myself to Charlie even before he sent you and your mother from the courtyard. Remember? But I didn't have to. People say I'm the spitting image of my father. Charlie recognized me the instant I stepped into the courtyard."

Crossing her arms over her chest, Priscilla stared him directly in the eye. "What did Pa say?"

"Say?"

"Did he admit it?"

"He didn't have to, Priscilla. He knows and I know."

"Then what've you been waiting for?"

The question was a cry of anguish, a plea for him to say it was all wrong, all a mistake, to take everything back. Lordy, how he wanted to. But he couldn't. Because it was true.

"Charlie and I made a bargain that first night."

"A bargain?" Her tone was one of unrelenting sarcasm.

"To keep it quiet until I cleared Joaquín."

"Until you cleared Joaquín?" Priscilla's voice trembled. "That was my deadline, too. By the time you cleared Joaquín, you would have fallen in love with me. After you cleared Joaquín, I would be able to convince Mama and Pa to accept you."

Will held her anguished gaze until she turned away. It was as if her anguish was his punishment, or his punishment was to cause her anguish. Or both. "For what it's worth, you succeeded in the first."

He watched her shoulders jerk. He knew she was fighting tears. So was he. For the longest time she stood staring at the ground, and he stood staring at her, as if to engrave every facet of her into his mind, as if that were necessary.

He wouldn't forget Priscilla. Not as long as he lived. And he would never forget the pain he had brought her.

"Well, I'll be going. I wanted you to know before I . . . before Charlie and I . . ." With a heavy heart he gave up and turned toward the house.

Eighteen

Before Will reached the house, Priscilla caught up with him.

"I'm coming with you."

"No." He neither broke stride nor glanced her way. She fell into step.

"I'm coming, Will." She skipped to keep up with his long legs. "It's all a mistake, you'll see. A terrible mistake."

"I don't want you in there, Priscilla."

They took the veranda steps. He stopped with a hand on the large iron door handle. "I mean it."

"I mean it, too. I'm coming."

She saw his jaws clench. His voice was strained, his tone pleading. "Please, don't."

"Why?"

"Because I . . . I've hurt you enough all ready."

She held his gaze, knowing he wanted to turn away. In her despair that seemed to be the only weapon left her, to force him to witness her anguish. "Do you think I won't be hurt if I stay outside? Get your head out of the sand, greenhorn." She jerked the door handle, squeezing his hand beneath hers. The door flew open and before he could stop her, Priscilla had sashayed through it, leaving him to follow.

"Pa," she called down the corridor.

Kate materialized from the courtyard. Her face was ashen. "He's in the library, darling."

Mama knows, Priscilla thought. Will had said she did,

but Priscilla hadn't believed it—hadn't wanted to believe it. Believing any part of the horrible lie would leave the door open for more of it to be true.

And it wasn't. It couldn't be. Pa wasn't a murderer. Not Pa. Not *her* Charlie McCain. Maybe someone else; someone else had taken that name. Hearing Pa's name, they had claimed it.

Will was on her heels. They reached for the library door at the same time. His hand covered hers. It was cold. It trembled, like her own.

"I wish you'd stay out here."

She shook her head.

"Priscilla, I . . ."

She looked into his eyes, eyes that bespoke the torment inside him. She'd seen that look before. Numerous times. Not as troubled as today, not as forlorn as today. But that same look—of a caged animal seeking freedom.

"If this is what it takes to set you free, Will Radnor, let's get it over."

Together they pulled open the door.

Charlie sat behind the desk. When they entered, his eyes fastened on her. "Miss Priss, what . . . ?"

"I tried to get her to stay outside, Charlie."

Charlie looked beyond her. "Kate . . . sweetheart?"

"Anything that affects you, affects us all, dear."

Priscilla reached the desk ahead of them. "Tell him it isn't true, Pa." She watched pain etch his face. "He thinks you're a . . . a murderer. Tell him it's a mistake."

She recalled the first time she'd realized Pa was getting older, the day she rode in from Chimayo. His sallow complexion, the wrinkles, his gray, wiry hair. At the time she'd thought it was from being confined to bed so long. The pain she saw today went much deeper. As she watched, a physical weight seemed to settle on his sagging shoulders, pushing him further into his chair.

Then Will moved. She watched the scene unfold as

though it were a nightmare from which she struggled to awaken. He reached to his waistband, drew out the little pistol.

Strange, she thought, she hadn't known he brought it. She tried to move toward him, to stop him, but her joints seemed locked in place.

Before she could react Will tossed the pistol to the desk. The clattering brought her to her senses. Recovering from the initial shock of thinking Will intended to shoot her pa, Priscilla focused on Charlie, who stared, as though mesmerized, at the small gun.

For the longest time, the only sound in the room was of four sets of laboring lungs; the four of them stared at the gun. Finally Charlie moved.

He unlocked the top right-hand desk drawer and withdrew . . .

Priscilla pressed her knuckles to her lips.

. . . a matching pistol. He tossed it to the desk where it slid into Will's. She recognized it. It was the same gun she'd shot tin cans with that long-ago morning when she was ten years old.

Will was right, the guns were alike. *A matched pair,* he'd claimed.

"It may sound strange," Pa was saying in a voice that didn't sound at all like his own, "but I'm relieved to get this over. I've known it was coming since the day I rode out of Philadelphia."

Priscilla thought she might faint. What did he mean? That he was guilty? That he had murdered Will's father? She gripped the desk. A part of her was sorry she hadn't listened to Will and stayed outside. Another part knew she had to stay right here and fight for the man she loved.

The dismal truth struck her a hard blow. For the *two* men she loved.

She stared at the guns. Will's story came back to her in bits and pieces—he'd been ten years old when he found his father clutching that gun. She'd been ten when she found Pa's gun. *A matched pair,* Will had said. His father had been dead; hers had been angry.

Dead, angry. None of it made sense. If Pa murdered Will's father, nothing . . . But he couldn't have. Not Pa. Not her beloved Pa.

Charlie moved again. Leaning to the side, he opened a larger drawer. With both hands, he lifted out an ancient ledger. *As tenderly as if he were holding a baby,* Priscilla thought. She stared at the ledger. The gold embossing had faded some but was still legible: Radnor, Radnor, & Kane, Attorneys at Law.

"The missing ledger." Will's voice drifted as on a hot summer breeze. "Old Mr. Peters said you'd taken it."

Priscilla fought back tears.

"Peters knew the truth, Will. Did he tell you that?"

"We all know the truth, Charlie."

"I don't," Priscilla cried. Will stared at Charlie, refusing to look at her.

"Well, sugar, I reckon it's time to set the record straight."

"You didn't murder his father. That's all you have to say, Pa. Not Will's father. You . . . you couldn't have."

"William Radnor was my best friend. Hell, he was the best friend a man could ever ask for. I miss him to this day. To this day I dream about that afternoon and ponder the choices. There were only two, an' many's the time I've wished I'd made the other one. Many's the time I've wished I'd let him kill me." Charlie's gaze traveled from Kate to Priscilla. Moisture glistened in his blue eyes. "But this is what I would have missed. You two ladies are more precious than . . . I know it's selfish, but . . . not knowing you . . . loving you . . . both of you . . ."

This was a nightmare, Priscilla thought, a nightmare. Any minute now she would awaken and find none of it true. "You didn't murder him," she cried. "You couldn't—"

"I'm getting to that, sugar. Will here and I are fixin' to

sit down at this desk and go over this ledger and when we're done, he'll know the truth."

"Charlie, there's no need—"

"Bear with me, Will. If for no other reason than to humor an old man, an old man who knew and loved you long before you grew to hate him."

Priscilla clasped her head in her hands to still its mind-boggling spins.

"All right," Will agreed. "I'll listen."

Priscilla watched him speak; his Adam's apple bobbed, as though the words were physical objects that had trouble passing through his throat.

"Kate?" Pa asked. "Is any of that good whiskey left, or did we finish it off the first night?"

"There's some left, dear."

"Then bring it, would you? And a couple of glasses. You ladies'll have to excuse us."

"I'm not leaving this room, Pa. I want to hear, too."

"Sure you do. And you will. Your mama knows the story as well as I do. While Will and I go over the books, she'll take you out to the courtyard and catch you up.

Priscilla held his steady, if solemn, gaze. She considered arguing but knew it would be wasted breath. Unwillingly, she relented, but her fear was so great it weakened her legs, and she thought at first she wouldn't be able to take a single step. Finally she managed to. Rounding the table, she hugged her father. He smelled of horses and cattle and Pa. She thought how they'd hardly had time to celebrate having him home before they were beset by another threat.

She made a mental note to never again put off anything. Not laughing or crying or—"I love you, Pa."

"I love you, too, sugar."

Straightening, Priscilla looked at Will and found his eyes on her. Muted messages of alarm and desperation passed between them. Everything in her cried to be in his arms. He needed comfort, too. She moved toward him. Stopped.

Her arms tensed with the need to touch him, to hold him. But she couldn't. And he couldn't. She saw it in his eyes. One touch and all would be lost.

Her mother returned with the whiskey.

"Run along, sugar," Charlie prodded.

"I'm going." She glanced from one man to the other. Suddenly the abject hopelessness of the situation overwhelmed her. Her eyes alighted on the matched pistols lying in the middle of the desk. She reached for them. "I'll take these with me, so you won't use them to kill each other."

Will's hand covered hers, stopping her.

"Leave them, sugar," Charlie said. "We're gonna talk. That's all."

Then they were alone.

The sound of the slamming door rebounded from the thick adobe walls of the library, accompanied by the angry jangle of Priscilla's retreating spurs. Will tried to shut out the sounds. He strove to exorcise the image of Priscilla, of her tears, of her pleas, of her hurt—if not for all time, at least for this moment.

This moment, for which he had lived his life, for which he had prepared since he was ten years old. At long last he stood before Charles Martin Kane, ready to confront him. Charles Martin Kane, murderer of his father—father of . . .

He watched Charlie pour whiskey into two glasses, hand him one.

"I didn't come to drink with you, Charlie. I came to take you back to Philadelphia."

Charlie set both glasses back on the desk. "Sit down, Will." He nodded toward the ledger. "Read it. Then we'll talk."

Will forced himself to focus the ledger. *The truth,* Charlie had said it contained. What truth? What truth could Will discover in an ancient book that would erase the reality he knew to be fact? The reality: his father's murdered body, Charles Kane's pistol clutched in his hand; Charles Kane's disappearance; the missing ledger.

The truth? Charlie McCain was a senile old man if he thought to change Will's mind with figures in a long-missing book; and if Will allowed himself to be led down this well-worn path of deception, he was a fool. A fool who wanted, desperately wanted, wished, prayed, to find a truth that would absolve Charles Martin Kane of a murder no one else could have committed.

A fool, who loved a woman so much he was tempted to walk out of this room and take it all back. Tell her he'd made a mistake, he'd been wrong, he hadn't meant it, it didn't matter, all that mattered was that he loved her, he'd forgive, forget . . .

A fool, who loved a woman so much.

Will glanced at Charlie. Tears glistened in his sky-blue eyes. As though unwilling to expose his vulnerability, Charlie ducked his head, rose quickly, and hobbled to the window. From the distance, he faced the room again.

"I know you've hated me a long time, Will. And with good cause. Not for what you think. I didn't murder your father in cold blood. But I left you fatherless. That, I did." Charlie ground the heels of his hands into his eyes, drying them.

Will looked away. Charlie continued in a voice earnest enough to sway the most callous jury.

"In a thousand silent ways, I tried to make it up to you, Will. I like to think I was a better father for it. Every time Priscilla scraped her knee or lost a tooth or fell off a horse, I thought of you with no father to pick you up and dust you off. Every time I dried her eyes or rocked her on my knee or kissed away her hurt, I thought of you with no father. Everything I taught her, I wondered who was teaching you. Every time she—"

"Leave Priscilla out of this, Charlie." The room seemed

to sway. The gold names on the ledger swam before Will's eyes.

"I can't leave Priscilla out of it. Neither can you."

Will glared at the old man. "I can if I have to. This is a matter of law and order."

"Then sit down and read that ledger."

"We're wasting time, Charlie. I'll tell you how we're going to handle this—"

"No, son, I'll tell you. Sit down there." Charlie limped back to the desk as he spoke. Will watched him sit in his worn leather-covered chair. He opened the middle drawer and reached inside, withdrawing a photograph at least as old as the ledger. He passed it to Will.

The photograph was tattered and dog-eared from years of handling. Will's hand trembled when he recognized the subjects—his father . . . and Charles Martin Kane. They wore old-fashioned black suits with starched collars and formal ties. Their arms were around each other's shoulders, their heads were tilted together, and they were laughing. Will's resolve returned.

"If I needed more proof, Charlie, here it is. You murdered your best friend."

"Turn it over. Read the back."

The ink had faded, but his father's scrawl was still legible—and recognizable.

To Charlie Kane, who'll always be the better man.
Glad you're joining the firm, old friend. I need you
to keep my nose clean and my ass out of trouble.
[Signed] William Penn Radnor III

Will dropped the photograph to the desk. It landed on top of the two Pocket Colts. "What are you trying to say, Charlie?"

"That you're right. He was my best friend. Like I said, the best friend a man could have. But we were different,

Will, as different as daylight and dark." After a dramatic pause, Charlie added, "As different as you and Miss Priss."

Moisture stung Will's eyes. He gritted his teeth so hard he felt his neck muscles quiver. Charles Kane must have been one hell of a lawyer. He knew all the tricks.

Charlie reached for the ledger and flipped pages, leaving it open about halfway through. "Sit down," he urged again. "This won't take long."

Will glared at Charlie. He had prepared for this encounter all his life, so why, how, had he allowed Charlie to get the upper hand? He should have taken charge. He should have—

Against his better judgment, Will sat. On the edge of the seat. With his heart in his throat. He had to get out of here. He had to take Charlie and get out of here.

Charlie handed him a single sheet of paper, a list of figures and dates. "Flip through the ledger. Compare the entries you find in your father's handwriting with this list."

Tentatively, as on insect feet, uneasiness crept up Will's neck. He eyed Charlie, suspicious of the man's motives, conscious now that the old man he faced was more than a worthy adversary. He was a damned skilled interrogator.

"Go ahead, Will. You owe it to yourself. The truth. After all this time."

At first glance, the figures in the ledger looked faded; then Will realized his vision was veiled with tears. What was Charlie up to? He squeezed his eyes in an effort to dry them. Charlie pointed to midpage. Will studied the entry.

His father's handwriting? It was different, slightly, from that above or below. He turned the photograph over and studied the faded handwriting, which moments before had been so familiar. He studied the list Charlie had handed him. The first item matched. The second. The third. Suddenly all Will's hatred and anger resurfaced. Except it wasn't the old hatred and anger.

This was a new hatred, a new anger, more potent than the emotions he had lived with for twenty-three years. Will slammed the ledger shut. He jumped to his feet. "How dare you try to muddy the water, Charles Kane? How dare you?"

"I'm not disparaging your father, Will."

"Disparaging my father?" Will yelled. "My father is dead. You killed him, Charlie."

"I haven't denied it."

Will's gaze locked with Charlie's. The room swirled around him in a dizzying rush. He paced to the window, stared out, past the veranda, beyond the barn, to the corral. All was still, quiet, as though nothing outside this room had changed.

And it hadn't. Nothing had changed for twenty-three years. He'd spent a month caught up in a fantasy, but nothing had changed. He turned on Charlie.

"My mother dried my tears, Charlie. My grandfather dusted me off when I fell off a horse. When you took my father, you took something much more precious away from me."

Charlie's face went ashen, and Will advanced. "I was the one who found his body, Charlie. Did anyone ever tell you that?"

Startled, Charlie clasped gnarled hands to his head. "My God, no . . ."

"I was ten years old, and I wore spanking new shoes, and I was full of hopes and dreams. You stole my dreams, Charlie. You murdered my father, and you destroyed my dreams."

Charlie sank back in his chair. He picked up the little guns and cradled them, one in each palm.

"My name was going to be on the door of that office, Charlie. Etched in the glass. Oh, it was . . . it is. But it was supposed to be beside my father's. My office was supposed to be next to his office. We would see clients together in the same conference room. We would try cases together, we would uphold law and justice together. Together, Charlie."

Charlie looked up. He stared into Will's angry eyes. He

didn't flinch. He didn't try to duck his head or look away. Will grasped the edge of the desk, breathed hard, deep. For a minute that was the only sound in the room, his breathing.

"I loved my father, Charlie. After you took him away from me, I vowed never to love another human being." He stood there, glaring at Charlie, breathing hard, while sensations as sweet and soft as a summer shower washed over him in wave after wave.

He didn't see Priscilla's face. He didn't feel her body. It was his love for her that swept over him. His enormous, limitless love for her. Tears stung his eyes.

He squinched them shut, hung his head. "Your evil knows no bounds, Charlie. Now you're taking her, too."

A long moment passed before Charlie spoke in quiet tones. "It doesn't have to be that way."

Will stood, head hung, eyes closed, willing his breathing to steady, his mind to clear. He heard Charlie rise, felt the man's hand on his shoulder.

"Sit down, Will. Let me have my say. You preach law and order, now let's see you practice it. I have a right to speak my piece."

Will sat. Truthfully, he had no choice. His legs were so weak, they probably wouldn't have carried him from the room. And Charlie was right. Even the most hardened killer had a right, under the law, to tell his side of the story.

"Like I said," Charlie began, "your father and I were about as different as two men can be. I was the serious type, not unlike yourself. Your father was fun-loving. He never met a stranger. Everyone loved him. I envied him that carefree, devil-take-all attitude. He enlivened my life. Enriched my life." Charlie nodded toward the photograph on the desk. "And like he wrote, I kept him out of trouble. Or tried to."

Picking up the ledger, Charlie thumbed through it absently. "I won't bore you with the depth of our friendship. That's not what you need to hear. The truth is that your father had gotten himself into some serious financial trouble. He liked to gamble and then, I'm not criticizing, Will, but your mother demanded the lifestyle she'd been born to. Your grandfather went along for a while, but well, I'm sure you knew Mr. William for the frugal man he was."

Will nodded. "Tight. That's what Mother called him."

Charlie returned to his chair, drew himself to the desk, and picked up the little pistols again. "I knew your father and grandfather were at odds over money, but as God is my witness, when I confronted your father with what Peters found in this ledger, I didn't know Mr. William had vowed to cut him off without another red cent."

Will watched Charlie heft the pistols in his palms, weighing them, lost in thought. Although what Charlie said was news, Will wasn't surprised. His mother had insisted on keeping a certain lifestyle. That's why she remarried a year after his father's death. She'd told Will as much.

"We need the money, Will," she'd said. "Your Grandfather Radnor doesn't understand." So she married a banker.

When Charlie didn't continue, Will prompted, "You went to my father with these figures?"

"Yes. I had to defend myself. I was in a precarious position. The only person outside the family admitted to the firm. And now the ledger showed I'd received moneys far in excess of what I had earned."

"Since it was in my father's handwriting, wouldn't Grandfather have taken your side?"

"Not likely. You grew up in the family, so you wouldn't understand what it's like to be an outsider. I was . . . expendable. But I had no intention of going to Mr. William. I only wanted your father to find some other way to finance his lifestyle; a way that didn't implicate me."

"And my father fired you."

"Yes. Took me by surprise, I'll tell you. Here we'd been friends through college, roommates through law school.

We'd practiced law together for years. And he fired me. Like I said, I didn't know how desperate he was."

"So, the next day you waited until Grandfather left the office; you went back, ostensibly to collect your belongings, and you killed my father."

Charlie rose, hobbled to the window, and stared out. At length, he turned and resumed the story. "Your father asked me to wait until Mr. William left for the day. When I got to the office, he was waiting. He told me then how desperate he was, that his father had refused him any more financial assistance. That if Mr. William learned about his embezzling, he would kick him out. I tried to convince him that I didn't intend to tell anyone, but he laughed."

Charlie's gaze fixed on the desk, on the pistols. " 'The way you preach law and order,' your father said, 'you couldn't keep this quiet. It'd eat at you and eat at you and one day you would explode.' "

" 'What kind of friend do you think I am?' I asked," Charlie said.

" 'You're the best kind of friend, Charlie. But you're an officer of the court first. My father's got you brainwashed.' We were in my office during this time. I'd brought a carton and was taking down personal things, putting them in the box. When I reached for the pistol case, he stopped me."

Charlie looked up at Will. "Like you stopped Priscilla . . . he grabbed my hand. Your father had this wild stare in his eyes. Before I realized what he was doing, he pulled out one of the pistols and pointed it at me. I never kept them loaded, so I didn't think anything about it."

Will jumped up. "Are you saying he fired at you?"

Charlie nodded.

"He would have known the guns weren't loaded."

Charlie held Will's troubled gaze, steady, infinitely sad. "He knew they *were* loaded."

"You're saying—"

"Let me finish. Just let me finish. That's all I ask." When Will settled back, Charlie continued.

"Instinct saved me. I'd been around guns long enough that even though I thought it was unloaded, I dodged. I'm here to tell you, when that bullet whizzed by my ear it took me by surprise. I lunged across the desk, but your father was out of control by then. He waved the barrel in my direction. I rolled away. He fired again. I reached for the second gun."

Will's heart pounded. *Self-defense.* That's what Charlie was claiming. Self-defense.

Disbelief swirled through Will's deep-seated hatred. Disbelief, weakened, he knew, by his love for Priscilla, by his desperate need to find a way to exonerate Charlie McCain.

"I didn't mean to kill him, Will. If you never believe anything else, I hope to God you can believe that. If not now, at least someday. I didn't mean to kill him."

Will sat, silent, stupefied. When he looked up, Charlie had taken his seat again. Like a defense attorney, who had finished presenting his case. Only Will had never seen a defense attorney who looked so defeated.

"If it happened like you say," Will challenged, "why did you run? Why didn't you stay and tell the truth?" He motioned to the ledger. "You had proof."

"Not then. Peters brought the ledger later that night. Later . . . while you were finding your father's body, I guess . . . Peters came to my apartment. He gave me the ledger only after I promised to leave town."

"Why?"

"Loyalty."

"Loyalty? You're talking about a law firm, dedicated to justice for all."

"This had nothing to do with law firms, Will. Nor with justice. The heir of one of Philadelphia's 'royal' families was dead. No outsider would be allowed to drag his name through the mud."

"Grandfather wouldn't . . ." Will's words drifted off. Hadn't he told Priscilla virtually the same thing, minus the royalty?

Charlie turned to the back page and shoved the ledger across the desk toward Will. "Peters left a signed statement . . . here in the ledger."

Will scanned the two-sentence statement:

To Whom It May Concern: Charles Martin Kane had no knowledge of nor any part in the embezzlement of Radnor funds. [Signed] Amon R. Peters

It said nothing about the murder, of course. Peters would have had no knowledge of that. But if his father embezzled . . .

Will indicated the statement. "Why did Peters do this?"

An expression of near hopelessness etched Charlie's face, aging him before Will's eyes. "He said I might need it someday."

Will slumped in his chair. Across from him sat the man he had hated as no human should be forced to hate, a man who represented all that was evil, all that was wrong with the world.

At least, Charlie had represented all that, until a month ago when Will arrived in New Mexico Territory and a golden-haired cowgirl, who dressed like Billy the Kid and smelled like horse sweat, climbed into that stagecoach and changed his life forever.

How could he love Priscilla and hate her father?

And how could he hate Charlie and expect Priscilla to love him?

Will stared at the open ledger, at the sheet of figures.

"Go ahead, Will. Study them. Decide for yourself."

Will looked up at Charlie, really looked at him—his ashen, wrinkled skin, his wiry salt and pepper hair, his sky blue eyes. He remembered the night he helped Charlie defend Spanish Creek against the Haskels; he remembered Charlie's reminiscings. Likely, Charlie had a lot more stories to tell, stories Will was hungry to hear. Neither his grandparents nor his mother had ever spoken freely of his father.

Now he knew why. Anything they recalled about his father, involved Charles Kane, too. Charlie and his father had been inseparable.

Until Charlie killed him.

Will jumped to his feet. He stared at the pistols, at Charlie again.

"Study the figures, Will."

"I've seen enough. Enough to convince me you're telling the truth about the embezzlement. But you still killed my father, Charlie. And I've . . . I've hated you all my life for it."

"I don't blame you, son. But now you love Priscilla."

Will turned away, reluctant for Charlie to see the truth in his eyes.

"Love is stronger than hate, Will."

Will clenched his fists. He strove to focus on Charlie and his father, on the twenty-three-year-old killing that might or might not have been self-defense.

He closed his eyes and tried to see his father's body, the blood pooling beneath him, the cluttered office, the pistol clutched in his lifeless hand.

He tried, but the only image he could call forth was of Priscilla. He saw her in the wickiup wearing that soft doeskin shift; he heard the little bells tinkle softly when he ran his hands through her hair.

He saw her beneath him, warm and passionate, while they made love—in the wickiup, in the mountains. Each time he held her, he expected it to be the last. Each time he kissed her he expected it to be the last.

Because each time he was with her, this day, this confrontation, loomed in their future.

Now it was over, but what had he accomplished? What had he learned?

". . . the sins of the fathers," Charlie was saying. "Whatever happened between your father and me, Will, whatever you choose to believe, don't let it interfere with you and Priscilla. If you love her . . ."

Will turned on him, astonished. *If he loved her?*

"I love her, Charlie. Don't ever doubt that."

Charlie ran a gnarled hand through his wiry hair. "Then why don't you hang around and see if we can work things out?"

Nineteen

Priscilla paced the courtyard, while her mother sat at the little table beneath the overhang. *Self-defense!* She'd known it had to be something like that. Pa wasn't a murderer. Not Pa. But to kill his best friend, Will's father. What a dastardly secret to have lived with all these years. Poor Pa.

But at least he hadn't *murdered* Will's father. Her relief was short-lived for suddenly another worry surfaced: It didn't matter what she thought. It was what Will thought that made a difference. What Will believed.

Turning, Priscilla ran down the path to the far end of the courtyard. Not to get away from her mother, but to escape herself, and the fear that rose in her chest and her throat and suffocated her. She felt like someone had stuck a horseshoe magnet to her body and pulled all her fears into a gigantic pile, forming one overwhelming mass of terror.

Kate came up behind her, took her by the shoulders.

"I love them both, Mama."

"I know, darling."

"But Will hates Pa. Even if he believes him, he's hated him so long, what if he can't ever . . . I mean, what if he can't believe . . . or forgive?"

"Sh, darling. Wait and see what happens."

"But I can't lose Will, Mama. I love him so much, so much it hurts."

"I know, Priscilla."

"I love him more than . . . more than . . ."

The truth hit Priscilla without warning, inundating, devastating her. Tears came in a great rush of sobs and she couldn't stop them. The truth, that she loved Will Radnor enough to leave, not only Spanish Creek, but Mama . . . and her beloved Pa, enough to go anywhere in the world with him, knowing she could never return.

She would change her name, she thought. When they married her name would be Radnor, then Will wouldn't ever have to be reminded of the past. But to leave . . . all this, the home where she'd been born, the parents whose love had sustained her through childhood woes and who would continue to sustain her . . . for the rest of their lives. But to live without Will—

The jangling of spurs alerted her.

"They're here, darling." Kate dropped her hands from Priscilla's shoulders and stood back. Priscilla turned slowly, filled with apprehension, yet, strangely ready to get through whatever lay ahead.

Charlie and Will stood side by side in the doorway, solemn-faced and silent. She looked from one to the other but could perceive no clue as to what the outcome had been. Then Charlie held his hand to Kate.

"Come on, sweetheart. Let's go see what Sog's cookin' up for supper."

Will held Priscilla's gaze. She heard her mother walk up the path. She saw the shadowy forms of her parents leave the courtyard, heard their footsteps on the tiled corridor inside the house.

Yet she couldn't move. She and Will stood in their tracks, drinking in each other, as though words were too painful, Priscilla thought. But the words had to be spoken.

"Did you believe him?"

"I don't know."

"Oh, Will."

"Maybe I just wanted to believe him."

"You wanted to?"

Suddenly, without being aware they'd moved, they stood in the middle of the courtyard, locked in each other's arms. Priscilla felt Will's heart thrash and knew hers did the same.

"I've never wanted anything so badly in my life," he said.

"Never?"

"Never." Clasping her face in his hands, he covered it with kisses. She opened her lips and felt him dip inside. She pressed herself against him and waited for her fear to abate. He pulled their faces apart. "Never," he repeated. "Never . . . ever."

"Oh, Will, I'll come with you. Now. Tonight. We'll get married and I'll change my name and you won't ever have to hear the name McCain again."

Her words ran out. She stood in his arms, breathless, trying to read the strange expression on his face.

"You'd leave Charlie? And Spanish Creek? And your mama? For me?"

"Of course, Will."

He cocked his head, stared at her. "What's this, 'of course, Will'?" The hint of a grin played at the corners of his mouth. "Ever since I've known you, you've worked tooth and toenail to save Spanish Creek and Charlie McCain, with no thought for anything or anyone else. Now you're ready to leave them, just like that?"

"Not just like that. They're my family. This is my home. Yes, I've idolized Pa. Maybe too much, I don't know. But none of it matters if . . . I mean, while you were in there with Pa, I realized . . . I mean without you . . ."

She watched a grin spread slowly across his face.

"You're going to make me say it?" she accused.

"Yes, I'm going to make you say it. Every word."

As seductively as she could manage under the weight of lingering fear, she pulled his face down until their noses touched. His eyes looked like huge brown marbles from this close. "I'll leave Spanish Creek and Pa and roam the world with you, greenhorn. If that's what it takes for us to be together."

This time when he kissed her, she was able to respond. Strange, what a grin would do to relieve one's fears. Some of them. When she pulled away again, he was ready to talk.

"You won't have to leave anything, not even Charlie." He nipped kisses to her face. "But it was nice to hear you say it. I never thought that day would come."

She pretended to be miffed but wasn't too successful. "What happened in there?"

"Charlie and I are going to try to work things out."

"How? What?"

"Well, I'm the only person left in the family who really cares. And, to tell you the truth, it's kind of nice being with Charlie. He's . . . well, he knew my father better than anyone else ever did. They roomed together in college and later in law school, then they practiced law together. I've never known anyone, not even my mother, who claimed to think more of my father."

"But you still don't believe him."

"I believe him."

"Something's wrong. You're not satisfied about something."

"I'm satisfied. My brain is, anyway. It may take a while for my emotions to catch up. I've lived for this day, and lately dreaded it, too long now. The records make it plain. Mr. Peters was the accountant, and it's obvious where my father changed the numbers in the ledger. Charlie has samples of my father's handwriting, and Mr. Peters made a statement in the back of the book, exonerating Charlie from embezzling Radnor funds."

"I'm so sorry."

He stared at her, not through her like he used to do. Now she understood. He'd worried about this day ever since he met her. Every time he looked at her, he'd seen Charlie and the end, the showdown.

"The time for sympathy is long past, Priscilla. If we were to go back and change part of the story, we'd have to change it all." He pulled her to him, pressed her body to his with a sweep of his hand. "And right now I feel like I've come home . . . to the only place I ever want to be . . . with you."

Suddenly she felt giddy, free, like a child again. Breaking loose, she took Will by the hand and fairly dragged him from the courtyard. By the time they reached the front veranda, Sog had begun banging the iron triangle that served as a supper bell.

Priscilla didn't stop.

"You that hungry?" Will called.

But she was headed for the barn. They passed Crockett and Jessie and Bart, all going the other way.

"What's wrong, Jake?"

"Nothing, Uncle Crockett."

"Where's the fire, Priscilla?"

"Nowhere, Jessie. Go ahead to supper. We're not hungry."

"We?" Will asked.

"We."

"Oh, sure. My stomach thinks my mouth has been sewed up with catgut, but *we*'re not hungry."

At Sargeant's stall, she dropped his hand.

"Saddle your horse, greenhorn."

"My horse?"

"Come on. Hurry." When she reached for her saddle blanket, he grabbed her by the waist and swung her around.

He was laughing. "I just rode in from almost a week in the saddle. I wouldn't step back on a horse for all the gold in Silver Creek Canyon."

She tilted her chin, teasing, challenging. "You don't know what you'll be missing."

"I don't intend to miss a thing, Miss Priss." With that he pulled her out of the stall and through the barn. They followed the same path she had taken earlier, when she ran from him, from his tale of murder and horror.

But this time they were together. Hand in hand, they walked, they ran, and by the time they reached the little burbling mountain stream, they were breathless.

"If we'd ridden, we wouldn't be out of breath."

"If we'd ridden, I'd be in no shape . . ." Reaching for her Will dragged her to him. ". . . to do what we came down here to do." Their gazes probed. Their smiles faded.

Sobered, they fell into each other's arms. He squeezed her to him, felt her body meld to his. He cradled her head to his shoulder and fought back tears. "I never thought," he began. "I never thought things would work out, could work out."

Priscilla lifted her face, stared into his loving gaze. "I never doubted it."

"But you didn't know—"

Using a tactic she'd learned from him, she covered his lips with hers, shutting out his words, closing out the past. While their lips played with wet and sensual abandon, her hands tugged his shirttail from his britches. When she caressed his bare skin, he shuddered.

Drawing his lips from hers, Will cast a longing glance around the little glen that lay cupped like the palm of a hand within a ridge of hills.

"This is my own special place," Priscilla told him, as if sharing secrets with a friend. "Where I come to lick my wounds and gather my wits. No one would dare disturb me here."

He kissed her, little kisses that set her on fire. "Good," he said between kisses. "Good."

They hurried, then, as though outrunning a prairie fire. Their lips joined while their hands rushed to disrobe, then to touch, skin to heated skin; body to begging body. He set her gently on their two spread shirts, knelt beside her; his gaze devoured her. Moisture filmed his eyes.

"I'm so happy, Priscilla, I don't know whether to laugh or cry."

She reached for him and he came to her, lay beside her, touching, his hands seeking, finding, caressing until she squirmed with eagerness. He fondled her breasts, tweaking a nipple, showering her with a fiery spray of desire. But when he dipped his head to take one in his mouth, she stopped him.

"Oh, Will, please. It's been so long. Hurry."

He moved over her then, possessed her lips, her body. She opened her legs to him, crossed them around his hips, pulled him deeper and deeper inside her. She caught her breath at the longing, the joy, the absolute pleasure of being with him, being one with him.

Will watched fire ignite in the sparkling blue depths of her eyes, and he knew he had found heaven. "What would you say now if I asked you to spend the rest of your life with me?"

She grinned. That sickly little grin, made stiff with passion. "Try me and see."

With his elbows resting on either side of her face and his body sunk deeply into hers, Will savored the moment he had been so sure would never come. "Priscilla McCain, will you, the best danged cowboy in New Mexico Territory, stoop to marry me, a known greenhorn?"

Her eyes smoldered. "I thought you'd never ask."

"I hope that means yes." He moved then, at last. They moved together, racing, not time, for they had all the time God in his wisdom would decide to give them. But they raced a passion that flamed ever hotter as they moved ever faster, together, in unison. Feeling her climax, Will allowed his, and it was as if the mountains had tumbled from their perches. Wave after wave of passion exploded inside him, releasing emotions he had held in check for twenty-three years. At length, he collapsed, pulling Priscilla to her side along with him.

"Of course it means yes, greenhorn," she whispered against his sweat-laved cheek. When their breathing steadied, she said, "Tell me again, now that I'm no longer your enemy."

"My enemy?" Will drew his head back, looked into her teasing eyes. "You were never my enemy."

"Same thing."

"Wrong."

"Tell me again," she repeated.

He raised on an elbow, cradled her head on his forearm, and traced a finger down her cheek. "I love you, Priscilla." Suddenly tears gathered in his eyes. He felt the sting. One rolled down his cheek.

She caught it on a finger. "Don't cry, Will. There's nothing left to be sad about."

"I'm not sad." He couldn't stop looking into her eyes; he had the strangest feeling he never could, that they were frozen here in this place, in this time, forever. Foolish, though, he thought, for the worst was over. Truly, now, the best was yet to come. Except . . .

"That was the first time we've ever made love that I didn't think the whole time that it would be our last."

"Oh, Will, I love you so much." She kissed his cheeks, where his tears had stopped; his lips, where passion was again incited.

"How long till Christmas?" he asked suddenly.

"Christmas? Well, this is August—five months, I guess. Why?"

"Do you think I might make the grade of cowboy before December?"

"Might. For a greenhorn, you definitely have possibilities."

He kissed her softly. "I'd sure like to take my wife to that Cowboy Christmas Ball. But I have a feeling a greenhorn would be about as welcome as a lamb licker."

She smiled that sweet, innocent, seductive smile. "You didn't come to New Mexico to be a cowboy, Will Radnor."

His heart caught at the reminder.

"You came to love me."

His gaze held hers. He felt lost in her, lost and wandering around, unable to find his way out. But who would want to find his way out of heaven?

"Lordy, Miss Priss, did I ever."

Epilogue

One month later.

"Get back inside, Priscilla."

"I'm looking to see if Mama and Pa have arrived at the cathedral."

"And every man in the plaza is looking to see you in your first pair of frilly drawers."

"Will, I'm holding the curtain over me!" Stepping back into Will's small room atop the cantina, Priscilla dropped the covering and looked down at her white pantaloons and camisole. "They really aren't me, are they?"

"Wait till we get finished. I'll think I'm marrying the wrong woman." He held out the corset. Priscilla eyed it.

"Sure you want to go through with this?"

"Yes." Taking the corset, she turned it this way and that.

"Here, let me." Will fitted the corset around her waist and under her breasts. "Never thought I'd marry a woman who knew less about feminine attire than I do."

"Keep what you know about feminine attire to yourself, Will Radnor. I don't want to hear it. Nor how, nor where you learned it. Not on my wedding day."

Will turned her around backwards. "Hold onto the bed post."

She grabbed hold, just as he began to jerk the lacings. She gasped.

"I never thought I'd have to dress my own bride, either."

"Then don't." *Gasp.* "I'll do it myself."

"There's no way in hell you can get yourself into all this gear, Miss Priss. You don't even know what half of it is." He jerked again. She gasped again.

"Would you stop belittling me? I should have found someone else to help."

"Who?" This time when Will jerked the laces, he kissed her nape and she let out a strangled sort of sigh instead of a full blown gasp. "Jessie's run off with Bart, so you couldn't have asked her."

"Do you think they're all right?"

"Jessie and her outlaw? Sure. They're probably already in Wyoming by now."

"I hope so."

"And you refused to ask the one person whose place it is to dress the bride—your mother."

"I wanted to surprise them, Will."

"You're fixing to. It'll be some surprise if they walk in on me dressing their daughter—before I marry her."

"They'll understand."

"You bet." He turned her to face him, nipped a kiss to her nose, and thrust a pile of crinolines in her arms.

"They know we've been . . ." She stepped into the first petticoat and squeezed the waistband while Will fastened it in back. ". . . together."

When she tried to pull a second petticoat up over the first, Will took it from her hand. "Knowing and seeing are two different horses." He dropped the second petticoat over her head, tugged it past her shoulders, over her breasts, and settled it at her waist.

"My parents are different." Three more petticoats followed.

"I suppose you're prepared to be as liberal-minded with our daughters."

"Maybe it'll be a son."

It was time for the dress. For a moment they both stared

at the white lace confection that hung on the hatrack beside the bowler Will had worn in from Philadelphia and the Stetson that had become his standard headgear. Priscilla sighed.

"Maybe I shouldn't have done this."

Will took her by the bare shoulders and kissed her tenderly on the lips. His fingers feathered their way across her chest to her breasts, which bulged above the corset and nestled in the resulting lace pockets.

"That gown is so beautiful, Will. Maybe I should leave it hanging—"

"Sh." Will's expression changed from teasing to serious. He took the dress from its hanger and lifted it over her head. She stood stock-still.

"I'm going to look like Wheeler Peak in wintertime."

"Can't hear you," he called from the other side of yards and yards of white lace ruffles.

The lace scratched, but he kept on tugging and shifting and finally freed her head. "You mean like a lamb licker at the Cowboy Christmas Ball?"

"That still has you worried, huh, greenhorn?"

"How could it not? You'll have to agree, it holds frightening connotations." When she tried to peek into the looking glass, he turned her away.

"Not till we're finished."

"But I may not—"

"Sh, cowboy." He fastened the dress, adjusted the ruffle over her shoulders, then sat her down, again away from the mirror. Standing back he scrutinized his work.

"I have to fix my hair." She fidgeted in the pile of petticoats and lace. The toes of her stockinged feet peeked out. "And my shoes. Where are my white slippers?"

Leaning into her, Will kissed her soundly. "Sit tight. I have a wedding gift."

"For me?"

"Who else?"

"But I didn't . . ."

He'd already left the room. When he returned it was with a pair of white kid knee-high boots, fashioned in the best Western tradition, with slender toes, slanted heels, and five rows of stitching on the tops.

Priscilla's mouth opened, but "Oh," was all that escaped.

Kneeling before her, Will lifted her skirts, found a foot, and held the boot while she stuck her foot into the top. Together, they worked her arch down until her foot settled into the soft leather.

"They fit."

"Of course, they fit. Do you think I'd let my bride walk down the aisle in a pair of boots that didn't fit?"

"But will it be . . . all right?"

Will kissed her. "When did you start worrying over propriety?"

"I . . . well, I . . ."

"I want you to be comfortable, and I know you're not going to be in that dress."

"And I want you to be happy. Should I change? Wear britches—"

"Priscilla, if you take that dress off, after all it took to get you in it . . ." While he spoke, he took her fingers and pulled her to her feet. "Close your eyes. Follow me. There. Stand still. Don't look." She felt him fluff her skirts.

"Now."

Her eyes flew open. Will stood beside her in his new black suit, silver bolo tie, and shiny black boots. Together they stared at her reflection in the looking glass. Her gaze found his.

"Lordy, you're beautiful. I never imagined my bride would be so beautiful."

Priscilla looked back at her own reflection. "That woman's beautiful. But I don't know her."

"I do. She's the woman I'm fixing to pledge before God to love and honor and respect for the rest of my life."

"Oh, Will . . ."

"Sit down," he said hoarsely. "Fix your hair so we can get out of here before I decide to lock you in this room and throw you on the bed and ravish your body."

Picking up the brush she began to untangle her hair. "After all the trouble it took to get me in this dress?"

"For what I'm thinking, every minute of it would be worth the effort."

After she rebraided her hair, entwining white satin ribbons and sprays of silk orange blossoms down the length of her one heavy braid, she scrutinized her reflection again.

"Maybe I should wear it in curls."

"You know how to make curls?"

"No."

"Well, neither do I, cowboy, so stop worrying."

Cathedral bells pealed with a suddenness that startled them both. Will drew her to her feet.

"Let's go get this over with." His eyes darted from Priscilla to the bed. "We don't want to waste the whole day outside."

Her palms were wet, but she didn't realize it until they reached the back staircase, and her hand slipped from Will's.

"What do you think he'll say?"

"Charlie?" Will's attention was drawn to the street beyond. "Looks like we're fixing to find out."

Kate and Charlie waited on the piñon-shaded walk outside the cathedral. Titus Crockett and Ol' Soggy Bottoms stood off to the side. Will ushered Priscilla across the empty street.

Kate saw them first. Will watched her mouth drop open. She nudged Charlie; he turned, frowned, froze in place.

"What's he thinking?" Priscilla whispered.

"Hell, Priscilla, he's your father. At least he's not carrying a shotgun."

It was the longest walk Priscilla could ever recall taking.

Her parents didn't budge from their position beneath the piñon tree until she stood before them. No one said a word.

Finally, Ol' Sog broke the silence. "I'll swear if it ain't Miss Jake all dolled up an' lookin' like an angel."

"Thanks, Uncle Sog." She wanted to hug him, but she was unable to move from the spot where she'd come to stand, directly in front of her pa.

"Mighty purty, missy," Crockett added in a voice that cracked with emotion.

"Thanks, Uncle Crockett."

"Darling," Kate whispered at last. Tears brimmed in her eyes. "Oh, why am I crying? Where did you get that gown? I didn't even know—"

"I wanted it to be a surprise, Mama."

"Well, it sure as shootin' is that," Charlie growled.

Priscilla stood stock-still. Her breath rose and fell. She knew her breasts bulged above the off-shouldered neckline every time she breathed. She tried to take shallow breaths.

"Well, I'll be," Charlie was saying. "I'll be."

"Don't you like it?" she asked finally, when neither of her parents seemed able to make a coherent statement.

"Like it?" Kate questioned. "It's . . . I mean, you . . . Sog's right. You look like an angel, my darling."

"We always knew that," Charlie responded.

"I wore it for you, Pa. The lace. And the ribbons in my hair. You always said I couldn't tie a ribbon. Well, I did, today. For you. Don't you like it?"

Moisture collected in the corners of Charlie's eyes. "Hell, sugar, you're the prettiest thing I ever laid eyes on. You've always known I felt that way."

"But you always wanted me to be a lady. So, I tried . . ."

Before she could finish, Charlie grabbed her in a bear hug. "Miss Priss, that's the prettiest dress I ever saw. For the prettiest girl in the whole danged world." He set her back and perused her from head to toe. "Fit for a lady—the perfect lady you've always been." He sniffled, shuffled his feet, and turned a deeper shade of red. "Hell, if it fit any better, ol' Will here'd've had to pour you into it with Sog's chili ladle."

Priscilla felt Will wince beside her; her own face grew hot.

"But for the record," Charlie added, "I'd've been just as proud if you'd worn britches and boots."

Priscilla recovered. Lifting her skirts she kicked out a booted foot. "Look what Will gave me for a wedding gift."

The appropriateness of wedding boots for Priscilla was discussed for a minute, then Kate moved them toward the cathedral. "We'd better go. The padre has already come to the door twice."

Priscilla glanced up and down the street. "Where's Joaquín?"

Charlie cleared his throat. "He lit out. Took Nalin into the mountains to find José Colorado. Then he's headin' west. Said he aims to take a job as a guide at some Easterner's hunting lodge up in the Rockies."

"I'll miss him," Priscilla said. "Was he all right?"

"Probably not," Charlie admitted. "Before he left we rode out to the canyon and looked over his horses. I told him I'd take care of 'em for him. Maybe he'll be back, maybe he won't."

Walking must have relieved Pa's nervousness, Priscilla decided, for he continued to talk as they walked side by side. Will and her mother followed, with Uncle Crockett and Uncle Sog bringing up the rear.

"Found something else out at the canyon," Charlie confided.

"What, Pa?"

"Found out what Avery was doin' hangin' around Spanish Creek. Didn't have much to do with you, after all."

"Humph!" Priscilla returned, mimicking his usual response.

"He was after that gold."

"Gold?"

"You know the tales. Gold in Spanish Creek Canyon."

"If there'd been gold in that canyon, we would have found it years ago."

"Looks like it. Anyhow, that's what Avery was doing. I found his tracks back in the tunnel and signs of digging."

"How'd know?"

"Reckon he saw that suit of armor and the other artifacts we have around the place, put two and two together and came up with dollar signs in his eyes. I figure he took those artifacts outta that trunk in the barn, too."

"Guess he wasn't absentminded, after all. He had gold fever."

"All adds up to the same dadburnt thing—shiftless, over-educated—"

Priscilla grinned. "Less than worthless . . ."

"On a ranch," Charlie finished.

They reached the cathedral then, and Charlie held the door for Will and Priscilla. Lit by candlelight, the aged adobe walls glowed like they'd been kissed by the setting sun. The air was sweet with incense and centuries worth of piñon smoke. Will tugged Priscilla to a halt. He whispered in her ear.

"Did you mean what I think you meant?"

"What?" she whispered back.

"What you said about it being a boy. Are we having a baby, Miss Priss?"

She leaned into him in the dimly lit interior of the centuries-old cathedral, feeling ancient and young, imbued with great intelligence and nonsensical innocence all at the same time. "I didn't think you understood."

"We didn't have time to talk about it. I intended to wait until later, but I couldn't. When will it be?"

"I don't know. I've never paid much attention to things like that. Are you . . . glad?"

"Glad? More than that. I never even thought about children. You're all I needed, wanted, and now we'll have a child, someone who's part of both of us, someone who . . ."

The outer door slammed.

"Sh, Charlie," Kate shushed.

Priscilla pulled Will toward the nave of the cathedral. "Then come on, greenhorn. Let's go make this legal."

MY WARMEST THANKS TO . . .

DAN PARKINSON—for sharing his wonderful story about a Colt Pocket Dragoon.

ANNE AND MIKE CHENNAULT—(She was my college roommate; he was her college sweetheart.) for showing us the beauty of northern New Mexico and for helping keep our friendship alive and well.

LOLA SMITH—for her lovely New Mexico guide books and for sharing with us the magnificence of the New Mexico sunsets.

AND TO MY EDITOR AT ZEBRA

CARIN COHEN RITTER—for editing that gives us both a book we can be proud to present to you, our readers.